Dear Reader,

Once upon a time, I was asked to contribute a book to a themed fairy-tale month. I jumped at the chance, but...which one? I scoured the internet and found hundreds of fascinating tales from across the world (not all compatible with romance!) before eventually settling on "Goldilocks and the Three Bears."

How about a fair-haired heroine who snacks on oat bars and for whom everything has to be just right? I mused. Named Orla ("golden princess"), perhaps. What if she's woken up in a bed she shouldn't be in by a darkly brooding bear of a hero who is still tormented by the loss of his wife and son, and isn't at all pleased to find her there? Shenanigans would ensue, I was sure. Heads would butt (quite literally!). And eventually, of course, love would prevail.

The result is *Undone by Her Ultra-Rich Boss*, and I hope you enjoy reading Duarte and Orla's story as much as I loved writing it.

Lucy xx

Lucy King spent her adolescence lost in the glamorous and exciting world of Harlequin when she really ought to have been paying attention to her teachers. But as she couldn't live in a dreamworld forever, she eventually acquired a degree in languages and an eclectic collection of jobs. After a decade in southwest Spain, Lucy now lives with her young family in Wiltshire, England. When not writing or trying to think up new and innovative things to do with mince, she spends her time reading, failing to finish cryptic crosswords and dreaming of the golden beaches of Andalucia.

Books by Lucy King

Harlequin Presents

Passion in Paradise

A Scandal Made in London

Lost Sons of Argentina

The Secrets She Must Tell
Invitation from the Venetian Billionaire
The Billionaire without Rules

Visit the Author Profile page
at Harlequin.com for more titles.

Lucy King

UNDONE BY HER ULTRA-RICH BOSS

Recycling programs for this product may not exist in your area.

ISBN-13: 978-1-335-58360-4

Undone by Her Ultra-Rich Boss

For questions and comments about the quality of this book, please contact us at CustomerService@Harlequin.com.

Harlequin Enterprises ULC
22 Adelaide St. West, 41st Floor
Toronto, Ontario M5H 4E3, Canada
www.Harlequin.com

Printed in U.S.A.

UNDONE BY HER ULTRA-RICH BOSS

For Charlotte, editor extraordinaire

CHAPTER ONE

'Quem és tu e que raios fazes na minha cama?'

In response to the deep, masculine, insanely sexy voice that penetrated the fog of sleep enveloping her, Orla Garrett let out an involuntary but happy little sigh and burrowed deeper into the cocoon of beautifully crisp, cool sheets she'd created for herself.

Duarte de Castro e Bragança usually paid her dreams a visit the night following the day they'd spoken on the phone. Every time his name popped up on the screen her stomach fluttered madly. The ensuing conversation, during which his velvety yet gravelly tones sent shivers racing up and down her spine, unfailingly left every nerve-ending she possessed buzzing.

They'd never met in person and their calls weren't particularly noteworthy—she ran an ultra-exclusive invitation-only concierge business of which he was a member, so they generally involved his telling her what he wanted and her assuring him it would be done—but that didn't seem to matter. Her subconscious inevitably set his voice to the photos that frequently appeared in the press and which she, along with probably every other hot-blooded person on the planet, couldn't help but notice, and went into overdrive.

It was unusual to be dreaming of him now when she hadn't spoken to him in over a month. Even stranger that he was speaking in his native Portuguese when he only ever addressed her in the faintly accented yet flawless English he'd acquired thanks to a British public school education, followed by Oxford.

But she knew from experience that there was little she could do to prevent it, and really, why would she want to even try? The moves he made on her… The way she woke up hot and breathless and trembling from head to toe… It was as close as she got to the real thing these days, not that the real thing had ever been any good in her albeit limited experience, which was why she gave it such a wide berth.

Besides, there was no harm in a dream. It

wasn't as if she harboured the secret hope that the things he did to her would ever become reality. The very idea of it was preposterous.

Firstly, quite apart from the fact that she steered well clear of things she wasn't any good at, getting involved that way with a client—any client—would be highly unprofessional.

Secondly, there was no way a staggeringly handsome, fast-living aristocratic billionaire winemaker would ever notice her in the unlikely event they did get round to meeting.

And finally, the entire world knew how devoted reformed playboy Duarte had been to his beautiful wife and how devastated he'd been when she'd died of an overdose six weeks after giving birth to their stillborn son, even if he was now reported to be handling the double tragedy with unbelievable stoicism.

No, her dreams were private, safe and, even better, unlike reality, completely devoid of the hyper-critical voice that lived in her head, constantly reminding her of how much she had to do and how, if she wanted to feel good about herself, she must not fail at any of it. In the dreams that featured Duarte, perfection wasn't something to strive for; it was a given.

'Hello,' she mumbled into a gorgeous pillow that was neither too hard nor too soft but just right.

'I said, who are you and what the hell are you doing in my bed?'

This time he did speak in English, his spine-tingling voice a fraction closer now, and, as a trace of something deliciously spicy wafted up her nose and into her head, warmth stole through her and curled her toes.

'Waiting for you,' she murmured while wondering with a flicker of excitement what he might do next.

Thanks to a last-minute let-down, she'd been working flat out for the past week, preparing his estate for the annual meeting of the world's top five family-owned wine-producing businesses. Her exhaustion ran deep. Her muscles ached. A massage, even an imaginary one, would be heavenly.

'Get up. Now.'

Well, that wasn't very nice, was it? Unlike those of Dream Duarte, who generally smouldered and purred at her before drawing her into a scorchingly hot clinch, these words were brusque. This Duarte sounded annoyed. Impatient. Where was the smile?

Why was the hand on her shoulder shaking her hard instead of kneading and caressing? And, come to think of it, why could she smell him so vividly? His scent had never been part of her dreams before…

Realisation started off as a trickle, which swiftly became a torrent, and then turned into a tsunami, crashing through her like a wrecking ball and smashing the remnants of sleep to smithereens.

With her heart slamming against her ribs, Orla sat bolt upright and cracked her head against something hard. Pain lanced through her skull and she let out a howl of agony that was matched in volume by a thundering volley of angry Portuguese which accompanied a sudden lurch of the mattress.

Ow, ow, *ow*.

God, that hurt.

Jerking back, she clutched her forehead, rubbing away the stars while frantically blinking back the sting of tears, until the pounding in her head finally ebbed to a dull throb and the urge to bawl receded.

If only the same could be said for the shock and mortification pulsating through her. If only she could fling herself back under the covers and pretend this wasn't happening with equal success. But unfortunately she couldn't and it was, so gingerly, with every cell of her being cringing in embarrassment and horror, she opened her eyes.

At the sight of the man sitting hunched on the bed, shaking his head and running his hands through his dark, unruly hair, her breath caught. She went hot, then cold, then hot again. Her stomach flipped and her pulse began to race even faster.

Yes, Duarte was actually here, very much *not* a figment of her imagination, and oh, dear lord, this was *awful*. He'd caught her asleep on the job. She'd all but invited him to join her in bed. And then she'd headbutted him—her most important, wealthiest client—and that was saying something when to even be considered deserving of an invitation their members had to have a minimum net worth of half a billion dollars.

At least she'd kept her clothes on when, energy finally depleted, she'd crashed out, which was a mercy, even if they were on the skimpy side, since it was hot in the Douro Valley in June. But how on *earth* was she going to redeem herself?

That he hadn't been expected back for another three weeks was no excuse. Her company promised perfection on every level. Their clients demanded—and paid outrageously for—the very best. This was the absolute worst, most mortifying situation she could have ever envisaged.

'I'm so sorry,' she breathed shakily, deciding that grovelling would be a good place to start as she pulled up the spaghetti strap of her T-shirt, which had slipped off her shoulder and down her arm.

Duarte snapped his head round, his dark gaze colliding with hers, and the breath was whipped from her lungs all over again. The pictures she'd seen of him in the press didn't do him justice. Not even slightly. They didn't capture the size or presence of the man, let alone his vital masculinity, which hit her like a blow to the chest and instantly fired parts of her body she hadn't even known existed. They didn't accurately reflect the breadth of his shoulders or the power of his jean-clad thighs that, she noticed as her palms began to sweat, were within touching distance. Nor did she recall ever seeing in any photo quite such cold fury blazing in the obsidian depths of his eyes or a jaw so tight it looked as if it were about to shatter.

'Can I get you some ice for your head?' she managed, inwardly wincing at the memory of how hard she'd crashed against him before remembering the emergency first-aid kit that she kept in her bag just in case. 'Painkillers, perhaps?'

'No,' he growled, his expression as black as night, tension evident in every line of his body. 'You can answer my question.'

Right. Yes. She should do that. Because now was not the time to be getting caught up in his darkly compelling looks that were having such a strangely intense effect on her. Now was the time for damage control.

'My name is Orla Garrett,' she said, praying that despite his evident anger Duarte was nevertheless reasonable enough to see the amusing side of the situation once she explained. With the exception of this lapse in professionalism, the service her company provided him with was excellent and that had to count for something. 'I'm co-owner and joint CEO of Hamilton Garrett. We've spoken on the phone.'

His brows snapped together and she could practically see his reportedly razor-sharp brain spinning as he raked his gaze over her in a way that made her flood with heat.

Should she hold out her hand for him to shake? she wondered, a bit baffled by the electricity that was suddenly sizzling through her. Somehow, with her still beneath the sheets and him still sitting on top of them not even a foot away, it didn't seem appropriate.

Far more urgent was the desire to surge forwards and settle herself on his lap. Then she could sift her fingers through his hair and check his head for bumps. She could run her hands over his face and examine first his impressive bone structure and then the faint stubble adorning his jaw. At that point he could wrap his arms round her and flip her over, set his mouth to her neck and—

Agh.

What was happening? What was she thinking? Was she *nuts*?

Appalled by the wayward direction in which her thoughts were hurtling but deciding to blame it on possible concussion, Orla swallowed hard and pulled herself together. She had to ignore the scorching fire sweeping along her veins and the all too vivid images cascading into her head, the reasons for which she could barely comprehend. There'd be time for analysis later. Right now, she needed to put some space between her and her client, so she scrambled off the bed on the other side and onto her feet.

'As per your instructions,' she said, fighting for dignity, for control, and smoothing shorts that suddenly felt far too tight and uncomfortably itchy, 'I've been preparing the guest accommodation for your conference. So far, all the bedrooms are ready except this one.'

Which was the one that looked to require the least work. The other five had been complete tips. Bed and bath linen had been left awry and crusty wine glasses had been abandoned on surfaces thick with dust. Downstairs had fared no better. Coffee cups overspilling with mould had littered the drawing room and empty wine bottles had filled a crate in the kitchen.

Trying not to gag at the smell, Orla had wondered what on earth had been going on here before reminding herself sternly that it was none of her business. Her job was to see that her clients' wishes were fulfilled and that was it.

'I've agreed the menus for the weekend with Mariana Valdez,' she said, hauling her thoughts back in line and focusing on the tiny stab of triumph she felt at having acquired the only chef in the world to currently hold ten Michelin stars, who was virtually impossible to hire for a private function, 'and all dietary requirements will be catered for. I've instructed Nuno Esteves,' the Quinta's chief vintner, 'to make available the wines you stipulated for dinner on the Friday and Saturday nights. The river cruise has been scheduled for the Sunday afternoon and the crew is prepping the boat as we speak. Everything is on track.'

Duarte shifted round to glower at her, clearly—and unfairly—unimpressed by what she'd accomplished under very trying circumstances. 'And all the while you've been sleeping in my bed.'

'No,' she said with a quick, embarrassed glance at the rumpled sheets, which didn't help her composure at all. 'I haven't. I booked into the hotel in the village, and I've been staying there. The nap was a one-off, I swear. Not that that makes it any better. It's unforgivable, I know.'

Not to mention inexcusable, even though excuses abounded. Duarte wouldn't be remotely interested in the fact that she'd been let down at the last minute by the team she'd put in place to carry out his requests and had had no option but to see to the situation herself, however inconvenient and however long the hours. It wasn't his problem that she'd somehow found herself in possession of the wrong set of keys and had had to break a window to get in so she could unlock the back door from the inside and proceed from there. Like all their clients, he paid a six-figure annual fee to have his every instruction carried out, without question, without issue, free from hassle and the tedious minutiae of implementation.

'I can assure you that it will never happen again,' she finished, mentally crossing her fingers and willing him to overlook the blip. 'You have my word.'

He let out a harsh laugh, as if unable to believe her word counted for anything. Then he gave his head a slow shake, at which her pulse thudded and panic swelled, because as the dragging seconds ticked silently by she got the sickening feeling that he wasn't going to forgive. He wasn't going to forget. The tension in his jaw wasn't easing and his mouth wasn't curving into a smile as she'd hoped. The anger in his dark, magnetic gaze might be fading but the emptiness that remained was possibly even worse. His expression was worryingly unfathomable and his voice, when he spoke, was icy cold.

'You're right,' he said with a steely grimness that made her throat tighten and her heart plunge. 'It *won't* happen again. Because you're fired.'

He couldn't think straight. His head throbbed from the earlier collision. His chest was tight and his muscles were tense to the point of snapping. It was taking every drop of his control to repel the harrowing memories that had been triggered by setting foot in this house for the first time in nearly three years. To contain the savage emotions that were battering him on all sides.

Frustration and surprise that his instructions had not been carried out correctly warred with fury that his fiercely protected privacy had been invaded. Shock on finding a beautiful, golden-haired woman fast asleep in his bed clashed with horror at the desire that had slammed into him out of nowhere at the sight of her. The grief and guilt that he'd buried deep had surged up and smashed through his defences and were now blindsiding him with their raw, unleashed intensity.

None of it was welcome. Not the swirling emotions, not the clamouring memories of his difficult, deceitful wife and tiny, innocent son who had never got to draw a breath, and certainly not the unexpectedly gorgeous Orla Garrett here, in his space, wrecking the status quo and demolishing the equilibrium he strove so hard to maintain.

'I'm sorry?' she said, sounding dazed and breathless in a way that to his frustration made him suddenly acutely aware of the bed, and had him leaping to his feet.

'You heard,' he snapped, striding to the window and shoving his hands into the pockets of his jeans before whipping round. 'You're fired.'

Her astonishing eyes widened. 'Because I took a nap?'

The reasons were many, complicated and tumultuous, and very much not for sharing. 'Because you're clearly incompetent.'

Her chin came up and her jaw tightened. 'I am many things, I will admit, but incompetent is not one of them.'

'Then what would you call this?' he said, yanking a hand out of his pocket and waving it to encompass the bed, the room, the house.

She flushed. 'A lapse.'

'It's more than that.'

'The circumstances are extenuating.'

'And irrelevant.'

She stared at him for a moment, frowning,

as if debating with herself, then she took a deep breath and gave a brief nod.

'You're right,' she said with enviable self-possession. 'I can't apologise enough for all of this. For hitting you in the head and, before that, implying that I was waiting for you. Obviously, I wasn't. I was asleep. Dreaming. About someone else entirely.'

Who? was the question that instantly flew into his thoughts like the sharpest of arrows. A husband? A lover? And what the hell was that thing suddenly stabbing him in the chest? Surely it couldn't be *disappointment*? That would be ridiculous.

Despite having spoken to Orla frequently over the last few years, which had presumably given her an insight into certain aspects of his life, he knew next to nothing about her. But that was fine. He didn't need to. Their relationship, if one could even call it that, was strictly business.

Whether or not she was single was of no interest to him. So what if her voice at the other end of the line had recently begun to stir something inside him he'd thought long dead? Given that he'd sworn off women for the foreseeable future, the wounds caused by his short but ill-fated marriage still savagely raw, it was intrusive and annoying and not to be encouraged.

'You've been working on the wrong place,' he said, angered by the unacceptable direction of his thoughts when he worked so hard to keep them under control.

'What do you mean?'

'I instructed you to fix up the accommodation at the winery. This is not the winery.'

Her brows snapped together. 'I don't understand.'

'This is Casa do São Romão, not Quinta do São Romão. So you've broken into what was once, briefly, my home. You've been poking your nose into places where you do not belong and sleeping in my bed. And in the meantime, the task I *did* assign you remains unfulfilled.'

She stared at him, confusion written all over her lovely face. 'What?'

'You've made a mistake, Ms Garrett,' he said grimly, although actually, to call Orla's actions 'a mistake' was an understatement. She'd invaded his space. Whether she knew it or not, she'd seen things he'd never intended anyone to see. Not even *he* had ever again wanted to have to confront the evidence of his torment, his grief and his guilt, which he'd indulged at length before locking away for ever. If this house had been left to rack and ruin, taking with it the memories contained within and turning them to dust, that would have been fine with him.

But at least the contract between him and Orla's company had come with an NDA. At least the truth about his supposedly perfect marriage would never emerge. The thought of it brought him out in a cold sweat. He judged himself plenty. He didn't need judgement from anywhere else.

'I can't have,' said Orla, visibly blanching, evidently stunned.

'Are you suggesting it's *I* who's made the mistake?'

'What? N-no. Of course not,' she stammered, the blush hitting her cheeks turning them from deathly pale to a pretty pink. 'There must have been a communication error. I'm so sorry. I'll make this right.'

There was nothing she could do to make anything right. What was done could not be undone. He should know. His son couldn't be reborn with a heartbeat instead of without one. He couldn't rewind time so that he could both erase the argument that had caused that and subsequently see what was happening with Calysta in time to stop her taking her own life. No one could. What he *could* do was get rid of Orla before he lost his grip on his fast-unravelling control.

'You have five minutes to get your things,' he said, his voice low and tight with the effort of holding himself together when inside he was being torn apart, 'and then I want you gone.'

CHAPTER TWO

ROOTED TO THE SPOT, Orla watched Duarte turn on his heel and stride off, her heart hammering and a cold sweat breaking out all over her skin. The floor beneath her feet seemed to be rocking and the room was spinning.

Oh, God, he was furious. He clearly didn't tolerate mistakes and she couldn't blame him, because neither did she. In fact, she hadn't made a single one since her engagement, which had come to an end four years ago. And even *before* that she'd done her level best to avoid them. Mistakes equalled failure and failure was not an option in her world.

As an overlooked, average middle child squashed between an older sister who sang like an angel and a brilliant athlete of a younger brother, she'd fought hard for her space in the family. She'd worked like a demon to get the best grades at school and siphon off some of the parental attention her more talented, more successful siblings attracted so easily. And it had worked. So well, in fact, that striving for excellence, for perfection, had become embedded in her DNA. Her sense of self-worth depended on it, she knew, and she couldn't imagine ever approaching a task with the expectation of anything less.

But she hadn't allowed her childhood insecurities to surge up and swamp her for years, and she certainly wasn't about to start now. Her blood chilled at the very idea of it. So it didn't matter at this precise moment how the mix-up here had happened when her company went to great lengths to ensure a project ran as smoothly as possible. An analysis of what had gone wrong would have to wait.

Nor was her opinion of Duarte's reaction to the situation of any relevance. She might think that his response was totally over-the-top when firstly, she'd never let him down before, secondly, there was still time to fix things, and finally, he had the unexpected bonus of a freshly gleaming home, but he was the client. He was clearly furious that she'd screwed up—although he couldn't possibly be as angry with her as she was with herself—and it was her job to reverse that. To get herself unfired. And not just because she had two decades' worth of hang-ups to battle. After years of grafting to prove her talent, her worth and her indispensability, of single-mindedly focusing on reaching the top, she'd finally been allowed to buy into the business. She had no intention of giving Sam, co-owner and joint CEO of Hamilton Garrett, any reason to regret that decision. Duarte earned them millions in fees and commissions—almost as much as all their other clients put together—and she would *not* be the one to lose him.

It wouldn't be easy but nor was it impossible. The coldness of his tone—worse than if he'd shouted at her, in fact—wasn't encouraging, but all she'd have to do, surely, was handle him the way she handled anyone who was reluctant to give her what she wanted. People always saw things her way in the end, and he'd be no different.

Taking a deep breath to calm the panic and channelling cool determination instead, Orla grabbed her trainers and strode out of the bedroom. She raced around the balcony that looked over the ground floor on all four sides of the house, until she came to the top of the wide, sweeping stone staircase.

'Wait,' she called, spying Duarte heading along a corridor, and hurrying down the steps. But he didn't stop, he didn't even show any sign he'd heard her, so she tried again. Louder. 'Conde de Castro. Duarte. Please. Stop. I can explain.'

He threw up a dismissive hand. 'No.'

'I'll do anything. Just name it.'

'It's too late.'

It couldn't be. That wasn't an option. 'How can I make this right?'

'You can't.'

She could. She *would*. She just had to figure out what he wanted. A discount, perhaps. Didn't everyone love a bargain, even wildly successful billionaires? 'I'll waive your fees for the next three years. Five. No, *ten*.'

'Your fees are a rounding error to me,' he said bluntly, continuing to power ahead with long, loose strides while she, still barefoot, remained hot on his heels. 'And if you think I'm continuing with my membership of your organisation, you are, once again, very much mistaken.'

Right. Not that, then. 'I'll make a donation to a charity of your choice.'

'You couldn't possibly match the sums I already donate.'

That was undoubtedly true.

Damn.

'I'll have someone else handle your account,' she offered, ignoring the odd sense of resistance that barrelled through her at the thought of it because desperate times called for desperate measures.

'No.'

Well, good. But on the other hand, not good. In the face of such intractability, she had little to work with here and she could feel the panic begin to return, but she banked it down because she wasn't giving up.

'Could you stop for a moment so we can talk about this?' she said, fighting to keep the desperation from her voice and thinking that while his back view—broad shoulders, trim waist—was a fine sight, it would be a whole lot easier to persuade him to see things her way if they were face to face.

'There's nothing to discuss.'

'Have we ever let you down before?'

'You've let me down now.'

'Your conference isn't for another three weeks. There's more than enough time to prepare.' Just about.

'That's not the point.'

Then what *was* the point? None of this made any sense. Yes, she'd made a mistake, and she winced just to think of it, but objectively speaking, it was hardly the end of the world. So what was going on? At no point during the course of their relationship had

Duarte come across as in any way eccentric. His requests were by no means as outrageous as some. Quite the opposite in fact. She'd always considered him entirely reasonable.

So could it be that he was just stubborn? Well, so was she. She stood to lose not just his business and her partner's respect and confidence in her but also quite possibly her emotional equilibrium, which relied on her continually succeeding at everything she did, and that wasn't happening.

'There must be *something* I can do to persuade you to change your mind,' she said, breathless with the effort of keeping up with him and adrenalin-fuelled alarm. 'Something you want.'

'There isn't.'

There was. Everyone had at least one weakness, and Duarte wasn't *that* godlike.

Think, she told herself as she continued to hurry after him. She had to think. What did he want that he didn't already have that only she could get him? What would he find irresistible? Impossible to refuse?

Desperately, Orla racked her brains for what she knew about him. She frantically sifted through a mental catalogue of interviews and articles, revisiting the phone conversations they'd had, grasping for titbits of information, for something, for *anything*…

Until—

Aha!

She had it. Thank *God*. The perfect challenge. It wouldn't be easy. In fact, it would most likely be immensely difficult, otherwise he'd already have achieved it. But making the impossible possible was her job. She had her methods. She had her sources. She frequently had to get creative and think flexibly. She'd find a way. She always did.

'How about a bottle of Chateau Lafite 1869?'

If Duarte had a fully functioning brain or any sense of self-preservation, he'd be sticking with his plan to shut this place back up and get the hell out of here so he could regroup and reset the status quo that had been shattered when he'd been informed that there was activity up at the house.

He'd only been back on the estate half an hour before the news had reached him. He hadn't waited to hear the details. His intention to spend the evening among the vines, which calmed his thoughts and grounded him in a way that nothing else could these days, had evaporated. A dark, swirling mist had descended, wiping his head of reason and accelerating his pulse, and he'd driven straight here, leaving in his wake a cloud of clay-filled dust.

He'd assumed whoever it was had broken in. He'd been fuelled by fury and braced for a fight. Then he'd found her, a golden-haired stranger in his bed, and the mist had thickened. Women had been known to go to great lengths to attract his attention. His wife, who'd gone to the greatest lengths of all by deliberately falling pregnant and effectively trapping him into marriage, had been one of them. So what did this one want?

The discovery of Orla's identity had cleared some of the mist, but it had made no difference whatsoever to his intention to eject her from his existence. He never deviated from a plan once made, whether it be a seduction, a marriage proposal or perpetuating a lie in order to assuage his guilt. Yet now, unhinged and battered, and with the name of the wine he'd been after for years and the whisper of promise hovering in the ether, he came to an abrupt halt and whipped round.

'What are you talking about?'

For a moment Orla just stared at him as if she hadn't a clue either, breathless and flushed, but a second later she folded her arms and squared her shoulders.

'You think I'm incompetent,' she said, her chin up and her eyes lit with a fire that turned them to a dazzling burnished gold and momentarily robbed him of his wits. 'Let me prove to you I'm not. I read in an article a while back that the only material thing you want but don't have is an 1869 bottle of Chateau Lafite. I will get it for you. Give me twenty-four hours.'

Incredulity obliterated the dazzle and the return of his reason slammed him back to earth. Seriously? She thought it was that easy? She had *no* idea. He'd been trying to get his hands on this wine, without success, for years. He'd tried everything. Persuasion, negotiation…he'd even toyed with the idea of bribery. What could she achieve in twenty-four hours? A couple of phone calls. That would be it.

'It's an exceptionally rare vintage,' he said scathingly, unable to keep the disbelief from his voice.

'I wouldn't expect it to be anything less.'

'Only three bottles exist.'

She stared at him for the longest of seconds, blanching faintly. 'Three?'

'Three,' he confirmed with a nod. 'And none of the owners is interested in selling.'

'Well,' she said, straightening her spine in an obvious attempt to recover. 'Not to you, maybe.'

But they would to her? What planet was she on? Delusion? 'You must be mad.'

'I've never felt saner.'

No. The colour had returned to her cheeks and her gaze now was filled with cool determination. She looked very sure of herself. Whereas he'd never felt *less* on solid ground. Spinning round like that had put him too close to her. Every cell of his body quivered with awareness. He could make out a ring of brown at the outer edges of her golden irises. Her scent—something light and floral, gardenia, perhaps, subtly layered with notes of rose and possibly sea salt—was intoxicating. The blood pumping through his veins was thick and sluggish. The need to touch her burned so strongly inside him that he had to shove his hands through his hair and take a quick step back before his already weakened control snapped and he acted on it.

'What makes you so sure you'll succeed where I didn't?' he said, crushing the inappropriate and unwelcome lunacy, and focusing.

'Experience,' she said. 'Tenacity. Plus, I never fail.'

Orla's tone was light but he detected a note of steel in her voice, which suggested a story that would have piqued his curiosity had he been remotely interested in finding out what it might be. But he wasn't. All he wanted was to forget that this afternoon had ever happened and get back to burying the guilt and the regret beneath a Mount Everest of a workload and getting through the days.

And in any case, she wouldn't be around long enough to ask even if he *was*. While he had to admire her confidence—however misguided—she would fail at this challenge and when the twenty-four hours were up she would leave. Which would mean having to find someone else to prepare the winery for the conference, but rare was the problem in business that couldn't be solved with money.

If it came to it, he would pay whatever it took. The conference was too important to screw up. Each year, in the belief that a rising tide lifted all boats, representatives from the world's top five family-owned wine businesses got together to analyse global trends, to solve any viticulture issues that might have arisen and generally to discuss all things oenological. This year it was his turn to host, the first since he'd taken his place as CEO three and a half years ago when the news that he was going to be a father had ignited an unexpected sense of responsibility inside him, which his own father had taken advantage of to retire.

There were those who couldn't see beyond the tabloid headlines and expected him to run the company into the ground by selling off all the assets and blowing the lot on having a good time, despite the twenty per cent increase in profit that had been generated since he'd been in charge. He didn't give a toss about them. He did, however, care about the business that had been going for nearly three hundred years. Its continued success depended on what people thought of his wines, and he was part of that package. He wasn't about to give anyone a reason to trash either his reputation or that of his company.

'So do we have a deal?' she said, jolting him out of his murky thoughts and recapturing his attention. 'Do you agree that if I succeed in acquiring this bottle of wine for you by this time tomorrow, you will recognise how good I am at my job and un-fire me?'

No, was the answer to that particular question. Orla had had her chance and she'd blown it. Duarte had a plan and he intended to stick to it. No allowances. No compromises. He'd been there, done that during his relationship with Calysta, regularly excusing her sometimes outrageous behaviour and ultimately sacrificing his freedom for what he'd believed to be the right thing, and he'd sworn he would never put himself in that position again.

Yet what if she did somehow succeed? he couldn't help wondering somewhere in the depths of his brain where recklessness still lurked. He'd be in possession of a bottle of the wine he'd been after for years. The headache of having to find someone else to finish the job she'd started would vanish. And then there was the sizzling attraction that was heating his blood and firing parts of his body he'd thought long numb and clamoured to be addressed.

Despite the reputation he'd earned in his twenties—which had been wholly deserved, he wasn't ashamed to admit—Duarte had no interest in romance these days. Love was a minefield into which he had no intention of venturing. It was messy and chaotic and could cause untold pain and resentment. In the wrong hands, it could be dangerous and damaging. Unrequited, it could be desperate and destructive.

Not that he'd ever experienced it himself.

He'd married Calysta because she was pregnant. A strange sense of duty he'd been totally unaware of previously had compelled him to stand by her and give their child his name. He'd never forget the moment he learned her pregnancy wasn't accidental, as he'd been led to believe. They'd been arguing about their lifestyle. He'd been determined to knuckle down and live up to his new responsibilities, she'd wanted to continue raising hell. In the heat of the moment, she'd yelled that she wished she'd stayed on the pill, and Duarte's world had stopped. He'd demanded an explanation, which she'd given, and at that moment any respect he'd had for her as the mother of his child had been blown to smithereens. He'd been taken for a fool, betrayed, his ability to trust pulverised, and the scars ran deep.

But it had been over three years since he'd slept with anyone, which was a long time for a man whose bedroom had once had a metaphorical revolving door. So perhaps that was why he was so aware of the flush on Orla's cheeks, the fire in her eyes and the way her chest still heaved with the effort of having raced to catch up with him. Maybe that was why he could so easily envisage her in his bed again, only this time with her wavy golden hair spread across his pillow as she gazed up at him, desire shining in her stunning topaz eyes and an encouragingly sultry smile curving her lovely mouth, focusing wholly on him instead of dreaming about someone else. If she was around, he'd have the opportunity to investigate this further and perhaps put an end to the sexual drought he'd been experiencing.

So, all things considered, he thought as the strands of these arguments wove together to form a conclusion, the pros of agreeing to her audacious proposal outweighed the cons. Changing the plan would be strategic, not weak. There'd be no need for compromises or allowances. The power, the control, would all be his.

'We have a deal.'

CHAPTER THREE

ORLA HAD LEFT Duarte's house with a longer to-do list than she'd had going in, but as she'd carted her things to the hire car she'd parked round the back first thing she'd refused to entertain the possibility of not getting through it.

She had to pour all her energy into delivering on her promise, she'd told herself resolutely, firing up the engine and driving away. She had to temporarily forget the fact that her job and all that was attached to it hung in the balance. She couldn't afford to panic. She needed all her wits about her if she was going to achieve what would no doubt turn out to be her toughest challenge to date.

The minute she'd arrived back at her hotel, after paying the site of the old winery a visit to scope out the venue she should have been focusing on, she'd called the office back in London. On learning, to her distress, that the mistake had been entirely hers, she'd doubled down on her efforts to fix it.

She didn't know how or why she'd misread the email that contained the details of Duarte's instructions but she hadn't wasted time dwelling on it. Instead, she'd been spurred into action. Since the Quinta was three times the size of the Casa and time was marching on, she'd sourced and hired a team from a local company to prepare it. A company new to her and an untested team, she'd recognised, but she had no doubt that she would be there to supervise.

Once that had been sorted, she'd set about tracking down the wine, which had been as challenging as she'd assumed. Although she reckoned she'd done a good job of concealing the sheer panic that had surged through her at Duarte's revelation that only three bottles of the wine he wanted existed, her confidence had been knocked for six. But she'd kept her cool, and on learning subsequently that all three bottles had been sold individually at auction fifteen years ago, she'd rallied. She knew the auctioneers well, and a ten-minute phone call had eventually furnished her with details of the sales.

The owners of the bottles she'd traced to Zurich and New York hadn't budged for anything. As for the bottle located in France, well, that had been a tough negotiation too, but ultimately a successful one—thank *God*—and as a result she was back at the top of her game, which was where she intended to stay.

There was no possible way that this evening Duarte would have the same impact on her as he had yesterday, she assured herself as she marched through the former manufacturing section of the winery, passing between rows of oak barrels that reached the roof and breathing in the rich scent of port that permeated the musty air. Those circumstances had been extraordinary, brought on by shock and, when he'd whipped round to face her in the corridor, so fast and unexpectedly she'd nearly crashed into him for the second time, the kind of proximity that punched her hard in the gut and flooded her with heat.

He'd looked at her for the longest of moments, she recalled, feeling a flush wash over her before she could stop it. That dark, hostile gaze of his had fixed to hers as if trying to see into her soul, and weirdly, time had seemed to stop. Her surroundings had receded and her focus had narrowed until all she could see was him. Her breasts had tightened and her mouth had gone dry. She'd felt very peculiar. Sort of on fire, yet shivery at the same time, and it had taken every ounce of strength to haul herself under control.

These circumstances, however, were anything but extraordinary. Given that they'd arranged this meeting an hour ago, there'd be no surprises. No head butts or strange spells of dizziness. No stopping of time, no galloping pulse and certainly no tingling of body parts. Her job was safe. She'd achieved the impossible and proved her value to him—and more importantly, to herself—and that was all that mattered.

Coming to a stop at the threshold of the room in which he'd told her to meet him, Orla pulled her shoulders back and took a deep breath. The anticipation and adrenalin crashing through her were entirely expected. The success of a project was always a rush, and with the added pressure of this one, and the sky-scraping stakes, the high was even higher.

On a slow, steadying exhale, she knocked on the door and at the curt *'Entra'* opened it. The room appeared to be half-office, half-sitting room. She briefly noticed a sofa, a coffee table, a sideboard and a pair of filing cabinets, but then her gaze landed on Duarte and yet again everything except him faded away.

He was sitting behind a desk, all large and

shadowy, with the setting sun streaming in through the open window behind him and bathing the room in warm, golden light. If she'd been able to tear her eyes away from him she might have admired the twinkling river that wound through the landscape and the gently undulating hills beyond, their terraces covered with vines that were dense with verdant foliage stretching to the horizon. She might have found serenity in the big, airy room with its cool flagstone floor and rough, whitewashed walls.

But to her bewilderment and distress she couldn't look away. She couldn't focus on anything but him. He was just so magnetic, so compelling, and now she was feeling anything but triumphant, anything but serene. Her skin was prickling and oxygen seemed to be scarce. The linen shift dress she was wearing was by no means tight—in fact, she'd deliberately chosen it because of its loose-fitting nature—yet when the fabric brushed against her body, shivers ran down her spine. She felt strangely on edge, alert and primed, as if waiting for something to happen, although she couldn't for the life of her work out what.

'Do you have it?'

The deep timbre of his voice scraped over her nerve endings, weakening her knees dangerously, and for a moment she wondered, did she have what? Her marbles? Her self-possession? Apparently not. Because despite her hopes and expectations to the contrary, his effect on her was still so intense she could barely recall her own name. The X-rated dreams that had invaded what little sleep she had managed to grab were cascading into her head, so detailed and vivid she was going dizzy, and God, it was stifling in here.

But enough was enough. She couldn't go on like this. It was totally unacceptable. She was a professional. She was here to work. She had to get a grip. And breathe.

'I do,' she said, giving herself a mental shake before stepping forwards into the room and setting her precious cargo on the desk, which unfortunately put her in a position where not only could she see him better, but smell him better too. 'There. Are you impressed?'

Duarte didn't respond. She doubted he'd even heard her. He was wholly focused on the box she'd put in front of him. Staring at it with what looked like barely concealed awe, he leaned forwards, undid the catch and lifted the lid.

Her gaze snagged on his hands as he carefully removed the bottle and slowly twisted it first one way then the other. Strong tanned hands, she noticed, a tingling pulse beginning to throb in the pit of her stomach. Long fingers with a light dusting of dark hair, neat nails. She could envisage them tangled in her hair, on her body, sliding over her skin and—

'Take a seat,' he murmured, popping that little bubble for which she was grateful, yes, *grateful*, not resentful.

Orla sat. She didn't know why. The plan had been to present him with the bottle, remind him of her competence and their deal, at which point he'd un-fire her and she'd get back to the business of preparing his estate for the conference. Sitting had not been part of anything. But then, nor had staring and hungering and magnetism, or indeed, weak, wobbly legs.

'Tell me how you did it.'

Right. So normally she didn't divulge her methods any more than she revealed her sources. Both were her currency, and her little black book of notes and contacts was worth a fortune. But in this case, since Duarte was directly impacted, she should probably disclose at least the bare bones of the transaction.

'I made a few phone calls,' she said, determined to ignore his potent allure and remembering instead the events of the last twenty-four hours. 'I tracked one bottle down to Zurich, another to New York and the third to France. This one came from there. I had it flown directly here from Nice and took delivery of it an hour ago.'

He arched one dark, disbelieving eyebrow. 'Just like that?'

Well, no, but there was no way she was going to go into how stressful it had been. How wildly her emotions had oscillated between panic and relief. How slowly the minutes had dragged as she'd waited first for responses to the approaches she'd made and then for the bottle she'd acquired to actually arrive.

So many things could have gone wrong. The plane could have crashed. The box could have been dropped. It could have been stolen en route. Anything. Her nerves had been shredded right up until the moment she had the wine in her hands. But he didn't need to know about the roller coaster of a ride she'd been on today.

'The logistics and insurance took some working out,' she said coolly, as if it hadn't taken every resource she had or wrung her emotionally dry, 'and it took a while to establish that the bottle had been meticulously stored with temperature and humidity control, but essentially, yes.'

Her explanation did nothing to remove the scepticism from his expression. 'So all you had to do was ask, and Antoine Baudelaire simply handed it over?'

If only. 'Not exactly.'

Duarte's brows snapped together, his eyes narrowing a little, and Orla shifted uneasily on her seat because this was where it possibly got a little awkward.

'Monsieur Baudelaire gifted the bottle to his daughter six months ago as a birthday present,' she said, mentally crossing her fingers that he'd be reasonable about the terms that had been agreed. 'It was her I negotiated with. First over the phone, and then over Zoom.'

'His daughter?'

'That's right. Isabelle.'

'What was the price?'

There was no point in pretending there wasn't one. Money hadn't worked. She'd had to get creative. 'She's organising a charity ball around Christmas time,' she said. 'She's been looking for a guest of honour to boost ticket sales and encourage auction donations. She now has one.'

The temperature in the room dropped a

couple of degrees and Orla shivered at the thunderous expression now adorning Duarte's perfect features. He sat back and she wanted to lean in to close the distance and capture his scent again, which was completely ridiculous.

'You pimped me out,' he said, a tiny muscle hammering in his jaw.

'I prefer to think of it as a provision of services in exchange for goods.'

'Of course you do.'

His tone was cold, his words were clipped. He was clearly furious, and her heartstrings twanged because by all accounts he didn't socialise much these days and the idea of a ball in all its gaiety must be deeply unappealing. But it was only an evening of his time. A fair swap, she'd figured, relieved beyond belief to have secured the bottle with relatively little trouble, even if it had taken a while to find out what it was that an heiress who had everything she needed and an overindulgent father might want.

'Believe me, you got off lightly.'

His face darkened even further. 'In what possible way?'

'She also wanted you to be her date.'

Isabelle had waxed lyrical about Duarte. She'd never met him but she'd read everything there was to read about him and pored over every photo. She was under the impression that she was the one to bring love back into his life, if only they could meet. However, if Isabelle could see Duarte's expression at this precise moment, she might have thought differently, because he now looked appalled as well as angry.

'She can't be much more than a teenager,' he all but growled.

'She just turned twenty. And you're thirty. I pointed that out. She eventually saw the better of it.'

It had taken some persuasion, and she'd had to call on every skill she possessed, but there was no way Orla was going to agree to *that*. It was one thing offering up his time and his influence, quite another to act the matchmaker. Her company left that up to others, and for some reason the mere idea of the stunning and no doubt perky Isabelle batting her eyelids at the gorgeous Duarte made her feel like throwing up.

'Am I supposed to be grateful?'

Quite frankly, yes. The infatuated girl had a crush on him the size of Portugal. She'd have clung to him like a limpet and been hard to prise off.

'I could always give the wine back,' she said, with a quick pointed glance at the wonky bottle that predated modern glass-making techniques and was standing on the desk in all its dusty, unassuming glory. 'All you have to do is say the word.'

The scowl on his face deepened. 'No.'

'OK, then.'

And that, she thought, as a deluge of relief and triumph washed over her, was how it was done.

Orla thought she'd won. Duarte could tell by the smug satisfaction on her face and the delight dancing in the depths of her eyes, and on a rational level he knew she deserved her moment of victory. She'd defied the odds. She'd achieved something that had always been out of his reach, and he ought to be impressed by what she'd accomplished because, objectively speaking, she was a genius.

On a deeper, more emotional, more turbulent level, however, the deal she'd struck to secure the wine sat like a rock on his chest, crushing his lungs and fogging his head. She'd involved him in her negotiations and allowed him no say in the matter. She'd used him to get what she wanted, and the feeling that he'd been manipulated—again—burned through him like acid, spinning him back to a time he'd been taken for a fool, a time he strove to forget.

With the memories of Calysta, her calculations and her volatility descending thick and fast, the fog in his head intensified. Emotion roiled around inside him. Every instinct he possessed was rising up to fight it. The need to regain the upper hand and to shift the balance of power back in his favour hammered through him.

It shouldn't be hard, he assured himself darkly. He held all the cards. Or at least he ought to. He was Orla's client. In a way, he was her boss. Yet he got the strange feeling that bending over backwards to please him simply because he paid her to do so was of little importance to her. Intense relief was woven through the triumph in her expression and it struck him now that there'd been a trace of desperation in her voice when she'd been running after him down the corridor yesterday afternoon, begging him to reconsider firing her. Something that hinted there was more at stake for her than the mere loss of a client.

With the arrogance of someone used to calling the shots and having his every order obeyed, he'd assumed uppermost in her mind would be keeping him happy, but what if all she really cared about was rectifying her mistake?

'Your strategy was a risky one,' he said, the odd, unexpected hit to his pride adding to the turmoil churning around his system and lending a chill to his tone.

'In what way?'

'You're counting on me to hold up your side of the deal.'

As the implication of his words registered, Orla's smile vanished. She went very still and wariness and tension gripped her frame. 'Are you saying you won't?'

And *now* he was back in control, he thought with grim satisfaction. 'I'm simply saying assumptions are unwise.'

Anger sparked in her eyes. 'If you renege on the terms I agreed my reputation will be destroyed.'

'You should have thought of that before you decided to use me.'

'It's one evening of your time and I *did* think of that,' she fired back. 'I read you had integrity, Duarte. I read you played fair. Is that not true?'

It was true, dammit. Just as he fought for his reputation to protect his business against the naysayers, he worked hard for his success and did things by the book. 'It's true.'

'I thought as much,' she said with a curt nod. 'So if I did take a risk it was a calculated one. I considered one evening a small price to pay for something you've been after for years. And yes, I suppose you could refuse to support the ball if you wanted to, but there are things at stake for me here that you couldn't even *begin* to understand.'

So he'd been right about the story. 'Like what?'

'My livelihood for starters.'

Which implied there was more. 'What else?'

'Isn't that enough?' she said, her chin and her guard back up. 'I've worked insanely hard for what I have. Don't destroy me simply because you can.'

And now he was even more intrigued. Why was *she* at risk of destruction, rather than her reputation or her job? What was really behind the offer to complete a challenge she must have known had a stratospheric risk of failure? What made her tick? And, come to think of it, what was she was doing here, seeing to his instructions personally? Who had she been dreaming about while asleep in his bed?

These were questions to which he sorely wanted the answers, he realised with a disconcerting jolt. He had no idea why. But then, nor could he work out why the fact that she'd used him as leverage in her negotiations didn't seem to matter quite so much now as it had a moment ago.

Perhaps the angry energy crackling around her, which gave her a stunning, dazzling glow, had short-circuited his brain. Or perhaps it was because, on reflection, he could see that what Orla had agreed with Isabelle Baudelaire was hardly outrageous. Once upon a time, before he'd met and married Calysta and duty and responsibility had become of primary importance, he'd frequented many a party. More often than not he'd *started* the party. And, as Orla had pointed out, it was only one night and it was for charity, so how tough would it be?

Furthermore, his acceptance of her terms would mean that *their* deal was on and she'd therefore be staying to oversee the preparation of his conference, which would bring benefits beyond mere convenience, because at some point over the last twenty-four hours he'd had to admit to himself that he wanted her. Badly.

What else could account for the change in his behaviour that had occurred the moment she'd mentioned the wine, when these days he *always* stuck to the plan? Why else would he have crashed out on the sofa in this stifling room last night instead of returning to his airy apartment in Porto that benefited from a sea breeze, as he'd intended?

He'd told himself it was simply a more efficient use of his time and better for the planet if he parked the helicopter instead of toing and froing between here and the city of his birth, a distance of some two hundred and fifty kilometres. But that didn't explain the heightened awareness he'd felt all day or the anticipation that had been rocketing through his system ever since he'd received Orla's text asking where they should meet. Or, indeed, the frustration and disappointment that he hadn't run into her today despite making himself wholly available.

No. He wanted to strip off the dress rendered see-through by the evening sun streaming in and tumble her to the sofa so much it was addling his brain, a brain that was already running on empty thanks to a severe lack of sleep. He'd had an uncomfortable night, and not just because his six-foot-three frame was too big for this room's compact two-seater sofa. Enveloped by the warm, velvety darkness, the still silence broken only by the cicadas chirruping in the vines, he'd tossed and turned, his imagination going into overdrive as he'd revisited the events of the day.

What if he'd kissed Orla awake instead of shaking her shoulder? had been the thought rolling around his head even though he was no fairy-tale prince. What if he'd capitalised on the brief flare of desire he'd caught in the depths of her eyes the moment before she'd leapt from the bed as if it were on fire?

His imagination hadn't cared about how inappropriate that would have been. His imagination had embraced hindsight, which recognised that she quite possibly felt the attraction too, and had gone wild, bombarding his head with visions of the two of them setting the sheets alight until he'd had to head to an old disused bathroom to take an ice-cold shower, where finally he'd found relief.

'All right,' he said, his mind teeming with ideas about how he might make the most of the situation that had landed in his lap. 'I'll honour your deal.'

'Thank you,' she said with a brief, confident nod, as if she'd expected his agreement all along. 'And the one between us?'

The one that meant he wouldn't have to find someone else to finish readying the estate, provided the chance to get the answers to the questions he had and offered him the potential to find out if she was as attracted to him as he was to her and, if so, do something about it? It was a no-brainer.

'That one too.'

CHAPTER FOUR

Oh, thank God for that, thought Orla, the tension gripping her body giving way to relief so intense it was almost palpable.

Things had taken an unexpected turn for the worse for a moment back there and the sudden potential reversal of fortune had sent her into an almighty spin, but she'd stayed cool and calm, and disaster had been averted. The mistake she'd made had been fixed. Her job was secure, her reputation was intact and her demons remained buried. Her work here was done. And now, with the adrenalin and stress fast draining away and the monumental effort of controlling her body's wayward response to his taking its toll, all she wanted to do was sleep because she was shattered.

Stifling a yawn, she pushed up on the chair arms and got to her feet, every muscle she possessed aching and sore, and she didn't even pause when he said, 'Where do you think you're going?'

'Bed,' she muttered, envisaging her gorgeously comfortable room at the hotel and almost weeping with need. 'It's been a very long, very eventful twenty-four hours.'

'Don't leave just yet. Stay and have a drink with me.'

Now, that did make her pause mid-turn. Because, despite her desperation to flee consuming every one of her brain cells, something about his voice seemed different. The chill had gone. His tone was smoother, lighter, less antagonistic and more like that of the man in her dreams.

Curious, her pulse skipping, she turned back and glanced down to find that he was looking at her with focus, with intent, and the tiny hairs on the back of her neck shot up. At the sight of the decidedly wicked glint in his eye, and the faint yet devastating smile curving his mouth, she shivered, and heat pooled low in her belly.

What was he up to? Why the glint? Why the smile? Why the abrupt one-eighty personality change?

She didn't want to know, she told herself firmly. She was tired and confused and her defences were weak. She should have ignored him and carried on with her exit. She shouldn't have allowed her curiosity to get the better of her. She didn't need glints and shivers. She needed respite from his effect on her and to recharge her batteries.

'Thank you, but no,' she said, crushing the tiny yet powerful urge to say yes and indulge her curiosity a little while longer because she had a plan to which she intended to stick.

'It doesn't seem right to drink this alone.'

He waved a hand in the direction of the bottle she'd acquired and her eyebrows shot up, shock momentarily wiping out the fatigue and the wariness along with the plan. *'This?'*

He gave a nod. 'Yes.'

'You're planning on *drinking* it?'

'I am.'

For a moment she just stared at him, scarcely able to believe it. Had he lost his mind? Perhaps yesterday's bump to the head had done more damage than had first appeared, because this wasn't just any old bottle of wine. This was special beyond words. Surely it wasn't for drinking.

'But it's over a hundred and fifty years old,' she said, aghast. 'It's worth a quarter of a million dollars. If you drank it, that would be it. History and a fortune blown in a matter of minutes. Shouldn't it be in a museum?'

'It *is* mine, isn't it?' he said reasonably, although she noticed that both the glint and the smile had faded slightly.

'Well, yes, but—'

'I never wanted it simply for the sake of owning it, only to admire it from a distance while it gathered even more dust. I've wanted it for its story, to savour and appreciate it and learn from it. So let Zurich and New York put theirs in a museum. I'll do what I damn well please with mine.'

'Of course,' she said, hastily back-pedalling, since, despite the easy way he'd delivered the explanation, he didn't look at all pleased at having his decision questioned and really she ought not to be antagonising him when she'd only just got her job back. 'It's none of my business what you do with it. But seriously, please save it for your guests at the conference. It would be completely wasted on me. I know nothing about wine. I'm more of a cocktails-with-an-umbrella kind of a girl.'

'Then I'll teach you.'

To her alarm, he surged to his feet in one fluid movement and made for the sideboard on the other side of the room, but she didn't want him to teach her, she thought a bit desperately. She wanted a break from the dizzying breathlessness that she couldn't seem to shake no matter how hard she tried. She wanted space. Sleep. And at some point she really ought to try and figure out why she'd messed up his instructions in the first place. 'What if I don't want to learn?'

'Isn't it your job to see to my every request?'

While the question that wasn't a question hung in the air, Orla narrowed her eyes and shot daggers at his back. Bar the immoral, the illegal or the unethical, it was, damn him, and it occurred to her suddenly that not only was he drop-dead gorgeous, but he was also determined and ruthless and clearly unused to hearing the word 'no'.

Not that that was remotely relevant at the moment. Why he would want her to share the wine was anyone's guess, but she had the feeling that she was still on somewhat shaky ground and he was the client, which meant that he was right. Within reason, what he wanted, he got. So she'd let him do his spiel, have one quick sip of wine and *then* she'd be off. 'Fine.'

'Excellent. Come and join me.'

Armed now with a decanter and a corkscrew, Duarte picked up the quarter of a million dollars that he was about to throw down his very tanned, very attractive throat and strode to a seating area where half a dozen glasses stood upside down on a tray in the centre of a coffee table.

Orla eyed the only seating option warily. The sofa wasn't a big one and he'd take up most of it. Perhaps she could drag the chair she'd been sitting on over. But no. It was solidly wooden and impossibly heavy. It wasn't budging, no matter how hard she pulled.

Taking a deep, steadying breath and assuring herself that it would be fine, that all they were doing was tasting wine, she moved to the sofa and sat down, wedging herself as tightly into the corner as she could. But, as she'd suspected, it wasn't enough. There was just too much of him. He was stealing her air, dizzying her with his proximity and robbing her of her composure, and she had the feeling that alcohol was only going to make things worse.

Yet she couldn't move. In fact, as she watched him brushing the dust off the neck of the bottle and carefully removing the cap, she wanted to scoot over and lean into him. She wanted to find out exactly how hard and muscled his chest might be. His shirt was unbuttoned at the top to reveal a tantalising wedge of tanned skin and gave her a glimpse of fine dark hair, and her fingers itched to investigate further.

'The grapes that made this wine grew when Queen Victoria was on the British throne,' he said, tilting the decanter and slowly pouring the contents of the bottle into it while she set her jaw and sat on her hands. 'Ulysses S Grant was the US president. Echoes of revolution and Bonaparte still sounded through France. It was a hot, dry summer in Bordeaux that year, a perfect climate for growth and harvest. The vineyard had just been bought by Rothschild. This was the first vintage to be bottled under their ownership. Nothing was mechanised. These grapes were picked by hand and transported by horse and cart. They were trodden by the feet of a hundred locals instead of going into a press as they do nowadays.'

His deep voice was mesmerising. The web he was spinning was lulling her into a sensual trance from which she didn't want to emerge. She was there, in France. She could feel the heat of the sun, smell the dusty earth that mingled with the scent of ripened grapes and snippets of French. She wanted him to tell her more. She wanted him to tell her everything. She could listen to him for hours.

'You paint a vivid picture,' she said, her

voice so unusually low and husky that she had to clear her throat to disguise it. 'You have a good imagination.'

He set the bottle down and glanced at her, his eyes dark and glinting with something that made her stomach slowly flip. 'So I've discovered.'

What did *that* mean?

'What if it's turned to vinegar?' she said, forcing herself to focus on the beautiful cut-glass decanter that was now worth a fortune, and not on the hypnotic effect he was having on her.

'It hasn't.'

'How do you know?'

'Smell the cork.'

Twisting round to face her, he held it under her nose and she instinctively inhaled, but all she got was him. Spice, soap, some kind of citrus. An intoxicating combination that muddled her head.

'Delicious,' she murmured, not entirely sure that was a word that could be used to describe the smell of a cork, but then, she wasn't entirely sure either that she actually meant the cork.

'Promising,' he said, and as he turned away to reach forwards and select a couple of glasses she got the strange feeling he wasn't talking entirely about the cork either.

He poured wine into each, watching the flow of liquid intently as he did so, and then nudged one in her direction. 'Here you go.'

'Do you realise there's around forty thousand dollars' worth of wine in that glass?'

'Forget the money.'

'That's easy for you to say.' It was all very well for aristocratic billionaires. For mere mortals, it was a small fortune. 'Forty thousand dollars in pounds would pay off a considerable chunk of my mortgage.'

'A fair point,' he said with a wry smile that flipped her stomach. 'But this is all about the senses.'

Hmm. Well. She didn't know that her senses would be up to much. They were frazzled, completely overwhelmed by him. He was all she could see…his voice was all she could hear. His scent had permeated every cell of her being and she wanted to touch and taste so badly it was becoming a problem. There wasn't a lot of space left for strawberries or compost.

'What do I do?'

'First you look at it, then you smell it, and finally you taste it.'

God, could he read her mind?

'Hold it against this,' he said, handing her a piece of white paper, which she took with fingers that were irritatingly unsteady. 'Tilt the glass. What do you see?'

Getting a grip, Orla did as he instructed and studied the liquid. 'It's a dark sort of reddish brown in the middle,' she said, her voice thankfully not reflecting any of the chaos going on inside her. 'Paler at the rim.'

'Wine browns as it ages and gets hazier.'

'This is very clear. Is that good?'

'It is. Now level it and swirl it around.'

'What does that do?'

'Two things,' he said, demonstrating in a way that bizarrely made her stomach clench. She valued competence. She appreciated it in others. She'd never found it sexy before, but in him, she did.

'First,' he continued, 'when the liquid touches the side of the glass the alcohol evaporates. What remains—the legs—indicates the viscosity or the degree of sweetness. Secondly, it maximises the surface area and releases the aromas.'

If she'd been in a test and had had to say what came second Orla would have been stuck for an answer. All she could think about now were legs. His legs. The long length of his thighs a foot away from hers and how powerful they might be beneath the denim of his jeans.

'What do you see?'

'No legs,' she said a bit breathlessly as she tore her gaze from his thighs and returned it to the glass. 'This must be very dry.'

'You're a fast learner.'

She'd had to be if she'd wanted to claim her place in her family. She'd worked hard and paid attention. The only area that strategy hadn't proven successful had been in the bedroom. She didn't know why. She'd tried her damnedest with her ex-fiancé Matt, yet nothing. It was immensely disappointing and insanely frustrating, and for the benefit of her emotional well-being she tried not to dwell on it much. 'I'm good at listening.'

'Let's see what else you're good at,' said Duarte, his eyes dark and glittering. 'Stick your nose in and sniff it.'

It was hardly the sexiest of instructions, yet she had an image of burying her nose into his neck, and longing thudded in the pit of her stomach. His nose, she noticed, was gorgeous. Straight. Perfectly proportioned. Aquiline, even, which wasn't a word she'd ever had cause to use before.

'What do you smell?'

'Cherries,' she said, the aroma of the wine

winding through her before gradually separating out into individual strands. 'Something herby. Rosemary maybe. And, weirdly, cheese.'

'You *are* good at this.'

He did the same, only way more expertly than her and for far longer. He considered, muttered something in Portuguese and made some notes on a pad on the table.

'Now taste it,' he said. 'Take a big gulp and swish it around. You should feel the alcohol at the back of your throat.'

'And then?'

'Swallow it and breathe in through your mouth and out through your nose. Note the textures and the astringency. Then take another gulp. That one you can either spit out or swallow.'

She would *not* react to that, she told herself firmly. She wasn't sixteen. But her imagination had other ideas. Her imagination had her getting up to lock the door to this room, heading back and then dropping to her knees before him.

Maybe that bang to the head had done more damage than she'd assumed to her too. She was dizzy and discombobulated, and when she tried the wine in the way he'd suggested, knocking it back instead of spitting it out, she could barely think straight, let alone take note of its textures.

'What do *you* think of it?' she said, struggling for control of her thoughts and setting her glass down before she dropped it.

'It's exceptional. Very vibrant for its age. Long finish. Impressive.'

'How strong is it?'

'Average. Why?'

'I'm feeling very light-headed.'

'That's unlikely to have anything to do with the wine,' he said, putting his own glass down before turning to study her with what looked like concern. 'It could be the heat.'

It was warm in here, that much was true. The sun at this angle bathed the room in abundant evening sunshine. But no, it wasn't the heat. That wouldn't account for the throbbing between her legs. It was him.

Her heart was thundering and her temperature was rocketing, and she could feel it happening inside her again—the strange combination of fire and ice that she'd experienced yesterday when he'd come to an abrupt halt and whipped round in the corridor. Her head was spinning but somehow, in the midst of the chaos, she noticed that he'd gone very still. Very alert. The tension vibrating through him was almost palpable.

As the seconds ticked by the air between them thickened, crackling with electricity. Awareness charged her nerve endings. His gaze dipped to her mouth for a second and her lips tingled. He was so close. All she'd have to do was lean forwards a little and she'd *finally* be able to find out what he felt like, what he tasted like.

'Orla?' he said, his voice very low and gravelly.

'Yes?'

'You need to stop looking at me like that.'

His eyes were blazing and she was dazzled. The rush of adrenalin that was shooting through her was making her feel reckless. 'How am I looking at you?'

'As if you want me to kiss you.'

'I do,' she breathed before she could stop herself, but oh, she *did*. She was going out of her mind. Sex was a problem but kissing would be OK, surely, if he was amenable.

'Well, why didn't you say?' he muttered roughly, clamping one hand to the back of her head to bring her forward and then planting his mouth on hers with a speed that suggested he was very amenable indeed.

She didn't have time or the resources to marvel at that. The inappropriateness of what they were doing didn't cross her mind once.

The heat flooding her body and the desire pounding along her veins were wiping her head of rational thought. All she could do was succumb to sensation.

She moaned and wrapped her arms around his neck, and the kiss deepened and intensified. The muscles of his shoulder bunched beneath her fingers as she ran them over him and this time he was the one to groan.

With an urgency that she would have found flattering had she been capable of thought, Duarte disentangled his hands from her hair and moved them to her waist. He lifted and shifted her and then, hardly aware of what was happening, she found herself astride him. He held her hips and tugged her towards him, and when she pressed against him, his erection rubbing her where she so desperately ached for him, she tore her mouth from his and gasped.

But that didn't deter him. He simply set his lips to her neck, lingering on the pulse hammering at its base, while she dropped her head back to give him better access and struggled for breath. With one hand he held her close. He slid the other down her thigh, slipped it beneath the hem of her dress and pushed it up.

Any minute now, she thought dazedly as

she burned up with want, her clothes would come off, followed by his, and then there'd be more touching and some body parts would want to be in others and it wouldn't all go wrong for her this time. There'd be no disappointment or despair. There'd be explosions and ecstasy and it would be perfect. More perfect than she could have ever dreamed, and her dreams had been pretty damn good.

But this wasn't a dream, this was reality. The heat and the desire coursing through her were real, which meant that she *could* feel passion, she *wasn't* frigid. She'd always thought she was a failure in the bedroom because she was unable to experience the kind of pleasure she'd heard was possible, but look at what was going on here. Fireworks. Genuine mini-explosions. For the first time ever.

So what if it *hadn't* been her? she thought wildly as he continued to wreak havoc on her skin. She'd only had one lover, her former fiancé, so she had little scope for comparison, but what if the failure had been his? Or maybe it had just been down to simple incompatibility that was nobody's fault.

She hadn't given sex another chance after her engagement had ended because, frankly, if she wasn't going to excel at it, why bother, but could she have missed out on four years of fun and games and even relationships unnecessarily? Need she not have been quite so lonely in all that time?

The questions now ricocheting around her head were huge, breathtaking and utterly overwhelming. On top of the clawing need and delirium, Orla could feel the emotion swelling up inside her, threatening to overspill and quite possibly manifest itself in tears, and that was an outcome she really didn't want to have to explain, so she wrenched herself away and scrambled off him.

'What's wrong?' Duarte muttered hoarsely, breathing hard as he looked at her with eyes that were glazed and burning.

She swallowed down the lump in her throat and tugged at the hem of her dress, as if covering up might provide some kind of defence against the potentially earth-shattering discoveries swirling around her brain. 'I need to go.'

'Do you? Why?'

Because her foundations were rocking and she needed time and space to deal with it. Because the strength of her response to him was scary in its intensity and she was out of her depth here.

'Because this isn't appropriate,' she said

desperately, grasping at the only excuse she was willing to give.

'It feels pretty appropriate to me.'

'You're a client.'

'That's irrelevant. I want you,' he said, his eyes dark and compelling. 'Stay.'

'I can't.'

It was one request she couldn't fulfil. Not right now, at least. She couldn't think straight. She didn't know what she was doing. She was totally out of control and it was terrifying.

'Thank you for the wine,' she managed, her head swimming and her heart pounding. 'See you at the conference.'

And then, before she fell completely apart, she fled.

In something of a stupor Duarte listened to the quick, rhythmic tap of Orla's heels on the stone floor of the *adega* fading away and reflected dazedly that if she thought she wouldn't be seeing him again until the conference in three weeks' time, she could think again. Because a kiss like that did not end there.

It had been hot, wild and wholly unexpected. One minute the conversation had been all about the wine, the next, their gazes had collided and the world had stopped. The hunger on her face and the need he'd seen shimmering in her eyes had lit a rocket beneath his pulse and turned him harder than granite.

Once she'd indicated what she wanted, he hadn't thought twice about abandoning the wine and kissing her. He'd acted purely on instinct, and the minute their mouths had met, desire had crashed through him, flooding every inch of his body in seconds. It still lingered, along with the memory of her in his arms, kissing him back with more heat and passion than he could possibly have imagined, as well as utter bewilderment at how suddenly and swiftly she'd backed off.

Was the strength of his response to the kiss down to the fact that it had been such a long time since he'd wanted anyone? It was impossible to tell. And what had spooked her? Again, he had no idea, although he could sympathise if she'd been caught off guard by the explosive nature of the kiss. The impact of it had hit him like a freight train too.

But for all the new questions racing around his head, one he'd had before had definitely been answered. She wanted him just as much as he wanted her.

So what happened next? he wondered as he leapt to his feet and began to pace around the room, repeatedly criss-crossing the lengthening shadows. Once upon a time, he'd have welcomed the obviously mutual attraction, capitalised on the kiss that had given him a rush he hadn't realised he'd been missing, and pursued Orla without hesitation, without doubt. But he was no longer that man. These days, he was battered and bruised and wary. These days, he had the responsibility for a billion-euro business to keep him occupied.

And yet, it wasn't as if he was after a relationship. Thanks to his marriage, from which he still hadn't recovered, he was never having one of those again. In fact, his blood turned to ice at the mere *thought* of it. Love was manipulative and commitment was a prison. And he didn't just have his own experience to base his opinions on. His parents' unpleasant and messy divorce had proved that long ago.

But sex with someone with whom he shared the kind of chemistry that led to unbelievable pleasure? The one-or-two-nights-only sort of thing he'd favoured before he'd married? That he could handle. That would be perfect.

He felt more alive, more energised this evening than he had in months, and he wasn't about to give that up. So he'd put in the groundwork. He'd allay any fears or doubts

Orla might have. Seduction had once come to him as naturally as breathing and it wouldn't take too much effort to brush off the dust and fire up his skills. He'd have her in his bed in no time. So, contrary to her parting shot, she wouldn't be seeing him in three weeks' time. She'd be seeing him tomorrow.

CHAPTER FIVE

WHAT A NIGHT.

Stifling a yawn and wishing she didn't feel quite so bleary-eyed, Orla climbed into the car and fired up the engine to drive the seven kilometres that lay between her hotel and Duarte's estate.

To say she hadn't slept well was an understatement. Two fitful hours, from three to five, was all she'd managed, and that was on top of the sleepless, stressful night before. She was therefore running on empty, which didn't bode particularly well for a day during which she needed all her wits about her, but at least she was fortified with coffee and the conviction that nothing was going to go wrong.

There was no reason it should, she assured herself as she turned out of the hotel's entrance and onto the road. She was meeting the housekeeping team she'd hired in an hour. She'd confirmed the time and printed off a copy of the instructions she'd already emailed to them, and all other arrangements were on track.

Of course, it would help enormously if she could stop thinking about what had happened yesterday evening. The memories of the kiss she and Duarte had shared had tormented her for most of the night, rendering her so hot and bothered that she'd wondered if she was coming down with something.

The heat and skill of his mouth moving so insistently against hers… The rock-hard muscles of his chest flexing beneath her hands… The glazed look in his eyes and the faint flush slashing across his cheekbones and the heady satisfaction of knowing she'd caused both… And then the abrupt, mortifying way it had ended.

She hadn't had the chance to contemplate the notion that the mediocre sex she'd experienced to date might not be her fault after all or regret the time she'd potentially wasted. She hadn't had the wherewithal to find out how the venue mix-up could have happened. Distressingly, she hadn't had the head space for anything other than the actual kiss itself.

But at least today she'd be so busy concentrating on the job she was here to do she wouldn't have time to dwell on these things. It wasn't as if she and Duarte's paths were going to cross. She'd made it very clear she didn't expect to see him until the conference and there was no earthly reason why someone like him would bother himself with anything as mundane as housekeeping. He had a billion-euro global wine business to run and presumably multiple demands on his time. So there'd be no awkward moments involving stuttering conversation and fierce blushing. No gazing at his mouth and remembering. There was nothing to worry about at all.

Orla swung off the road and onto the wide, sandy drive that led to the Quinta, the awe rippling through her as fresh as it had been when she'd rushed over the day before yesterday, shortly after her initial, monumental mistake had come to light.

As conference venues went, this one was spectacular. The house had been built on the north bank of the Douro at the beginning of the eighteenth century, the year the estate was bought by an ancestor of Duarte's who'd travelled from the UK to try his hand at making port. Against a cloudless azure sky the white walls of the three-storey building sparkled in the early morning sunshine beneath a terracotta tiled roof. Green shutters were open at the ground-floor windows that stretched out either side of the huge oak front door, and at those above on the next floors up.

Behind the facade, the original building had gradually tripled in size and been regularly modernised. It now boasted ten en-suite bedrooms, countless reception rooms, a dining room that could seat fifty, and a ballroom, which was where the meetings would be taking place. At the rear, the courtyard that was decorated with jewel-coloured mosaics featured a fountain in the shape of a cherub holding aloft a bunch of grapes. And beyond that, a vine-covered pergola stood over a wide stone patio that ran the length of the house and had stunning views of the terraces.

Over the years, the success of that intrepid eighteenth-century winemaker had led to the expansion of the business and the acquisition of further estates, and almost all of the winemaking had since moved to Porto. But, given its size and idyllic setting, this magnificent building had been used for entertaining for the past three centuries and still was.

Quite honestly, Orla still couldn't work out how she'd got it so wrong. The house she'd originally and incorrectly identified as the venue for the conference was lovely—now that it wasn't a complete tip—but it wasn't a patch on this.

She should have questioned the keys that didn't fit, she thought for what had to be the thousandth time. She should have paid more attention to the odd curious glance she'd received over the ten days or so, which she'd attributed to miscommunication as a result of her poor attempts at Portuguese. She shouldn't have been so confident she knew what she was doing that she hadn't triple-checked the instructions.

However, now wasn't the time for unfathomable conundrums. Now was the time to focus on the day ahead, a day free from distractions and lapses in concentration, a day devoid of slip-ups.

Everything was going to go brilliantly, she reminded herself as she pulled up at a wing of the house to the rear, the tradesmen's entrance, got out and bent to retrieve her satchel from the back seat. She had her lists and the order of play. She knew what she was doing, and, more importantly, she knew what everyone else was doing. Everything was under control.

'Bom dia.'

At the sound of the deep voice somewhere behind her, Orla jumped, narrowly avoiding hitting her head on the roof of the car, and whirled round. Her heart gave a great crash against her ribs and then began to race. Duarte was striding her way, his gaze fixed on her, a faint smile hovering at his mouth.

Oh, no, she thought, her heart sinking as the memory of last night's kiss, the wantonness of her response and the way she'd been all over him instantly slammed into her head and flooded her cheeks with heat.

This was bad.

Very bad.

What was he doing here? Why wasn't he doing something brilliant with wine? What had happened to their paths absolutely not crossing? So much for a day free from distraction and loss of focus. Ten seconds in his vicinity and already panic was beginning to flutter inside her. Already she was on edge and wired in a way that had nothing to do with the copious amounts of caffeine she'd consumed earlier. But what could she do? She could hardly order him to leave. It was his estate.

'Good morning,' she replied, hitching her satchel over her shoulder, locking the car and deciding that denial and professionalism while she figured out a way to get rid of him were the way forward here.

'Did you sleep well?'

No. She hadn't. She'd slept appallingly. 'Perfectly well, thank you,' she said, setting off for the back door. 'You?'

'Barely a wink,' he said as he fell into step beside her. 'You kept me up for hours. Literally.'

Her pulse thudded, her mouth went dry and she very nearly stumbled. Why would he say that? How did he expect her to respond? Was she supposed to apologise?

She'd never been in this situation before, working in such physical proximity with a client. She didn't know how to handle it. But she was pretty sure that if he'd decided to start flirting with her it wasn't going to help at all. It wasn't helping much that despite his allegedly rough night he still looked unfairly gorgeous. No washed-out skin or dark, saggy bags under the eyes for him. *He* hadn't had to slather on the concealer or paper over the cracks.

'Did you finish the wine?' she asked as she walked through the door he held open and into the beautifully cool house.

'I lost the taste for it.'

What a frivolous waste.

Heroically resisting the urge to roll her eyes, Orla started down the long flagstone-floored passageway that led to the kitchen and tried to ignore how near he was. The passageway was as wide as the Douro. There really was no need for his arm to keep brushing against hers. Every time it did, tiny shivers scampered through her body. She even felt them in her toes, for goodness' sake.

'So what are you doing here?' she asked, aiming for politeness and trying not to let her frustration show.

'I thought I could lend a hand.'

With what? What did he think he was going to do? Make up a bed? Did he even know how to? Judging by the mess she'd found at his house, assuming it had been caused by him, it didn't seem likely.

'I have everything under control,' she said, deciding that on balance it was probably better not to be thinking about beds, hands or, in fact, any other body part of his. 'I'm meeting the housekeeping team here in,' she glanced at her watch, 'half an hour.'

'Local?'

'Yes.'

'I'll help translate.'

'The team leader speaks excellent English.' Honestly. Did he really think she wouldn't have thought of that? 'You pay a hefty fee not to have to bother with any of this, Duarte,' she said pointedly while just about managing to retain her smile. 'You really don't need to stick around.'

'I want to.'

But why?

Unless…

Her eyes narrowed as an unwelcome thought occurred to her. 'Do you think I'm going to screw up again?'

'Not at all. But you can answer one question for me,' he said, striding ahead of her into the vast kitchen and taking up a position against an expansive stretch of work surface.

Orla made for the enormous wooden table that stood in the middle of the room and had three centuries of food preparation scored into its surface and sat down. 'What do you want to know?'

'Why are *you* here, seeing to things personally?'

Well, at least *that* was a question she could answer. 'I was let down at the last minute by the team I'd put in place to carry out your instructions,' she said with an inward wince as she laid her satchel on the table and opened the flap. 'They're the best. I use them all the time. Fly them across continents. But they got struck down by a bug. All of them at the same time. It's never happened before. I spent two days trying to fix up a replacement but then decided it would be quicker and simpler to do it myself.'

It had been a frantic, stressful time and in hindsight, *that* was probably why she'd misread his email.

'But why are *you* here?' she asked, wondering if it had really been that simple. 'You weren't due back for another three weeks.'

'I had business in the States. It wrapped up early.'

Which in some ways had been a good thing, she had to admit grudgingly. While his happening upon her taking a nap hadn't been ideal, imagine if her mistake hadn't been uncovered until the day of the conference. There wouldn't have been time to fix things. He'd have been even more furious, and justifiably so. She felt faint at the mere thought of it.

'So when you think about it,' he mused with a nonchalance she didn't trust for a second, 'neither of us is meant to be here. Fate, wouldn't you say?'

She would say nothing of the sort. 'I don't believe in Fate.'

'No, I don't imagine you do,' he said with a quick, dazzling grin. 'You're too practical. But mistakes aside, you're dedicated.'

'*One* mistake,' she corrected, determinedly blinking away the dazzle and reminding herself that practical wasn't boring, practical was good. 'Which is being rectified. And it's my job.'

'Which you love.'

'I do,' she agreed as she began removing her laptop and notebooks from her bag. 'Who wouldn't? It involves opulence. Outlandish, unforgettable, once-in-a-lifetime experiences. VIP events. Unimaginable excess and extravagance.'

It also required stellar organisation, infinite skill when it came to persuasion and negotiating, and the ability to think on her feet. Every single day demanded and expected more from her than the day before, and she was one of the best. Usually.

'Recently, I arranged an engagement proposal on an iceberg,' she said, as much to remind herself of her competence as to prove it to him. 'Once, a client wanted to have a private dinner in front of the Mona Lisa.'

'I ought to up my game.'

Orla reached for her clipboard and thought that Duarte's game was quite high enough. They spoke at least twice a month. His requests ranged from arranging private jets to reserving tables at impossible-to-book restaurants and much more besides, and they were frequent. While most of what he wanted hovered at the bottom of the outrageousness scale, last year he'd asked her to recreate a perfume long since out of production for his mother as a birthday present. That had been a challenge. 'You keep me busy.'

'I could keep you busier.'

Orla froze in the middle of attaching her lists to the clipboard and shot him a startled glance. What did he mean by that? She couldn't work it out. His words were innocent enough but the way he was looking at her was anything but. He was sort of *smouldering* and quite suddenly she was finding it a struggle to breathe. He'd gone very still and his gaze had dropped to her mouth, which went bone-dry, and oh, dear God, was he thinking about last night? Was he planning a repeat?

She was so hopeless at this, she thought desperately, her heart thundering while a wave of heat crashed over her. But *this* shouldn't even be happening. She shouldn't be burning up with the urge to get to her feet, throw herself into his arms and take up where they'd left off. She shouldn't want him to spread her out over the table and feast on her.

The speed and ease with which he could make her lose control was confusing and terrifying. It was as if there were wicked forces at play, luring her into the unknown, over which she had zero control, and if there was one thing she hated, it was that.

But now cool-headed logic battled against hot, mad desire, and she feared it was losing—

And then, relief.

Blessed, blessed relief.

'I think I hear a van.'

By the end of the day, Orla could stand it no longer. Her nerves were in tatters and her stomach was in knots.

As she'd hoped, the work side of things was going splendidly. The house had buzzed with activity. The housekeeping team she'd organised was as efficient and excellent as she'd been assured. Rooms were in the process of being cleaned and laundry pressed. Anything that could be polished shone, and vacuum cleaners had hummed throughout the building all day. Her mistake was well underway to becoming history and her satisfaction on that front was deep.

But, as she'd feared, Duarte was proving to be a menace. While she'd been handing out instructions and emphasising priorities, he'd donned a tool belt. Subsequently, everywhere she'd turned, up he popped, sometimes with a hammer, other times with a screwdriver, and once, when a basin tap was discovered to be leaking, with a wrench. At one point she hadn't seen him for an hour and had dared to hope that he'd gone for good, but unfortunately he'd returned with lunch. For everyone.

There seemed to be no end to the man's talents and it was driving her nuts. She couldn't stop thinking about the smouldering. The tool belt, combined with olive combat shorts and a white polo shirt that hugged his muscles and highlighted his Portuguese heritage, was such a good look on him, she could hardly tear her eyes away. His smile, which he wielded frequently and lethally, laid waste to her reason every time she caught sight of it. So far today she'd knocked over a vase, temporarily mislaid three of her precious lists and spent a good fifteen minutes she could ill afford to spare gazing out of a top-floor window at where he was methodically clearing leaves from the pool, having waved aside protests from the team of gardeners handling the outdoors.

She didn't like it. Any of it. Not the loss of focus, not the weakening of her resolve, and she particularly hated the sinking sensation that if things continued in this vein, a serious slip-up was only a matter of time.

She couldn't allow that to happen, she thought grimly as she stood at the back door and watched the convoy of vans carry off the three dozen housekeeping staff for the night. She was striving for excellence here and for that she needed to stay on the ball. Right now, not only was she *not* on the ball, she wasn't even anywhere near it. She felt as if she was walking a tightrope. One wobble and she'd tumble to the ground, where her insecurities lay waiting to pounce.

So enough was enough. Forget the fact that Duarte was a client who ought to be kept happy at all times. Forget that this was his house. She couldn't carry on like this. She had to find him and get rid of him. Whatever it took.

Beside the pool, Duarte unbuckled the tool belt and dumped it on a lounger. He emptied his pockets of his keys, wallet and phone, then stripped off his polo shirt. After removing his belt and adding it to the mounting pile of belongings, he dived into the cool, fresh water with relish.

The day had been surprisingly enjoyable and unexpectedly revelatory, he reflected as he began to swim lengths, the heat in his body and the tension in his muscles easing with every powerful stroke. He'd already come to the conclusion that, despite initial impressions, Orla was exceptionally capable. Why else would she be joint CEO of her company and how else could she have acquired the elusive wine? But who'd have thought competence would be such a turn-on? She issued crystal-clear instructions, could mentally turn on a sixpence and solved problems with head-spinning speed. She was like a highly efficient, well-oiled dynamo. She demanded excellence and got it, and the longer he'd watched her in action the more insistent the desire drumming through him became.

Whether or not she still wanted him, however, was as clear as mud. She'd spent most of the day trying to avoid him. He strode into a room and she marched out. He'd brought her lunch—since the oat bars she snacked on were hardly the kind of sustenance needed for a long day's work—and she'd responded not with appreciation, as one might have expected, but with a huff of barely concealed disappointment. When avoidance had been impossible, she'd opted for ice-cool professionalism, as if she hadn't melted in his arms and kissed him so passionately last night.

Her frosty attitude towards him didn't bode all that well for his intention to entice her into his bed, Duarte had to admit as he turned and started a length underwater, but he had no intention of giving up. She wasn't the only one with goals. Once he set his mind to something, nothing swayed him. So he'd stick to the plan—perhaps even ramping it up—and she'd succumb soon enough. The women he'd wanted in the past generally had and he didn't see why Orla would be any different.

Coming up for air, he caught sight of her marching across the grass towards him. He swam to the side of the pool, his pulse hammering with an intensity that could have been caused by the exercise but more likely was because of her, and rested his arms on the tiled edge just as she drew to a stop right in front of him.

'Duarte,' she said in the clipped tone he'd become used to over the last twelve or so hours and which, perversely, fanned the embers of desire and sent it streaking through his veins like fire.

'Orla,' he murmured, letting his eyes drift from her fine ankles, up her shapely legs and over her shorts and T-shirt, which were close-fitting enough to make him want to get his hands on the skin beneath and trace her shape.

'We need to talk.'

Oh, dear. That sounded serious. He'd never been a fan of 'talking'. At least, not about anything that mattered, anything that might hurt. Shortly after the deaths of first his son and later his wife, his mother had tentatively suggested therapy. Beleaguered by unimaginable grief and excoriating guilt, he'd instantly shut that conversation down and sensibly she hadn't revisited it. What had happened was his fault, he knew, and he didn't deserve to work through it and come out the other side. He deserved to burn in hell.

'What about?' he drawled, pushing the unwelcome memories down and burying them deep.

'You. More specifically, this…' she waved a hand around '…*situation*.'

Interesting.

What precise situation did she mean?

Assuring himself he could easily deflect the conversation if it headed down a path he'd rather not follow and somewhat relieved that the idea of 'talking' had deflated his desire when his shorts now clung to him like a second skin, Duarte heaved himself out of the pool. He gave himself a shake and strode over to the lounger. He reached for his polo shirt and used it first to rub his hair dry and then to blot the water from his chest. When he was done, he stalked over to the table that could seat twelve and draped it over the back of one chair before dropping himself into another.

'I'm all yours,' he said, leaning back and stretching out to let the evening sun do its thing.

When Orla didn't respond he glanced up at her. She looked dazed. Flushed. She swayed for a second and he briefly wondered if she was about to pass out. Today had been scorching and long. It wasn't beyond the realms of possibility.

'I'm sorry?' she stammered.

'You wanted to talk? About me and a situation.'

She blinked and snapped to. 'Yes. That's right. I do.'

'Fire away.'

'Okay.' She cleared her throat and tucked a lock of wavy golden hair that had escaped her ponytail behind her ear. 'Yes. Good. I just wanted to say thank you for your help today. It was…appreciated.'

She didn't sound as if it was. The moment's hesitation suggested his presence here today had been anything but appreciated, which was intriguing. 'You're welcome.'

'However, there's no need for you to be here tomorrow.'

'It's no trouble.'

'Really. I wouldn't want to put you out.'

'You won't.'

'I'm sure you must have somewhere better to be.'

She was wrong. For once, he had time on his hands, and while there was always something in the business that required his attention, he could afford a few days off to focus on this latest project. He had the feeling that it would be more than worth it. 'I don't.'

Her stunning eyes flashed with annoyance. 'Well, you can't stay here.'

'Why not?'

'You're getting in the way and putting me off my stride.'

'Your stride looks fine to me,' he said, his gaze dropping to her long legs and lingering.

'You're being deliberately obtuse.'

'Then clarify it for me.'

She let out a sigh of exasperation and threw up her hands in what looked like defeat. 'I can't concentrate while you're around,' she said hotly. 'You're too distracting. I need to be able to do my job to the best of my ability and you're preventing me from doing that.'

Her admission jolted through him like lightning, electrifying every nerve ending he possessed. So she *was* affected by him. She was just remarkably adept at hiding how she felt. It was surprisingly satisfying to know. 'I bother you.'

She gave a nod, her jaw tight, as if she was loath to have to admit it. 'Yes.'

'And yet you're still brilliant.'

'I am,' she agreed. 'And I've worked very hard to be. But I won't be brilliant if I keep dropping things and losing lists. You're making me do that. You mess with my head. All day I've been on tenterhooks waiting for some disaster to happen because I'm not paying enough attention, and I can't have it.'

'I think you're overestimating my powers.'

'You couldn't possibly understand.'

'So explain.'

'I have to be in control,' she said, glowering down at him and shoving her hands in the back pockets of her shorts, which did interesting things to her chest. 'I need everything to be perfect. All the time. I can't accept second best. It's just not in me.'

'You're a high achiever,' he replied with a nod. 'I get that. So am I.'

She shook her head. 'It's more than that. For high achievers, the goal is important but mainly it's about the journey. My older brother and younger sister are classic examples of that, so I should know. Nothing fazes them. If something goes wrong they dust themselves off and pick themselves up. They see it as a lesson learned. For me, it's all about the goal, which I have to reach no matter what. It's not about the journey. I couldn't care less about that. I just want results. Failure sends me into a spin. I sink into a pit of self-doubt and despair and it's not a good place for me to be. Ergo, I can't fail.'

So that was why she'd been so desperate to get her job back after he'd fired her. As he'd suspected, rather disappointingly, he found, it had had nothing to do with him. 'That's a lot of pressure.'

'You have no idea,' she muttered vehemently. 'It's fine if I stay on track. Not so much if I don't. Which is what's happening here.'

'I make you panic?'

'Yes.'

'Because I distract you.'

She scowled. 'What do you want? A medal?'

No. He just wanted her. She looked like a goddess standing there in the sun, her hair gleaming beneath the rays, fire in her eyes. A frustrated and annoyed goddess, it was true, but she was magnificent none the less, and desire hammered hard in the pit of his stomach.

'I want you to admit you want me as much as I want you,' he said, focusing every drop of his attention on her so he didn't miss a thing. 'I want you to admit you can't stop thinking about our kiss.'

'Fine,' she snapped, clearly at the end of her tether. 'I *am* attracted to you. I *can't* stop thinking about our kiss. It kept me awake all last night. It's been plaguing me all day. It's—*you're*—driving me nuts.'

'Then I have the perfect solution.'

She frowned at him for one long moment, her expression wary and her body tense. 'What is it?'

'Sleep with me.'

CHAPTER SIX

FOR A SPLIT SECOND, Orla thought she'd misheard. That she'd been so dazzled by the sight of him—his broad, muscled chest, tanned, bare and glistening in the evening sunshine—she'd lost her ability to think.

And to be honest, briefly, she had. Duarte had hauled himself out of the pool and she'd practically combusted on the spot. All she'd been able to do was stare and drool. When he'd lowered his gaze from her face to her legs just now, leisurely perusing the bits in between, she'd been so transfixed that she hadn't even been able to take a breath, let alone summon up a protest at his blatant and outrageous scrutiny.

Her brain had clearly been starved of oxygen by that because she hadn't meant to confess how strongly he affected her. 'Whatever it took' had not meant exposing her vulnerabilities to a man who already wielded far too much power over her. It had not meant admitting to an aspect of her personality that she'd been told, by a therapist she'd seen once when her engagement ended and she spiralled into a pit of self-doubt and hopelessness, was a flaw.

Could she have been subconsciously hoping that he'd sympathise and retreat? If she had—and frankly, she had no idea why that would have been the case when she barely knew him—it had badly backfired. All she'd done was give him ammunition. However, what was said was said and it was too late to take any of it back, and in any case the conversation had taken an unexpected turn.

Surely he couldn't have said what she thought he'd said. And if he *had*, then surely he had to be joking. But he didn't look as though he was joking. His expression was filled with dark, dangerous intent and his voice had dropped an octave, just as it had the evening before when he'd asked her to stay.

'You've lost your mind,' she managed once she'd unglued her tongue from the roof of her mouth and regained the power of speech.

'Not in the slightest,' he said with a cool, even tone that she would have envied had there been space for it amongst all the heat and desire crashing around inside her. 'By your own admission you're distracted because you're attracted to me. That attraction won't go away just because I do. It's too powerful. It will linger. Fester. Swell until it grows out of all proportion, and then you really *will* be distracted. Then you really *will* make mistakes.'

He didn't sound quite so cool now. He sounded like he knew what he was talking about. 'Are you speaking from experience?'

The shrug he gave was careless, but she could practically see the shutters slamming down over his eyes and his guard shooting up, which suggested she was right. Who? When? How fascinating.

'If you want your concentration back, you need to get what's throwing it off course out of your system,' he continued, interestingly leaving her question unanswered. 'Demystify it and it loses its power. We want each other. You're driving me as mad as I apparently drive you. So let's do something about it. Scratch the itch and it goes away.'

Seriously?

No matter how certain Duarte sounded, to Orla that didn't make any sense. Eradicate the attraction by indulging it? She might not have much knowledge on the subject but she didn't think it worked like that. What if it didn't go away? What if it got stronger? *More* distracting? And if sleeping with Duarte was so good that she ended up with further itches that needed scratching, how on earth would *that* help?

'What if it doesn't?' she said, her head fogging at the thought of feeling even more for him than she already did.

'That's never been my experience. Once is generally enough.'

For him, maybe, but what about the women he took to bed? What about her? 'I'm really not sure it's a good idea,' she said with staggering understatement.

'Incredible sex is always a good idea.'

Well, yes, perhaps in *theory*, but she wouldn't know, and the whole idea of sleeping with him felt recklessly dangerous. Not only could she find herself way out of her depth, but also she really didn't fancy making a fool of herself, which was what could well happen if hell froze over and she did throw caution to the wind to take Duarte up on his suggestion.

According to the gossip columns, he'd bedded hundreds of women in the years preceding his marriage. Beautiful women. Experienced women. Imagine if something started between *them* and she got it all wrong. Imagine if her inability to truly enjoy herself in bed hadn't been down to her ex or simple incompatibility but was in fact because of something in *her.* What if the sparks and heat she felt in his vicinity didn't last? What if his effect on her somehow disappeared beneath the pressure to perform, to excel? The humiliation would be unbearable. She'd never be able to work with him again. She wouldn't even be able to look him in the eye.

But on the other hand, insisted a little voice in her head that was becoming increasingly loud, what if it didn't? What if she was overthinking this and quite possibly missing out on not only the opportunity to turn a failure into a success but also some apparently pretty scorching sex in the meantime?

Didn't she owe it to herself to see if she couldn't rectify the situation that had been bugging her for years? She was nearly thirty. How much longer was she going to put it off? And perhaps Duarte was right and just the once *was* the way to get it out of her system. He had vastly more experience than she did, so maybe chemistry *did* work like that. Out of sight, out of mind hadn't exactly been a success. Look at how her night had panned out.

Something had to give here, and she had to at least *try* and find out what she was capable of, she thought, the possibility of it beginning to drum through her. She'd never experienced lust before—which presumably was what all this was—and who knew when the next opportunity might come along? Surely the effect he had on her—so wild and intense—had to mean that anything between them would be better than good.

Deep down, she longed to know whether the reality could live up to her dreams, and what was the worst that could happen? That it didn't? That she felt nothing and had to fake it? Well, that wouldn't be a problem. She excelled at *that*. Her ex hadn't guessed for a moment that her panting and moaning was calculated and strategic rather than spontaneous and instinctive, and if it came to that, nor would Duarte.

'Incredible is a bold claim,' she said, her mouth as dry as the desert and her heart thundering like a steam train.

His dark gaze glittered in the setting sun. 'Incredible is a guarantee.'

Was it? He seemed so sure. Did she dare? To grab the chance to right a wrong and experience some allegedly hot sex with the most attractive man she'd ever met, a man who astonishingly seemed to want her as much as she wanted him, and wasn't really a professional conflict of interest? Why, yes. Despite the potential for failure, apparently she did. 'All right.'

* * *

For a big man Duarte moved with impressive speed. Barely before she'd had time to blink he was up and off the seat and closing the distance between them with single-minded intent. He stopped an inch in front of her, planted a hand on the small of her back and drew her in.

'Here?' she managed breathlessly, as her senses swam and her skin beneath his palm burned. 'Now?'

'Do you have a problem with that?'

The heat swirling in the depths of his eyes as he stared down at her took her breath away and her thoughts spun for a second. Ludicrous thoughts, such as when had she last examined her bikini line? What underwear was she wearing? Did it matter? Would he even notice? Given the focus and intensity with which he was looking at her, she doubted he would notice a thousand champagne bottles popping simultaneously behind him. And her body was all right. She kept herself in shape and depilated. It would probably be best to strike while the iron was hot and just get on with it, before she talked herself out of it.

'No,' she said huskily, lowering her gaze to his mouth and feeling a surge of longing so overwhelming she didn't quite know what to do with it. 'No problem at all.'

She put her hands on his bare chest and his hold on her tightened and then he was kissing her, hot and hard. Her heart thundered and fire licked along her veins. She slid her hands up, over warm skin and taut muscles, skimming over his shoulders, until her fingers came into contact with his thick, soft hair. She held his head and he pulled her hips to his, and when she felt the steely length of his erection against her she gasped.

Taking advantage of the break in kissing, Duarte, breathing heavily, removed her T-shirt and, ah, yes, now she remembered. Her underwear was practical and sturdy rather than sexy and feminine, cotton not lace, designed for comfort while at work in the heat. Not that he appeared to mind. He seemed more intent on getting her horizontal. He manoeuvred her round and down and then she was lying back on a double sun lounger, free to ogle him as he reached for his wallet and extracted what she presumed was a condom.

God, he was gorgeous. And he clearly knew his way around a female body. But what would someone like him—former international playboy, looks of a god—expect? Presumably incredible sex required incredible input on her part, but what ought she to be doing? His skills were evidently extensive, while hers were very much limited, and how on earth was she supposed to get an A-plus when she hadn't even revised for the test?

She'd close her eyes and trust her instinct, she told herself firmly. She'd stop thinking and focus on feeling. She was a fast learner. She'd pick up the clues quickly enough. There'd be no problem.

Duarte joined her on the lounger and lowered his mouth to hers, kissing her deeply while she closed her eyes and moaned. Her hand went to the nape of his neck and his moved to her breast. She arched her back, pressing herself against him harder, seeking the tingles she'd experienced the night before, but they remained annoyingly elusive.

Why was that? she wondered frustratedly as he rubbed his thumb over her nipple and she sighed with what she hoped he'd interpret as ecstasy. What was she doing wrong? And, come to think of it, where was the reason-wrecking heat and all-consuming need off to? She could feel it dissipating and she tried to recapture it but to no avail, and no, no, no, no, *no.* This wasn't meant to be happening. She wasn't meant to be panicking that she was going to mess it up. She was meant to be doing *this* and doing it well.

Duarte ran his hand down her body, and in anxious desperation Orla writhed in a way designed to indicate passion, in an attempt to reignite it inside her, but it was as if she were watching the proceedings from somewhere far, far away, and she wanted to cry with despair and frustration.

So much for getting the craziness out of her system. Right now, it wasn't even *in* her system. With all her overthinking, she'd killed the mood. For her at least. But she needn't kill it for him, and who knew, maybe his desire for her would be strong enough for both of them?

Panting hard and frantically hoping to relocate the need that had been tormenting her for days but was now stubbornly absent, she trailed her fingers down his back and round to the button of his shorts. She started undoing it, feeling the hard length of his impressive erection beneath her hand, when he suddenly put his hand over hers and stilled her movements.

'What are you doing?' she said huskily, looking up at him with what she hoped was an encouragingly seductive smile. 'Why are you stopping?'

His eyes were dark and glittering, and a

deep frown creased his forehead. 'This isn't doing it for you, is it?'

What? Damn. Why couldn't he have believed her pants and moans, the way her ex had? Why did he have to notice she was struggling to focus? He wasn't helping by putting a halt to things. Couldn't he see that?

'Just carry on,' she murmured, trying to shake his hand off hers so she could continue undoing his fly. 'It'll be fine.'

He stared down at her, as if unable to believe what he was hearing. *'Fine?'*

Oh, dear. Now she'd offended him. 'I meant, I'm sure it'll be incredible,' she said with a batting of her eyelids and a twist of her hips. 'There'll be explosions and ecstasy. Whatever. It's all good.' Or it would be if she could get out of her head. Probably.

'It is far from all good,' Duarte said grimly, disentangling himself from her, sitting up and moving to the edge of the lounger.

Orla missed his heat immediately and inwardly railed at her inadequacy. There really was no hope for her. 'I'm sorry,' she said, feeling quietly mortified and very exposed.

He looked at her, his eyes stormy and every line of his body rigid. 'You never have to apologise for changing your mind.'

'I haven't changed my mind,' she said, keen

to make that clear despite the hopelessness she could feel descending. 'That's not it at all.'

'Then what is it?'

'I started thinking about excellence and expectations and got a bit sidetracked.'

His eyebrows shot up. *'Sidetracked?'*

'Well, yes. You must have slept with lots of women. I, on the other hand, have only slept with one man, not very successfully. You're way more experienced than I am. I have no tricks.'

He retrieved her T-shirt and handed it to her and she put it back on, feeling a little chilly now. So much for hoping her lack of success at sex might have been the fault of her ex or incompatibility. It was clearly neither. It was her. There was something wrong with her.

'What are you doing tomorrow?'

Orla swallowed hard. Right. He was obviously no longer interested and it was back to business. 'The same as today, I expect,' she said, determined not to care. Making sure everything went smoothly and avoiding him, most likely. Only instead of being distracted by memories of the kiss on his sofa, she'd be trying not to think of what had happened here.

'Take the day off.'

What? 'I can't.'

'Everyone here knows what they're doing, right?'

'Well, yes…' Apart from her obviously. She didn't have a clue.

'And you have a phone in case of emergencies.'

'I do, but—'

'Then you can take the day off.'

Why was he so insistent? Why wasn't he simply marching off and going in search of someone who *did* know what they were doing? 'What for?'

'Further research into excellence and expectations,' he said, his deep, hot gaze holding hers so she couldn't look away even if she'd wanted to. 'And tricks.'

Oh.

Oh.

Maybe he was still interested. Orla's pulse skipped a beat and then began to race but she ignored it because she knew now that that translated into precisely nothing. So what would be the point in pursuing things? It would be a disaster again and there was only so much humiliation a person could take.

'There's no need for that,' she said thickly, her throat tight with disappointment and regret.

'There's every need for that,' he countered.

'You're not the only one with goals, Orla. I'm not accustomed to mediocrity either, especially when it comes to sex. So take the day off.'

Orla considered taking the day off a mistake. Duarte knew this because he'd picked her up from her hotel half an hour ago, after she'd done what needed to be done at the Quinta, and she'd already mentioned it half a dozen times. She'd cited professionalism. She'd muttered something about there being a problem with the tablecloths. She'd repeatedly asked herself what she thought she was doing. Out loud.

He, on the other hand, considered it anything other than a mistake. He'd never had a woman in his arms simply going through the motions. He didn't like it. Either his skills were rustier than he'd imagined or Orla required a different approach. Whichever it was, he wanted to get to the bottom of what had sidetracked her. His desire for her was so strong that if something wasn't done about it soon he could suffer permanent damage. His male pride was wounded and demanded satisfaction, and it was more than three long years since he'd last slept with anyone.

So if overthinking was her problem then he

had to get inside her head and disrupt from within. He sensed there was a volcano bubbling beneath her surface that needed erupting. He also had the intriguing feeling that the sex she'd previously had, *not very successfully*, was involved, and that, therefore, also merited investigation.

'Where are you taking me?'

With any luck, by the end of the day, to heaven and back. 'The river.'

'Why?'

'Because while you're here you should see more of the local area than just the Quinta. It's beautiful off the beaten track. Nature at its most excellent.' Not to mention far away from work and reality and ideal for his purposes. 'And speaking of excellence, where does your need for it come from?'

'You don't waste time.'

He took his eyes off the road for a split second and cast her a quick glance to find that she was looking at him both shrewdly and suspiciously. 'I don't see the point,' he said, totally unperturbed by this. Orla was skittish and wary and easily spooked by matters of a carnal nature, but she was also trapped in a moving car. He could afford to be direct. 'My badly bruised ego demands answers.'

'I'm a lost cause.'

'How do you know? We've barely even begun.'

'Experience.'

Ah.

'Also, were you not there last night?'

'I was very much there,' he said, remembering how soft and warm she'd been in his arms, how divine she'd smelled and tasted, and feeling a pulse of heat low in his pelvis. 'Even if you weren't.'

'I was to begin with, before getting sidetracked.'

Duarte crushed the pressing yet wildly inappropriate urge to pull over and find out if she still felt that good and reminded himself of his plan to find out what made her tick. 'So back to my question…'

'I'm the middle of three siblings,' she said on a sigh. 'My older sister is an opera singer. A contralto. She's with the Met and lives in New York. My younger brother plays rugby for England. My parents were generally to be found either at a concert hall or on a touchline somewhere. There wasn't a lot of time left for me, you know?'

'No,' he said. 'I wouldn't know. I'm an only child.'

'So you got all the attention.'

He caught a note of wistfulness in her voice,

guessed that she was imagining a happy family unit that was all hearts and flowers, and the cynic in him felt compelled to burst that particular bubble.

'Not exactly,' he said flatly, his hands flexing on the steering wheel. 'My parents divorced when I was twelve. Acrimoniously. They were so busy hurling insults at each other, there wasn't a whole lot of time for me either.'

That hung between them for a moment, then she said softly, 'I didn't know that. I'm sorry.'

'No need,' he replied, really not needing her pity. 'It's been eighteen years and they're civil to each other now. We all rub along well enough. But for a decade I did end up seeking attention elsewhere. Everywhere, actually.'

'You found it. In spades.'

'I did.' And he hadn't regretted a minute of it. Until he'd met Calysta and lost his head.

'I had to work for mine,' she said, putting a stop to his turbulent thoughts before they could head down that dark and twisted path. 'And my only option was school. I studied hard, all the time, making sure I came top of the class every term and acing every test.'

'Did it work?'

'It did. The first time I got a hundred per

cent in a maths exam my parents took us all out for a meal to celebrate and *I* was allowed to choose the restaurant. I was eight and it was the best moment of my life, so I didn't stop. I carried on aiming for the top and claiming what snippets of attention I could. Luckily, I really enjoyed studying.'

'What about friends?'

'What friends?' she deadpanned.

She had high expectations of herself. She probably had high expectations of others that were hard to live up to. As he'd thought, the pressure she put on herself must be immense. 'How did you become joint CEO of Hamilton Garrett?'

'I didn't bother with university,' she said. 'There was nothing I was interested in apart from organising and making everything just so, and there isn't a degree for that. After I left school I became an executive assistant at a bank and worked my way up until I became the aide de camp for the bank's president. I left there to start at what was then plain old Hamilton Concierge Services. My aim was always the top and after a lot of blood, sweat and tears I got there last year.'

'Impressive.'

'Just focused and determined.'

'Is there anything you *don't* excel in?'

'Not much. But then, I tend to steer clear of things I know I won't be good at.'

'Such as?'

'Opera singing and rugby,' she said drily.

'That's it?'

A pause. 'There may be other stuff,' she said, hedging in a way that piqued his curiosity.

'Like what?'

'Just stuff.'

'Sex?'

It was an educated guess, based on the last couple of nights, but he could feel her blush from all the way over here and he knew he was right. She was satisfyingly easy to read.

'It's complicated.'

'So it would seem.'

'Anyway,' she said briskly. 'I think that's quite enough about me. What about you? The business press sings your praises almost weekly. You're said to have the Midas touch when it comes to wine and sales and things, and you're good at fixing sinks and fetching lunch. You pursue excellence, too.'

'But not at the expense of all else.' He had friends. He didn't fear failure. Not professionally, at least. On a personal level, it was a different matter altogether. He'd failed his wife and son so badly the guilt and regret still burned through him like boiling oil. But he learned from his mistakes. It wouldn't happen again. Ever.

'You think it's a flaw,' she said, a touch defensively.

'Don't you?'

'No. Why on earth would it be? Why wouldn't you want to be and do the best you can? Besides, the pursuit of perfection keeps me on an even keel and I like feeling good about myself.'

Was it the only thing that made her feel good about herself? That didn't sound healthy, but then, what did he know? He was hardly a role model in matters of self-worth. He'd spent a decade wreaking havoc across Europe trying to find his. Thanks to his unforgivable role in the deaths of Arturo and Calysta, it still remained elusive.

'But you are not alone in thinking it's a problem,' she continued, refocusing his attention before it tumbled down that rabbit hole of pain and guilt. 'I once went to a therapist who suggested the same thing.'

'Why did you need a therapist?'

'I didn't. My mother arranged it and I was in too bad a place to summon up the energy to refuse. My engagement had ended and I was wallowing in a vat of self-doubt and despondency.'

'But not heartbreak?' he said, astonished to hear she'd been engaged when by her own admission she didn't even have friends.

'Well, yes, that too, obviously.'

'What happened?'

'We discovered we weren't suited. My expectations of him were too high apparently, which again I don't see as a problem, even if he did. I mean, what's wrong with wanting and expecting things from people, including the best?'

'Nothing.'

'Quite.'

'As long as what you want and expect isn't beyond what they can give, of course.'

Orla didn't seem to have a response to that. As he swung the Land Rover off the road and onto a bumpy track, Duarte glanced over to see she was looking at him shrewdly, a faint frown creasing her forehead. The memory of their conversation about attraction, the moment she'd asked him if he was speaking from experience in particular, flew into his head and his chest tightened as if gripped by a vice. She was astute. All this talk about therapy and relationship expectations was making him uneasy. If she decided to turn the conversation back to him, asking the kind of questions he'd been asking her, probing into the deeply personal, the roiling of his stomach would get worse and that was hardly the plan for today.

So it was a good thing, then, that, as he pulled up beneath the wide-spreading branches of an acacia tree, they'd reached their destination.

'We're here.'

CHAPTER SEVEN

'HERE' WAS A deserted bend in a stretch of the river that flowed close to the border with Spain but still within the district of Bragança. On both banks, terraces planted with vines were carved into the steep hills that descended to the shore. Just beyond the spot where Duarte had stopped, a golden sandy beach protected by a dense forest shimmered in the hot midday sun. It was secluded and beautiful, quiet and tranquil, and couldn't have reflected Orla's inner state less.

She was just so confused, she thought despairingly, hopping down from the Land Rover and seeking distance and air by wandering down to the shore. By Duarte and his effect on her, but also, more pertinently, by herself. She didn't understand what she was doing. She knew she shouldn't have accepted his invitation to spend the day with him. She had myriad excuses to decline—principally work and the mortification of the evening before—yet she'd found a counter argument to every single one of them.

Why had she done that?

Could it be because she simply wanted to find out more about him? Their interactions over the phone and email were naturally all about him and what he needed from her, but here, so far, the conversation had been all about her. Adept at deflection, he'd largely remained an enigma. So had she accepted it to correct a perceived imbalance that had her constantly on the back foot? Or really, did she just burn with the need to uncover the stories that lay behind the shadows that occasionally flitted across his expression and the guarded wariness that she sometimes caught in his gaze?

If it was the latter, she reflected, lifting her hand to shield her eyes as she gazed at the stunning panoramic view, she wasn't doing a very good job of it, because apart from the brief yet illuminating glimpse he'd given her into his upbringing, the conversation on the way here had hardly corrected any imbalance. On the contrary, it had tipped the scales further in his direction.

What on earth made her want to tell Duarte everything about herself? Why had she brought up the subject of her ex? His way of plain speaking must have rubbed off on her, but whatever had prodded her to mention it, she wished she hadn't. His comment about not expecting more than someone was able to give had stuck in her mind. Was that what she'd done with Matt? Had her expectations been unfairly high? While breaking off their engagement shortly after he'd been made redundant, he'd called her draining, unsupportive and impossible to please. At the time, she'd believed that if he couldn't match up, if he wasn't good enough to get another job, that was his problem, but maybe it wasn't that simple.

Adding to the general chaos filling her head was the suspicion that she'd agreed to today because, despite the disaster of last night, she actually wanted a conversation with Duarte about expectations and tricks. She wanted to know what his goals were, particularly with regards to her. It was entirely possible that deep down, against all the odds, despite all the evidence, she still had hope. Her pulse had skipped a beat when he'd pulled up outside her hotel. Sitting next to him as he drove her here had made her stomach churn and she'd felt as if she couldn't breathe even though the Land Rover had no roof and oxygen abounded.

It was madness, none of it made any sense, and, for someone who always knew what she was doing and where she was going, this flip-flopping of thoughts, the loss of control and her irrational behaviour was a worrying state of affairs. The most sensible, safest thing to do, therefore, would be to tell him she wanted to go back, but that ship had sailed because she didn't.

With a sigh of exasperated helplessness, Orla turned round and walked back to the Land Rover, where Duarte was heaving a cool box out of the boot with impressive ease. Perhaps she'd find some kind of comfort by attempting to rebalance the scales of personal information. Probing into the tragedy of his family might be a step too far, but there were plenty of other things she wanted to know. If *she* was the one asking the questions for a change, perhaps she'd be able to claw back some sense of control.

'How did you find this place?'

'It's part of the estate,' he said, handing her a blanket and taking the cool box and a basket to a flat, grassy, shady spot at the edge of the beach. 'A well-kept secret passed down the generations.'

Part of the estate? Just how big was it? They'd driven for nearly an hour to get here, the road winding up through hill after hill before dropping into the valley. It had to be vast. 'It's spectacular.'

'It's the perfect place for a picnic.'

And what else? Seduction? Who else had he brought here? Lovers? His wife? 'Do you come here often?'

'Not for years. As a university student I brought a girlfriend here once. I haven't been back since.'

With inexplicable relief, Orla laid out the blanket. Duarte dropped to his knees, opened the cool box and began setting out the food, a mouthwatering selection of cold meats and cheeses, tomatoes, olives and rolls. Then from the basket he produced a clear bottle half filled with ruby-coloured liquid, and two glasses.

'What's that?'

'Our wine.'

Their wine? Hmm. She sat down and frowned. 'Is it still drinkable?'

'Should be.' He poured a measure into each glass and handed her one. 'I've been meaning to say thank you.'

'You're welcome.'

'I was impressed.'

It was odd how her pulse gave a little kick at that. 'You didn't look it.'

'You'd succeeded where I'd failed,' he said with a wry smile. 'My pride may have been dented.'

Was that what it had been? With his confidence, he didn't seem the type, and when she recalled how icy he'd become on hearing how she'd acquired it she had the feeling there'd been more to it. 'Is your pride really that fragile?'

'As an eggshell. Hence why we're here.'

Right. Last night. Goals of his own. Research into expectations and tricks… And what had they been discussing again? Ah, yes. The wine.

'Why didn't you finish it the other night?' she asked, at least ten degrees warmer than she had been a moment before.

'I don't drink alone.'

'Why not? Too great a temptation?'

He gave a slight shrug. 'Something like that.'

Not something like that, Orla decided. Or at least not *just* something like that. Could he have been responsible for the terrible mess she'd found at the house ten days ago? Could drowning his sorrows have been the way he'd handled the deaths of his wife and child? Had he been there, done that? It did seem to be the obvious explanation, and rumour had it he had disappeared for two whole months. However, that was a question she *wasn't* going to ask. That was way too personal.

And in any case *this* glass of wine was making her think of the kiss in his office-slash-sitting room. Of legs. Of tasting and touching and an overwhelming of the senses. She'd let her head get the better of her too then, she thought with a sigh that she stifled with a sip of the wine that was indeed as delicious now as it had been a couple of days ago. Truly, she was her own worst enemy.

With a 'Help yourself!' Duarte handed her a plate, and waited for her to take her pick of the smorgasbord before filling his own. Orla sat back and crossed her legs and tried not to ogle as he stretched out on his side and propped himself up on an elbow.

'This is delicious,' she said, nibbling on a chicken leg, then wiping her fingers on a napkin and contemplating what to sample next.

'The cafe in the village is superb.'

'Do you cook?'

It was hardly the most exciting of conversational topics but she was finding it hard to keep her mind off his hands. She could recall them on her body and, despite the heat of the sun, shivers were skating down her spine. But she'd been here before and wasn't the definition of madness doing something over and over again, expecting different results?

'Occasionally,' he said, breaking open a roll and stuffing it with slices of *presunto*. 'I eat out a lot.'

'For work?'

'Yes. Before I took over as CEO, I was in charge of PR and marketing. It involved a lot of wining and dining.'

'I bet you were good at that.'

He flashed her a quick, dazzling grin. 'I was very good at that.'

He was very good at everything. Except, she rather thought, answering some of her questions truthfully.

'So how did you become CEO?' she asked, popping a piece of soft, creamy cheese into her mouth and almost groaning with delight as the flavour burst on her tongue.

'My father wanted to retire,' he said smoothly. 'The timing was right.'

'Any charges of nepotism?'

'Some.'

'Disproved?'

'I would hope so.'

'I signed you up shortly after.'

He regarded her thoughtfully. 'You're good with dates.'

'I have to be. For my job. So where do you live?' she asked before he could start questioning her about dates of a different kind, which, in her case, were non-existent. He'd once described Casa do São Romão as his home, and maybe it had been for a while, but no one had been living there for a long time.

'I have an apartment in Porto.'

'That's a long way.'

'It is,' he agreed with a nod.

'Do you go there every evening and return every morning?'

'No. I've been staying here. At the Casa. Where I first found you.'

She spun back to the moment this had all begun, remembering how hostile and grim-faced he'd been back then—was it really only four days ago?—and her heart skipped a beat. Was he sleeping in the bed she'd slept in? On the same sheets? For some reason that felt incredibly intimate and her cheeks heated.

'What's the story there?' she asked distractedly, trying to get the fluster and the blush she could feel hitting her face under control.

'What do you mean?'

Oh, no.

Her heart gave a lurch and her gaze flew

to his. He'd gone very still, the lazy smile nowhere to be seen, his guard sky high, and she wished she could retract the question because she genuinely hadn't meant to ask. But now she had, she wasn't about to take it back. The curiosity had been killing her. 'The house was a total mess.'

His eyes shadowed for a moment. 'Yes.'

'What happened?'

'The cleaner quit.'

She didn't believe that for a moment. 'You should have asked me to find you another.'

'It must have slipped my mind.'

No, it hadn't. She doubted it had even crossed his mind, and part of her wanted to press him on it, but his jaw was rigid, his eyes were dark and his expression was filled with…yes, *anguish*.

Her heart turned over and her throat tightened, and she ruthlessly quelled the questions spinning round her head. She couldn't make it worse for him. This time of year had to be awful enough anyway. His son had been stillborn in early May. His wife had died six weeks later. Three years ago next fortnight, in fact. On both occasions her company had sent flowers, a wholly inadequate gesture, she'd thought at the time, if conventionally appropriate.

'I believe we were going to have a discussion about tricks,' she said, now deeply regretting the fact that she'd invaded his privacy and desperately seeking a way to lighten the mood.

As she'd hoped, the anguish faded and a gleam lit the dark, stormy depths of his eyes, and some of the tension gripping her muscles eased.

'I'm intrigued by the ones you think I know.'

'Well, obviously I don't have details,' she said, putting her plate to one side, her appetite gone. 'But I've read the gossip. You've slept with a lot of women.'

'You shouldn't believe everything you read.'

'Do you deny it?'

'No.'

'How many?'

'I've never kept count.'

'That many? You *must* have tricks.'

'I don't,' he said simply. 'What I do have is instinct. I watch, listen and learn. There's no manual and there are no expectations other than that everyone has a great time.'

Everyone? How many women did he have at once? God, the sun really was scorching today. 'Do you really think that the only way to get rid of attraction is by giving in to it?'

'Yes.'

He sounded adamant, but surely his wife had to have been the exception. Presumably in marriage, the continuation of attraction was a bonus rather a hindrance. But then, what did she know? She was hardly an expert. She'd once planned to marry a man to whom she'd only very tepidly been attracted, which boggled the mind because if she compared the effect Matt had had on her with that of Duarte, well, there *was* no comparison.

'As I mentioned,' she said, determinedly ignoring the unacceptable longing to know more about his marriage when she'd already probed far too much, 'my experience is limited.'

He arched one dark eyebrow. 'The ex-fiancé?'

'Yes. And it wasn't all that great.'

'How long were you engaged?'

'Six months. We dated for a year before that.'

'You implied you had no friends.'

Well, no, she didn't. At least, none that she'd call good and none that lasted. Her hours were long, longer since she'd bought into the business and half of it was now her responsibility. She didn't have much time for socialising. And that was fine. 'I work a lot.'

'So how did you meet?'

'Via a dating app.'

She'd been twenty-four and lonely, not to mention still a virgin, thanks to her determination to outperform all her targets at work. She'd wanted to rectify that, since it had somehow felt like failure. Matt had seemed perfect, as driven professionally and personally as she was, and the future had looked so golden she'd forced herself to simply accept the fact that the sex was lukewarm at best.

'How did he propose? On an iceberg?'

As if. 'Over breakfast one morning. He's a tax accountant. He said it would make good fiscal sense to pool our resources, which in hindsight, explains a lot.'

'When did it end?'

'Four years ago. A long time, I will admit,' she said in response to his arch of an eyebrow, 'but crappy sex isn't hard to miss, especially when it was probably all my fault anyway.'

'How the hell would it be your fault?'

'I think I might be frigid.'

'You are far from frigid,' he said, his gaze drifting over her before settling on her mouth. 'You just need to think less and trust in the chemistry. Ours is outstanding, by the way, and that's unusual.'

'What a waste.'

'You also probably need to be in control.'

She stared at him, the ground tilting beneath her for a moment, and said, 'Do you think so?' even as a tiny voice in her head went, Well, *duh*.

'You said so yourself.'

'I was talking about work.'

'Why would it be different in other areas?'

Hmm. Perhaps it wouldn't. She'd never analysed control as an issue before. But, thinking about it, events beyond her control were generally the ones that sent her into a panic, which was why she tried so hard to mitigate them. So maybe he had a point.

'And in light of that,' he continued, his gaze lifting to hers, the heat blazing in his eyes hitting her like a punch to the gut, 'I should tell you that you can do anything you want to me whenever you want.'

Her mouth went dry and her breath hitched. 'Seriously?'

'Completely. You'd be one hundred per cent in charge. You could decide what you like and what you don't like and you could stop any time.'

'Would that make a difference?'

'You'll only know if you try. Give yourself instructions. Give *me* instructions. You're good at that.'

She was. And it was tempting because she wanted to experience rockets going off and bone-melting bliss. But then, there was the night of the kiss and yesterday, and the possibility that history would repeat itself, at which point she'd have to catch the next plane home with her tail between her legs and hand his account to a colleague, which wasn't an attractive prospect.

'You don't take instructions,' she said.

'No, I don't. But for you, I'm prepared to make an exception.'

'Why?'

'Because I want you. You're stunning and sexy as hell. And passionate, beneath the surface. It seems a shame to let all that go to waste. And I like you.'

For a moment, Orla was speechless. She was too busy gazing at him and melting like butter in the sun to be able to even think straight. He thought her stunning? He liked her? Had he taken another bang to the head?

'But what if you don't like what I do?' she said eventually.

'I very much doubt that would be possible,' he said, his voice low and so very certain. 'There are no rules. Just do what comes naturally.'

Oh, to have his confidence. But she'd never done anything naturally. She didn't trust in instinct. She studied and planned and practised until everything she did was perfect. She proofread her emails three times before hitting send. When she had to give a presentation she didn't leave anything to the last minute, oh, no. She had it ready weeks in advance, all the better to practise it, practise it and practise it some more. She just didn't understand how instinct—uncontrollable and unpredictable—could be more reliable than careful, considered preparation.

But maybe this wasn't something that could be studied. There was no test, at least, not that she knew of. And what was she going to do? Embrace celibacy, live half a life, in case she continued to fail? That sounded like failure of a different kind. And rather cowardly. So could she change the habit of a lifetime and switch from study to instinct?

Perhaps there was only one way to find out.

Her heart was by now crashing against her ribs so hard she feared one might crack, but Orla drummed up every drop of courage she possessed and said, 'Lie back.'

A muscle in Duarte's jaw jumped and an

unholy glint lit his rapidly darkening eyes. 'See?' he said, a wicked grin curving his mouth as he slowly rolled over, using his elbows to prop himself up. 'I told you that you were good at giving orders.'

'Don't talk. I need to concentrate on doing what comes naturally.'

'Ironic.'

'Shh.'

If he wasn't going to be quiet she was going to have to put his mouth to an alternative use. Would that be a good place to start? The right place?

No.

There was no right place. She'd start wherever she wanted to start. And right now, she wanted to explore his body, in detail and at length. Determinedly silencing the hypercritical voice in her head that was desperate to analyse what she was doing and assess her performance, Orla moved across the blanket, avoiding the remnants of lunch, and knelt beside him, stretched out before her like her own personal banquet.

With her breath in her throat, she leaned forwards and began undoing the buttons of his shirt, taking her time, savouring every inch of gorgeous tanned skin that her movements exposed. But it was awkward at this angle.

She felt like a doctor examining a patient—not the ideal scenario to be envisaging—so she shifted, yanked up her skirt, and in one smooth movement she was sitting astride him, and ah, yes, this was better. From here, she could put her hands on his shoulders, and with his help remove the shirt altogether.

As she began to trace the muscles of his chest and then lower, of his abdomen, he tensed and let out a long hiss, and when she lifted her gaze to his face she saw that his eyes were dark and stormy and his jaw was rigid.

He wanted her. A lot. She could feel the hard steel of his erection pressed against her soft centre, and suddenly, unexpectedly, a rush of liquid heat poured through her and settled low in her pelvis. Her head spun and her pulse raced, but she wasn't going to analyse it. She wasn't going to think about anything. Instead, she was going to kiss him.

Bending forwards and training her gaze on his mouth, Orla planted her hands on the blanket and lowered her head. Her lips settled on his and she tentatively slid her tongue between them to meet his. As she explored him, slowly and thoroughly, her eyes fluttered shut and sparks danced in her head. Her senses took over and it wasn't even a conscious decision that she'd had to make. She was far too drugged for that. He tasted of rich wine and delicious wickedness. His spicy, masculine scent wound through her, intoxicating her further.

She could feel his restraint as he kissed her back, in the rigidity of his body and the curling of his hands into fists at his sides. To know how strongly she was affecting him gave her the biggest of kicks and the confidence to tear her mouth from his and move it along his jaw. The feel of his stubble against her skin made her shiver and his breathing was harsh in her ear. When her mouth closed over the pulse hammering at the base of his throat, he actually growled.

Badly in need of air, Orla drew back dazedly, genuinely panting, and looked down, and somehow, *instinctively* maybe, her hands had made their way to his chest. His heart was thundering beneath her palms, almost as hard and fast as hers, and oh, look, now they were sliding down over hot skin and a light dusting of hair that narrowed down and disappeared beneath the waistband of his shorts.

She was burning up. Her T-shirt was too tight. She was struggling to breathe, and without thought, without a care, she whipped it off and tossed it to one side. Her bra—lacy today, as if subconsciously she'd *known* that this was a possibility—followed a moment later, leaving her bare from the waist up and exposed to his gaze. But the brush of a breeze made no difference to her temperature, not when Duarte was looking at her with such blazing hunger.

'You're killing me,' he said roughly.

He sounded tortured and for a split-second Orla wondered whether she was doing something wrong, but there *was* no right or wrong, she reminded herself firmly. There was just heat and desire, and to her giddy delight she was still feeling it all.

But she wanted more. Much more.

'Touch me,' she murmured, her voice scratchy and low.

With one swift move, Duarte shifted her down and pushed himself up, one arm sliding round her back to hold her in place. Orla was still catching her breath when his other hand landed on her waist, but she nevertheless felt the sizzle across her skin, as if she'd been branded.

'More,' she gasped, wrapping her hands round his neck and sinking her fingers into his hair while he obliged her by sliding his hand up her side to her breast.

He cupped her there, stroking her feverish

flesh, and oh, it was so very different to the night before. Tingles were spreading through her entire body, tiny sparks of electricity that she felt from the top of her head to the ends of her toes and made her tremble. She groaned, she couldn't help it, and this time there was nothing fake or forced about it. This time it had risen up from somewhere deep within her.

She was dizzy with longing. Able to focus on nothing but the sight of his large, tanned hands moving over her skin and the burn they left in their wake. She was growing increasingly desperate to find out what she was capable of, to do something to ease the gnawing ache intensifying inside her. Breathing hard, she reached down. With trembling fingers and a banging heart, she undid his belt then grappled with his fly. Duarte shifted so that she could shove his shorts and underpants down, and then he was in her hand, velvety hot and as hard as iron.

But running her fingers over him wasn't enough. She wanted him in her mouth, to taste him, to find out if he liked that, *how* he liked that, so she planted a hand on his chest and pushed him back. He let out a soft gasp of surprise, but when she scooted down his body and closed her mouth over him, doing to him exactly what she wanted to do, his gasps became harsher, more ragged, and shudders racked his powerful body.

Nature was marvellous, instinct was wonderful, and oh, he *did* like that. He liked every lick, every stroke. And so did she, she liked it a lot, but the clawing ache was relentless now and she badly wanted him inside her. She lifted her head and looked at him. His eyes were dark and dazed and his jaw was clenched, tension gripping every muscle of his body.

'Condom?' she managed, her pulse hammering and her breath coming in sharp, shallow pants.

'Basket.'

The roughness of his voice, almost a growl, scraped over her nerve endings and, about to expire with need, Orla reached over and found it.

'I hope you don't think I'm using you,' she said shakily as she ripped the packet open.

'You aren't but I couldn't care less if you were,' he said through gritted teeth, taking the condom and applying it with impressively swift efficiency while she rid herself of her knickers.

Catching her lower lip with her teeth, she lifted her hips and sank down onto him, her breath hitching at the incredible feel of him, so big and deep inside her. She leaned forwards to kiss him, her hands on his shoulders for support, and began to move. She couldn't help herself. It was as if her body had a mind of its own and she was merely along for the ride.

And what a ride it was becoming. Her blood was on fire. Her bones were melting. Their kisses were generating enough electricity to power a small country and with every wild roll of her hips, sensation blazed through her.

So this was the result when you let things happen naturally, she thought dazedly, as the pressure inside her grew. This was what it was like to moan and groan and sigh without intending to.

Duarte clamped one hand on the small of her back and the other to the back of her neck, pressing her more tightly against him and angling her head to deepen their kisses, as if able to read what she needed and taking care of it. And she found she was all right with that. She was all right with everything. More than all right, in fact.

Her movements were becoming wilder, more uncontrollable. Kissing was impossible and she was unbearably hot. Her body didn't feel like her own. It was being driven by a need that defied analysis—huge, overwhelming, breathtaking. She ached all over, the tension filling her agonising. Her heart was thundering, the pressure was building and she was racing in the direction of something that was barrelling towards her.

And then somewhere in the recesses of her brain, she was aware of Duarte reaching round and pressing his fingers against her with mind-blowing accuracy, and suddenly, with a cry she just couldn't contain, she shattered into a million scorching pieces. Wave after wave of pleasure crashed over her, so intensely she saw stars. Pure ecstasy flooded her entire body and she found she was shaking all over, fighting for breath, for sanity, and convulsing around him.

And when he thrust up one last time, impossibly hard and deep, a great groan tearing from his throat as he pulsed into her over and over again, triggering tiny aftershocks of delight, she knew that it had been perfect. Wonderfully, gloriously, perfect.

CHAPTER EIGHT

UTTERLY SPENT, HIS mind blown and his body boneless, Duarte flopped back, taking Orla, sweat-slicked and limp, with him. He was breathing hard and reeling, scarcely able to believe what had just happened. When he'd suggested she take the initiative and run with it, he'd expected she would need a lot more persuasion. He'd anticipated something resembling a slow burn. Instead, he'd encountered a wildfire.

He couldn't remember the last time he'd come across such enthusiasm. Or experienced such exquisite agony. He'd never had any trouble relinquishing control when it came to sex, but how he'd managed not to touch her at first he had no idea. The thoroughness with which she'd explored him… The torture she'd subjected him to… When her mouth had closed over him he'd nearly jumped out of his skin. When his orgasm had hit, he'd almost passed out.

Orla carefully lifted herself off him, making him wince slightly as she did so, and immediately he missed the soft, warm weight of her body. He was filled with the urge to pull her back into his arms and relight the fire that burned between them, because, despite the fact that he hadn't yet got his breath back from the last quarter of an hour, he wanted more. A lot more.

Which, he thought with a disconcerting jolt as he turned away to deal with the condom with surprisingly shaky hands, was…unexpected.

He hadn't been lying when he'd told Orla that in his pre-marriage experience, one night had generally been enough to satisfy any desire he'd felt. He'd been easily bored and had enjoyed variety, constantly seeking the attention he'd craved in new people. But apparently he'd changed in more ways than one in the last few years, because not only could he take or leave attention these days, he was far from bored with Orla and the thought of variety made him want to recoil in disgust.

Which meant what? What did he want from her? More of this, absolutely, but nothing permanent, that was for sure. So something temporary, then. Sex for as long as she was here, perhaps. That could work. In fact, that would be ideal, because it would both assuage his rampant desire for her until it burned out altogether and provide a much-needed distraction. The anniversary of his wife's death, which never failed to challenge his ability to keep the crushing pain of betrayal and the overwhelming guilt under control, was rapidly approaching. An affair with Orla would be infinitely preferable to seeking solace at the bottom of a bottle, which was how he'd handled both the immediate aftermath of the tragedy and the anniversaries of the last two years.

Wanting more with her was no cause for concern, he assured himself as he rolled back to face her and propped himself up on his elbow while the plan in his head solidified. It wasn't as if he wouldn't be able to send her on her way when it was over.

What *was*, potentially, a worry was whether she'd be on board with the idea. She'd agreed to a one-time thing. That might have been enough for her, a tick in a box, a failure overcome. The control was still in her hands—she could easily turn him down—and that put him faintly on edge, but he'd just have to persuade her to see things his way because this felt like a win-win opportunity to him and he was not going to pass it up.

'So you were right,' she said huskily, still sounding a little breathless.

'About what?'

'I'm not frigid.'

She certainly wasn't. She was the opposite. She was as hot as hell. Volcanic, in fact, just as he'd imagined. So why on earth, when she pursued excellence on all fronts, had she'd chosen to marry a man who'd never been able to tap that? 'There really isn't anything you don't excel at, is there?'

She stretched languidly, tousled and flushed, half naked and stunning, and gave him a wide, satisfied grin. 'Not a lot, no. And anyway, back at you.'

She was wrong. He did not excel at everything. Far from it. He let his emotions cloud his judgement. He had a tendency towards self-absorption. He failed to protect those for whom he was responsible, and the consequences of these weaknesses of his were devastating and irreversible.

But that wasn't what this afternoon was about, so he shoved to one side the memories and the guilt, focusing instead on the gorgeous, pliant woman beside him, and said, 'Just imagine what we could do with more practice.'

'More practice?' Orla echoed softly, staring at him wide-eyed as surprise and delight mingled with the lingering traces of pleasure. 'I thought that once was generally enough.'

'So did I,' Duarte murmured, his gaze dark and hot as it slowly and thoroughly roamed over her. 'But I was wrong.'

'So what are you suggesting?'

'An affair. For the next three weeks, until the conference is over and we both leave. I'm not after a relationship, Orla. I have neither the time nor the inclination. But I do want you and I want more of this. So what do you think?'

Quite frankly, Orla thought that she'd never been so relieved to hear anything in her life. Even Isabelle Baudelaire's *'Oui, bien sûr'* in response to her request for the wine paled in comparison.

Because what had just happened had been the most intense experience of her existence, and she knew with absolute certainty that once wasn't going to be nearly enough. How could it be when it had been so unbelievably good? She wanted him again, right now, and how that was possible when she could still barely feel her toes she had no idea.

That he didn't want a relationship was fine with her. Why would he? He'd had the perfect marriage, which had been tragically cut short. His wife was irreplaceable. Peerless, even. Who could ever compete with a ghost like that?

But she didn't want a relationship either. One was quite enough, and the thought of another, which would inevitably end in deep disappointment and endless self-recrimination, was enough to bring her out in hives, and she too didn't have the time.

But she did want more sex with him, and whether or not itches were scratched or multiplied she didn't care. She ought to do more research. What did once prove anyway? And she needed to know just how excellent she could be, he could be, they could be together. She wouldn't get distracted. She excelled at multitasking. It was only three weeks. It would be hot, intense and fun, and when the conference was over she'd walk away with happy memories and no regrets.

'An affair it is.'

For Orla, the next few fabulous days were revelatory, in both expected and unexpected ways. Having handed her the key to unlock the secret to spectacular sex, Duarte had unleashed a devil she hadn't even known she'd been guarding. The first time she'd experienced the heady heights of earth-shattering bliss by the river had just been the start of it. He'd taken it upon himself to prove to her exactly how much pleasure her body could endure, which had turned out to be a *lot*, and by the end of the day she'd been completely drained, so lethargic, her body so boneless, she'd barely been able to move.

Control was a powerful thing, she'd realised as she'd lain there in the glow of the afternoon sun, catching her breath yet again, stars dancing in her head. But so was having the kind of confidence that meant you could temporarily let it go. And that was what he'd given her—confidence—over and over again.

The realisation that she was capable of excellent sex, that she'd finally overcome an obstacle that had been bothering her for years, had been so overwhelming that at one point during the afternoon she'd had to take a moment by going for a wander alone along the shore.

Perhaps she should take more risks, she'd thought, gently kicking at the cool water lapping at her feet. Perhaps she shouldn't simply avoid things she didn't think she'd be any good at. Because maybe, just maybe, she'd turn out to be the opposite. And look what could happen when she *did* take a risk. Yes, there was always the possibility of failure, but should she *not* fail, the results could be astounding.

From that afternoon on, when she wasn't overseeing progress at the Quinta or engaged with other work-related matters, Orla was in Duarte's bed. Or he was in hers. Whichever was closer.

She'd learned that he'd lied about not having tricks. He had plenty, every single one of them astonishing, and in the pursuit of excellence she'd developed a few of her own, one of which she'd tried out in the shower yesterday morning.

In the belief he'd gone off for his habitual early morning swim and she was on her own, she'd switched on the water, lathered herself up and started singing. Terribly. Which was why she generally didn't do it, whatever the genre. But on that occasion, she'd had a song in her head about happiness and rooms without roofs that was driving her nuts and she'd thought, what the hell?

She'd had the fright of her life when a few minutes later Duarte had appeared and asked who was strangling the cat. To cover her mortification, she'd dragged him into the shower with her and then done her very best to wipe the moment from his head, which had only reinforced her newfound belief that the outcome of taking a risk could sometimes be spectacular.

If he had concerns about the beast he'd released, he didn't show it. On the contrary, he was with her every step of the way, as insatiable as she was, as if he, too, were making up for lost time. And maybe he was. Whenever he appeared in the press these days he was conspicuously on his own. If he had had a liaison of any kind, he'd been exceptionally discreet. If he hadn't, if she was the first person he'd slept with since his wife, well, that didn't mean a thing.

'Come for a swim with me,' Duarte said, jolting her out of her thoughts by tossing the sheet aside, getting out of bed and distracting her with the view.

A swim? Orla shivered and her pulse skipped a beat. He'd never invited her along before and she was more than all right with that. So why the change of plan?

'I should get to work,' she murmured with real regret because, although it wasn't going to happen, she'd like nothing more than to mess about in the water with him.

'It's still early.'

'I don't have a costume.'

'No need,' he said, a wicked smile curving

his mouth as he threw her a towel. 'There's no one else here.'

She caught it and set it to one side. 'Another time, maybe.'

'I'll make it worth your while.'

She frowned. 'Why the insistence?'

'Why the evasion?'

'All right,' she said with an exasperated sigh since he clearly wasn't going to let this drop and the sight of him all naked and perfect was robbing her of her wits anyway. 'I can't swim.'

His dark eyebrows lifted. 'Really?'

'I was never taught. I can't ride a bike either. Overlooked as a child, remember?'

'You could have learned later.'

'Well, yes, I suppose I could have,' she said, instinctively bristling at the faint but definitely implied criticism, 'but by that point it had become another thing to not be able to do and another thing to avoid. I know it's pathetic. I don't need you to judge.'

'It's not pathetic and I'm not judging. I'm just surprised.'

'It's not *that* uncommon.'

'I will teach you.'

No, he wouldn't, was her immediate response to that. There was no way she was getting in a pool and making a complete and utter fool of herself. Especially not naked. And especially not in front of someone like him, who seemed to be brilliant at everything he did. Besides, she'd become so adept at avoiding anything that involved a beach or a pool she barely even thought about her inability to swim any more.

But now she *was*, she found herself wondering, bizarrely, whether it wouldn't be quite nice to be able to go on holiday somewhere hot at some point. Not that she had the time to go on holiday, or, in fact, anyone to go on holiday with, but two weeks in the sun with no way of cooling off had always been her idea of hell. Come to think of it, three weeks out here, working in the relentless heat and constantly covered in a thin film of sweat hadn't been much fun either from that point of view, and if she was being brutally honest she'd longingly eyed up the pools both here and at the Quinta on more than one occasion.

So maybe she ought to accept a lesson or two. Duarte had taught her about wine. He'd taught her about sex. If she was willing to risk it, he could teach her how to swim, she had no doubt. She trusted him, she realised with a warm sort of glow, and interesting things did tend to happen when he took it upon himself to improve her education. So might this not be a golden opportunity to knock another thing off her activities-to-avoid list?

'All right,' she said, gathering up her courage and assuring herself that, quite frankly, nothing could be more embarrassing than being caught singing in the shower. 'Let's go.'

'Are your hands supposed to be where they are?'

At Orla's side in the pool, Duarte watched her paddle her arms and kick her legs and grinned. 'Absolutely.'

'Only I'd have thought one on the stomach and one on the back would make more sense than one on my bottom and the other on my breast. I feel you might be taking advantage.'

There was no might about it. He took advantage of her every time he got the chance, and where his hands were was no accident. He couldn't stop wanting to touch her. Her skin was as soft as silk and her body was warm and lush. Fortunately for the relentless and mind-boggling need he had for her, she was equally as disinclined to pass up such an opportunity. As he'd suspected, beneath the slightly uptight surface bubbled a volcano that erupted with only the tiniest provocation, and he was more than happy to supply that.

The idea of an affair with Orla really had been one of his best and teaching her to swim hadn't been such a bad one either, he thought, removing his hands from her body with some reluctance and letting her go. Not only did it provide ample opportunity for close proximity and direct contact, but it had also occurred to him that by avoiding anything she wasn't good at and deliberately not trying new things, she must have missed out on a lot. For some reason, he hadn't liked the thought of that and it gave him immense satisfaction to be able to do something about it, although for the life of him he couldn't work out why. But then, he didn't know why he'd invited her for a swim in the first place either when generally he used the time to clear his head and restore the order that she so easily destroyed.

'There,' he said, shaking off the profound sense of unease that came with confusion and focusing instead on her progress across the width of the pool. 'You see? You're swimming.'

'Am I?'

At the edge, she stopped and blinked as she looked back, as if only just realising what she'd achieved. 'Oh, my God, I *am*. You're good.'

'It's not me,' he said, feeling something unidentifiable strike him square in the chest and frowning slightly. 'You're the one who had the courage to try and then gave it one hundred per cent.'

The beam she gave him was more blinding than the hot morning sun that was rising above the hills. 'I did, didn't I? How can I ever thank you?'

'There's no need to thank me,' he said as the brilliance of her smile sizzled through him and ignited the ever-present desire, which was something he *did* understand, at least. 'But if you really insist, I can think of something.'

Orla spent the next week overseeing operations that were going so smoothly they didn't require much attention, which was fortunate because her thoughts were becoming increasingly filled with Duarte. She couldn't get enough of him or the conversations they had. They'd talked about work and travel, family and upbringings—everything, in fact, apart from past relationships, as if by unspoken but mutual consent that subject was off the table.

Yesterday, she'd expressed an interest in the winemaking process and he'd taken her on a tour of the vineyard. This morning she'd swum ten full lengths of the pool: three breaststroke, three backstroke, four crawl. Now she was floating about the place, feeling really rather pleased with herself about everything and unable to keep the smile off her face, until reality intruded in the shape of an email from a flower arranger that immediately zapped it.

The ultra-demanding client for whom she'd arranged the iceberg marriage proposal was celebrating it tomorrow with a huge party in a marquee in the grounds of her parents' stately home. Requirements had been extremely detailed and uncompromisingly inflexible, so the news that the ornamental cabbages due to take a starring role in the thirty floral displays had not turned up was not ideal, to say the least.

Half an hour later, however, contrary to Orla's hopes and expectations of an easy fix, 'not ideal' had become 'catastrophic'. Pacing the kitchen, she'd contacted everyone she knew, calling in favours and making promises in return. She'd tried to beg, borrow or steal, but all to no avail, and, as she hung up on the last of her options, panic was beginning to bubble up inside her and a cold sweat coated her skin.

This was her fault, she thought, swallowing down the nausea. She'd become so preoccupied with Duarte and the incredible way he made her feel that she'd taken her eye off the ball. She should have put in a call to all the contractors involved in tomorrow night's event and confirmed the arrangements. She shouldn't have assumed that just because everything was going smoothly here, she could rest on her laurels elsewhere.

So what was she going to do? she wondered, anxiety spreading through her veins and burrowing deep. How was she going to fix this? She didn't have a clue. She couldn't think straight. Her head was nothing but white noise. She was useless, a complete waste of space. What on earth had made her think she deserved any kind of success? Her pulse was thundering and her chest was tightening. She couldn't breathe. *She couldn't breathe.*

'Orla? Are you all right?'

Duarte's voice filtered through the thick, swirling fog and she was dimly aware of him stalking towards her, vaguely wondering what he was doing there when he'd told her he'd be working at the house today, but mainly thinking, no. She wasn't all right. She wasn't all right at all. The room was spinning and she was hot and dizzy and quite possibly about to pass out.

But she didn't. Seconds before she toppled like a ninepin, a pair of large hands landed on her upper arms, keeping her vertical and holding her steady.

'Look at me.'

Like that was going to help. Looking at him would just make her dizzier. It always did. But sitting was good, she thought woozily as he pushed her down into a chair. Sitting would definitely stop her crumpling into a heap on the floor.

'Breathe.'

'I can't,' she croaked. Her throat was too tight and, because he'd dropped to his knees in front of her and was leaning in close, he was stealing all the air.

'Breathe with me.'

He placed her clammy hand in the centre of his chest and held it there, covering it with his warm, dry one, and she didn't even have to think about focusing on the rise and fall she could feel beneath her palm. All her senses narrowed in on that one thing, the warm solidity of his body acting like a sort of anchor, calming the chaos whirling around inside her as she instinctively followed his lead until eventually her heart rate slowed and the panic subsided.

'Thank you,' she murmured shakily, faintly mortified and not quite able to look him in the eye as she reluctantly took her hand back.

'What happened?'

'I had a panic attack.'

'Why?'

'There's a national shortage of ornamental cabbages.'

'What on earth are ornamental cabbages?'

'Bedding plants,' she said, lifting her eyes to his and seeing the fierce concern in his expression turn to puzzlement. 'For an engagement party tomorrow night. The iceberg proposal. But there aren't any. Anywhere.'

Duarte sat back on his heels and rested his forearms on his knees, his frown deepening, as if he couldn't see the problem. 'So use something else.'

If only it was that simple. 'Nothing else will do,' she said. 'The bride-to-be was very specific. It's a disaster. A complete and utter disaster.'

At the thought of it, tendrils of renewed panic began to unfurl inside her and her breath caught, making the dizziness return.

'It doesn't have to be,' he said with enviable calm. 'If you can persuade Isabelle Baudelaire to part with a two-hundred-and-fifty-thousand-dollar bottle of wine, you can persuade this bride-to-be to accept an alternative to ornamental cabbages.'

She stared at him, holding his gaze and

taking strength from his steadiness until her head cleared and she could breathe once again. Well, when he put it like that, she probably could. Cardoons had been suggested by one of her contacts. They were as bold as ornamental cabbages, if not bolder, stunning in their own way, and supply wasn't an issue. 'Cardoons might work.'

'And no one will ever know.'

But that wasn't really the point. '*I* will,' she said, swallowing hard. 'I'll always know I screwed up.'

'*You* didn't,' he countered. 'This is not your fault.'

Debatable, but irrelevant. 'I'm still responsible. The buck stops with me.'

'It's a hiccup. Which you will fix. And everything will be fine.'

'It won't be fine,' she said. 'It won't be what the client wanted. It won't be perfect.'

'It will be almost perfect.'

She shook her head in denial. 'Almost perfect is not good enough.'

'It's more than enough.'

It wasn't. It never had been. Second-best wasn't in her mindset. 'That'll do' was not a phrase she'd ever used. She could understand why he didn't get it. No one ever did.

'You are exceptional at what you do, Orla,'

Duarte continued in the same steady vein while she continued to resist. 'I've seen you at work here and watched how you've managed people and handled problems. Focus on the many things you've achieved and trust yourself.'

That was easy for him to say, and it gave her a kick to know that he thought her work exceptional, but she doubted his entire life imploded when he made a mistake. She'd bet he didn't live with a super-critical inner voice that constantly drove him to achieve more and be better. That battered him with insinuations of worthlessness when he was down and made him feel he *deserved* to be overlooked.

He was impossible to overlook. He just had to walk into a room and all heads swivelled in his direction. He came across as supremely confident in who he was and what he did. He was out to prove nothing.

Whereas she was out to prove…

Well, she wasn't quite sure what she was out to prove. Which was odd when she'd always known exactly what drove her. But right now, suddenly, she wasn't sure of anything. Because to her shock and confusion, as everything he'd said spun around her brain like a demented, out-of-control top, she was wondering whether she oughtn't ease up on herself a little. As he'd once pointed out, she did put an immense amount of pressure on herself. She always set herself goals that were slightly out of reach, forever needing more to silence the judgemental devil that lived in her head.

Announcing she'd acquire for Duarte the bottle of Chateau Lafite 1869 was a case in point. It had been a nigh on impossible task. She hadn't slept. She'd been too wired, too focused on the goal. She'd felt no great sense of triumph at having achieved the inconceivable in itself, only at what it had meant for her job and her emotional well-being.

She'd lived like this for the best part of twenty years. She'd never considered perfectionism a flaw—despite what that therapist she'd seen once had insinuated—but maybe he'd been right after all and it was. She knew from experience that it wasn't an irritating little personality quirk. At times it could be hellish. But maybe true perfection was impossible anyway, and if it was, then the pursuit of it was not only wildly unrealistic but also incredibly unhealthy.

How much longer could she go on like this? she wondered, her stomach and her thoughts spinning. She had no time for friends or hobbies. Her to-do lists were out of control. She was heading for burnout. Her doctor would certainly be pleased if she took her foot off the pedal. Her cortisol levels were stratospheric.

And mightn't it be nice to live in the moment for a change instead of either analysing her performance on tasks gone by or thinking about everything she had to do next? Happiness and contentment weren't things she'd ever really thought about, but could she honestly say she was happy? No. She couldn't. Not in the way her siblings were. They were far more sorted than she was. They took setbacks in their stride. They didn't wallow in recrimination and self-doubt when things went wrong. *And* they had the whole relationship thing nailed. Her sister was married and her brother had a long-term girlfriend. She, on the other hand, had been planning to marry a man with whom she had less-than-mediocre sex simply because she refused to admit defeat. She hadn't been jealous of them for years. She found she was now.

So could she unravel two decades' worth of perfectionist traits and allow that good enough *was* good enough? The thought of it made her feel even more nauseous than before, and every cell of her body was quivering with resistance, but something had to change. She couldn't carry on like this. So perhaps she could try it and see how it went, however terrifying.

'You're right,' she said, taking a deep breath and bracing herself for a giant leap into the unknown. 'Cardoons will have to do.'

Noting that the colour had returned to Orla's cheeks and the strength to her voice, Duarte got to his feet and took a surprisingly unsteady step back before turning on his heel, shoving his hands in his pockets and stalking out. He needed air, the more of it he could get and the fresher it was, the better.

Thank God he'd been around to stop her falling, he thought grimly as he emerged into the bright afternoon sunshine and inhaled raggedly, his pulse still hammering at the memory of the sight of her standing there about to swoon. Why he'd changed his mind and opted to work from here instead of staying at the house he hadn't a clue. It wasn't as if he couldn't stay away from her. He wasn't *that* desperate. He was totally in control of the effect she had on him. He didn't *need* to know where she was or what she was doing. He'd decided to head to the kitchen because he was thirsty and felt like an ice-cold beer, not because he'd caught sight of her through the window pacing up and down the flagstones with such a wretched expression on her face that his heart had almost stopped.

But none of that mattered. All that *did* matter was that he'd been in the right place at the right time and a good thing too because if she'd cracked her head on the stone floor she could have hurt herself badly. She could have lain there in pain—or worse—for hours.

Orla evidently wasn't as indestructible as she liked to make out. She had insecurities and vulnerabilities and that meant that he was keeping an eye on her. He wasn't ignoring another woman's emotional well-being. He'd learned that lesson. So from now on, he was sticking to her like glue.

CHAPTER NINE

ORLA SAT ON the terrace at the Casa, nursing a cup of steaming coffee in the early morning sunshine and contemplating the idea that Duarte was about as ideal a man as it was possible to get. He inspired trust. He could read her body as if he'd studied her for an exam and her mind as if he could see into it. And he was good company.

When she thought about how patient he'd been while she'd freaked out about ornamental cabbages, she melted. He hadn't scoffed about the triviality of bedding plants. He hadn't diminished what to her were very real, very significant concerns. He'd handled her with care and perception and talked her off the ledge, and every time the memory of it slid into her head, she found herself grinning like a fool.

And he might have had a point about the whole 'good enough' thing, she'd grudgingly come to admit. Her demanding bride-to-be had raved about the cardoons, deeming them infinitely superior to the apparently rather lacklustre ornamental cabbage. A minor problem with the drains here had been swiftly, if imperfectly and only temporarily, resolved—which was…well, not too bad, actually. She'd spent years believing that her sense of self-worth was tied up in excelling at everything, but perhaps it didn't have to be that way. Perhaps she could find it in something else. Or even, maybe, someone else…

But Duarte was wrong about one thing. The chemistry that sizzled between them was far from fading. It burned like a living flame inside her, growing stronger every day. Colours were brighter. Smells were more intense. She knew when he was around even if she couldn't see him. Her skin would break out in goosebumps and then, a moment or two later, there he'd be.

In fact, all her senses appeared to be heightened and she felt on top of the world. Her swimming was improving in leaps and bounds. Work was going brilliantly. Progress at the Quinta was steaming ahead and she'd just signed up another ultra-high net worth client, who, happily for her company's bottom line, showed every indication of being all for opulence and extravagance.

Everything was perfect.

Her skin prickled and she couldn't help grinning when a moment later she felt Duarte sweep her hair to one side and drop a hot kiss at the base of her neck.

'I need to go to Porto this evening,' he murmured against her skin, making her shiver and wonder whether there was time for a quickie. 'I have a meeting first thing tomorrow.'

Well, maybe not quite that perfect, she amended, her spirits taking a sudden dip as the blood in her veins chilled. He'd been extremely attentive lately, ever since the ornamental cabbage incident, in fact, and she'd got used to having him around. She didn't like the idea of eating supper on her own. But it would be fine. It wasn't as if she'd miss him or anything. She'd only known him a couple of weeks, and she was hardly addicted to the sex. Honestly. She'd spent innumerable evenings alone. She'd occupy herself with work, just as she usually did.

'OK,' she said, feigning nonchalance with a casual shrug. 'No problem.'

He moved round her and dropped into the seat opposite. 'Come with me.'

At that, those spirits of hers bounced right back and her heart gave a little skip.

Well.

She *could* decline, she told herself, battling the rising urge to grin like an idiot. To prove to herself that she could take or leave him, that she *wasn't* addicted, perhaps. But God, she didn't want to. She wanted to spend the night with him in Porto. She wanted to see where he lived and what he did outside this lovely bubble they currently existed in. The world wouldn't collapse if a problem arose and she wasn't there. She had her phone and she'd keep it on.

So the hyper-critical voice in her head warning her she was straying into dangerous territory could pipe down. This *wasn't* one of those risks she'd contemplated while paddling at the edge of the river. She was still leaving once the conference was over. She wasn't going to develop any unwise ideas about what this affair of theirs either was or wasn't. But nor was she going to waste a single minute of it.

'I'd love to.'

That evening, Duarte flew her to Porto by helicopter, a forty-five-minute journey that was, in equal parts, terrifying and thrilling.

Terrifying because, despite having organised more such trips than she could count, she'd never actually taken one herself and it was alarming to be hurtling through the air in what amounted to little more than a tin can. And thrilling, because she recalled his asking her to research helicopter options and arrange the lease shortly after he'd signed up to her company's services but never in a million years had she imagined she'd one day occupy the passenger seat.

From the airport they travelled straight to his apartment on the coast, which could not be more different to the properties on the wine estate. It stretched across the entire top floor of a fifteen-storey modern block of what she supposed was cutting-edge design. Light flooded in through acres of glass and bounced off the many reflective surfaces. Rich, gleaming wood and cream marble abounded, and the views of the sea from virtually every angle were stunning. While Orla was a fan of a perfectly positioned cushion or six and the occasional colour-coded bookcase, she could see how this décor would suit Duarte. It was warm, unfussy and unashamedly masculine.

'Nice place,' she said as she walked out

onto the vast, lushly planted terrace and joined him at the balcony.

'Thank you.'

He handed her a glass of *vinho verde* and the brush of his fingers against hers sent shivers scuttling down her spine in a way that really she ought to be used to by now but which still caught her by surprise.

'Have you lived here long?'

'Two and a half years.'

He must have moved here soon after his wife had died, she mused, taking a sip and feeling the deliciously cool white wine slip down her throat. It was on the tip of her tongue to ask, because increasingly she found herself wondering about the woman he'd married. What had she been like? The press had painted her as great a party animal as he'd been, but she longed to know more. And what of the overdose? Had that been an accident or deliberate?

However, she couldn't ask. The subject was still far too personal for a brief affair, however intense. Besides, it would ruin the mood of a beautiful evening, so she crushed the curiosity, turned away from the pink-and-gold-streaked sky, and instead focused on the table that sat beneath the pergola strung with fairy lights.

'What's all this?'

'Dinner.'

Well, yes, she could see that, but as she moved closer to peruse the dishes set out on the table her heart began to thud so hard she could feel it in her ears. It was more than dinner. A couple of days ago she and Duarte had had a conversation about culinary loves and hates. And here she could see a platter of langoustines and a dish of plump black olives. A bowl of vibrant guacamole, a basket of ridge-cut crisps and, on a wooden board, sliced impossibly thinly, medium rare steak. All her favourite things.

Her mouth went dry and her head spun for a second. She could totally see how he'd bedded so many women back in the day when he'd lived fast and played hard. Being the object of his attention was like standing for too long in the midday sun—dazzling and dizzying.

'God, you're good at this,' she said, wondering if it would be rude to delay dinner by dragging him off to one of the three bedrooms so she could show him her appreciation properly.

He glanced up from the candle he was in the process of lighting and shot her a wicked grin. 'What, specifically, are you referring to?'

'The whole seduction thing.'

He went still and something flickered in the depths of his eyes, gone before Orla could even begin to work out what it was.

'Well, as you know, practice makes perfect,' he drawled with a shrug, but she noticed that his smile had hardened a fraction and suddenly, inexplicably, she felt a bit sick.

Could she have offended him? she wondered, the wine in her stomach turning to vinegar. Impossible. His past was no great secret. For years his exploits had been plastered all over the front covers of the more salacious global press. She was merely stating a fact. There was no need to feel bad.

'Right,' she said, her throat nevertheless strangely tight.

'Take a seat.'

'Thank you.'

'What would you like to do tomorrow while I'm in my meeting?' he asked, his gaze cool, his expression unreadable.

'I'm not sure.'

'Have a think and let me know.'

While Orla slumbered peacefully in his bed, Duarte sat on the balcony in the warm, still dark of the night, staring out into the distance, feeling anything but peaceful.

Dinner had turned out to be unexpectedly awkward. Conversation, for once, had flowed like concrete. And it was all because of that comment of hers about his seduction techniques.

It had stung, he thought, vaguely rubbing his chest. He didn't know why. When applied to his exploits prior to his marriage, it was nothing less than the truth. He'd revelled in the chase and honed his skills to razor-sharp perfection. Yet there'd been no calculation in his decision to have delivered to his apartment all Orla's favourite food tonight. No ulterior motive. They had to eat and it had simply seemed the easiest option. Besides, their affair was blazing. Seduction was unnecessary.

Perhaps, with hindsight, inviting her here had been a bad idea. At the time, he hadn't even had to convince himself that he needed to keep her close so he could keep an eye on her. He'd acted purely on instinct. The last two weeks had been a heady rush of lazy conversation and endless pleasure. As he'd confessed by the river, he liked her, even more so now than he had done then. She was clever and perceptive, self-aware and quick to learn. She had a smile that he wanted to bottle so he could take it out whenever he needed a moment of sunshine, and he found her scent on his pillows so soothing that staying at the Casa didn't bother him any more. Thanks to her original mistake it was unrecognisable anyway, and besides, the new memories they were creating there were doing an excellent job of erasing the old.

Missing even a second of that when she'd soon be gone for good had been deeply unappealing, and he hadn't thought twice about issuing that invitation. But he should have, because it had been rash and reckless and smacked of a man with a shaky grip on his control.

What he'd been thinking over the last fortnight he had no idea. He didn't need to know what made her tick. Her innermost thoughts and opinions were of no importance. She didn't need to know anything about the city of his birth or the place where he lived. And God knew why he'd taken her on a tour of the vineyard the day before yesterday. It wasn't as if he'd wanted her to be impressed by the changes and innovations he'd brought to the business, even though she had been.

He'd come to suspect that the stab to the chest he'd felt when she'd swum a width of his pool on her own had been one of pride. The way she'd handled the cabbage crisis had filled him with admiration, and none of that was necessary. It suggested emotional intimacy, and, unlike intimacy of the physical kind, that played no part in anything. He had no business taking it upon himself to make her see what she was missing out on, living her life the way she did. Instead of ordering all her favourite food last night they should have just eaten out. This was sex without strings and that was it.

But as long as he remembered that there was no need for concern, he told himself, ruthlessly silencing the little voice in his head trying to protest that it might have become more than that. Tonight had been a mistake and some of the things he'd said and done over the last couple of weeks had been dangerously unwise, but there was no point in overanalysing anything or attaching to it a greater significance than it warranted. What was done was done and regrets were pointless. The swimming lessons and conversation could stop easily enough. It was just a question of control.

Tomorrow he'd be in a meeting most of the morning, and when he was done he'd take Orla back to the Quinta. Once there, he'd spend the days they had left proving to her and himself exactly what this fling of theirs was. He'd keep his distance by day and make up for it by night, until she was gone, and everything would be fine.

The following morning Orla was taken on a private tour of Duarte's port house, where she discovered a taste for dry white port and a fascination for the history of his family.

The original founder, Duarte's ancestor, might have come from a humble background, but flushed with vinicultural success, he'd married into the local aristocracy, and ever since then the family's wealth and connections had multiplied. Offspring attended the world's finest schools and best universities, before generally taking up a position in the business.

Judging by the oil paintings that hung on the walls of a gallery built specifically for that purpose, Duarte's looks had been passed down the generations along with his staggering personal wealth. And he'd definitely ended up with the best of them, she'd thought dreamily as she'd stood and stared at his portrait for so long someone had asked her if she'd wanted a seat.

In comparison, she felt rather inadequate and insignificant, so to counter that she visited the most beautiful book shop she'd ever seen, followed by a *pasteleria* famed for its custard tarts, and the exquisite perfection she'd found in each had made her feel a whole lot better.

At first, Orla had been relieved to be on her own. That awkward moment before dinner last night had been followed by some horribly stilted conversation and then some mind-blowing yet strangely soulless sex. This morning, just before Duarte had left for his meeting, she'd tried to apologise, although she wasn't quite sure what she was apologising for, but he'd looked at her as if he hadn't a clue what she was referring to before kissing her senseless and telling her his car was at her disposal. It was all baffling, not least the switch from soulless to smouldering, and because she felt as though she was suddenly on shaky ground she'd welcomed the breathing space his meeting gave her.

But by the time she arrived back at the airport, she was unexpectedly sorry he hadn't been there to share the experiences with her. At the port house, she'd kept turning to ask him something about one ancestor of his or another, but of course he wasn't there. In the Livraria Lello she'd come across a book about the history of seventeenth-century winemaking in south-west Spain and had wanted to know if he already had it and, if not, whether he might like it. She'd missed him, which was ridiculous when they'd only been apart for a handful of hours and the morning had started off rather oddly, but it was what it was.

She was also filled to the brim with a warm sort of glow that she just couldn't seem to contain. For the best part of a decade she'd organised the lives of other people and, while she loved her job, when it came to things like marriage proposals on icebergs, she couldn't help but feel the occasional pang of envy. This was the first time ever that someone had arranged something solely for her. From the moment they'd taken off yesterday evening she'd barely had to lift a finger. She'd been sublimely fed, luxuriously chauffeured around and, despite the odd uncomfortable moment, been taken care of most excellently. Duarte had made all that happen—for her—and as a result she felt ever so slightly giddy.

'How was your meeting?' she asked when he joined her in the private lounge at the airport, her heart banging against her ribs at the sight of him because the man in a beautifully cut charcoal-grey suit really was something else.

'Productive,' he said, shrugging off his jacket and rolling up his shirtsleeves with an efficiency that left her weak-kneed and breathless. 'I signed a new contract to supply the biggest department store chain in the States.'

'We should celebrate.'

His ebony gaze collided with hers, glittering with a sudden heat that stole the breath from her lungs, and everything fell away, the noise, the lights, the people, everything. 'Hold that thought.'

She held that thought all the way back to the Quinta. She couldn't have shaken it even if she'd wanted to. Forget the landscape. She'd admired it on the journey out. All she could admire now were his hands. His forearms. His profile, complete with the sexiest pair of sunglasses she'd ever seen on a man.

When not occupied with flying the helicopter, his hand was on her thigh, skin on skin, just high enough for her to wish it was higher, covering her where she needed him. She felt increasingly feverish, hot and trembling as if she were on fire. Her stomach was fluttering and her head was buzzing. The pressure in her chest matched in intensity the throbbing between her legs. She was burning up with wanting him and her heart felt too big for her chest. If she didn't have him inside her soon she was going to explode.

The minute they'd touched down on the estate and Duarte had switched off the engine, Orla unclipped her seatbelt, her hands shaking. He took off his headset and unbuckled himself, but before he could jump out she launched herself across the gap and planted herself on his lap. She smothered his gasp of shock with her mouth and started kissing him with all the wild, unidentifiable tangle of emotions swirling about inside her, until he put his hands on her head and drew her back, his eyes blazing.

'Stop.'

'No,' she breathed raggedly. She didn't want to stop, ever.

'We can't do this.'

What? 'We can.'

'You'll snap the lever.'

'Who cares?'

'I do,' he growled, nudging her off. 'It's my helicopter and I need it functional. Get in the back.'

Orla didn't have to be told twice. With less dignity than she'd have ideally liked, she scrambled between the seats and into the small utilitarian space designed not for passengers but luggage. She landed on the rubberised floor, and a second later Duarte was on top of her, pressing her down with his warm, hard weight and kissing her with a fierce, desperate need that matched her own.

She didn't want finesse. She had no idea what he was muttering in her ear, her Portuguese just not up to that, but she caught the urgency in his voice and guessed that he had no time for it either. While she yanked his shirt from the waistband of his trousers, he shoved her skirt up, dispensed with her knickers and grabbed her knees. He clamped his hands on her hips and shifted, and then his head was between her legs, his mouth on her, hot and skilled.

At the electrifying sensations that lanced through her like lightning, a groan tore from her throat and her chest heaved. Her hands found their way to his head, and her back arched and then, suddenly, she was crying out as spasms of white-hot pleasure racked her body.

She was only dimly aware of Duarte moving to rummage around in his overnight case. She was limp. Blitzed. She'd never shattered so fast and hard that she'd very nearly passed out. Yet, unbelievably, when he lifted her hips and slid into her with one powerful thrust, it triggered a fresh wave of ecstasy that detonated the aftershocks and had her shuddering and shaking all over again.

She wrapped her arms around his neck and her legs around his waist, her heart filled to bursting, and when he hurled them both over the edge into a bright, dazzling shower of stars she wondered how, when the conference was over, she was ever going to let him go.

That was more like it, thought Duarte, rearranging his clothes while his heart rate slowed and his breathing steadied. Frantic and desperate and unexpectedly intense, but, at the end of the day, just sex.

He helped a flushed and dazed Orla off the helicopter, grabbed his bag, and then, with the intention of implementing his plan to avoid her by day at the forefront of his mind, without looking back, strode away.

'Wait.'

He instinctively stopped and spun round. 'What?' he snapped, irritated beyond belief that he didn't even seem to be able to resist her voice and determined more than ever to keep his distance the minute he'd dealt with this.

'I bought these for you.'

She held out a bag, and for a moment he just stared at it as though it were about to explode.

'Little custard tarts,' she said with a warm smile. 'Your favourite, you said.'

Yes, well, he'd said too much lately. Given away too much. But that stopped now. *'Obrigado.'*

'You're welcome. And thank you for taking me to Porto and arranging everything. No one's ever done anything like that for me before.'

Her eyes were shining and his stomach clenched with even greater unease. What was going on? Why was she looking at him so...*tenderly*? She'd better not be getting any ideas.

'It was hardly a proposal on an iceberg or dinner in front of the Mona Lisa.'

'Doesn't matter. I don't need grand gestures that are frequently style over substance. I had a really great time.'

'Good,' he said bluntly, mentally adding to his plan the need to figure out how he was going to pulverise any potential yet very much misguided expectations she may have. 'I'm returning to the house. I'll see you tonight.'

CHAPTER TEN

THREE DAYS LATER, after weeks of azure skies and glorious sunshine, the weather changed. As a result of a front moving in from the west, the pressure plummeted and a thick layer of cloud lay heavily over the estate.

All morning, Orla had felt on edge, her stomach with a strange sense of foreboding that had nothing to do with anything on the professional front.

Everything for the conference, which was now in four days' time, was either ready or about to be. Guests had been assigned rooms and arrival details had been finalised. The wine had been retrieved from the cellars and food and staff were arriving, including Mariana Valdez, who thankfully defied the stereotype of the illustrious yet temperamental uber-chef by being utterly charming.

On a personal level, however, it was an entirely different matter. Ever since they'd arrived back from Porto, Duarte had been distant and brooding and worryingly monosyllabic. Citing work, he'd been around less during the day and she found that, as in Porto, she missed him. He'd continued to rock her world at night, more so than before, in fact, which was definitely *not* a cause for complaint, but, while he was at least physically present then, emotionally, she sensed, he was always miles away.

But at least the reason for that wasn't hard to figure out. Today was the anniversary of his wife's death, and if the weight of that knowledge sat like a lump of lead on her chest she couldn't imagine what he must be going through.

She'd woken early this morning, the date flashing in her head like a beacon, and lain there next to him, listening to the gentle rumble of his breathing, her mind racing and her heart aching. How was he going to handle it? Would he want to be on his own? Would he accept her support? Should she brace herself for rejection? Silence? Should she even mention anything?

They weren't exactly friends, and she supposed a brief affair—however intense—wasn't designed to encourage that kind of intimacy. But at the same time, he'd be hurting.

How could he not? He might look like a god but at the end of the day he was only human. The whirlwind fairy-tale romance had ended in tragedy. The love of his life was gone for ever. It had to be agony, and if it was solely up to her she'd be there for him. But what would he want?

In the end she'd decided to play it by ear. Whatever Duarte wanted, whatever he needed to get through the day, whether it be space, silence or sex, she'd provide it. She'd be sympathetic and supportive. She could do that, despite her ex once having told her otherwise as their engagement limped to an end. This wasn't someone who'd lost his job due to a corporate restructure and then endlessly moaned about not being able to find a new one without actually putting in all that much effort to facilitate that. This was a man who'd lost his son and beloved wife within six weeks of each other. While it was possible that perhaps she'd been a little harsh on Matt, Duarte's situation could not be more different.

Yet now, tonight, with the rain hammering down outside and the window of opportunity rapidly closing, Orla couldn't stand it any longer. Of all the scenarios that had played out in her head, the status quo had not been one of them. However, all day Duarte had acted as if nothing was different. He'd woken up and she'd braced herself for whatever might be coming her way, but he'd merely reached for her and rolled her beneath him. Then, after grabbing a coffee and a croissant, he'd opened up his laptop and got to work, just as he had yesterday, the day before and the day before that.

Perhaps denial was his coping mechanism. Perhaps he didn't need comforting or to talk about it. The trouble was, because she was aching for him, she *wanted* to talk about it. She *longed* to comfort him. The urge to bring it up had been clamouring inside her all day, swelling and intensifying to an unbearable degree, and if she didn't ask him about it now, when they were at her hotel and privacy was plentiful, then when?

'So how are you feeling?' she said, pulling the sheet over her naked, still languid body, shifting onto her side and propping herself up on her elbow as Duarte emerged from the shower room in a white towel wrapped round his hips and a cloud of steam.

He headed for the window and closed the shutters, treating her to a lovely view of his bare back in the meantime.

'That's the fifth time you've asked me that this evening,' he said tersely. 'And I'm still fine.'

But was he? Really? How could he be?

'You haven't been fine since we got back from Porto,' she said, forcing herself to focus on the mystery of his attitude lately and not his near nakedness. 'You've been distracted and distant.'

'I've been right here.'

'I mean emotionally.'

'What do emotions have to do with anything?'

Right. Well, for him, nothing, obviously. Unfortunately, she was riddled with the things, and they were demanding attention with increasing insistence, which meant that she couldn't let this go.

'You know, if you wanted to talk to me about anything, anything at all, I'd listen,' she said. 'Like you listened to me when I was going on about plants.'

He turned, his expression puzzled. 'What on Earth would I want to talk to you about?'

For a moment, she couldn't breathe. Her lungs had frozen and her throat had closed up. OK, so that hurt, she thought, forcing out a breath. That stabbed at her heart and then sliced right through the rest of her. But she had to persevere because he was clearly in denial and that couldn't be healthy. 'I understand it might be difficult.'

'What might be?'

'Well, today.'

'Why? What's so special about today?'

Surely it didn't need to be said. Surely he didn't need to be reminded. 'It's the anniversary of your wife's death.'

Duarte went very still. His brows snapped together in the deepest frown she'd ever seen on him and he seemed to pale beneath his tan. Shock jolted through her and her eyes widened. The air thickened, the only sound in the room the sound of rain hitting the window like gunshot.

Had he forgotten? No. Impossible. It had only been three years. He wasn't the sort of man to let the anniversary of the death of a much-loved wife slip by unnoticed. He couldn't be. She had to be mistaken. It had to be denial, after all.

But the tiny seed of doubt that had taken root in her head was growing a foot a second, and before she could stop herself she said, 'Did you forget?'

'Apparently I did,' he muttered, his jaw so tight it looked as though it was about to shatter.

She gasped and clapped a hand to her mouth. 'Why? How?'

'What business is it of yours?'

His tone was flat, brutal, and hit her like a blow to the gut, even though she knew that the answer to his question was none, no matter how much she might wish otherwise. They weren't in a relationship. They were just having an affair, and one that would soon be over. She had no right to pry. No right to feel eviscerated by the fact that he didn't want to share anything of meaning with her when she'd shared so much. She had no right to anything, but he was toppling off the pedestal she'd had him on, and suddenly that mattered. She wanted to know why. 'How could you?'

'We can't all be perfect.'

'But she was your soulmate,' she said, too agitated and distressed by the notion that he might not be the man she'd thought he was to heed the warning note in his voice. 'The love of your life. I don't understand.'

'Leave it, Orla.'

'But—'

'I said, leave it.'

Still reeling with the shock that had nearly taken out his knees, Duarte grabbed his T-shirt off the bed and yanked it on as if it might provide some kind of protection against the detonation of his world.

Orla's reminder of the date had landed like a grenade that had then gone off. He couldn't believe he'd forgotten. How the hell had it happened? He had no idea, but it did make sense of a lot of the things that had been baffling the life out of him today. Such as the curious glances she'd been casting his way. The bizarre tiptoeing around him and the constant questions about how he was feeling. The concern in her expression and the sympathy in her eyes, which he hadn't been able to fathom and which had only added to the unease that had been gripping him for the last forty-eight hours.

Around lunchtime he'd wondered if she'd started to regret their affair. If she wanted to put a stop to it for some reason that may or may not have had something to do with his strategy of keeping his distance, and had been trying to figure out a way to let him down gently.

The idea that she regretted anything about what they'd been doing had left a strangely sour taste in his mouth, and he'd recoiled in denial at the thought of their affair ending early. But he needn't have worried about that because he'd been wrong. She'd simply remembered the date, that was all, and why wouldn't she? At the time, her company had sent flowers. She'd handwritten him a personal message of condolence. And being good with dates was part of the job, she'd once told him.

He needed to get out of here, he thought grimly as he discarded the towel and pulled on his shorts and jeans. He'd already revealed too much. When, too stunned to exercise his customary caution, he'd admitted he had indeed forgotten the significance of today's date, Orla had been horrified. She'd looked at him as if he'd told her he drowned kittens for fun. She clearly found him severely lacking and he needed no judgement, from anyone, least of all from her. That was precisely what he'd been trying to avoid by allowing the myth of his marriage to perpetuate and the truth to remain buried.

So he ought to leave, pack up his things at the Casa and fly straight to Porto. Before he said or did something he'd *really* regret. Like telling her the truth. He'd have to be insane to do anything as stupid as that. He'd never uttered a word of it to anyone. If he did, to her, if he gave her even half an inch, she'd take a mile. She'd bulldoze her way through his fractured defences and poke around at the exposed weaknesses they were designed to protect. She'd uncover the man he was behind the facade, and she would find him weak. Shameful. Abhorrent.

And yet he was so sick of the secrets, the lies and the guilt. Not even his parents knew the whole truth of what had gone on during the course of his relationship with Calysta. He carried the burden alone, and because he wasn't as good at shouldering it as he liked to tell himself, it was crippling.

He didn't know how much longer he could hold it together. For weeks now, he'd been fraying at the edges, the gruelling schedule he'd adopted to keep a lid on his emotions and get through the days taking its toll. His mother was worried. He'd become short with his staff. It couldn't continue.

So what if he *did* tell Orla what had really happened? Could he trust her to listen without judgement? The feeling that somehow he'd let her down curdled his stomach. He wanted to set the record straight. He wanted to be able to let go of the guilt.

After she'd spilled the truth about her pregnancy Calysta had regularly tried to get him to talk, to no avail, and he was all too aware that if only he had, if only he'd listened, things could have turned out differently.

Might that be the case here? Could shedding the crushing load somehow be cathartic? And what if Orla *wasn't* sickened by the real him? What if somehow she understood? What if she was able to shed some light on the quagmire of his soul?

'I'm sorry,' she said hoarsely, jolting him out of his thoughts as she slid off the bed, still wrapped in the sheet, and reached for her clothes. 'I should never have brought it up. How you choose to handle this is entirely up to you. I should go.'

'No.'

Her gaze snapped to his, her eyes wide with surprise. 'What?'

'Stay.'

'Why?'

He silenced the voice in his head insisting he had to be insane to be considering doing this. The NDA Orla had signed still held. He had nothing to lose and possibly everything to gain. It would be fine.

'Because I want to tell you what really happened.'

At that, Orla went still, a shiver of apprehension rippling through her as Duarte stalked into the bathroom to hang up his towel.

She had never seen him look so serious,

she thought, her heart thudding heavily as she slipped on her T-shirt and the pair of knickers she'd discarded earlier. So haunted and desolate. So completely the opposite of the former playboy she'd caught the occasional glimpse of over the last couple of weeks. She had the unsettling feeling that whatever he wanted to tell her was momentous. It was going to turn everything she thought she knew about him on its head, and that was happening already. Already his halo was shining a little less brightly than before.

Was she ready for that?

God only knew.

But she had told him she'd listen, and this *was* what she'd wanted. To discover the real man behind the image, whoever that might be. The curiosity about his wife and the marriage they'd had, not to mention the shameful jealousy she'd failed to overcome, had become unbearable. And who knew, if he wasn't dealing with everything as stoically as the world believed, maybe she could try to help him in the way he'd helped her to make a start at overcoming her issues? All she had to do was keep calm in the face of any seismic revelation, which would be a challenge when she was gripped with trepidation, but she'd just have to handle it.

'All right,' she said, settling back against the pillows as Duarte sat down in the armchair that stood in the shadows in a corner of the softly lit room. 'I'm listening.'

He rubbed his hands over his face and then shoved them through his hair. 'Calysta was far from my soulmate,' he said grimly. 'And I didn't love her. In fact, I loathed her.'

Right. Orla swallowed hard, trying to absorb the shock of that when every cell of her body wanted to resist what she was hearing.

'But what about the fairy tale?' she asked, thinking of the pictures she'd seen spread across the pages of *Hello* that March. The bride, beaming, beautiful in white. Duarte looking darkly—although, come to think of it, unsmilingly—handsome in his navy suit as they stood side by side on the battlements of a castle just outside Sintra.

'There was no fairy tale,' he said flatly. 'It ended up being more of a nightmare. We'd been dating for a month when she told me she was pregnant. I married her out of a sense of duty. I felt responsible for her and the baby. That was it.'

No. She didn't want to believe it. She wanted to clap her hands over her ears and screw her eyes tight shut. Yet why would he lie? 'And what about Calysta?' she asked, faintly dreading an answer that would make a mockery of the photos and destroy further an already tarnished image of perfection. 'Did she marry out of duty too?'

He let out a harsh laugh that chilled her to the bone instead. 'Oh, no,' he said, his voice tinged with bitterness. 'She claimed to love me.'

Her throat tightened. 'Claimed?'

A shadow flitted across his face. 'As I said, we'd only known each other a month.'

So what? She'd known him less than that and—

Well.

No.

Her feelings, whatever they might be, weren't important right now.

'What happened to make you hate her?' she said, determinedly stamping out the emotions hurtling around her system, and focusing.

'We got married when she was twelve weeks into the pregnancy. A couple of months after that we had a discussion about the future. I wanted to focus on building a secure, stable life for our son, she hadn't let up socialising and wanted to carry on. Things got increasingly heated. I told her in no uncertain terms that the partying was to stop and she told me that she'd got pregnant on purpose but really wished she'd chosen someone else.'

And there went another piece of the lovely fantasy, crashing to the ground and shattering. 'What sort of woman *does* that?'

'One who's all alone in the world and desperately wants a family,' he said. 'Her parents died when she was young. She was very insecure.'

'She was very beautiful.'

'Yes,' he said with a frown. 'She was. I wanted her and I pursued her. But she was clever. She held out.'

'Was she the mistake you referred to when you were telling me about the dangers of letting desire go unaddressed?'

He gave a brief nod. 'It made me want her more. It made me dull-witted and blind.'

'What did you do when you found out?'

He sat back, closed his eyes and pinched the bridge of his nose. 'Lost it,' he said gruffly. 'I realised I'd been trapped. I felt like a fool. I felt somehow betrayed. We had a monumental argument. Two days later I took her to the hospital because she hadn't felt any movement for a while and Arturo had previously been very active. A scan showed that he no longer had a heartbeat.'

That hung between them for a moment during which Orla's eyes began to sting and her heart ached so badly it hurt. 'You don't believe the two events were linked,' she said, barely able to get the words past the lump in her throat.

'Why not?' he said bleakly.

'Is there any evidence for that?'

He shrugged. 'There's no evidence to the contrary. And Calysta certainly blamed me.'

Whatever the truth, the grief and the guilt must have been unbearable. On top of the betrayal he'd already been feeling, he had to have been torn apart. She couldn't *begin* to imagine what it must have been like. 'What happened after that?'

'We buried him and I went back to work, but it was all a blur. We stopped speaking and she was out every night and eventually I told her I wanted a divorce. A week later she took an overdose and died.'

'Deliberately?' she asked, and held her breath.

'I don't know,' he said on a shaky exhale. 'The inquest was inconclusive. All I do know is that I should have noticed what was going on. However I felt about her, she was my responsibility. If I hadn't been so wrapped up in bitterness and resentment, I'd have been able to help. But I was a wreck on all fronts and my judgement was screwed.'

'You were young.'

'I was twenty-seven,' he said with a slow shake of his head. 'Not that young.'

'She can't have been well.'

He regarded her thoughtfully for a moment, his brow creased, then he gave a shrug. 'You're probably right about that. She was very volatile. One minute she was the life and soul of the party, the next she was under the covers with the blinds closed to shut out the light. And she had to deliver Arturo, which must have been hell.'

'She could have been depressed.'

'Or she could have decided that if I was never going to love her then life wasn't worth living.'

Her heart stopped for a second. Did he truly believe that? If he did, no wonder he was still so affected by what had happened. 'Did she see anyone afterwards? A doctor? A counsellor?'

'Not to my knowledge.'

'That's a shame.'

'Believe me, I know,' he said bitterly. 'I live with the guilt of it every single day.'

'I'm not judging.'

His eyebrows lifted. 'Aren't you?'

'No. Of course not.'

'You have impossibly high expectations of people.'

'Well, yes. But—'

His mouth twisted. 'But this is only sex, so you have no expectations of me at all.'

What? Where on earth had *that* come from?

'That wasn't what I was going to say,' she said, utterly bewildered by his observation, which was so very wrong. 'I was going to say, I've never been in a position like that, so how could I possibly judge? How could anyone? But I do know that what happened wasn't your fault.' Everything else might be up in the air right now, she knew *that* down to her bones.

'Everything points to the fact that it was,' he said roughly. 'It *feels* like it was.'

A strangely fierce need to protect surged up inside her. 'No. You're wrong. It was just an impossibly tragic set of circumstances, initiated by a woman who might have had issues, but was also selfish and manipulative,' she said, wishing she could rewind time and rewrite his history. 'I'm not surprised you're angry.'

'I'm not angry. I'm guilty.'

'You are guilty of nothing.'

'I refuse to believe that.'

'You have to.'

'I can't.'

He suddenly looked devastated, as if the weight of the world was crushing him, and the backs of her eyes stung.

'What do your parents say about it all?' she said, swallowing down the boulder in her throat.

'They believe the myth.'

So he'd been handling this all on his own? It made her heart ache for him even more. 'How did that come about?'

'Assumptions were made from the moment Calysta and I got together,' he said. 'In the aftermath they continued, and I was in no fit state to correct them. I was too busy drowning my grief and guilt in wine.'

'Here.'

He nodded. 'The villa where we'd lived on the outskirts of Porto held too many memories. I spent two full months here—you saw the evidence—and then returned to work, coming back only when I needed to escape. There were enough people waiting for me to screw the business up without me giving them more ammunition. It was easier to accept the pity and the sympathy than to explain. I'm not proud of that.'

No, that much was clear. He was tortured by all of it. He blamed himself, and she could see why, but he shouldn't. He'd done what he'd thought was the right thing and been punished for it. He hadn't had the ideal marriage. He'd had a terrible one.

She'd been right to suspect that her view of him would be turned upside down by what he had to say but she hadn't expected the truth to be quite so gritty. Her perceptions of perfection, of him, were shattering all around her. It was huge, overwhelming, and she didn't quite know what to do with it all.

'Do you want to carry on talking about this?' she asked, taking refuge in something that thanks to him she *did* now know how to handle.

His eyes glittered. 'No.'

'Then come back to bed.'

CHAPTER ELEVEN

CONTRARY TO HIS EXPECTATIONS, Duarte didn't feel better after telling Orla the truth and he didn't feel lighter. After a fitful night, he flew to Lisbon first thing for a meeting with his lawyer about the acquisition of a vineyard in California, an exciting opportunity that would open up new markets and at any other time would have given him immense satisfaction. But there was no sense of triumph. The catharsis he'd hoped for didn't materialise. Instead, all day his stomach churned with a strange sense of dread.

There was no point pretending he didn't know the source of his apprehension. He'd had ample time to figure it out. Instead of returning to the Quinta immediately after the meeting had finished, as had been his original plan, he'd headed to the beach, where he'd spent the afternoon surfing the angry waves of the Atlantic beneath a bruised sky the colour of the Douro's slate-based soil in an effort to unravel the chaos swirling around inside him.

He'd allowed their affair to spiral out of control, he knew now with unassailable certainty. From the moment he'd threatened Orla with scuppering the agreement she'd made with Isabelle Baudelaire, he'd arrogantly assumed that he was in charge, and that that was where he'd remain. But he'd been wrong. Somehow, without his even being aware of it, the power had been gradually slipping away from him until she held it all, and he hadn't even considered that a possibility. Once again, he'd been so consumed with the present that he'd been blind to the danger of the future.

She'd sneaked through his defences and stolen control of his thoughts. She'd had him changing his plans on a whim and behaving in a way that he simply didn't recognise and certainly couldn't explain. Such as teaching her to swim or encouraging her to believe that life didn't have to be perfect, that it was all right to fail. What business of his was any of that?

Things between them had become too intense. He'd wanted a distraction, sure, but he'd never expected to it to take over so completely. He'd never anticipated the attraction intensifying instead of dissipating. Somewhere along the line their affair had turned into something that was more than just sex, despite his efforts to convince himself otherwise. He'd told her the truth about his marriage because he felt he could trust her with it, which was stupidly rash and beyond dangerous. It was true that they'd been working well together for several years now and she'd signed an NDA, so she couldn't do anything with the information, but that didn't mean it was all right to be sharing with her something so intensely personal, something that no one else knew.

And when had wanting to live up to her expectations become so important? He had no idea about that either. All he knew was that the moment she'd told him to come back to bed last night was the moment he'd realised how petrified he'd been of her judgement. How badly he *hadn't* wanted her to find him shameful and abhorrent. The relief that had flooded through him when it had become clear that she didn't had nearly had him weeping with gratitude.

He'd sworn he would never again allow a woman to hold all the power, he reminded himself grimly as he angled the helicopter and the Quinta came into view far below, and he had no intention of breaking that vow. He would not allow emotion to cloud his judgement and he would not end up in a position where he could be held accountable for someone else's well-being and destroy that someone along the way.

So he had to end things with Orla before he was in so deep that happened and he couldn't get out. She represented too great a threat to the way he wanted to live his life, free from the responsibility and commitment that experience had proven he couldn't handle. It wouldn't be fair to her, either, to let things carry on. He'd caught the way she looked at him sometimes, with stars in her eyes and a dreamy smile on her face. He didn't deserve stars and dreams. He'd never deserve her, so there was no pointing in wanting her any more.

All was set for the conference. There was no need for her to remain in Portugal. He'd told himself to back off once before and been too damn weak to follow it through, but this time it would be different. This time, the minute he landed, he'd track her down. He'd tell her it was over and send her home, whatever it took, and absolutely nothing was going to stop him.

Finally.

As the familiar rumble of the Land Rover cut through the still of the night, Orla jumped off the bed and ran to the window. Headlights lit up the road to the hotel but she could just about make out the shape of Duarte in the driving seat, and God, it was good to see him. He'd been gone *such* a long time. Because he'd been due back mid-afternoon and her texts had gone unanswered, she'd been going out of her mind with worry. She'd been on the point of calling the police when she'd received a reply from him asking where she was.

Waiting for him to return had been agonising. She'd done a lot of thinking while he'd been away and come to a number of conclusions that she ached to share with him. Given the lull in activity at the Quinta, the calm before the storm as it were, she'd had to do *something* to fill the time and it was inevitable that her thoughts would be filled with him, with herself, with them.

Especially after last night.

She understood him so much better now, she thought, her heart thundering as he got out of the car and slammed the door behind him. He was racked with guilt that in her opinion was very much misplaced. No wonder he'd flipped out so badly when he'd found her asleep in his bed the day they'd met. She'd invaded his privacy and caught a glimpse into his carefully guarded soul. She'd dug up the truth he'd kept buried and he'd resented that.

Every time she recalled what he'd been through, she wanted to weep. No one deserved to suffer such torment and it broke her heart that he'd had to deal with it alone. Had she been able to help him last night? God, she hoped so, but who knew? He'd been quiet this morning before he'd left for Lisbon.

She'd been so wrong to place him on a pedestal, she'd realised over a cup of tea this afternoon. He'd never claimed to be perfect. That had been all on her. She'd taken the bits of him he'd allowed her to see and judged him accordingly. But she'd been foolish to do so. No one was perfect. And what on earth gave her any right to judge anyone anyway?

Her ex had been right all along. She hadn't been particularly supportive or sympathetic when he'd needed it. The minute he'd told her he'd been axed as part of a strategy to reduce headcount, he'd plummeted in her estimation because she'd thought he clearly hadn't been good enough to be retained. But that had been grossly unfair of her. The loss of his job hadn't been his fault and she should have recognised the massive collapse of confidence he'd suffered because she experienced the same on the rare occasion she failed.

She *did* have expectations of people that were unjustly high, she'd thought, accepting the guilt washing over her that was nothing less than she deserved. She did judge. And because of it, she subconsciously pushed people away. Colleagues, potential friends, the occasional fiancé… She'd always told herself that she didn't have time for relationships of any kind, but in reality she'd always been pretty unforgiving of other people's foibles, and no one needed that kind of pressure. As a result, she was always on her own, which had never bothered her before, but now, she found, did. A lot. She hadn't realised how lonely she'd become until she'd met Duarte and embarked on an affair during which she was with him pretty much all day every day.

Most things in life, she'd discovered in the course of her soul-searching, weren't as black and white as she'd always assumed. They lay somewhere in the grey, the middle ground. And, while this was uncharted territory for her, it was territory that she was determined to explore because she was beginning to think that, contrary to the beliefs she'd held for so long, there was actually little good about perfectionism and having impossibly high expectations. Both made for isolation and loneliness. Both inevitably led to wholly unnecessary disappointment.

If she was being brutally honest, to discover that Duarte had feet of clay, that he was as flawed and fallible as she'd learned she was, was something of a relief. Now that she'd allowed 'good enough' into her way of thinking she'd been worrying about being able to match up to him. But now she felt that perhaps she *could* match up. At least she hoped so. Because she didn't want this to end. She wanted him. For far more than an affair. She wanted him for ever, because she was head over heels in love with him.

From the moment she'd taken his call and signed him up shortly after his marriage three and a half years ago, she'd been fascinated by him. Every time his name had popped up on her phone her heart beat that little bit faster. For every request he'd made she put in that little bit more effort. The reality of the man far outclassed any dream she'd ever had. He was patient. Thoughtful. Not to mention hot as hell and able to make her come in under thirty seconds. And he'd shone a light on some of her deepest, darkest fears and reduced them to the faintest of shadows.

But how did he feel about her?

Their affair wasn't just about sex. It never

really had been. Right from the beginning he'd looked out for her. He'd taught her how to swim and shown her another, better, way to live her life. He'd given her belief in herself that didn't come from the pursuit of perfection, and he'd told her the truth about his marriage. All that had to mean something, but what?

Did she dare to find out?

It would be a massive risk, she thought, her heart hammering even harder as she heard footsteps thud along the corridor outside her room. They hadn't known each other long. They both had issues that needed working through. But perhaps it was a risk she ought to take, because they could be so good for one another. And now she knew there was no ghost to compete with, what was stopping them from carrying on and seeing where things went?

At the sharp rap on the door, Orla practically jumped a foot in the air. She spun round from the window and headed to open it, her feet barely touching the floor. Her heart was fit to burst with hope and anticipation, her smile wide and giddy as she flung back the door, but at the sight of the expression on Duarte's handsome face, she froze.

His jaw was tight and his eyes were dark.

He looked tense, on edge, and something about the way he was standing sent a bundle of nerves skittering through her. He seemed braced for something, something unpleasant.

A cold sweat broke out all over her skin and her pulse began to race. Had something happened? What? She couldn't tell. His face was completely unreadable.

'Come in,' she said, instinct warning her to proceed with caution as she stood to one side to let him pass.

But he didn't move an inch. 'I won't, thanks.'

What? Why not? 'Bad meeting?'

'The meeting was fine.'

'So what's wrong?' Because something was definitely up. Could it be a delayed reaction to last night's conversation? If it was, whatever he needed from her, she'd give it to him. She'd give him everything. Especially if he actually came into her room.

'Nothing's wrong,' he said, thrusting his hands into the pockets of his trousers. 'How was your day?'

'Professionally uneventful, personally illuminating.'

He frowned at that, just for a moment. 'Everything ready for Friday?'

'Yes.'

'Good. Then your services are no longer required.'

Oh? What did that mean? 'Well, I wouldn't put it quite like that,' she said with the hint of a knowing grin despite the faint ribbon of anxiety beginning to wind through her. 'My...*services*...are available until Sunday.' Hopefully even beyond.

'I'm serious,' he said. 'You should go home. Tomorrow.'

The smile slid from her face. Tomorrow was Wednesday. The conference started on Friday. What was going on? 'I should be here in case things go wrong.'

'They won't.'

'When did you become the expert?'

'I'll call if there's a problem.'

Her pulse sounded in her head. Her mouth dried, and as the truth dawned, her stomach rolled. 'You're not joking, are you?' she said with difficulty. 'You really want me to go.'

'Do I look like I'm joking?'

No. She'd never seen anyone appear to be joking less. His jaw was so tight it looked as if it were about to crack. He was pale beneath his tan, but there was no mistaking the intent behind his words. He was resolute, impenetrable. He was batting away every point, every protest she made, and would continue to do so.

And then it hit her like a blow to the head that *she* was the unpleasant business. While she'd been carefully picking up the pieces of her shattered foundations and putting them back together in a different, better way so that she could dream of a future with him, he'd been revving up to tell her to leave.

'Why?' she managed, her throat impossibly tight.

'Your work here is done.'

'And what about us?'

'There is no us.'

His face was utterly unreadable and it was horrible. Who *was* this? Where was the man she'd fallen in love with? She didn't recognise the ice-cold stranger before her.

She swallowed hard, feeling nauseous and faint. 'There could be.'

A muscle hammered in his jaw. 'There won't be.'

'Does this have anything to do with last night?'

'No,' he said with the barest of shrugs. 'I've simply had time to reflect on things and come to the realisation I've had enough.'

While she'd come to the realisation that she hadn't had nearly enough.

The pain that shot though her at that was swift and harsh. It pulverised reason and made her desperate. It made her reckless. 'I'm in love with you.'

The only indication he even heard her was a flicker of something in the depths of his eyes, but it was gone before she could identify it. 'I regret that happened.'

Orla stared at him, frozen in shock, the air trapped in her lungs while the world about her collapsed. And then, charging through the rubble, came fury. He *regretted that happened*? What the *hell*? How dared he dismiss her feelings like that, as if nothing they'd shared mattered, as if *she* didn't matter? How could he be so brutal? After everything? The hot, wild tangle of emotions swirling through her coalesced into one cold, hard lump and settled in her chest, and then, blessedly, she could feel absolutely nothing.

Up until this very moment, despite how this little chat had developed, she would have given him the benefit of the doubt. She'd have slept on it, tracked him down in the morning and tried to figure out what was behind all this. But not now. Now he'd drawn an indelible line in the sand and obliterated both what they'd had and what they could have had. Which meant that she wasn't going to hang around when she was very obviously not needed. So, contrary to his instructions—instructions! As if *he* had the right to dictate what she was to do when this was her *job*—she wouldn't be here tomorrow. She'd leave tonight. He and his bloody conference didn't deserve even a second's more consideration.

'Well, that seems to say it all, doesn't it?' she said numbly.

He gave a curt nod. 'I believe so.'

'Goodnight, then.'

'Goodnight.'

And with that, he turned round and strode down the corridor, leaving her standing there, stock still, chilled to the bone and wondering what the hell had just happened.

Duarte didn't recall getting to his car and driving back to the Casa. It was only when he switched off the engine and killed the headlights that he realised that his palms were sweating and his entire body was trembling.

With relief.

That was what it had to be, he told himself as he shakily stepped down from the Land Rover and inhaled great gulps of air.

Because he'd done what he'd set out to do and he hadn't faltered. He hadn't been blown away by the dazzling smile she'd greeted him with. He'd ruthlessly ignored the tsunami of pleasure that had rushed through him at the sight of her, and he'd resisted the fierce urge to push her back, slam the door and tumble her to the bed. When she'd told him she was in love with him he'd steeled himself so successfully that the overwhelming desire to sweep her into his arms and never let her go hadn't even made it into his head. He'd remained strong and in control at all times, even in the face of her evident shock and anger once she'd finally got the message.

As a result, he'd avoided a highly dangerous liaison that would have inevitably ended up in pieces. He didn't want to hold Orla's emotions in his hands. He couldn't be responsible for them. He didn't want her love. He wasn't capable of returning it. He'd only destroy it.

But disaster had been averted, he thought grimly as he stalked into the dark, quiet house. Tomorrow she'd leave. He was safe. More importantly, *she* was safe. So it was all good.

Thanks to the savage anger coursing through her veins like fire, Orla held it together as she packed up her things, checked out and then drove the two hundred and fifty kilometres from the hotel to the airport in the early hours of the morning. She spent the entire duration of the first flight back to London grimly thanking her lucky stars that she'd discovered Duarte's true colours before humiliating herself by begging him to let her stay. He wasn't at all the man she'd thought he was and she'd had a narrow escape, she'd told herself over and over again in the taxi from Heathrow to her flat. Such a narrow escape.

It was only when she walked over her threshold and closed the door on the world outside that she fell apart. Exhausted, miserable and wretched, her armour falling away and vanishing into thin air, she dumped her bags in the hall and sank to the floor.

The pain that lanced through her then was unlike any she'd felt before. It sliced open her chest and tore her heart to shreds. It whipped the breath from her lungs and put a sting in her eyes. She thought she'd been devastated when Matt had broken up with her, but that was a scratch compared to this. This was true agony.

How had things gone so badly wrong? she wondered as the sting became tears that seeped out of her eyes and flowed down her cheeks. They'd been going so well. She'd had no sign that anything was amiss. Apart from the strangely charged moment she'd handed him the custard tarts on their return from Porto, perhaps. At the time, she hadn't paid it much attention. She'd been too starry-eyed from the scorching encounter in the helicopter and too overwhelmed with emotion for nuance. But now she thought about it, his jaw had been rigidly tight then too. Perhaps she'd gone too far, overstepped a line.

And she'd done it again by pressing him on his marriage. Deep down he couldn't have wanted to talk about it. It was a harrowing tale. She should never have indulged her curiosity. She should never have forced him to relive it. Yes, she'd tried to backtrack and leave him in peace at the time, but she wouldn't have been able to for long. It would have festered until the belief that she was right would have pushed her to demand the truth anyway.

What had she been thinking? What on earth had made her believe that she could possibly help? She knew nothing of what he'd been through. Nothing. She wasn't right. About anything.

She'd been so stupid to allow herself to fall in love with him, she thought on a heaving, painful sob. She'd been swept away by the romance of the location and the situation and read too much into everything. Despite the intensity of their affair, the conversation and the thoughtfulness, they hadn't had a real relationship. They'd barely stepped off the estate. It had been a one-scene fantasy. The perfect fantasy, in fact, until reality had intruded and smashed it to bits.

She'd been a fool to believe in it and as deluded as Isabelle Baudelaire to assume that she could be the one to bring him back to life and teach him to love. She wasn't that person. She wouldn't ever be that person. It was truly over. There was no coming back from this. So what on earth was she going to do now?

CHAPTER TWELVE

At eight o'clock in the morning Duarte addressed the team Orla had been working with and updated them on her departure. The news that she'd left without so much as a goodbye was greeted with looks of surprise and expressions of disappointment. He, however, did not share either sentiment. He'd have only been surprised if she'd defied his order to go, and all he felt was relief.

Everything had turned out exactly as he'd planned and, as he stalked into the bustling kitchen of the Quinta in search of the coffee that he needed to get through the day after a largely sleepless night, he felt as if he could breathe for the first time in weeks. He was free. Of commitment, of responsibility, and, more importantly, of all the emotions he'd felt whenever he'd been with her.

He'd definitely done the right thing in sending her away, he told himself as he retrieved two cups from the cupboard, frowned, and returned one. He'd soon get used to being on his own again. He'd only known her properly for three weeks. By Monday he'd be back in Porto, back to work, and what had happened here would fade until it became nothing more than a distant memory.

Besides, it wasn't as if he couldn't manage this coming weekend. He ran a billion-euro business. He could handle a two-day conference. How hard could it be? He didn't need Orla and her unsettling insights. He wasn't going to miss her in the slightest. He was perfectly all right. Couldn't be better, in fact, and everything was going to be fine.

But it wasn't fine. It wasn't fine at all.

Thanks to Orla's meticulous planning and preparations, the conference itself went off without a hitch. The weather had improved and the Quinta looked spectacular. The food and drink had been exceptional, issues had been discussed and problems had been solved. Any doubts anyone may have had about his ability to run his company had been well and truly squashed.

However, this boat trip up the Douro, to round off the weekend, was proving problematic.

Duarte hadn't given much thought to the route. He'd left the logistics up to the crew. But he should have insisted on knowing the plan, because they were heading for the spot where he'd taken Orla for a picnic and now, no matter how busy he'd been over the last couple of days, no matter how hard he forced himself to focus on the tour and entertain his guests this afternoon, she was all he could think about.

Despite his intentions to the contrary, he had missed her. The Casa was quiet and empty without her vibrant, dazzling presence, yet filled with the memories that they'd created together, which fractured his sleep. To his intense frustration, he'd been seeking her out all weekend. Every time it hit him that she wasn't there, bleak disappointment struck him in the chest, as confusing as it was unwelcome. And increasingly, when he thought of the way he'd sent her home, he didn't feel relief. His stomach invariably knotted and a weight sat on his chest, the regret so intense it made his head spin. His appetite had disappeared and a dull heaviness had seeped into every cell of his body.

Yesterday evening, after his guests had retired for the night and the staff had returned to the village, he'd headed for the vines, hoping that the peace and tranquillity of the hills and the warm scent of the earth would soothe the chaos swirling around inside him as it so often did. But he'd found no solace there. In fact, with no guests to distract him, his unsettled thoughts had turned to Orla even more and she'd become a burr, sticking to his skin, impossible to remove.

Today, the creeping restlessness had expanded and spread, its tendrils reaching into every inch of him, and it was now crushing him on all sides. He stood at the polished wood railing that ran around the bow of the cruiser, staring at the bend in the river around which lay the beach, breathing in deep lungsfuls of air while inside his guests helped themselves to a sumptuous buffet. But nothing he did seemed to relieve the pressure. It was in his head. In his chest. Everywhere.

His knees shook and he gripped the railing so tightly his knuckles went white, but it was too much, and suddenly, unexpectedly, something inside him snapped. His defences splintered and a wild rush of emotions, thoughts and realisations rained down on him.

He missed her, he loved her, and he'd been the biggest of fools to have taken this long to realise it. He'd been thinking about her for months, long before he'd actually met her. Making spurious requests to fill in the time between the genuine ones, just so he could hear her voice. That was how he'd ended up with the helicopter. He could have easily told his secretary to liaise with her. He hadn't had to get personally involved. But their conversations had triggered fantasies that had become addictive, fantasies that he knew now had come nowhere close to the reality, and he hadn't wanted to let that go.

For three years he'd been petrified of a relationship. Of commitment. Of letting anyone get too close and then destroying them with his staggering self-absorption and emotional obstinacy. But there was nothing terrifying about what he'd been doing with Orla. He *liked* the way he'd behaved with her—before he'd screwed everything up—*and* the fact that traces of the man he used to be had returned. She was not Calysta and this was not the same.

For days he'd been resisting and denying the points she'd made about his marriage with every bone in his body because he was too afraid of the possibility of a relationship opening up and him wrecking it. But perhaps Orla was right. Perhaps none of what had happened had been his fault. The terrible day of the scan, the obstetrician had talked about a heart defect as the most likely cause of Arturo's death in the womb, but he'd barely listened. He'd just recalled the savage argument two nights earlier, and the link between the events had seemed so damn obvious. He'd held himself to blame ever since, but maybe he had to accept that it had simply been nature at its most cruel.

And as for Calysta, after Arturo's funeral he should have been around more instead of immersing himself in work. However much he'd despised her at that point, however much he'd been grieving for the son he'd badly wanted despite the circumstances of his conception, he should have considered what she'd been going through. But he would never have loved her the way she'd needed him to, whatever the circumstances, and she would never have been able to accept that.

So could he let go of the guilt? He wanted to. God, how he wanted to. Because he wanted Orla back. He wanted her trust and her love. He wanted it all.

But whether she'd even agree to see him was anyone's guess. The look of devastation on her face when he'd told her he was sorry she'd fallen in love with him still haunted his dreams. Out of sheer fear, he'd been cruel and callous. He felt sick and his chest ached to think of it.

Could he fix the godawful mess he'd made of things? He'd do his damnedest to try. As he'd once told Orla, he too had goals, and this was his biggest, most important one ever. So he'd do whatever it took, however long it took, and this time he would not screw it up.

Releasing his white-knuckled grip on the rail, Duarte turned on his heel and stalked into the cockpit to address the captain.

'The trip is over,' he said, his jaw set and his entire body filling with resolve. 'Turn the boat around.'

'Orla!'

Orla had barely stepped out of the lift when Sam Hamilton, her co-CEO for the time being, accosted her in the lobby of their fifth-floor offices in London's West End.

At his expression, the little hairs at the back of her neck shot up and her pulse skipped a beat. The last time he'd looked this serious, three days ago, in fact, he'd told her he planned to retire within the next twelve months, and if she wanted it the business would be hers. The news should have had her punching the air in triumph. Instead, she'd just about managed to muster up a weak smile and mutter a half-hearted 'thank you', but that had been it. Despite the endless talking-tos she'd given herself recently, she was still so damn sad about Duarte.

But enough was enough. A weekend of moping about, immersed in self-pity and misery, was plenty. Any more ice cream and she'd turn into a pistachio. Who needed a relationship anyway? How many of them failed? She didn't know the statistics, but she knew it was a lot, and she wanted none of it.

No. Instead, she'd decided it was time for change. She was going to focus on her issues. She'd figured her insecurities and fears would exist whether she failed or succeeded, so she'd start with them. She'd always associated her sense of self-worth with a need to achieve, but why did it have to be that way? Why couldn't she find it elsewhere? Say, from her job? From friends? From who she was, which wasn't *so* bad really? So she was going to be less unforgiving. Of herself and other people. She'd learn to accept criticism without getting all defensive about it and start to build some proper, healthy relationships.

She'd forget about Duarte and the bittersweet memories soon enough. Just because she thought about him constantly didn't mean that she would for eternity. She'd talk herself out of it eventually. She talked herself out of things all the time. And, quite honestly, so what if she had fallen in love with him? It was nothing to be ashamed of, although it was regrettable that she'd told him. Unfortunately, you couldn't choose whom you loved and you couldn't make them love you in return. You just had to accept things as they were, and try to avoid the chaos, mess and misery that was love for a very long time.

At least the super-loud, super-critical voice in her head had gone. She wasn't perfect, nothing in life was, and that was OK. She *was*, however, utterly drained by all this self-analysis on top of everything that had transpired before and, quite frankly, she could do without the hassle of whatever it was that had Sam in such a state so early. But she was a professional, so she'd take it in her supremely capable stride.

'Sam,' she said, plastering a smile to her face and hoisting her satchel higher onto her shoulder as they set off across the lobby. 'Is there a problem?'

'We've had a complaint.'

Oh? Her heart plummeted. No wonder he was agitated. Complaints were unwelcome, and, thankfully, rare. 'What is it?'

'It's more a case of who.'

Her eyebrows lifted. 'Who?'

'Yes. He's in your office.'

'Who is?'

'Duarte de Castro e Bragança.'

Orla froze mid-step, her head spinning and her heart suddenly pounding. No. That couldn't be the case. What did he have to complain about? Sam had informed her that the conference had been a success from start to finish, although apparently the river cruise had ended rather abruptly and ahead of schedule. And why was he in *her* office anyway?

'Can't you deal with it?' she said, her stomach clenching at the thought of him in her space, breathing her air and looking around her things. 'He's your client now.'

'I believe that's the complaint.'

What? He was the one who'd necessitated the switch with his brutal dismissal of her. So how dared he saunter in here and turn her world on its head again? This was *her* space. Her *sanctuary*.

Well.

Whatever.

Duarte didn't bother her any longer. Did Not Bother Her. She had no need to be distressed by this latest turn of events. She was immune to his charms now. She'd handle him with polite professionalism, get to the bottom of his so-called complaint and then she'd send him on his way.

'Fine,' she said flatly, setting her jaw and straightening her spine. 'Leave it with me.'

At the sound of the door to Orla's office opening, Duarte, who'd been pacing up and down in front of the window, oblivious to the view, oblivious to anything other than the drumming of his pulse and the desperate need to put things right, spun round.

Orla closed the door behind her and then turned to him, and a wave of longing crashed over him. He'd missed her. He'd missed her immeasurably. How on earth could he have sent her away? What had he been thinking?

'Good morning,' she said with a practised smile that didn't reach anywhere near her eyes, and which he hated, but then, he hadn't expected an easy ride. He deserved the ice and the bristling even if it did chill him to the bone and fill him with shame.

'Good morning.'

She strode over to the desk and sat down, so cool, so professional, so hard to read now. 'Have you been offered coffee?'

'I have,' he said, seating himself in a chair on the other side of her desk and linking his hands to stop them shaking.

'Good. So. I understand you have a complaint.'

'I do.'

'What is it?'

'I called to speak to you and was told that you'd given my account to someone else.'

'Yes,' she said with a brisk nod. 'To Sam. My co-CEO.'

He swallowed with difficulty. 'Why?'

'Because he's excellent.'

'That's not what I meant and you know it.'

'We crossed a line, Duarte,' she said bluntly,

her voice completely devoid of expression. 'Do you honestly think we could have carried on working together after what happened at the Quinta?'

'Which part in particular are you referring to?'

'All of it.' She swivelled round to switch on her computer. 'It was a mistake from start to finish.'

'You don't make mistakes.'

'I do. And I've discovered recently that that's fine.'

He frowned. They'd been many things, but a mistake was not one of them. Did she really think that? Had he done that to her with his cowardice and fear?

'Was there anything else?'

Oh, yes. He wasn't done. Not by a long shot. He'd prepared a speech. He'd been practising. 'I've barely begun.'

'Well, I have a meeting in,' she glanced at her watch, 'ten minutes. So I can give you five.'

Then he didn't have a second to waste. This was the most important moment of his life. His entire future happiness depended on it. He took a deep breath and focused. 'I wanted to apologise for our last conversation,' he said gruffly, regret pouring through him at the memory of it. 'For the way I behaved. It was appalling and unnecessary, and when I think of it I am deeply ashamed.'

'Accepted,' she said with a dismissive wave of her hand.

'I wanted to explain.'

'No explanation necessary.'

His heart began to pound. 'You were right about everything.'

'Not any more, I'm not. I'm through with all that.'

What did that mean? Was she through with him too? A bolt of pure panic shot through him. 'I'm in love with you.'

She stared at her monitor, utterly still for a moment, and then she clicked her mouse and adjusted her keyboard. 'That's…regrettable,' she said, and typed in what could have been her password.

Not that he was capable of that level of logic. He was reeling with the shattering realisation that he'd blown it. For good. The flatness of her tone… The way she couldn't look at him… Her choice of words, which was no coincidence… One mad, terrible conversation that had been driven by the demons that he'd foolishly allowed to override everything else and he'd ruined the best thing that had ever happened to him.

Suddenly Duarte couldn't breathe. The shock of what he'd done and the realisation that it was undoable had winded him. His vision blurred. His chest was tight. He couldn't speak for the pain scything through him.

'You'll be in good hands with Sam' came her voice through the fog. 'And now, if you'll excuse me, I really am very busy.'

Yes, he could see that. Whatever it was that she was looking at was demanding her full attention. She was scrolling and typing, scrolling and typing, while his world was splintering into a million tiny pieces.

'Right,' he said gruffly, his throat sore, his entire body trembling. 'I see. In that case, I won't waste another second of your time.'

He got up in a daze. Turned to leave, grateful for the fact that his legs would get him out of here. But then at the door, his hand on the handle, he stopped. No, dammit. That *wasn't* it. He wasn't having this. He'd come here for a reason. He had things to say and they needed saying. He'd vowed on the boat to do whatever it took and that was precisely what he *would* do.

Squaring his shoulders and taking strength from the determination and adrenalin rocketing around his system, Duarte spun back, and froze at the raw, naked misery that crumpled Orla's face for a split second before it disappeared and her expression was once again unreadable.

But he'd caught a glimpse behind the mask, thank *God*, and, while it killed him to see, it also had hope and relief roaring through him because she wasn't as indifferent to him as she was trying to make out. She wasn't indifferent at all.

Why, oh, why couldn't Duarte have left? Orla thought desperately, her heart racing as he slowly stalked back towards her. She'd been doing so well, holding the emotions raging through her at bay and clinging on to her dignity even though it had taken every drop of strength she possessed. So well to steel herself against his declaration of love, which meant nothing when the memory of Tuesday night was still so raw.

Why had he had to turn around at that precise moment when the pain of what she'd lost had become too much? There was no chance he hadn't caught the brief slip of her deliberately icy facade. Gone were the nerves she thought she'd detected in him a moment ago. He was all steely purpose, his jaw set and his eyes glinting darkly as he bypassed the chair he'd earlier vacated and came to perch on her desk, so close she could reach out and touch him if she wanted to.

'I still have four minutes,' he said, gripping the edge tightly as he gazed down at her.

Orla pushed her chair back, out of his mind-scrambling orbit, and sat on her hands. 'Three and a half actually.'

And that was three and a half too many. How long would her strength hold out? Already, his proximity was battering away at her defences. Already she could feel herself weakening.

'I'm so, so sorry,' he said gruffly. 'For everything that I said on Tuesday night. I was terrified of my feelings for you. I wasn't ready to let go of the past. Ever since Calysta died I've been wrapped up in the idea that because what happened to her was my fault, I can't be responsible for someone else's emotions. But you were right. About so much. Especially the guilt and the blame. And if I've been wrong about that, then I'm wrong about the rest of it. I love you, Orla. I think I've been falling in love with you ever since I asked you to research helicopters for me when I didn't even need one.'

Her heart thundered in her ears, and, with her armour suffering blow after blow, she simply couldn't keep the icy front up any longer. 'I offered you everything,' she said hoarsely as all the hurt and pain broke through to batter her from every angle.

'I know.'

'You were cruel.'

His expression twisted and the sigh he gave was tortured. 'I know.'

'You hurt me.'

'Irrevocably?'

'I don't know.'

He stared at her, regret and sorrow filling his gaze, and then he swallowed hard and gave a nod. 'I understand,' he said roughly. 'Right. Well. That was all I wanted to say. I should go.'

He pushed himself off the desk and, in a split second that seemed to last a year, Orla's brain spun. Was she really going to let him leave? After everything he'd told her? When it had to have cost him so much to say? Despite everything she still loved him madly and she wanted nothing more than to throw herself into his arms and never let go.

But was she brave enough to do it? Just because he'd recognised his hang-ups didn't mean they were going to disappear overnight. But then, she thought, her heart hammering wildly, nor were hers. Was this one of those risks worth taking? Yes, it absolutely was.

'No. Wait,' she said before he could take a further step.

He stilled, his gaze snapping to hers, so wary, so hopeful it made her chest ache.

'I'm sorry too.'

He shook his head and frowned. 'You have nothing to apologise for.'

'I do. I should never have pushed you into talking about something you weren't ready to face.'

'I might never have been ready and I needed to face it.'

'There are things I've also had to face. Things that you've helped me to deal with.'

His jaw clenched, the tiny muscle there on the right pounding away. 'What are you saying?'

She took a deep breath and rose from her chair. 'We could continue to face them together.'

He nodded slowly, once, and her pulse skipped a beat. 'We could.'

'I've missed you.'

'Not nearly as much as I've missed you.'

He opened his arms then and whether she threw herself or he pulled her into them she didn't know. All she knew was that he was kissing her as if his life depended on it, and all her doubts and fears were being swept away on the wave of hot desire and delirious joy that was rushing through her.

'I love you,' he muttered against her mouth as his hold on her loosened. 'Very much.'

'I love you, too.'

'I've been so blind. So stupid. I'm so sorry

I hurt you.' He pulled back slightly and the remorse on his face tore at her heart. 'I'll never forgive myself. How can I ever make it up to you?'

'You can start by locking the door.'

'What?'

'Lock the door,' she said again softly as she started to undo the buttons of his shirt just in case there was any lingering confusion. 'And then, my darling, you can show me exactly how sorry you are.'

'Ah, I see,' he said, a glint appearing in his eye as he did as she instructed and then took her in his arms and sat her on her desk. 'I thought you had a meeting.'

Back on the buttons, her whole body vibrating with love and happiness, Orla smiled up at him, leaned forwards and murmured in his ear, 'I lied.'

EPILOGUE

The South of France,
three months later

THE LATE SEPTEMBER evening sunshine bathed the privately-owned chateau on the outskirts of Nice in warm golden sunshine. The air was heady with the scent of the lavender that was planted all around, and in the vast, lavishly appointed ballroom five hundred guests had dined on lobster and lamb before parting with millions in the wildly extravagant auction. Ten minutes ago, a band had taken to the stage and the dance floor was filling with men in tuxedos and women in silk.

Out on the terrace that overlooked the city and the sparkling azure Mediterranean beyond, Orla was wrapped in Duarte's arms, eyes closed, smiling softly and swaying to the sultry beat that was drifting out through half a dozen pairs of French doors.

Champagne had been flowing for hours, but she hadn't needed any of it. She was bubbling with happiness and overflowing with love enough as it was.

The last three months had been unbelievably brilliant. Four weeks after Duarte had made all her dreams come true that horrible then fabulous morning in her office, she'd packed up her flat and moved to Porto. She could do her job from anywhere and his apartment needed a cushion or two. When not travelling for work, they spent the weeks in the city and the weekends at the Casa do São Romão.

Today, at lunchtime, they'd flown to Nice for Isabelle Baudelaire's charity ball and checked in to the finest hotel in the city, where they'd idled away most of the afternoon in bed before getting ready.

'One evening of your time,' she murmured against the warm skin of his neck. 'Worth the sacrifice, do you think?'

'Most definitely.'

'Isabelle told me that because of you she sold double the number of tickets she'd expected to and increased the auction donations by half.'

'I'm not sure that was anything to do with me,' he said, the vibrations of his voice sending shivers rippling through her. 'She rivals you for tenacity and skill.'

It was *all* to do with him, she thought dreamily. When he smiled, which he did frequently these days, he was irresistible. 'I wonder who won the trip to the Arctic.'

'I did.'

She leaned back and stared up at him in shock. 'Heavens, why?'

'For the icebergs.'

At the look in his eye, the expression on his face, she went very still and her breath caught. 'What?'

'The Arctic has icebergs,' he said, then frowned. 'But now I think about it, I seem to recall you saying you didn't care much for style-over-substance grand gestures, so that might have been a bad idea. And in any case the trip's in December, and I don't think I can wait that long.'

Her heart thundered and the ground beneath her feet tilted. 'Wait that long to do what?'

'To give you this. I've been carrying it around for days. You should have it before it gets lost.'

'This' was a diamond the shape and size of an almond in a ring of platinum. It sparkled in the setting sun, and when he slid it onto the third finger of her left hand her vision blurred and her throat tightened.

'I love you, Orla,' he said, softly, tenderly. 'More and more each day. Will you marry me?'

She swallowed back the lump in her throat and threw her arms round his neck. 'Yes, of course I will,' she said in between kisses. 'I love you, too. So much.'

'Sorry about the Arctic,' he murmured when they finally broke for air.

'Don't be,' she said, her heart swelling with joy and love. 'It's perfect.'

* * * * *

Head over heels for
Undone by Her Ultra-Rich Boss*?*
Then you're sure to get lost in these other Lucy King stories!

A Scandal Made in London
The Secrets She Must Tell
Invitation from the Venetian Billionaire
The Billionaire without Rules

Available now!

Razing the Dead

Sheila Connolly

BERKLEY PRIME CRIME, NEW YORK

THE BERKLEY PUBLISHING GROUP
Published by the Penguin Group
Penguin Group (USA) LLC
375 Hudson Street, New York, New York 10014

USA • Canada • UK • Ireland • Australia • New Zealand • India • South Africa • China

penguin.com

A Penguin Random House Company

RAZING THE DEAD

A Berkley Prime Crime Book / published by arrangement with the author

For information, address: The Berkley Publishing Group,
a division of Penguin Group (USA) LLC,
375 Hudson Street, New York, New York 10014.

ISBN: 978-0-425-25713-5

PUBLISHING HISTORY
Berkley Prime Crime mass-market edition / June 2014

PRINTED IN THE UNITED STATES OF AMERICA

10 9 8 7 6 5 4 3 2 1

Cover illustration by Ross Jones.
Cover design by Rita Frangie.
Interior text design by Laura K. Corless.

ACKNOWLEDGMENTS

Most writers use people and places they know when they write a book—it's so much easier than starting from scratch. This was particularly true for me with this book.

Anyone who has spent time in the Philadelphia area in the past few decades or who is familiar with the skyline will most likely recognize the man who inspired the character of Mitchell Wakeman in this book. Likewise, anyone who knows the township of East Goshen in Chester County should be able to name the individual who inspired Ezra Garrett. As it happens, I knew and respected both of them (they're both gone now) and I hope they'd be pleased with the characters I created for them.

My family lived in Chester County for decades, close to the Paoli Pike, so it was easy to write many familiar places into the book. But despite that long association, until recently I had never explored the site of the Battle of Paoli, also called the Paoli Massacre, even though I drove past the historic marker for it hundreds of times. Nor had I ever studied the story behind that event, but to put it in simplest terms, that small battle had a significant impact on the early course of the American Revolution. Today there is little more to see than a level grassy field,

but the war memorial there is one of the oldest in this country.

Like many battles, it was chaotic—made more so because it was a sneak attack fought by night—but that gave me the opportunity to ask, "what if . . . ?" As a result, I created a plot element that I believe is consistent with what we know. My apologies if I have offended any purists who dislike authors who tinker with history—I have been one of you.

Many details of the story reflect real places. The Chester County Historical Society is a delightful institution with excellent collections, but I have given the place a director who is neither based upon nor resembles any actual employee there. Ezra Garrett's farm did indeed belong to a single family for at least two centuries, until it was sold to QVC in the 1980s. The portion that lies along the Paoli Pike looks much as it always has.

In crafting this story, what I wanted to convey was how much our history is still with us. The past is not dead but lives on in unexpected ways.

Thanks as always to my tireless agent, Jessica Faust of BookEnds, and my eagle-eyed editor, Shannon Jamieson Vazquez of Berkley Prime Crime, for sustaining this series and giving me an excuse to visit Philadelphia regularly. Thanks, too, to the wonderfully supportive mystery community, including organizations such as Sisters in Crime and the Guppies as well as the great crowd of writers I count as friends. And of course, thank you to all the readers who follow Nell Pratt as she grapples with managing a Philadelphia museum, trying to sort out her love life, and solving those murders that keep springing up around her.

Three can keep a secret, if two of them are dead.

—Benjamin Franklin

CHAPTER 1

I was standing at the sink making a stab at clearing up the breakfast dishes when Special Agent James Morrison of the Philadelphia FBI came up behind me, wrapped his arms around my waist, and kissed my neck. So much for dish washing.

"When do you have to leave, Nell?" he asked.

"Ten minutes ago, and I still have to get dressed."

"Anything important on your calendar this morning?"

I turned to face him, which put us in contact from the neck down. "I don't want to be late." I was lucky that I held a job that let me call my own hours—I was president of the Pennsylvania Antiquarian Society, so in theory I could come and go as I chose. But I preferred to set a good example for the rest of my staff, which meant that under normal circumstances I arrived early and left late. But circumstances over the past month had been anything but normal.

Actually, I would be happy to be late—again—because time with James felt . . . precious. It was barely a month since he had nearly bled to death under my hands, and the scar that curved along the inside of his arm was still raised and red. The Philadelphia FBI office had been generous in allowing him a month's leave to recover—in tacit recognition that it was their fault he'd gotten injured in the first place—but we were nearing the end of that grace period, and I had noticed James becoming increasingly restless as his health improved.

But for now? It looked like I *was* going to be late again.

I was surprised a while later when he rolled to face me, and said, "I think we should look for a bigger place."

Wait—*we*? Admittedly, I had been spending most of my time at his apartment near the University of Pennsylvania in Philadelphia, returning to my own small house in the suburbs only now and then to swap out clothes. Until now we'd been careful not to talk about anything long-term. We'd been living in the present, waiting until he recovered. I'd originally moved in to take care of him—I've always acknowledged to myself and anyone else who would listen that I'm a lousy caregiver, but I'd felt I owed it to him. Besides, there was no one else to do it. While he might have deep Philadelphia roots, on a day-to-day basis he was as much of a loner as I was.

But a serious discussion had been looming on the horizon, like a coming storm. After all, we weren't young, and we should be old enough to know our own minds. On the other hand, I'd been married once for about fifteen minutes and it

hadn't worked out, and I'd lived alone since, and James had never been married, a fact that continued to mystify me. I mean, he was smart, good-looking, held a responsible job, and could be tender and funny and sexy when he took off the strong-silent-FBI-agent mask.

There was no question that the last month, here with James, had been . . . like nothing in my life. James hadn't been a demanding patient. If anything, he'd been too stoic at first, never admitting when he was in pain, never asking for anything, not even a Tylenol. Thank goodness that phase hadn't lasted more than a week or two. After that a new and unexpected James started to emerge, one with a sense of humor and an element of playfulness that his serious FBI persona hadn't previously let him show.

But *we*? As in *together*, with our names on a lease? Or even a mortgage? I fought a moment of panic and realized he was looking at me oddly because I hadn't answered him. I scrounged up a smile, and said, "Are you asking me to move in with you? Like, officially?"

"For an intelligent woman, you can be kind of dense. Yes, Nell, I think we should look for a place for both of us, together."

"Oh. Well, then, yes, you're right." *Damn it, Nell, you were going to try to get over your fear of commitment, weren't you?* I took a deep breath and looked him in the eye. "Yes, James, I would be delighted to live with you. But right now I need to leave for work, and I can't blame my late entrances on your medical crises forever. Because you're about ninety-seven percent back, right?"

"I am, and I don't want you to use that as an excuse to

move out again. My lease is up the end of August, and I'm sure someone would grab this place in a minute. So we've got a little time to work out the details."

"Good." I leaned over and planted a kiss on him, then backed away so he couldn't pursue it. "Then I'm going to work. Shoot, look at the time!"

"I can drop you off," James volunteered.

"Then you'd better put some clothes on."

Ten minutes later we were out the door. Normally I could have walked to the Pennsylvania Antiquarian Society from James's apartment, especially in the nice summer weather. I'd found I enjoyed the walk—unless it was raining, in which case I could drive—and all the walking was doing wonders for my waistline. Well, that and all the worrying I'd done over the past month. If you're not a stress eater, worrying is a rather good way to lose weight.

"You have plans for today, apart from your meeting with your boss?" I asked, as he pulled up in front of the bluestone portico of the venerable Society building. It was only an hour later than my normal arrival time. Well, maybe an hour and a half.

"Get a haircut. See if any of my suits still fit. Talk to Cooper and see when I can start back at work. I feel ready, and my doctor's okayed it. You want me to call a Realtor?"

"Oh. Uh, yes, I guess." *Nothing like showing unbridled enthusiasm, Nell.* "See you later." After a serious kiss, I climbed out of the car and went up the steps. I nodded at Front Desk Bob, a retired policeman who staffed our reception area, and headed toward the back hall. While I waited for the balky elevator to make its stately descent, I greeted the massive marble statue of Edwin Forrest in his role as

Coriolanus that guarded the back hall. "Don't worry, Edwin—I'm going to see to it that you get moved to a better place, where more people will see you." Luckily, there was no one around to hear me talking to a sculpture, but I had a lot of strong feelings about Edwin.

Upstairs on the third floor, I stopped by my assistant Eric's desk. "Good morning, Eric. Anything I need to know about?"

"Mornin', Nell. Actually, there is. Mitchell Wakeman called and asked for an appointment with you, so I penciled him in for eleven. Is that okay?"

That left me all of half an hour to get my head around this meeting. I didn't know Wakeman personally, but I knew that he was a major player in Philadelphia development and construction—he'd had a finger in every major building project that had happened in the city for the last couple of decades. I'd have to Google him to remind myself of the details. "Did he say what he wanted?"

"No, he just said there was something he wanted to discuss with you. The man himself, not his assistant. I can cancel if you want."

Based on his comment, Eric must have recognized the name, and Eric was a lot newer to Philadelphia than I was. Maybe Wakeman wanted to give the Society a whole lot of money—or upgrade our creaky century-plus-old building. Hey, I could dream. But his visit could be an opportunity, and if it was, I was going to grab it. "No, that's fine. I'll be happy to talk to him. Do you know if Latoya's in?" Latoya was the Society's vice president for collections, who managed all the stuff that was inside the building, and there was a lot of it.

"I believe so."

"Then ask her if she can come see me ASAP."

"Will do."

"Thanks, Eric."

I barely had time to sit down behind my desk when Shelby stuck her head in the door. "Everything okay?" she asked. "'Cause you've been keeping kind of irregular hours. For you, that is."

I gestured her in, and she pulled the door shut behind her. Shelby had been one of my first hires at the Society. In fact, she had replaced me as development director when I was unexpectedly bumped into the corner office. But more than that, we were friends. "Everything is peachy-swell. Hunky-dory. Pick your own term."

"Things are going well with Mr. Agent Man?"

"Swimmingly." I hesitated, then said in a lower voice, "He wants us to find a place together."

"About time!" Shelby said, grinning. "So, he's back in fighting form?"

"He is, and he's talking with his boss today about going back to work. I have to say we're tripping all over each other at his place, and mine's not any better, plus it's kind of out of the way for him. We need more space. And more closets."

"Well, congratulations. I'm happy for you. He's one great guy." She cocked her head. "But you don't look exactly thrilled."

"Is it that obvious? Look, I know he's a terrific guy and we get along pretty well, but . . . what happens if it doesn't work out?"

"Then you find another place to stay. You gonna sell your house?"

"Thus far our discussion about this move has been about three sentences long, so I don't know." I lived in what had

once been a carriage house behind one of the gracious Main Line mansions in suburban Bryn Mawr. The exterior of the house was still gracious, but inside, it had been chopped up into offices by a succession of professionals. At the moment it was owned by a group of psychologists. I wondered how easy my place would be to sell—it was kind of small and had no land attached, and it was in somebody else's backyard. Something I'd have to think about. If James and I took the next step. *If?*

Shelby stood up. "Well, I'd better get to work. But let me say this: If you let him go, you're an idiot. Get over your fear of whatever and move forward."

"Thank you, Doctor. That's what I plan to do." Maybe.

We were interrupted by Latoya. "You wanted to see me, Nell? Oh, hi, Shelby."

"Hi, Latoya," Shelby said. "I was on my way out. You want to have lunch, Nell?"

"Let me get back to you on that, Shelby. I've got an appointment at eleven, and I'm not sure how long that will run."

When Shelby left, I turned my attention to Latoya. We'd had a rocky relationship ever since she joined the Society a few years earlier, back when I was still director of development. As vice president for collections, she usually had conveyed the sense that fundraising was somewhat inferior to collections management. She'd had some difficulty adjusting to my unexpected promotion to president—which had made me her boss. I hadn't wanted to force the issue, but now that I was settled in the position, it was time for me to take a firmer hand. It was hard to do, but I knew it was best both for me and the Society. I just hoped Latoya would adjust to our new working relationship.

"Is this about the registrar position?" she asked bluntly.

"It is. What progress have you made?"

"Actually, we've had a lot of applications since we posted the position. Which I will say surprised me, but given the economy, I guess I ought to have expected it. Unfortunately, many of the applicants simply aren't qualified for a senior position here."

"Have you considered moving Alice into the position?" Alice was an intern, very young but very talented.

"She hasn't said anything to me, and I'm not sure she wants it. To be honest, I really don't think she's ready. She has the ability, but not the depth of experience. I hope she'll stay on, though. Do you disagree?"

"Actually, no. I think you're right. Her job description may change a bit, depending on the skills the new registrar brings to the table. Well, keep looking and keep me informed. The collections here are still superb, and we're in sore need of someone who can work with the new software and finish sorting them out. We really need to dig out from under all the stuff we've got piled up." Not only was the documentation of the Society's collections mired in the past, but we'd been handed a mountain of uncataloged material by the FBI recently, and we were bursting at the seams.

"I'll do that." Latoya stood up, then hesitated. "Nell, we really do need to do something to improve our image in the public eye. Almost all of our publicity lately has been about theft and murder, and I can't imagine that our members are happy about that. Not to mention our donors and the board."

As if that was my fault? "I recognize that, Latoya. If you have any ideas, I'd love to hear them. Maybe we should have an all-hands staff meeting devoted to this, to find out what

people have been saying about us and figure out how to fix it." Now that I didn't have to worry about James from day to day, I could devote more energy to my own responsibilities.

"Good idea. Let me put my ideas on paper, and we can talk."

"Sooner rather than later, please."

"Right." Latoya left, but as soon as she had cleared the door, Eric stuck his head in.

"Mr. Wakeman is downstairs. Want me to bring him up?"

"Please." The man was early, and I hadn't had time to check out what we had in our records about him or think through what he might want. When Eric left to retrieve Wakeman, I figured I had about three minutes, so I did a quick online search about my guest. My fuzzy memory was more or less correct: he was a big-time developer in Philadelphia and the surrounding counties. Which didn't give me a clue about why he wanted to see me.

Two and a half minutes later, Eric ushered in a tall, greying man in his fifties, whose expensive clothes seemed to have a mind of their own and were flying in several different directions—necktie loose, shirt coming untucked. But I was pretty sure he wasn't here for a fashion consult.

I stood up and extended my hand. "I'm Nell Pratt. What can I do for you, Mr. Wakeman?"

He shook it firmly. "I'm working on a new project, and I want you to help."

Music to my ears.

CHAPTER 2

Mitchell Wakeman sat heavily in one of my antique guest chairs, legs sprawling. "Nice to meet you, Ms. Pratt. I've been seeing your name in the papers a lot lately."

I was never sure how to respond to statements like that. It really would be nice to get some press for something related to Philadelphia history instead of my involvement with its crime rate. I hedged a bit. "And how did that lead you here to the Society?"

Wakeman nodded once, as if noting my tacit acknowledgment of the events he was talking about. "I'll come to the point. Please keep the details of what I tell you on the q.t.—we're still in the preliminary planning stages and I don't want to spread it around yet. You know, drive property values and construction costs up in the neighborhood."

"I understand, and I hope I am always discreet about any confidences. What are you asking for?"

"Now that the economy is turning around a bit, I think

the time is right for a project I've been nursing along for a while—a multipurpose development in Chester County."

"Multipurpose? Meaning a combination of residential and commercial?"

"Yes, but even more. It's a unified development that brings together everything you need, kind of like a little community of its own. You know—housing, restaurants and cafés, shops, dry cleaner, maybe even some medical offices."

"Like a retirement village for senior citizens?"

"For all ages. Condos first, then maybe houses in a later phase."

"Sounds interesting. Will this be in commuter range?"

"Good question. Like I said, it's in Chester County, so it's in commuting range. Plus SEPTA's been talking about extending one of its lines out farther that way. I'd like to encourage that. I've initiated very preliminary discussions with management there about a sort of public-private venture, but nothing is set in stone yet."

"I live near the Main Line. So, this would be out beyond that?"

"Yeah, that's where the land is." He leaned forward and lowered his voice a notch. "I've got a nice parcel of land in Goshen, a working dairy farm until recently. I knew the owner for years—his family owned the place for centuries. When he hit ninety, Ezra decided to sell before his kids started squabbling over what to do with it. I was happy to take it at a fair price. The deal was already done when he passed last year, but he had a life interest in it."

"This all sounds wonderful, Mr. Wakeman, but where does the Society fit in this?"

"You know about Duffy's Cut?"

"Yes, of course." Duffy's Cut had been in the news a lot over the past couple of years—it involved the tragic death of over thirty Irish immigrants working on the "cut" or railroad cutting in Malvern, a town in Chester County, in the early nineteenth century, and the cover-up by the railroad company, which had buried the bodies fast and never reported the deaths. They'd been found only recently. "Various historians and members of the media have done some research on it here. How does that apply?"

"Frankly, I don't want another Duffy's Cut to happen on my project. It's not just the legalities about digging up old bones—I can respect that. What I want is to be ready if something like that comes up, so I'm not caught with my pants down. Goodwill is important in making a project like this work, and it's hard enough without worrying about any messes in the press. You see what I'm saying?"

"I think so," I said cautiously. "You want the Society to look into the history of the property you are considering to make sure there aren't any unpleasant surprises hidden there? Or, if there are, to make sure you're prepared to handle them?"

"Exactly." He sat back and smiled at me. "Can you do that?"

I thought for a moment. He was right to come to the Society. We had the best collections of documents about Philadelphia history anywhere, although there was a good small historical society in West Chester. But I still wasn't sure what he was asking. "Do you want to hire a researcher to look into this?"

"You mean one of your hourly intern types who'll take a year or two? No, I want the best. I want someone working

on this pretty much full-time until I'm sure you've turned over every rock and nothing crawls out."

Full-time? I wasn't sure I could help him there. Our staff was pretty limited. There was Rich, an intern whose main job was to slog through the Terwilliger Collection, mainly documents from generations of local Terwilligers—Pennsylvania movers and shakers who went back to the early eighteenth century. The family had included several Society presidents, and its latest member, Martha Terwilliger, was on the Society board. The short answer was, Rich was fully occupied and Marty wouldn't be happy if I tried to divert him from "her" project. That only left new intern Alice, who was untried. She'd been hired in part to keep her benefactor uncle happy, although so far she'd done a great job for us. But no way was she ready to tackle a major research project like the one Wakeman was proposing. Still, I didn't want to tell him that we couldn't handle it or send him off to one of the local universities to find a historian, who would probably want to write a book about it anyway. And academic historians were slow, because they insisted on being careful and accurate, with footnotes on every page. I didn't condone the quick-and-dirty approach, but I thought we could deliver what he wanted. "Mr. Wakeman, I'll be blunt. We don't have enough staff at the moment to provide what you need. But we can recruit and hire someone qualified to take on this project on a full-time basis, if you're willing to pay for it. And we do have all the resources here on site."

"Of course I'll pay for it," Wakeman said impatiently. "But I want somebody good, and I want whoever it is to keep his or her mouth shut until I'm ready to go public with this."

"That's not a problem. I take it you want this to happen immediately?"

He grinned. "Yeah, like, last week. How much you gonna charge for this?"

I named a figure that equaled six months' salary for one of our interns—plus fifty percent. I figured the extra would cover speed and silence, of course, and I knew he had the money.

Wakeman didn't blink. "When can you start?" he asked.

"As soon as I can identify him—or her."

"Let me know. I'll want to meet him—or her. And if this goes right, there might be something extra in it for the Society."

"I'm sure that would be welcome."

Wakeman stood up. "Great. Here's my card. Give me a call when you have somebody for me to talk to." He turned and strode out, and I frantically gestured to Eric to see him out of the building, since Wakeman couldn't use the elevator without a key. Pitiful security, I knew, but it was all we had.

After they were gone, I sat at my desk for a few moments, stunned. I recognized this as a true opportunity: Wakeman Property Trust was a major player in the greater Philadelphia area and was rolling in money. If we did a good job, there would definitely be rewards, tangible and intangible. And we were clearly the best organization to dig into the history of that particular plot of land. The problem would be finding someone who could do it.

Well, Marty Terwilliger was a good person to start with. She knew everybody in Philadelphia and was related to half of them (including James). Funny—I hadn't seen much of her in the past few weeks. Of course, I hadn't been around much myself in the past few weeks because of James. But

it was definitely time to climb back in the saddle. I picked up the phone and dialed Marty's cell.

She answered on the fifth ring. "Nell? What's up?"

"Nothing bad, I promise. I've got a research project I'd like to discuss with you. Can you do lunch today?"

I heard what sounded to me like a hand clamping over the phone and a rumble of voices. Then Marty came back. "One? At that place around the corner?"

"Great. See you there."

I checked my watch: twelve fifteen. The meeting with Wakeman hadn't taken long, because he'd come right to the point. I hated bits of time that weren't long enough to start anything but were too long to waste. I decided to spend it doing some more online research into Mitchell Wakeman. From my days as Society fundraiser, I was sure he had never been a member of the Society or given us any substantial amount, so I wondered what had made him think of us. It was gratifying to know that we had a solid reputation—apart from a few recent problems—but Wakeman could have hired just about anyone in the business. How hush-hush was this project of his? Had he come to us because he thought none of his construction colleagues would see what he was up to? The next time I looked up, it was twelve forty-five, there was a stack of printouts on my printer, and Shelby was leaning on my doorframe smiling.

"Earth to Nell?"

"Have you been standing there long?"

"Maybe. What had you so absorbed?"

"I'll explain over lunch if you want to come along. I'm meeting Marty around the corner in twelve minutes, so we should get going. Say, have you seen much of Marty recently?"

Shelby wrinkled her brow. "Come to think of it, I haven't. Maybe Rich is too tied up with general stuff to work on the Terwilliger materials?"

"That never stopped her before. I've been so distracted that I hadn't even noticed she wasn't around. But she said yes to lunch quickly enough when I called today. Maybe there's something else going on in her life."

"Heaven forbid Martha Terwilliger should have a life!" Shelby said in mock horror. "Let's go find out."

Marty, unfazed by the August heat, was waiting outside the restaurant when Shelby and I arrived. We gathered her up and ducked into the air-conditioned restaurant as quickly as possible and found a quiet table in the back. Once we were settled with tall glasses of iced tea in front of all three of us, Marty looked me over critically.

"You're looking good. How's Jimmy?"

"Are those two statements related?" I parried.

"I'd say yes," Marty said. "Has he asked you yet?"

"Asked me what?" I said, stalling.

"Yeah, what?" Shelby said, smiling and looking back and forth between us.

"About moving in together," Marty replied.

I struggled to answer. How come she knew before I did? "Yes, he mentioned something like that this morning."

"You gonna do it?" she asked. Marty didn't bother withbeating around the bush. But I supposed she had a right to be interested, since she was the one who'd introduced me to James and the one who'd glued me back together when he'd been injured, and forced me to step up to take care of him. "Your house is cute, but it's not adequate for two people. Kind of like a burrow built for one."

"Marty!" I protested. "It's a perfectly nice Victorian carriage house, but I know it's small. And how the heck do you know anything about it? Have you even seen James?"

"We had lunch a couple of times while you were at work."

"So, was this your idea or his?" I was working up a head of steam. Was Marty trying to manipulate my life now?

"His. He asked me how I thought you'd react. I told him you'd back off, and then you'd waffle for a while, and that he should just wait it out because you two belong together."

Great. My own life was not my own, apparently. "Shelby, were you in on all this, too?"

"No, ma'am!" she said quickly. "But I do agree with Marty. Why don't you skip the waffling part and go straight to yes?"

"Hey, give me like fifteen minutes to think about this, okay? Besides, a few other things have intervened. Which is what I wanted to talk to you about." I looked around the room: midweek, after one, the restaurant was sparsely filled, and there was no one seated at a table near us. "I had a very interesting discussion with a certain prominent local developer this morning."

"Mitchell Wakeman, right?" Marty said.

"How did you know?" I asked. The woman was uncanny.

"Before you ask, no, he's not a relative, and no, I didn't send him to you." She grinned at me. "He figured out where to come all by himself."

One question answered, to my happy relief. "I'm glad to hear that. How, then?"

"Because you say *prominent*, *local*, and *developer* in one sentence, and he's the obvious choice. What did he want?"

"Time-out," Shelby interrupted. "Who is this guy? I

mean, I know the name, and I know his reputation, but he's never been involved with the Society."

"You haven't been around Philadelphia very long, have you?" I said. "He and his various companies more or less shaped the current skyline of the city. He's had a finger in every pie in half the state. He's been on boards and panels and who knows what around here. Does that about cover it, Marty?"

"In a nutshell. He's one of the good guys. Politically connected, but he uses it for good, not evil. He's made tons of money, but legally, and not by trampling or squeezing anybody for it. Never been a member or given us any money." By *us* I knew Marty meant the Society, to which she was fanatically devoted, just as her father and grandfather had been. "What did he want?"

"You mean I actually know something you don't?" I smiled at Marty. Our salads arrived, which kind of quashed conversation for a few minutes. Plus I suddenly felt a little funny talking about this in public after Wakeman had specifically asked me to keep things quiet. I decided to change the subject, at least temporarily.

"So, now that James will be going back to work, I should be in the office more. I feel like I've been out of the loop for a while." All too true: the first couple of weeks of looking out for my injured warrior had been kind of rough. Sure, I'd had plenty of accumulated sick leave and vacation time, but I was also the relatively new president of a venerable institution, so I was torn between nursing and doing my job. It would be a relief to get back to normal, if I could remember what that was. "What have you been up to, Marty?" I said innocently.

Shelby picked up my drift. "You know, I haven't seen much of you, either. Something new going on?"

Marty seemed to be at a loss for words, which was unusual.

"Marty, are you blushing?" I asked with a grin.

"No!" she protested quickly. "Well, maybe." She smiled, kind of. "I'm seeing someone."

"Ooh, tell us!" Shelby said before I could say much the same thing. Marty had been married a time or two, but as far as I knew she hadn't been involved with anyone for a couple of years now.

"What's his name? Do we know him?" I asked.

"I'm not going to play twenty questions with you. He's a professor at Penn, specializing in urban history and economics. Widowed, grown kids. And before you ask, not related in any way, shape, or form to the Pennsylvania Terwilligers."

"So how did you meet him?" I pressed.

"I went to a lecture he gave. He was interesting, so I hung around to ask him a question after. Things kind of went from there. And that's all I want to say right now."

"Stay away for a couple of weeks, and the earth shifts on its axis," I sighed dramatically. "But I'm happy for you, Marty. I hope it works out."

"Just like you and Jimmy, huh?" Marty shot back.

And we finished the lunch with non-business-related girl talk. After, standing outside the restaurant, I said, "Marty, do you have time to come back and talk to me about this mysterious special project of Wakeman's? Shelby, you're welcome to join us. Based on what he said, I think this is about local history, which isn't exactly up your alley, but you've come up with some good stuff in the past. If you aren't too busy."

"Hey, lady, anything that puts me in the good graces of a local power broker works for me," Shelby said happily. "Let's do it!"

CHAPTER 3

Settled once again in my office, I began, "Before we get into it, anybody have any new thoughts on the registrar position? Latoya told me she's been getting applications but that many of the people simply aren't qualified."

"Alice is working out well," Marty volunteered. "She's smart. Or maybe I mean *intuitive.* I can't see her chained to a computer all the time, but she's great with descriptions and making connections."

"I agree with both your points. Latoya and I discussed her earlier, though, and I'm not sure she's ready for it, nor would it send the right message to bump her up to the position right now. Which leaves us nowhere. Latoya hasn't found any candidates that she likes. Maybe it's just that it's summer and things are slow."

"Or nobody wants a job that's both boring and unlucky," Marty said. "I'll ask around again. Have you talked to Jimmy about it?"

"Why would I?"

"In case you haven't noticed, the FBI uses analysts. Maybe somebody over there wants a change of pace. Or maybe he'd remember a good candidate they didn't hire. Can't hurt to ask."

"I suppose." I made a mental note to mention it to James later. "Now, back to the Wakeman project. Here's the deal: Mr. Wakeman approached me directly because he's planning some sort of mega-development out in Chester County, and he doesn't want to run into any problems like Duffy's Cut."

"What's Duffy's Cut?" Shelby asked.

"How much time have you got?"

"Hey, this is business, isn't it? Take all the time you want, boss."

"Okay, you've both been to my house in Bryn Mawr. The train that serves the town is now the SEPTA R3, but it's always been known as the Main Line. It's what's left of the main line of the Pennsylvania Railroad, which served all the upscale communities west of the city. The 'old money' families."

"They took trains? I thought they all had chauffeurs," Shelby said with a smile.

"Well, some of the gentlemen had to get to their clubs, so the train was simple," interjected Marty.

"Anyway, the Main Line used to end in Paoli, and then it was extended to the next town over, Malvern," I continued. "Now, the Malvern stretch was originally built for a different railroad in the nineteenth century. When the bosses needed laborers back then, they'd take immigrants straight off the ships in Philadelphia—mostly Irish and mostly those with no local connections. In 1832, dozens of them died on the Malvern railway job in a cholera epidemic, and nobody ever notified the relatives back in Ireland, and the railway all but

destroyed the evidence. The bodies were buried in a ditch under the tracks and more or less forgotten. When the bodies were finally discovered in 2009, archeologists saw what they thought looked like evidence of blunt-force trauma, so the site was declared a crime scene rather than a dig. There are some nasty rumors that some of the workers may have been killed off to stop the spread of the disease."

"That's awful!" Shelby exclaimed.

"Exactly. When the mass burials were uncovered, it became a big issue, of course, with various factions blaming others retroactively, and then the current railroad wouldn't let the historians finish the dig, which only made things worse. I read all about it at the time—it's kind of in my backyard, it's local history, and it's a compelling story. Anyway, Wakeman's property is only a couple of miles away, and he doesn't want to run into any surprises like that or set off another firestorm among local historians. Malvern and the local towns are already pretty sensitized to the issue, so he wants to be sure that everything is clean and aboveboard. That's why he came to us—he wants somebody to do a thorough history of the site he's optioned, to make sure there aren't any bodies there, literally or figuratively. Worst case, if there are, he wants to be ready to manage the situation."

"Wouldn't hurt our reputation much, either," Marty said. "Did he tell you exactly where the site was?"

"He said it was a dairy farm. He bought it before the old owner died, but he's only taken possession of it recently. He also said it's near a rail line, but there's some talk of extending that, and I think that would figure into his development plans."

"What's he want to build?" Shelby asked.

"He called it a mixed-use development that combines

housing, commercial space, recreational stuff—a whole package. I was impressed, if it's true. I mean, I've seen enough ugly suburban sprawl, so if he can do it efficiently, with a solid plan and with the local communities on board, I'd have to applaud. If it all checks out, I'd like to help him. The only problem is, we don't have anyone available to do the work right now at the Society. We're already short-staffed. Either of you have any ideas about where we can find somebody qualified for a short-term appointment?"

Everybody was silent for a couple of minutes, apparently thinking hard. Then Marty said, "Did he mention money?"

"He said he'd pay the salary of a researcher, if we needed to hire one. We didn't get into anything about supporting the institution, if that's what you're asking, but he kind of hinted. So, Marty, you know everybody and everything that matters about eastern Pennsylvania. What's your take on this project? Is it something we should be part of?"

Marty contemplated the ceiling. "I've known Mitch Wakeman and his wife for years, but sort of socially, and we're not close. He lives way out in the burbs, with said wife and a bunch of his kids. I've never heard anything negative about him, and as far as I know he is a good planner, and doesn't jump into a project unless he's pretty sure he has the funding lined up, so he's left no half-built messes behind. As for the project itself . . . I think I know the parcel he's talking about. Plenty of room, but he is going to have to look at access roads, water supply, wastewater, all that stuff. I don't think any of them is a deal-breaker, if he's got enough money to put into it. The train upgrade might be harder because there are a bunch of different agencies involved, but I'm not sure it's essential to the project."

Marty leaned back in her chair. "He's going to need local approvals from the township out there. I don't know what Wakeman's relationship with that bunch is like, although I think it's a good bet that he knows them already. And I'm sure he's thought about all of this. The Society's role is a very small part. Still, it's nice of him to think of us."

"Great, so you're in favor of going ahead? Do we need board approval?"

"I'll talk to them, but I don't think anyone will have a problem—well, unless one or two of them have butted heads with Wakeman in the past, which has been known to happen, because he can be kind of, well, abrupt. Let's hope not, anyway. It won't cost the Society anything if we can find a warm body with a brain to take it on, and it'll make us look good. Assuming, of course, that we don't find something like another Duffy's Cut that puts the kibosh on the project or drags it out for years."

"And what would do that?"

"Let's not borrow trouble," Shelby said. "First you need to find a researcher. What's his timeline? Or maybe I mean, when did you tell Wakeman you'd get back to him?"

"Uh, I don't think I said. But ASAP, at least with a yea or a nay."

"Maybe Ethan knows a grad student . . ." Marty said, her expression softening.

Shelby and I exchanged a look. "Ethan being the man of the moment?" I asked. "Does the man have a last name?"

"Uh, yeah. Miller," Marty said, then shut up again.

"A grad student might be a good choice, if he knows anything about local history," Shelby commented.

"I'll ask," Marty muttered. "So, what're you going to tell Jimmy about the whole moving-in-together thing?"

Nice deflection, Marty, I thought. "I, uh, don't know. We'll have to talk about it." My cell phone rang in my bag. I fished it out: James. Marty and Shelby wouldn't mind my answering. I punched the button to connect. "Hey there. Were your ears burning?"

"What? Oh, I get it. Say hi to Marty."

"And Shelby," I added. "So, what's up?"

"You free for dinner tonight?"

"Out? Are we celebrating?"

"Close enough. I'll meet you at the Society at six, okay?"

"Fine. See you then." We both hung up. I looked up to see Marty and Shelby watching me with closely matched smiles.

"Ah, true love," Shelby cooed.

"You two are the very soul of romance," Marty added.

I refused to take the bait. "Come off it, guys. This is my place of business. He and I will get mushy over dinner tonight, and no, you can't tag along."

"Wouldn't anyway—I have plans," Marty said, looking smug.

"So, we're about done here. Marty, you're going to ask Ethan if he knows of any eager researchers who want to take on a short-term project like this. Shelby, maybe you can do a little digging about Wakeman and see if there's anything we need to know—and check out his record on charitable donations while you're at it. Oh, and I'll ask James if there are any leftover FBI analysts who might fit the registrar position. Anything else?"

Shelby stood up and saluted. "No, ma'am. That about covers it. I'll let you know if I find anything interesting."

After she'd left, I turned back to Marty. "This thing with Ethan serious?"

"Maybe. Look, I'll lay off you and James if you don't ask any questions about Ethan. If there's anything you need to know, I'll tell you."

"Deal."

Having sent Shelby and Marty off with their marching orders, I whiled away the rest of the afternoon with paperwork and correspondence and all the other stuff that keeps an institution going. At five, Eric popped his head in.

"You need anything else, Nell?" he asked.

"No, I'm good. Look, Eric, thanks for covering for me over the past few weeks. I know I haven't been around much, but I hope things will get back to normal now."

"I was happy to help out. And I'm glad Agent Morrison is back on his feet. It must have been hard on you."

"It was, but we're past that now. Thanks for asking. I'll see you in the morning."

Eric left, and the rest of the administrative staff on the third floor trickled out until I was the last one. I'd mentioned getting back to normal, but what *was* normal? I'd been in charge of the place for over a year now, and every time I thought things had settled down, another crisis erupted. Sometimes I wondered how we managed to keep the doors open and staff employed, but we had. Sometimes I wondered how I had managed to survive all of it—and a few times it had been a close thing—and come out of it with renewed enthusiasm for what I was doing. The Society and the history that it held were worth fighting for . . . although I really

would prefer it if people stopped fighting and just enjoyed the bounty of the place.

I was lost in thought when James called to say that he was downstairs waiting for me. I gathered up my bag, turned out the lights, and went down to meet him.

I almost didn't recognize him. The haircut made a big difference—he'd gotten kind of shaggy over the past month, but a major scalp laceration did not lend itself to regular trims. And I'd forgotten how good he looked in a suit. Had anything else changed? Maybe a little. His face seemed thinner, and there were a few more lines at the corners of his eyes, but they just added dignity. I felt almost tongue-tied. "Hey," I said brilliantly.

"Hey yourself," he said, smiling.

"Damn, you look good."

"Thanks. I can't button the jacket—I need some serious gym time. But it's summer, so nobody should notice. You ready to go?"

"Are we walking?" I asked, and James graciously escorted me down the stone steps of the Society.

"I thought we'd go to Vetri—that's close."

"Nice! If I'd known, I would have dressed for it."

"You look lovely."

I bit off a remark along the lines of "What, this old thing?" I was trying to learn to accept compliments, and James's were always sincere. "Thank you. So this really is a celebration?"

"I hope so. I've been cleared to go back to work. You're back on the job full-time. And we made it through, you and I."

"That we did," I said, taking the arm James offered, establishing our status as a couple for all the world to see.

CHAPTER 4

We strolled slowly, given that the heat of the day still lingered in stone and concrete. Since the restaurant was only a couple of blocks away, we arrived quickly despite the leisurely pace, and once inside we were seated immediately.

"Wine?" James asked.

"Please," I said, and watched as he ordered a bottle of white. When the waiter had departed, I said, "You know, you look very pleased with yourself."

"Shouldn't I be? I'm fit again, I've got a job I enjoy—plus my boss now figures he owes me because he didn't listen to me when it counted—and I've got you. Not necessarily in that order. Nell, I can't thank you enough for sticking by me over the past month. I know it wasn't easy."

"No, it wasn't, but I wanted to be there. After what happened . . ." I stopped, unsure how to go on. "The aftereffects linger on," I finally said. When he started to protest, I held up a hand. "No, I'm not having flashbacks or waking up in

a sweat at night. It's just the stress of being understaffed at work, and we're having trouble filling this registrar position, which keeps getting bigger and more complicated. We're still not done with the conversion to the new software system, and then there's the flood of new items, thanks in part to all the FBI stuff you dropped on us, and we'd barely made a dent in that when things hit the fan. So, as I said, it's not over until we're fully staffed and things are running smoothly again." I took a sip of my wine. "Marty said I should ask whether you knew anyone who might be interested in the job. You don't, do you?"

James thought for a moment. "Actually, I might know somebody who would be a good fit for that position, but he may surprise you. Let me talk to him and see if he's interested."

"Does he have a résumé?"

"I don't know if he's written one lately. It's kind of an odd situation . . . No, let me check with him, and then we can talk about it."

We lapsed back into silence for a moment. "Is there something else that's bothering you?" James asked.

"You told Marty about what you asked me this morning," I said bluntly. It still rankled, although I wasn't sure why.

"What? Oh, you mean about finding a place together? Is that a problem?"

"I guess I'm not happy that she knew before I did. You might have asked me first."

He cocked his head at me, looking genuinely confused. "I'm sorry, I didn't mean to overstep, but you know Marty . . . Wait, are you saying you don't want to?"

"No, not exactly. But I want to think about it, okay? I mean, spending this past month with you has been . . .

interesting, and parts of it have been intense, but I haven't had time to look at the big picture."

He looked down at his wine glass and swirled the contents rather than look at me. "Is that one of those 'it's not you, it's me' lines?"

"No! I'm happy that you've asked, but I need to figure out what I want, and what works for us together."

He looked at me then, and his eyes were less warm than they had been. "I told you, my lease is up at the end of the month. When do you think you'll have an answer?"

Suddenly my eyes were filled with tears. "Oh, James, you only asked me this morning. It's a big step for me. Just give me a little time, please?"

The waiter appeared to refill our glasses and take our orders, providing a welcome break. Why was I being such an idiot? I loved James. He was smart, sexy, gainfully employed, and he said he loved me. What else could I possibly want?

The problem *was* me. I had trouble trusting people, and I didn't let them get too close. I knew it was an issue, but I'd never figured out how to get around it. Yet, if there was ever a time to work it out, this was it. I knew it was an insult to James, that my hesitation signaled I didn't really trust him, not all the way, when he'd been up-front about how he felt without pushing too hard. Heck, he had every right to push—he wanted to get on with his life. Why didn't I?

Once our food arrived, it gave us something else to focus on. The wine was smooth, the food was delightful, but the company was . . . subdued. It certainly didn't feel much like a celebration anymore, and that was my fault, which I regretted. After passing on dessert but agreeing to espresso, James settled the bill, and said, "Are you coming home with me?"

"If you want me to," I said.

"Always," he said, and he smiled to show he meant it.

I woke up in the morning before James and I lay still in bed, thinking. James and I had been thrown together intimately, in more ways than one, for the past month, but I still knew in the back of my mind that I had a place that was all mine, one I could escape to if I needed. Was I ready to give up my escape hatch? To the world it looked like I had all my ducks a row—great guy, good job, nice life. What more did I want? I rolled over to find James watching me. I smiled at him. "How many bedrooms?"

He smiled back with what looked like relief. "Three? That way we each get office space."

I liked the idea of a hidey-hole with a door, all my own. "Sounds good."

We moved on to talk particulars. James's third-floor row house walk-up was probably better suited to a graduate student than to a senior special agent for the FBI, but it had worked for him, at least until now. He had few possessions and didn't seem to care much about "things." In contrast, I was a collector—pretty items that caught my eye, heirlooms I treasured that had belonged to my grandparents, and a lot of stuff that just seemed to accumulate. As my stuff migrated, his place had become increasingly crowded. It hadn't been too bad when James had been laid up, but now that he was more himself, we kept bumping into each other. Not that that was always a problem, but still. We discussed parking spaces and the like, then James asked, "Nell, you're sure about this?"

"Yes, I am." Maybe. I wasn't sure I was sure, but I was

going to work very hard to convince myself. "Now, let's celebrate for real."

I made it to work on time, but only by skipping breakfast. I picked up a large coffee on the way.

"What's on the calendar today, Eric?" I greeted him as I arrived at my office.

"Mr. Wakeman called again, asked if you had some time free this afternoon to look at something. You don't have anything scheduled, but I didn't want to book it without checking with you first. Should I call him back?"

"Sure. Anything else?"

"Ms. Terwilliger called, said she might have someone for that thing you told her about. I assume you know what she means?"

"I do. Did she say if she'd be coming in today?"

"She didn't mention it. You want me to call her, too?"

"I'll do it, after I've talked with Mr. Wakeman, since the calls are kind of related." Eric looked game but confused. I decided to take him into my confidence. "Hey, come on into my office and I'll explain."

Eric followed me in and shut the door. "Is this something secret?"

"Not exactly, but let's keep it low profile. You know who Mr. Wakeman is?"

"Kind of—I Googled him after that last meeting. Big local builder, right? I see his name on construction sites a lot."

"Exactly. He's done a lot for the city. Anyway, he's hatching a new development in the suburbs and he doesn't want to run into any archeological or historical surprises at the site, so he's asked us to look into it for him. It's a very

responsible thing for him to do, and I'm pleased that he came to us. But since we're a bit shorthanded at the moment, we'll have to recruit somebody short-term to do it. That's where Marty's call comes in—I asked her if she knew anyone who might fit the bill."

"Got it. Is this project hush-hush?"

"It's still in the planning stages, so the less said the better for now. Not that I don't trust you, Eric, but you never know who's going to overhear something in the city and run with it. If everything goes well, the site will get a clean bill of health and we'll come out smelling like a rose. Maybe with a nice contribution to go with it."

"Let's hope so. Thanks, Nell, for filling me in. I'll call Mr. Wakeman for you now."

I barely had time to take a sip of my coffee before Eric told me that Mitchell Wakeman was on the line. I picked up. "Good morning, Mr. Wakeman. What can I do for you?"

"I wondered if you'd like a tour of the site, so you know what we're talking about?"

"I would like that. When did you have in mind?"

"This afternoon? I could pick you up about three—it's maybe an hour away, out toward West Chester."

"That sounds good, if you're willing to drop me off in Bryn Mawr on your way back."

"No problem. I'll come by at three, then. Thanks." He hung up. He knew I wasn't going to be doing the research myself—I couldn't claim to be a local historian—but I figured that the big cheese at the Wakeman Trust preferred to talk to his counterpart at the Society, and that would be me. Actually, I was kind of intrigued by the idea of seeing a major development project like this from the ground up,

literally. Assuming it was done responsibly and tastefully, without upsetting the neighbors or the ecology.

And I'd get a ride home out of it. Though "home" was a loaded term right now . . . I shook myself and picked up the phone to call Marty, and she answered quickly. "Hey, Nell. I think I've got a researcher for you. You want to meet her?"

"That was fast. Give me a quick rundown, will you?"

"Penn grad student, needs some cash because her grant funding dried up all of a sudden. Doing a masters on urban planning, majored in American history in college. Smart, and a hard worker."

"Sounds just about perfect. Marty, how do you do this? Come up with people at the drop of a hat?"

"Ethan's her advisor. It's a good fit, isn't it?"

"It is. Look, Wakeman offered to take me on a tour of the site at three this afternoon. If this person's free, she could come over here and talk to me at two, and if I like her, I can introduce her to Wakeman and we could go out together and see what's what."

"Good idea. I'll call her and let you know." She hung up. Why did I talk to so many people who hung up abruptly? Was that better or worse than the ones who rambled on and wouldn't get off the phone? Anyway, I was glad that the pieces seemed to be falling into place nicely.

Eric rapped on my doorframe. "Nell, there's a guy downstairs, says Agent Morrison sent him over to talk to you. You want to see him?"

I wasn't sure I knew what James's idea of a registrar candidate would be like, but I was willing to talk with the man. My goodness, this morning was moving at an incredible

pace. Maybe the stars had realigned while I wasn't looking. "All right. Can you go down and bring him up?"

"Will do." Eric disappeared.

I straightened what little there was on my desk and tried to get my head into interview mode. Maybe I should send this person straight to Latoya, but James had pointed him toward me, so I might as well talk to him first. At least I knew what the registrar's job required in the way of qualifications, having interviewed quite a few people for it in recent months. Whoever we hired needed to have solid computer skills and some serious database-management experience. A background in history, particularly for the Philadelphia area, would be extremely helpful. Someone who really cared about local history would be even better.

Eric returned quickly, and I looked up from the job description I'd retrieved from my file to greet the newcomer—and then adjusted my gaze down: the man was in a wheelchair.

CHAPTER 5

The man didn't smile. "I'm Benjamin Hartley. James Morrison said you have a position open. Don't get up." He looked to be fortyish, with close-cropped hair, and not exactly happy. He rolled his wheelchair closer to the desk and extended his hand. I shook it; his grip was as strong as I would have guessed. "Not what you expected, huh, Ms. Pratt?"

"I'm Nell," I answered with a smile. "Frankly, Mr. Hartley, I wasn't expecting anybody, not this fast. I only mentioned it to James last night. How do you know each other?"

"Went to college together. Then he went with the FBI and I went to into the military. We stayed in touch."

All right then. A military guy? I wondered why he was here for this position, and how he could possibly fit. "What did James tell you about the job?"

"That it's mainly computers and historical stuff."

"Do you have a résumé?"

"Nope. Just got out of rehab—physical, not alcohol or

drugs—and I haven't had time for that kind of stuff. But I need a job."

Nobody would accuse this guy of sucking up to a potential employer, or of pulling his punches. But if James vouched for him, I had to assume he had a good reason. Even out of loyalty to an old friend, he wouldn't send over someone totally unqualified. "You haven't interviewed for a job for a while, have you?"

"No. Why?"

"Because you're giving me a lousy first impression. Why are you here?"

"Because I need to work, and I've got the qualifications."

I took a moment and counted to ten. "Okay, let's back up. You're no longer in the military?"

"Right. I'd had enough of that. And if you're wondering, I'm in this chair because of a stupid car accident, after I got out. At least I've got decent insurance."

"You're cleared physically to work full-time now?"

"Yes." He didn't elaborate.

I suppressed a sigh. To be honest, the registrar position didn't require a lot of interaction with other people, just technical skills. "Why the attitude, if you want a job here? Are you pissed off because you think this is a charity offer? I assure you it's not. We need someone in this position—but it has to be someone who can do the job."

Ben looked at me for a moment, and finally he smiled, which changed his face altogether. "Sorry, you're right—I'm being rude. It's just that I'm kinda new to this whole disability thing, and I don't want anybody's pity. I want to work, and I can do the job. Can we start this over?"

"Happy to. Welcome, Mr. Hartley. Tell me, why do you

think you're suited to the position of registrar at the Pennsylvania Antiquarian Society?"

"It's Ben, please. I've got an undergrad degree in history, and ten years in data management for the US Army. I'd just gotten out, hadn't even started looking for something new, when this happened." He waved at his legs. "But the rest of me still works fine."

"Thank you for telling me. I never know these days which questions are politically incorrect and which ones you could sue me for. Are you from Philadelphia?"

I was willing to discount his hostile entrance—he was having a hard time dealing with being in a wheelchair, both physically and psychologically. Once he started talking, Ben relaxed and became a much more pleasant person. He was intelligent and well-informed about computer issues—or at least, better than I was. And he knew something about history and the local scene. Mobility wasn't really an issue for the position, except for retrieving files off a high shelf now and then, but someone could help out with that. Could he maneuver through the stacks? Easy enough to find out. We already had handicapped access to enter the building from the side street. I decided I liked him.

"You considering other people?" he asked after several minutes.

"To be honest, we had a fair number of applicants for the position because of the general economy, but most of them don't have the credentials. You're the best qualified by any standard. Let me bring in my VP for collections, Latoya Anderson. The position reports to her."

I picked up the phone and punched in Latoya's number.

"Latoya, could you come to my office for a moment? I'd like you to meet a candidate for the registrar position."

She appeared thirty seconds later—not hard, since her office was just down the hall. "You might have given me some warning, Nell."

"I would have, but I was as surprised as you. Latoya, meet Ben Hartley. He's applying for the registrar position. Before you ask, no, I haven't seen his résumé."

Latoya appeared bewildered for a moment, looking at Ben and then back at me as if to see if I was joking. Then she pulled herself together and sat down in the chair in front of my desk. "Tell me about yourself, Ben. What interests you in working at a place like this?"

Now that he was warmed up, Ben handled himself well, and I watched the two of them interact, feeling encouraged. Latoya and I had had our disagreements, but she was a professional, and she had the best interests of the Society at heart. I didn't think she'd be petty enough to reject Ben just because I'd been the one to bring him in, and he was responding to all her questions appropriately. After a few minutes, Latoya stood up. "Thank you for coming in, Ben. Nell and I need to discuss your application, but I promise we'll get in touch with you shortly. I'll be down the hall, Nell." She left quickly.

"How'd I do?" Ben asked me.

"Not bad. Could you work with her?"

"She always have a stick up her butt?"

I stifled a snort of laughter. "Yes, she does. But she is good at her job, and she knows the collections."

"Fair enough. Yes, I believe we could work together."

"What do you think of the work? Feel you'd be up to the job?"

He nodded once. "I believe I could handle it, if you'll give me the chance."

"Let me confer with Latoya. But I will call you either way, I promise. Thanks for coming in. Oh, by the way, the job would start, like, yesterday. We are so behind, you would not believe it. Is that a problem?"

"Nope. Except I'd need some time off on a regular basis for rehab sessions."

"We could work that out. I'll see you out." I escorted him out of the office and to the elevator, then called to alert the front desk that he was on his way down so they could take him to the handicapped lift. Then I headed for Latoya's office.

She was at her desk. "What do you think?" I asked.

"He's qualified." She said it with a noticeable lack of enthusiasm, but then, I'd seldom seen Latoya excited about anything. "Where'd he come from?"

"James Morrison recommended him—he's a personal friend of James's. But that doesn't mean we're obliged to hire him, if you object."

"Why would I object? He's the best of the lot so far, or at least he talks a good line, and I have no reason to doubt him. And there's a kind of symmetry—bringing in a guy the FBI recommended to handle a load of stuff that the FBI dumped on us. You want to call him, or shall I?"

"I will. And he's available to start immediately. Do you have time to acquaint him with the software and the collections?"

"I'll make time."

"Latoya, are you sure you don't have any issues with

hiring Ben? I'd rather hear them now than have you looking for him to fail."

She gave me a cold look, but I didn't flinch. Finally she said, "All right, I'll admit I feel as though he's being shoved down my throat. The collections staffing is my responsibility."

"Latoya, I recognize that, and I'm not challenging you here. You've done a good job with attempting to recruit suitable candidates. If Ben can't do the job, he should be treated like any other employee. Agreed?"

Latoya straightened up and looked me in the eye. "Fair enough. I didn't mean to imply—"

I cut her off before she could finish that statement and erase any positive progress we'd made. "Thank you for agreeing to give him a chance."

My, weren't we all sweetness and light? But I wasn't going to complain. And just like that, we'd filled the position. I needed to let James know. Back at my office, I hit the speed dial for him.

"Agent Morrison," he responded crisply. "Oh, sorry. Hi, Nell—I was trying to get back into the routine. What's up? Did Ben call you?"

"Was he supposed to call first? He showed up, interviewed, and it looks like he's hired. Even Latoya seemed to like him. So, thank you. But if he's faking it, it'll be on your head."

"I'm not worried. He's a good guy who's had a hard time lately, but I'm sure he can handle it. You're welcome. I may be home late tonight—lots to catch up on here."

"Oh, about that—Mitchell Wakeman invited me to go tour his development site in Chester County, and I asked if he could drop me off in Bryn Mawr after. Is that all right?"

"So you'll stay out there?" He kept his tone neutral.

"Yes, for tonight." I started to make excuses, like I needed to find some clean clothes, but then I stopped myself. It was still my house, and I wanted a little alone time with it.

"Okay. We can talk tomorrow. Gotta go." He ended the call.

Which left me feeling vaguely unsatisfied. But, hey, I'd said yes to him starting a real estate hunt, hadn't I? I got up and ambled down the hall to Shelby's office.

She was surrounded by stacks of paperwork but looked up when I arrived. "Hey there. Before you ask, I don't have time for lunch if you want me to finish this anytime soon." She waved at the piles in front of her. "You need something?"

I flopped into a chair. "No, not really. Things just seem to be moving awfully fast. In a good way. James sent us a possible registrar candidate, and he's already been interviewed and I think we're offering him the job. Marty says she has a good possibility for the Wakeman research slot, and I'm going to meet her this afternoon. And the man himself invited me to go out and look at the development site this afternoon. Oh, and I told James we could go ahead and look for a bigger apartment."

Shelby sat back in her chair and laughed. "Lady, you weren't kidding when you said things were moving fast! But it *is* all good, isn't it?"

"I think so. I hope so." I hauled myself up out of the chair. "I'll let you get back to work. I'm going to go find a sandwich and wait for Marty's pick of the day to arrive."

I left the building to get a sandwich and was surprised that the streets of the city seemed positively calm compared to the whirlwind that had been my morning. At least things

were falling into place, although it might have been easier if they'd been spread out a little more. But I couldn't complain. I rewarded myself with a bag of potato chips to go with my tuna on rye and ate lunch in the break room at the Society.

Lissa Penrose, Marty's latest find, arrived seven minutes before her scheduled appointment at two. At least I'd had time to finish my sandwich. She turned out to be a tall, self-assured woman who looked to be in her later twenties, with straight, shoulder-length brown hair and glasses that hovered between hip and nerdy. Given what I guessed her age to be, I wondered if she had worked for a while or traveled or done something else before returning to school—she seemed a bit past the usual age, although these days a lot of younger people were returning to school rather than trying to find satisfying work.

I stood up and offered my hand. "Welcome, Lissa. I'm glad you could make it on such short notice."

She shook briefly but firmly. "Thank you for seeing me so quickly."

"Please, sit down. How much did Marty tell you?"

She sat. "Just the outline—that there's a developer who wants to vet a large suburban property before he proceeds with a major development project there, and he wants the Society to review any potential historical problems. I assume he has other people working on other aspects, such as any possible contamination of the site and the water supply."

A smart young woman. "Good heavens, you're already way ahead of me! I hadn't even considered the contamination question. Are you thinking there might be some overlap with the Society's part, if there was an old factory or something on the site?"

"Exactly. We should be prepared to coordinate. If I get the gig, of course."

"Good thinking. So give me the snapshot version of your credentials." Good thing I was in interview mode today.

"Born and raised in the Philadelphia suburbs—north of the city. Went to Juniata as an undergrad. Then my mother got sick, so I spent a couple of years taking care of her. She died last year, and since she left a little money, I applied for a graduate program at Penn and got in. But the money didn't stretch as far as I'd hoped, even with a grant, so something like this would be perfect."

"It is short-term, you know. Three months max."

She nodded. "I know. But Marty gave me an estimate of what it pays, and that would go a long way for me."

"How do you know Marty?"

"I don't, really. I know Ethan—he's my advisor—and I've run into Marty several times in his office. She's like a walking encyclopedia of who's who in Philadelphia, isn't she? Ask her what a particular neighborhood in the city was like in 1840 and she can tell you who lived there and who built the houses on that block. It's amazing."

Either Ethan kept people waiting, or Marty was at his office a lot. "It is a gift, and we're very lucky that she's involved with the Society. You know Philadelphia yourself, obviously. Your undergrad degree was in history?"

"History and urban planning—I hoped to work for the city, in their community redevelopment department, but then life kind of got in the way."

"Have you used the Society's collections before?"

"I have, although not extensively. But this would be a very focused project, wouldn't it?"

"It would." I made a quick decision: she was a good fit. "I don't know if Marty told you, but the developer—by the way, it's Mitchell Wakeman—wants me to see the building site this afternoon. Would you like to tag along?" Why not see how she got on with the person she ultimately had to please?

"Sure, I'd love to. I know something about Chester County, but I can be more efficient about researching it if I'm familiar with the specific part he's looking at. Tell me, what if we do go ahead with the historic assessment and we find something, like that George Washington slept there—could that derail the project?"

I considered her intelligent question before answering. "That's complicated, I think. In undertaking any project like this, I'm sure you know there are a lot of people you have to keep happy—local governments, the federal government, environmentalists, historians, neighbors. How much clout each group has varies a lot, and I don't know if just one of them can put the kibosh on it. They might be able to delay it with lawsuits and the like. Does that worry you?"

"Not really—you're paying a flat fee for the project, not on an hourly basis, right? So even if I've mined all your resources before the three months is up, would I still be paid the full amount?"

"As long as you get the job done and Mitchell Wakeman is satisfied, I don't see why not. But it's his call."

"I know. Right now, I'll take what I can get, and this sure beats waitressing."

"I hope so."

CHAPTER 6

Front Desk Bob announced Mitchell Wakeman's arrival just before three, and the unusual level of respect in his voice suggested that even he knew who he was dealing with. I gathered up my things and, with Lissa trailing behind me, I went down to greet him.

"Mr. Wakeman, good to see you again. Do you have time for a quick tour of the Society?"

He seemed restless, as if the stately grandeur of the Society's lobby made him uncomfortable. From all I'd heard and read, he was pretty much a no-nonsense and hands-on construction guy, so maybe he really didn't feel at home surrounded by all this shiny marble. "Maybe another time. Who's this?" he asked, nodding at Lissa.

"This is Lissa Penrose. We're considering her to fill the researcher position you described to me. With your approval, of course."

Lissa stepped forward and offered her hand. "It's a

pleasure to meet you, Mr. Wakeman. From what Nell has told me, it sounds like you're proposing an ambitious project."

I thought she hit just the right note with the man—respectful without being fawning. Points to her.

"Nothing I can't handle." He turned back to me. "I'll trust your judgment about who to hire—I'm told you know your stuff. You ready to go?"

"Yes. Do you mind if Lissa comes with us? She should see the site, so she knows the context."

"Sure, fine. Let's go—I'm double-parked."

We went out the door. His nondescript sedan was parked directly in front of the steps. No fancy cars or chauffeurs for Mitchell Wakeman, apparently. Silly me, to have expected the trappings of wealth from a multimillionaire developer. I got in front, and Lissa slid into a seat in the back, and then we set off for Chester County.

Wakeman drove efficiently and not overly aggressively, and with the low mid-afternoon traffic we made good time. We engaged in impersonal small talk on the way. I tried to probe discreetly about the man's interest in local history, and he proved reasonably well informed, although not particularly reverent about the past that was still much in evidence around us.

When we reached the suburbs, he said to me, "You live out this way?"

"Yes, I've lived in Bryn Mawr for a while now. I guess I like to keep my work and my life separate. I like to have a place to escape to. I like the contrast. Does that make sense to you?"

"Yeah, sure, I get that."

"You live even farther out, don't you?"

He glanced briefly at me, as if surprised that I knew. "I do, for a lot of the same reasons. Nice country, west of the city. Open space."

"And you're proposing to put a major development in the middle of it? Sorry, I don't mean to be rude—I'm just trying to understand how you see this."

"I understand. I guess the bottom line is, I want to do it right. People are moving out that way, and they're going to need housing. I want to show that it's possible to create a community that has all the things people want, but without dropping it like a flying saucer in the middle of a place and wondering why the people who've lived there for years are pissed about it. I respect the history of the area, and the geography and the ecology."

"That sounds admirable. Are there any other examples of that kind of development?"

He tossed off a couple of names that meant nothing to me. "Thing is, it takes big money to put together the whole package, not just a bunch of houses and a couple of stores in the middle of nowhere. I've got the money, so I can make it happen. Does that sound crude to you?"

Was he smiling? "No, just practical. And I see your point. Trying to do it piecemeal means you run the risk of the whole project losing steam, and then you're left with a half-finished mess."

"Exactly. Almost there." I turned away from him to look out the window and check out where we were and realized we'd reached Paoli, on Route 30, a road I knew well, since it ran close to my house. Past the train station he turned off to the left. "Hey, you in the back—you've been quiet. Do you know where we are?" he asked as we drove along.

Lissa spoke up promptly. "We just left what was once the Philadelphia and Lancaster Turnpike, which was the first incorporated major toll road in the country," she said, just loudly enough to make herself heard. "We're on the Paoli Pike, that leads to West Chester, which became the county seat in 1786. But we're not going that far, are we?" I noted that she pronounced Paoli correctly: pay-o-lee. People who didn't know the region and had only read the name often got it wrong.

Wakeman looked pleased by her response. "Nope, we're stopping just this side of it."

I watched the houses roll by, the space between them increasing the farther we went. I loved this time of year: everything was lush and green, which somehow made it quiet, apart from the cicadas. But inside the car you couldn't hear them. Wakeman drove through a couple more town centers, usually no more than a few public buildings, such as local government offices and post offices, and a scattering of stores. Sometimes it was hard to believe that we were no more than thirty miles from Center City. We passed a sign for a stable, and there were sleek horses grazing in a field by the road. A mile or so farther on, Wakeman turned onto a smaller road on the right, which climbed a hill, then he turned in to an unpaved gravel driveway on the left. A hundred feet farther he stopped the car and turned off the engine. "This is it."

We all climbed out of the car and stood looking out over the rolling hills to the south. I knew the town of West Chester was only a couple of miles down the road, as was a shopping center, but here all was serene and unspoiled.

"Let me show you what we're planning," Wakeman said, after giving us ample time to take it all in.

I looked down at my shoes. I hadn't been planning on a hike when I'd dressed in the morning. "Uh, I don't think I've got the right footwear."

"No problem. I always carry boots in the trunk—a lot of construction sites are muddy. Let's see if we can find something to fit you."

If Mitchell Wakeman had appeared uncomfortable in the venerable rooms of the Society, here he was clearly in his element—expansive, enthusiastic, talkative. He quickly found boots for both Lissa and me, even if our feet slopped around inside the too-large boots, and appeared ready to walk the entire site with us, outlining each detail.

"Before we set out," I said as tactfully as I could manage, "could you tell us about the general layout? How much land are you talking about? Where's the center going to be?"

Wakeman pulled a rolled plan from the trunk and laid it out on the hood of the car. "We're here, at the top of the hill." He pointed to the center of the map.

That much I could have figured out for myself. I looked around me: nice old stone farmhouse at the top; a ramshackle wooden dairy barn just down the hill from the house, with an adjoining tall silo; various dilapidated sheds, whose use I couldn't identify, scattered around. "How much land do you have altogether?"

"About a thousand acres, irregular shape," Wakeman replied promptly. "We plan to build on no more than a third or it in the first phase. We want a mix of housing and open space, plus a buffer zone along the perimeter roads. I've got options on some of the abutting properties if we want to expand in the future."

"A thousand acres?" I said, incredulous. "How on earth did you find a single parcel that big in this day and age?"

"Told you—the Garrett family's been here since seventeen-whatever. Ezra was a great old guy. One of eleven kids. Ran a dairy operation here all his life. I got to know him through a couple of civic organizations we both belonged to. And he was smart. Some people might have figured he'd be sentimental about keeping the old place in the family, but he knew damn well the land was worth more as housing than as a dairy farm. I'd guessed it would come to that, so that's why I approached him. I did tell the kids that I'd keep the old farmhouse as a community center—they liked that."

"The underlying property must have been part of a Penn land grant, although I doubt that the Garretts were the first owners, but I can check," Lissa said suddenly. "Either way, it's amazing that they've kept the land together this long."

"That's the kind of information I'm looking for—Melissa, is it?"

"Lissa," the girl corrected him quietly.

"Lissa, got it. You dig into all that stuff. Great selling point when the houses are built—own a piece of history, going all the way back to William Penn." Wakeman turned away and surveyed his domain. "So, basic facilities up here, kinda behind the hill so you won't see it from the road—market, post office, café, a couple of doctors' offices, bank, that kind of thing. Houses set back, scattered around. We keep the trees when we can, plant some new ones to fill in. No ticky-tacky rows of matching buildings, even for the condos. The lots might be small, but the houses'll be staggered so you aren't looking into your neighbor's bedroom,

you know? My planning people tell me most of the residents, at least in the beginning, won't have children, so no strain on the local schools. Golf course on the far side." He waved vaguely to the east, or maybe it was the north—I couldn't tell. "Hey, it's easier to show you. Follow me."

He struck off up the hill, his long legs leaving us behind. Lissa and I exchanged a look and followed.

Thirty minutes later we had covered what felt like the entire thousand acres, although that might have been a small exaggeration. We'd made a big loop around the perimeter, with Wakeman making grand sweeping gestures all the way. I had to admit the man had a vision for the place, and he seemed committed to doing it right, making the new buildings fit into the landscape. His enthusiasm was obvious, and I admired that; he'd been doing this a long time, and it was heartening to see someone who still enjoyed his work after so many years.

"Let's finish up down by the road—I want you to see how it will look to anyone passing by." He pointed down the hill toward the Paoli Pike, the way we had come in.

It was well after five o'clock, and still hot. I was sticky and sweaty, and my feet hurt. I wanted to go home and take a nice, cool shower. But I also wanted to remain in Mitchell Wakeman's good graces, for the benefit of the Society—besides, he was my ride home, and maybe he could drop Lissa at a train station along the way. I dredged up a smile and said, "Sounds great." Lissa shot me a dirty look, but heck, she was younger than I was, so she couldn't complain.

We dutifully trooped down to the bottom of the hill and looked back up at the skyline. If I squinted, I thought I could see a hint of Wakeman's vision for the place.

He was still talking, energy undiminished. "And like I said, we'll keep a lot of this part as a buffer, maybe halfway up to the ridge there. Keep that nice little pond over there." He pointed. "Scenic. Reeds. Geese sometimes. Besides, it's too wet to build on, so might as well keep it." He stopped suddenly. "What the hell? Nobody's supposed to be dumping there." He took off abruptly toward the pond, loping downhill on his long legs. But when he reached it he stopped and stood staring down at the water. He seemed frozen.

I picked my way through the marshy grass, stumbling a bit in my too-big boots, until I came up beside him and looked down to see what had seized his attention.

I should have guessed that things had gone a bit too well today and I would have to pay the cosmic bill.

Before us bobbed the body of a dead man, facedown in the pond.

For once, it seemed, the industrial titan Mitchell Wakeman was at a loss. "What the . . . ? Who is it?"

"How on earth should I know?" I snapped.

Lissa had finally made her way down to stand beside us. She looked at the pond, and said, "Oh." Then she turned quickly, walked to the edge of the road, and threw up.

I'd been through this before. I pulled out my cell phone and hit 9-1-1.

The good news is, out in the suburbs, where there are lots of small towns, the police station is never far away. The bad news is, because these are small, peaceful towns, there are seldom police officers on staff who have much experience investigating deaths. In five minutes, a squad car arrived and two youngish uniformed cops climbed out. I'll give them credit for doing things correctly, all by the book: they

approached us and looked down at the body and nodded sagely; they asked us who we were and what we were doing there; and then they escorted us back to Wakeman's car and told us to sit there and stay put. Then they walked away so that they were out of earshot, conferred briefly, and made another call.

Five minutes after that, another car arrived, and two more officers climbed out. One was older and clearly had more authority. He spoke briefly with the first officers, then came up to Wakeman, who was leaning against the car with a thousand-mile stare on his face, and introduced himself. His deference suggested that he recognized Wakeman's name if not his face. Then he turned to Lissa and me, and we explained again how we had come to be in an idyllic cow pasture on a fine summer's day, staring at a corpse. Who nobody had yet identified. The cops had wisely left the body right where it was, presumably to avoid mucking up any potential evidence.

"What happens now?" I asked. I had a passing familiarity with Philadelphia procedures, but I wasn't about to assume they were the same here.

"We wait for the coroner," the officer said promptly. "That's who decides if it's an unnatural death and figures out who it is. He'll be here any minute—the county office is right down the road."

For a brief moment I nursed the hope that whoever it was had fallen into the pond (which looked about a foot deep) and drowned. Or chosen a rather unlikely method of suicide, in plain sight of a well-traveled road. I couldn't convince myself that either was likely.

"Will you be handling the investigation?" I asked, more

to make conversation than because I cared. I knew I had nothing to do with this death. I couldn't swear to Wakeman's innocence, but why would he have brought me all the way out here to witness his discovery of the body?

"Depends on what the coroner has to say, and who it is." The senior officer looked over at Wakeman, standing a dozen feet away sucking on a cigarette, and asked, "That's *the* Mitchell Wakeman, right?"

"Sure is," I said.

"What's he doing here?"

"You'll have to ask him." I didn't know what details of the project had gone public, and I wasn't going to talk out of turn.

The coroner arrived. The senior officer conferred with him, and then the pair of them went back to the pond, and the coroner took pictures of the body, the pond, the field, a pretty flower . . . well, probably not that last one, but it seemed that way. I was getting punchy. After the coroner had taken the appropriate photos, he enlisted the assistance of a junior officer and together they extricated the body from the pond, which, as I had guessed, turned out to be shallow but muddy. They laid the body on the grass at the edge of the pond and stared down at it. The coroner shook his head and said something, then knelt and fished a wallet out of the dead man's hip pocket and flipped it open to look at the driver's license. He looked up at the senior officer and nodded, then stood up again.

This was beginning to feel like watching a television show with the sound turned off. Whatever conversation there was was drowned out intermittently by the sound of passing cars, some of which slowed to see what all the activity was

about, only to be shooed on by one of the younger officers. I watched the senior officer walk over to Wakeman and exchange a few words, then the two of them went over to where the body lay, and looked down. Wakeman shook his head; apparently he didn't recognize the man.

Then Wakeman came back to where Lissa and I were still standing. "Sorry to have dragged you into all this," he said.

"Don't be. You didn't have anything to do with it. Did they tell you who the guy was?"

"Local, according to the cop—he's the zoning officer for the township. Which I guess makes it likely that he's tied into the project, because that seems like the only reason he'd be here. Like I said, sorry."

"I'm sorry, too. It's clear this project means a lot to you, and this isn't going to make it any easier. Can we go?"

"Not yet. I think the local cops have decided they're in over their heads, since I'm kind of a public figure, and they've called in some bigger guns, and I talked to some people, too. They should be here shortly, and they may want to talk with us. So we sit tight for now."

I nodded, then turned to Lissa. "You okay?"

She shrugged. "I guess. I've never seen a dead body before, not outside of a hospital. It wasn't quite what I expected."

"I know what you mean." All too well.

We sat for a while, saying nothing. It seemed to incongruous, to be sitting in the midst of the bucolic splendor of a Chester County summer while a body lay on the grass below, discreetly covered with a piece of plastic. We talked sporadically about insignificant things. At some point, Lissa said, "You know, you wouldn't know it to look at it now, but a lot of history took place around here. As I said earlier, that

road down there has been a major road since the late seventeen hundreds. Washington and his hapless troops were all over the place around here, and we're not all that far from Valley Forge." She stopped for a moment, then looked past me and nodded toward an approaching car. "Looks like the cavalry has arrived."

A plain car pulled up behind the police cars and parked. The door opened—and James stepped out.

I didn't know whether to laugh or cry.

CHAPTER 7

We regarded each other across twenty feet of driveway. I felt I had the advantage: I figured the local cops had indeed recognized this death was beyond their scope and had asked the FBI to step in—which they had every right to do—so seeing an FBI agent here was not altogether surprising. What the odds were that James would pick up that case, and that he'd find me here in the middle of yet another murder investigation, I couldn't begin to guess. For a brief, wistful moment, I wondered if this was where I was supposed to sob gracefully and fling myself into his manly arms and let him comfort me, but I stifled it. We were both here as professionals and should act accordingly.

He made the first move. Wakeman and the senior cop were deep in conversation a few yards down the hill, so James approached me first.

"I don't believe it," he said in a low voice. "What are you doing here?"

"Getting a grand tour of the proposed development site from the developer himself." I nodded down the hill at Wakeman. "What are you doing here?"

"The local police put in a call for help, but I'm pretty sure it was your developer pal who asked. Whoever caught the call thought a nice suburban death would be a soft entry back into the game for me, so I got sent. It never occurred to me that you'd be involved." He leaned back, because Lissa had come up behind us.

I made the introduction. "Lissa, this is Special Agent James Morrison, from the FBI. He's been called in to help out the local police with the investigation. James, this is the person Marty recommended to handle Wakeman's research into this site. Although she may not be interested after today." Dealing with dead bodies—recent ones, at least—had not been part of the job description.

"Good to meet you, Agent Morrison. I take it you know Nell?" Lissa asked, her composure returned.

"Uh, yes, we're . . . we've . . ." James fumbled for an answer.

I rescued him by saying, "I'll fill you in later, Lissa. James, don't you need to check in with the local authorities?"

"I do. I assume they told you to stick around?"

"Yes, since we discovered the body. And Wakeman was our ride, anyway."

"We'll sort it out." James turned away and started down the hill to where the main players were gathered, waiting.

"I can't wait to hear the story," Lissa said drily as she watched him go.

I was torn between admiration for her observational skills and an urge to swat her, and say, "Hands off, he's

mine." Very mature of me. I settled for "We might as well sit down to wait—this may take a while."

We sat in Wakeman's car, leaving the doors open, our feet pointing downhill, and watched the machinery of a police investigation grind along. "You said something about being involved in murder investigations? Do you know what happens now?" Lissa asked, indicating the police.

"Well, I've only seen things from the civilian side, but I'll tell you what I know. The coroner's here and he's identified the body and apparently declared the death a crime, since they called for reinforcements. That means there will be an autopsy to determine the exact cause of death and when it happened. Then they'll start interviewing people. Apparently, the victim is a local guy, so they'll start with his wife, if he had one, his colleagues and friends around here, and then anyone who might have wanted him dead."

"Sounds logical enough. Why did they call in the FBI?"

"Manpower, for one—most police departments don't have a lot of staff these days. Access to information, for another—the FBI can look at phone records, financial information, all that stuff, a lot more quickly. They've got better forensic facilities, too. And I'd guess that the fact that Mitchell Wakeman is involved means there'll be more public attention to this, even if he had nothing to do with it, so I'm going to guess the locals are covering their butts."

"You think the project will go forward?"

It seemed a little early to ask, but Lissa was probably worried about this job opportunity drying up. "I'd guess yes. Unless someone can prove that Wakeman committed the crime himself or had direct knowledge of it, both of which seem unlikely. He's probably looked into most of the history

carefully already. He just wants our official seal of approval—not that I'm suggesting you sugarcoat whatever you find. He seems very heavily invested in this project, and I don't mean just financially."

"I agree—he seemed really enthusiastic when he was showing it off. I like his vision for this place," Lissa said.

I watched Mitchell Wakeman talking to the group of police and James; he was remarkably patient. "I'd like to think he's honest and he really does care, but I can't say that I know him well. Look, if you'd like to back out now, I'd understand."

Lissa smiled, more to herself than to me. "No, I'm good with it. It's a shame about that poor man, but after all, it isn't the first time people have died here, and we had nothing to do with his death."

We fell silent again. The shadows were lengthening and swallows were swooping above the meadow, snagging slow-flying insects. I watched James at work. He seemed to have things well in hand. He was talking to the officers, but he appeared neither too deferential nor too assertive. He knew he was on their turf and he didn't want to create any more friction than necessary, but somehow he managed to make it clear that he was in charge without ruffling any feathers. It didn't seem like his reentry into work was proving too taxing, I was glad to see.

I just wished I didn't have quite such an up-close-and-personal view of it.

I watched as the coroner's van loaded up the covered body and sped off toward West Chester, then James and the local police chief conferred with Wakeman. After a lot of nodding, the group split up, with James and Wakeman coming toward us. Lissa and I stood up.

"Ladies," Wakeman said, "I know you probably have questions, but I need some time to think about how this is going to proceed. I didn't expect anything like this. Agent Morrison says he'll see to getting you two home, so I'll leave now. I'll be in touch."

"I understand," I said—and I did. "I hope everything works out for the best."

We stepped away from his car, and Wakeman pulled out. Thirty seconds later I saw his car on the Paoli Pike below, headed toward West Chester.

"What now?" I asked James.

"Have either of you eaten?" he said.

"Uh, it's been a while. I'd ask you both back to my place, but I don't think I have any food."

"I hear the Iron Hill Brewery in West Chester is nice," James said. "We can eat, and then I'll take both of you home."

"Deal," I said.

It took us no more than five minutes to reach the restaurant, and we even found a parking space on the street. Inside, the place was comfortably filled, but we got a table quickly and ordered a locally brewed ale and exotic pizzas all around. When the waitress left to fill our orders, I asked, "How much can you tell us? Or can't we talk about this?"

"You were on the scene before I was, obviously." James looked around carefully, but there were few people in earshot, and they all seemed deep in conversation with their tablemates. "How did Wakeman react when you all found the body?"

"You mean, did he set us up to witness his reaction? I doubt it. As far as I could tell he was honestly surprised—he started out annoyed that somebody was dumping stuff on

his site, until he got closer and realized what it was we were looking at. He seemed pretty legitimate to me."

"Did he recognize the victim?"

"I don't think so. I think the coroner told him who it was. Why? Is there some reason he should have known the guy?"

"What was the man's name?" Lissa asked.

"George Bowen, a township employee in charge of land use and zoning, among other things."

Lissa and I exchanged a look. "Do you know if he was involved in Wakeman's project?" I asked.

"On some level, probably, though it seems highly unlikely that the head of a major corporation would be talking directly to a small-town local official—Wakeman's probably got about eight layers of people to do that. On the other hand, we can't dismiss it altogether."

"Are the police handling the local interviews?" I asked.

"They were going to talk to Bowen's wife—some of them know her, and they live close by. They'll talk to his township colleagues in the morning. They're better equipped to handle that than I am, but I may sit in."

"What was the cause of death?" I prompted.

"According to the coroner, a blow to the head, possibly in combination with being strangled, and his best guess before an autopsy was sometime late last night—certainly after dark. And before you ask, we don't yet know if it happened where he was found or somewhere else. We'll be sending a couple of our forensic people over."

"So if this man was hit on the head *and* strangled, he was murdered?" Lissa asked. "How awful." We all grew quiet. I surprised myself by reaching out and taking James's hand; he in turn looked startled, then smiled and clasped it in his.

We kind of lost a few moments looking at each other. "I'm glad you're here," I said quietly.

Lissa was watching us with some amusement. "So, Agent Morrison, Marty tells me you're her cousin?" she said, shifting conversational gears. As well she should, for all our sakes.

"Yes, but don't ask me to explain how," James said. We all laughed, then kept the conversation on lighter topics and away from murder.

Our pizzas appeared and we dug in happily. I hadn't realized how hungry I was, but everything tasted good. It was full dark when we finally emerged from the restaurant, and we hadn't worked out who was going where. I had said I wanted some alone time at my house—but that was before we'd stumbled into another murder. But now there was Lissa to consider. So I saw three choices: James took me home and deposited me on my doorstep, then took Lissa back to the city; the three of us crashed at my place, which would definitely be a strain on my hospitality; or we stuck Lissa on a late train and had some personal time together, which seemed kind of unfair to Lissa, who had seen the same body that I had and had every right to be upset. Why did all this have to be so complicated?

In the end, James made the decision. "Let me take you home, Nell, and then I'll take Lissa back with me. Where do you live, Lissa?"

"Near Penn," she said. "But I could take a train."

James brushed off her offer. "That's near me, so it's no bother. Nell, does that work for you?"

What could I do but agree? I'd asked for space, and I was going to get it. "That's fine."

Late in the evening, it took no more than half an hour to reach my house. I got out of the car and was surprised when James did, too. "I'll walk you to your door," he said.

The door was ten feet away. But it was dark. I hadn't been home in ages, so I'd left no lights on. James took my arm and guided me to it, and waited while I found my keys. Then he looked at me and said softly, "You all right?"

I nodded. "Yes. It wasn't . . . awful, and I didn't know the man. Maybe I'm getting jaded, after what we've been through. But thanks for asking."

James leaned in and kissed me, the kiss gentle, warm. Then he broke it off, sooner than I might have liked. "I'll talk to you in the morning."

"Hey, are you all right yourself? First case and all? Maybe, since I'm in the middle of it, you should step back?"

"That doesn't worry me—and it has nothing to do with us, right? You're just a bystander this time. Good night, Nell." He turned and went back to his car, and like a schoolgirl I watched as he drove off until I could no longer see him.

Then I let myself in to my dark, empty house. It was very quiet, and once I turned on the lights I could see it was also rather dusty. When had I last spent any time there? Weeks, at least. I stalked to the tiny kitchen and opened the refrigerator: pathetic. I filled a glass with peach iced tea and wandered around while I drank it.

I could have gone with James and Lissa, back to the city, back to James's apartment. Why hadn't I? Did I value my independence more than my relationship with a great guy? Where would that leave me in forty years? Sure, there were no guarantees in life, and an FBI agent was always in danger, more or less—as I knew only too well. But being scared

of possible negative outcomes in the distant future was a stupid reason to avoid living life in the now.

Well, I'd said yes to finding a place together, hadn't I? Okay, maybe it was a qualified, halfhearted sort of yes, but it was still a yes. He understood—I thought. Now all we had to do was find a place that made us both happy—and I had no idea what that would be.

I took that much-needed shower and went to bed. Alone.

CHAPTER 8

The next morning I woke surprisingly early, given the events of the prior day, and lay in bed reviewing what was going on. I should have checked with Latoya to confirm whether Ben Hartley, our new registrar, would be starting today. I had no way of gauging whether his military computer skills would translate to cataloging antique items and documents, but data was data, wasn't it? And James had recommended him—shoot, yesterday we'd been too distracted to talk about Ben. I reminded myself to find out a bit more about Ben's backstory and how he and James had kept in touch.

I couldn't do much about Lissa's position until I knew if there would actually be a need for it now, and under the circumstances I wasn't about to badger Mitchell Wakeman about that. But I meant what I had said to Lissa the day before: this planned development was a big project, and unless all evidence pointed directly to Wakeman or a member of his project

crew, it probably wouldn't derail the project. Of course, that assumed the murder was solved and the killer identified sooner rather than later. Lissa had seemed surprisingly calm throughout the whole experience—after she'd thrown up. And she was observant. Of course, being able to read people wasn't quite the same as being able to read documents, but her apparent competence was reassuring.

Okay, moving on. James had said he was going to start the process of finding a new place for us to live—of course, that had been before he'd been assigned to the Wakeman case. Did I want to get involved in house or apartment hunting? Well, maybe first we should pin down what we were looking for. I liked living in the suburbs: I liked the privacy of a freestanding house; I liked the open space; I liked being someplace that was away from work. I liked having choices for commuting. James lived in the city, in an apartment. Would he want to stay in the city? Style-wise, my little carriage house was late Victorian, and while I hadn't gone overboard with decorating it in a true Victorian spirit, I liked that it was older and had a history of its own. James's apartment was definitely modern, stark, rectilinear. Where would we find a middle ground?

Enough. I jumped out of bed and started my day.

I arrived at the Society early, at least compared to recent days, but Eric had beaten me to the office anyway. "Mornin', Nell. Coffee?"

Eric and I had long since worked out a coffee agreement: whoever arrived first made the first pot. "Sure. Did I miss anything yesterday afternoon?"

"While you were out finding bodies?"

"Shoot, did it make the papers already? How did they find out so fast? It was only the one body."

"Since Mr. Wakeman was involved, it did—you know he's news. Speaking of whom, he's already called this morning."

"Did he want me to call him back?"

"No, he left a message, and I quote: 'Project is a go. Lissa can start ASAP.' Make sense to you?"

"It does. That's good news, I think. A man of few words, isn't he? But decisive. So we will have a new, short-term intern. Can you figure out what paperwork we'll need? Funding will come from Wakeman or some subsidiary of his, and it's a term appointment—three months."

"Will do. Right after I get you that coffee. Oh, and Latoya said that other new hire would be starting day after tomorrow."

Bless Eric. I'd hired him because Shelby knew him, and he was a nice kid and needed a job, but he had far surpassed my expectations. By now I couldn't imagine running my office without him.

Coffee in hand, I settled myself in my office and contemplated where to begin. I should call Lissa, but I wasn't sure if I had her phone number. Should I call Ethan at Penn to get it? I didn't have his phone number, either, although that should be public information. Marty would know it, though . . .

As if by magic, Marty materialized at my door. "Someday I'll figure out how you do that, Marty," I said. "I was just thinking about you."

Marty dropped into a chair. "Good things, I hope. How'd Lissa work out?"

"What, you haven't heard?"

"Heard what?"

"We went out to see the site yesterday and found a body. Eric said it was in the paper."

"You've got to be kidding! No, I haven't had a chance to look at the paper this morning. This was a body on Wakeman's patch?"

I nodded. "It was. The three of us were walking the grounds and we found him in a pond."

"Anybody know who he is?"

"Apparently an official with the township there. You don't have any friends or family in Goshen, do you?"

"Maybe. Old neighborhood, there—mostly Quaker, way back when. What was the guy's name?"

"George Bowen, I think. James will know."

"Why?"

"Because the local police called in the Mounties, and he got the case."

Marty laughed heartily. "You're kidding! I would've loved to see that little meeting! They really think they need the FBI out there?"

"I think that was Wakeman's involvement. You know he wants only the best."

Marty gave one of her ladylike snorts. "What's your take on Wakeman, now that you've spent some time with him?"

"Overall I'm impressed. He seemed like a straight-arrow guy, I guess. Not at all pretentious. He was really excited about this development project of his, and happy to show it off. At least, until we found the body."

"Did Wakeman know the dead guy?"

"He said not."

Marty shot me a look, and I wondered if I had sounded more skeptical than I intended. But she didn't pursue it. "So, you took Lissa along on this little jaunt?"

"Yes. I thought it made sense—she could get a feeling

for the physical lay of the land. And I wanted to see how she got along with Wakeman, although they probably won't run into each other again."

"What did you think of her?"

Something in Marty's tone made me look more carefully at her. "She's smart, and she's very calm—didn't panic about the body, and she asked intelligent questions. She was older than I expected, but she explained that she'd taken some personal time off before going back to school. Wakeman okayed her. How did you come to recommend her?"

"I met her at Ethan's office, and he said good things about her. And she needs the money."

Marty sounded a bit abrupt, even for her. In the time I'd known her, Marty hadn't been involved with anyone, or at least not seriously. And she'd kind of hidden her involvement with Ethan, although since I'd been a little preoccupied, I could have missed the signs. Was she worried that Ethan had some interest in Lissa? I felt I was treading on shaky ground with my next question—although Marty had never hesitated to involve herself in my private life, I rationalized. "Do Ethan and Lissa have a history?"

Marty shrugged. "Maybe. I haven't asked."

"Okay," I said cautiously. "But you have no problem if the Society hires her for this project for a couple of months?"

"Nope. If Ethan vouches for her, she'll do a good job." Marty's tone made it clear that she wasn't going to comment further.

"Fine. Do you know where I can reach her? I want to tell her the project is moving forward."

"Sure." Marty pulled a scrap of paper out of her pocket and scribbled a number on it, then handed it to me. "That's

Ethan's office—his assistant should know where to find Lissa."

"Thanks. Was there something else?"

"When's your registrar showing up?"

"Day after tomorrow. I left it to Latoya to deal with the formalities, since he'll be working for her." I did a double take. "Wait, how did you know we'd made an offer?"

"James told me that he was thinking of recommending Ben and asked if I thought Ben could handle the job."

"Hang on. You know Ben, too? Why was there any question about whether he could handle the job?"

"I don't know him personally. James wanted to know what the job requirements were. Ben's had a rough time since the accident, and he hasn't worked lately, which looks bad on his résumé. But he's smart and hardworking, and he'll want to prove himself."

"Will he fit in here?"

Marty smiled. "With this crew of misfits? I wouldn't worry. Just don't expect him to be real sociable."

I sighed. But at least the registrar position didn't require a whole lot of social interaction, just computer skills and a good eye. And as for those, anyone I hired would have to demonstrate them directly, whatever his or her baggage and background. "Ask Latoya about his start date. And don't co-opt him to do all the Terwilliger stuff first."

"Would I do that?" Marty said, batting her eyes with exaggerated innocence. She stood up. "I'm going back to the processing room, by way of Latoya's office. See you later."

She had no sooner walked out the door when Shelby appeared. Good thing I hadn't planned to get anything like work done this morning. "Hi, Shelby—what's up?"

Shelby took the chair that Marty had vacated. "You've got a new corpse, I hear."

"Did my name come up in the paper?" I asked, almost afraid to find out.

"Nope, but Mr. Wakeman's did, and I knew where you were going yesterday afternoon, so I put two and two together. How many does this make?"

"Too many. And to top it off, James caught the case when the FBI was called in to help."

"My, my—just like old home week. What is the great Wakeman like?"

"Surprisingly normal, for a multimillionaire mogul. He seems to like what he does, and he had a great time showing us his plans for the place."

"So this body in the pond won't slow the project down?"

"Apparently not, according to him, because we have the go-ahead to start the historic research on the site. Best case, the murder investigation will be wrapped up quickly and we'll do the research here and give him a gold star and everything will go as planned." That had to happen sometime, didn't it?

"Let's hope so. They're sure it's not an accident?"

"So the coroner says."

"What a shame," Shelby said, then pivoted the conversation away from murder to ordinary Society business.

After she left I tried to remember what I'd originally planned for the day. I heard the phone ring, then Eric call out, "Agent Morrison for you."

I picked up. "Hello. Is this official business?"

"Just wanted to see if you had time for lunch. I can bring sandwiches."

"A working lunch? Sure. Here?"

"One?"

"Okay. Uh, there isn't a problem with anything, is there? Have you solved yesterday's murder?"

I could hear him chuckle. "I may be good, but I'm not that good. I just wanted to touch base with you. See you at one." He hung up, leaving me slightly confused. But that was a state I was used to.

"Eric?" I called out. "I'm having a quick lunch with Agent Morrison at one, here in the building. You have something to keep me busy until then?"

He appeared in my doorway with a sheaf of papers. "Sure do."

CHAPTER 9

At one, I went downstairs to let James in. I was beginning to wonder if I might as well go ahead and give him a key, since he was at the Society so often. He arrived on time carrying a bulky bag. I had to admit he was looking good, considering what he'd been through over the past month. Concussions were sneaky, and sometimes left nasty aftereffects, but he hadn't complained. It was back to business as usual.

But the old, serious James was back, and I realized how much I would miss the warm, funny James now that he was back to work.

We decided to eat in the first-floor conference room, which was usually empty. After we had doled out food, I asked, "Are you okay?"

"Why wouldn't I be?" he responded.

"First day back and a lot of running around yesterday. You got thrown into the deep end pretty fast."

"I'm fine, Nell. Really. I wanted to talk about yesterday, and what we've learned."

"By the way, Wakeman called early this morning and left a message, and said that the project was still on. Is that true?"

James took a large bite of his sandwich. "Close enough. It's not as though the township called a meeting last night and hashed it all out, but I gather the relevant parties put together a conference call and decided that the project was important to the community and, barring any legal issues, it would go forward as planned."

"You think Wakeman leaned on them?"

"I don't know, but I don't know if it would have been necessary in any case. You want the details on the dead man?"

"Please." I picked up my sandwich and started eating, chewing while I listened.

He opened a file but rattled off the key points without looking at it. "George Bowen, age fifty-seven. Engineer by training. Lived in the township and worked for them for about ten years. Wife who works in West Chester. Two kids, both married and living out of state. Volunteered for a lot of civic activities. Interested in local history. All-around nice guy, from what everybody says."

"Do you believe 'everybody'?" I made air quotes as I said the last word.

"No reason not to."

"So nobody had a reason to want him dead."

"Not that we've found, but it's been only a day."

"Have your forensic guys done their bit yet?"

"At first light this morning. Mr. Bowen did not die at the pond but somewhere else yet to be determined."

"How do you know this?"

"There's no evidence of a struggle or an attack in the area around the pond, which would have held impressions since the ground around there is soft and damp. There are, however, some interesting footprints leading up to the pond, but they couldn't follow them through the grass to the point of origin."

"So you're saying someone carried George Bowen to the pond?"

"You do ask all the right questions. Yes, he was carried. He weighed about one eighty, so it would have taken a strong man to carry him without dragging, and there are no signs that he was dragged—that we would have seen."

"Obviously the field isn't exactly well lit. Could a strong man have slung the body over his shoulder and carried him across the field from somewhere else? In the dark?"

"Like a fireman's carry? Maybe."

My questions just kept bubbling up. "Why the pond? I mean, it's kind of close to the road. Anyone driving by would have noticed someone dumping a body there."

"It would have to have been in the middle of the night, when it was darkest, and there was the least traffic. That squares with what the coroner said about time of death. Still, getting him there had to be quick. You're right—nobody could stroll around with a body and expect not to be noticed for long. As for your first question, so far all we know is that the pond is not where he died. You saw for yourself that it's not deep enough to hide a body, so maybe the body was dumped there simply to distract our attention."

"So you've narrowed the search to a strong man. Does that help?"

"Not a lot," James said cheerfully. He must have been used to it. "His wife came home about six but he wasn't there. She wasn't surprised, because the township holds a lot of after-hours meetings, and sometimes they run over into dinner. She ate and watched television for a while. She was mildly worried when he wasn't back by the time she went to bed, but not enough to act on it. I gather it's happened before."

"Did they have problems?"

"Not that she'd admit, but she was obviously upset, and people under those circumstances usually fall back to the 'don't speak ill of the dead' mode. No doubt the police will be talking with her again."

"So he could have been having an affair, and maybe the other woman's spouse or boyfriend or whatever found them together and went ballistic?"

"It's a possibility, but there's no evidence. Yet. But it's early days."

"And that's all you've got?"

James gave me a smile tinged with exasperation. "Nell, this happened yesterday, and we've just started. But, yes, there's nothing obvious jumping out. The guy lived within his means, had a small balance remaining on his mortgage. His kids are happily married and solvent. No unexplained money coming in or going out of his bank account, no overextended credit cards. If he wasn't dead, he'd be a model citizen."

"But he is dead. So what happens now?"

"We continue to investigate. If we don't turn up anything on George, we look at people who might have something at stake in this property, or in the development going forward. People in the township, or in any other townships that might

have been competing for the project. People on Wakeman's management team. We'll keep widening the circle and digging deeper."

"Sounds like archeology, doesn't it? That reminds me, what about the research on the history of the site?"

"What about it?"

"Should we—Lissa or the Society—be looking for anything that might provide a motive?"

"Ah, Nell—things aren't always all about the Society, or history, or you."

I was stung, oddly enough. "Hey, I was there, remember? At the same time that this guy coincidentally ended up dead in the pond when Mitchell Wakeman was showing off his dream project to a pair of wonky historical researchers. Are you saying to ignore any historical information that might be relevant? Without even knowing what it is?"

"I'm sorry, I didn't mean to hit a nerve. No, I won't rule out a connection, but I'm not going to make any assumptions about it, either. Is that fair?"

"I guess," I grumbled. This was stupid. I was not a crime investigator; I managed a building full of history investigators. Past and present did not often collide, and when they did, they seldom resulted in corpses. But it was unsettling nonetheless.

"I missed you last night," James said softly.

"Me, too. You got rid of Lissa?"

"Are you jealous that I went home with a younger woman?" He smiled.

"No, not really. If anything"—I leaned in close—"I'm guessing Marty thinks Lissa's got her eye on Ethan. But don't you dare tell her I said that."

James raised one hand, and said solemnly, "I am an agent of the federal government. I know how to keep secrets."

"This is Marty we're talking about."

"There is that. But you don't have to worry, Nell. We're good, you and I."

"We are." At least, I hoped so. Oh, how I hoped so.

"But you've got to remember, Nell, that what I've told you today has to remain between us. I shared it with you only because you're already involved, so you have a right to know at least some of the details."

"What if Lissa asks questions? She was there, too."

"Just tell her you don't know anything beyond what's in the papers and that it's an ongoing investigation, which is true."

"Speaking of which, how did the papers get onto it so fast?"

"I can't say for sure," James said, "but it's possible that Wakeman and his people put the story out there to make sure they look transparent."

That was an angle I hadn't considered. "What about Marty?"

James looked pained. "Why would she stick her nose into this?"

"Because she's Marty. Are you going to swear there wasn't a Terwilliger living in West Chester in seventeen-whatever?"

"No. If she asks for details, just point her to me, okay?"

"I'll be happy to." Enough about the crime, since there wasn't much information to go on—yet. "So, what's the story on Ben? Or can't you talk about that without breaking all sorts of confidences?"

He sat back and thought for a moment before answering. "Look, I know there are a lot of things you as an employer can't ask or consider in hiring someone, at least in theory. I know you well enough to know that your main goal is to find someone who can do the job for the Society."

"Why are you dancing around the question? Is there something that I should know that I'm not supposed to ask about?"

He sighed. "Not exactly. Okay, you already know that I met Ben in college. We weren't exactly best friends, but we hung out together, along with some other guys. After college he joined the army and stayed on for quite a while, as a number cruncher, an analyst, not a combatant. Then he left, and he was trying to figure out where he fit in the private sector, and then the accident happened—by the way, it wasn't his fault. He got T-boned by a drunk and ended up in the hospital for a while and then in rehab. He's understandably bitter about it. I'll tell you in confidence that he's had trouble adjusting to civilian life in a wheelchair—he used to be an active guy. What he needs most right now is to have a job, one that lets him feel useful and productive again. He's smart and he's got the skills, and I think he can do what you need here. But there may be some speed bumps along the way, because this is far from a military organization."

I had to smile at that. "You think? Thank you for telling me, and you know I'll keep it to myself. I might have to share this with Latoya, but I will only if I think it's necessary."

"Don't handle him with kid gloves, Nell," James said. "Let him do the job. Just give him a little time to settle in, okay?"

"Of course." I gathered up my lunch trash and stuffed it back into the original bag. "Was there anything else?"

"Where will you be tonight?"

"Where do you want me to be?"

"With me."

So simple. Shouldn't it be? "Okay. Dinner?"

James smiled. "I brought lunch. You can figure out dinner."

"Deal."

And we went our separate ways, slowed only by a rather steamy kiss before we emerged from the old conference room.

CHAPTER 10

When I got back to my office, I found Lissa there waiting for me, chatting with Eric. "Hi, Lissa," I greeted her cheerfully. "How come you're here? Did you hear?"

"Ethan asked me to check some references for him. Hear what?" she asked.

"Wakeman wants to go ahead with the project—he apparently isn't the type to let a little problem like a dead body stand in the way of progress. Was that why you're here?"

"I'll admit I wanted to know if you'd heard anything. Does that mean I can get started? "

"Come on in and we can talk about where we go from here. Eric, did you manage to figure out what paperwork we need? Mr. Wakeman and his crew may have plenty of money, but that doesn't mean they pay their bills on time, and I'd rather get this on his desk before he gets distracted." *By more than a body*, I added to myself. But busy men were

busy men, and I should send paperwork to him before he forgot who we were and what he'd asked us to do—and what he'd promised to do for us.

"On your desk, Nell."

"Thank you. Lissa, come on in."

She followed me into my office and took the chair I pointed to. "I should start by asking, are you okay?" I asked.

"What do you mean?" she replied, looking confused.

I sat down behind my desk. "Well, after finding the body yesterday. Sometimes you think you're fine at the time, but it catches up with you later. I won't hold it against you if you want to back out, after what you saw."

She looked down at her hands briefly, then back at me. "It's not a problem, really. I mean, I know I threw up, but after that I found the whole procedural part kind of interesting. I hope you don't think that makes me weird or something."

I thought I'd reserve judgment on that for now. People cope with traumatic events in different ways, and if Lissa's way was to observe details in order to distance herself, that was fine with me.

"Besides," she went on, "I really do need the money."

"I understand. Mr. Wakeman seems to approve of you, so I'll get the paperwork in the pipeline as soon as possible. So tell me, how do you plan to approach this? I don't intend to interfere with however you want to do it, but I'm curious. You should know up front that I got into this field via fund-raising, so I wasn't trained as a historian or a researcher. I don't always know all the details."

Lissa nodded once. "Okay. As I understand it—before having done any real research—Mr. Wakeman bought a thousand acres of Chester County farmland that has been

continuously owned and managed by the same family since the seventeen hundreds. I'm sure he's got a small army of real estate lawyers who have done title searches to make sure the title is clear. I would review all of those, because who knows? Sometimes modern lawyers don't understand the language of seventeenth-century deeds. Just double-checking, plus I can give Wakeman a nice folder of reproductions of all the original documents, even if all he does with them is use them for PR and impressing the homebuyers."

"Do I detect some cynicism?"

She shrugged. "Maybe. But this is the modern world, and nobody's going to buy that land just to keep the pretty views. I'd rather see Wakeman follow his vision than watch another cookie-cutter development go up."

"I agree, for what it's worth. So, say you've made sure the title is clear—what next?"

"I think I mentioned that it's worth checking for any old factories or trades that occupied any part of the farm. For example, early paint factories left a lot of nasty chemicals in the soil, and remediation is expensive. And there are other polluters. Again, he's probably covered all that, but sometimes nobody recognizes the hazards from a factory that's not even there anymore."

"Okay," I said cautiously. I was way out of my depth here, but it all sounded interesting. "You're familiar with the Duffy's Cut story?"

"The Irish cholera victims? Of course. Really sad. But that should have nothing to do with the Garrett property—the railroad is a couple of miles away."

"But what about other historical events? I guess my question in this context would be: what kind of archeological

discovery could delay the project? Say, the equivalent of an ecologist finding that some rare and unique tree frog has made its sole habitat in the middle of the property?"

"My guess is that's Mr. Wakeman's primary concern, or at least why he invited the Society to the party. He can hire plenty of biologists and pollution experts, so my task is to look at the history of the place. As I said, I'd start with the deeds. And then I'd start looking at contemporary accounts in local collections. Here at the Society, of course, but a lot of things still hide out in other institutions. And even if they've been transcribed, there are often things that are missing or misinterpreted, so it's best to see the real documents. I'm sure the people at the Chester County Historical Society will help."

I nodded in approval. "I would think so. I've heard they've got good people there. It all sounds great, Lissa—exactly what Mr. Wakeman needs. Let's hope there are no more unpleasant surprises. Will three months be long enough?"

"I think so, unless I have to travel. But most of the materials should be right here. Thanks for giving me the chance, Nell."

"You're qualified, and better yet, you're here on the spot. And you've already started."

"Thank you." She cleared her throat. "If you don't mind my saying so, I read some of the online reports about other . . . complications you've been involved in."

"And yet you came back?" I said in mock horror. "I'm sorry that my abysmal luck seems to be slopping over to this project."

"Not your fault, is it? How could you have known there would be a body there?"

"Thank you for the vote of support. I really was hoping that this would be a clean-and-simple project, but I should know better by now."

"That's okay. The history will still be there waiting, no matter what happened to that poor man. And no doubt Mr. Wakeman has enough pull to see that it's all cleared up as quickly as possible. All quite legally, I'm sure."

I couldn't argue with that. "You want me to show you around the office, introduce you to the rest of the people you're likely to run into here?"

"Sure, that would be great."

Outside my office, Eric stopped me. "Latoya confirms Mr. Hartley will be starting tomorrow morning. You want to see him then?"

"Sure. I'll see if Latoya has shown him around. He'll have to figure out the software for himself, because I'm clueless about it, but he can ask her. You can go ahead and set up a time, unless I've got something else scheduled that I don't know about."

"Will do, Nell."

I guided Lissa in the direction of the processing room, where the collections and items that needed to be cataloged were kept, awaiting attention. It was a large, open space with shelving around the perimeter and large tables in the center of the floor. Normally it was a comfortable space, but since the FBI had deposited what could be years' worth of items seized under a wide range of circumstances and had asked us to figure out exactly what they had, the space had become a lot more crowded. I pushed open the doors, led Lissa in, and gave her a minute to scope it out.

Interns Rich and Alice were already in the cataloging

area. Ben would sort of be their boss, officially responsible for cataloging and entering all collections into our electronic database.

"Rich, Alice, meet Lissa Penrose," I said when I had their attention. "She'll be working on a short-term project looking into the history of the land for Mitchell Wakeman's Chester County development project." It wasn't like the project was exactly secret anymore, since George's Bowen's murder had been splashed all over the news media.

"Hey, Lissa," Rich said, raising a hand in greeting. "Whoa—that the place where they found the body yesterday?"

Just as I'd guessed. "That's it. And before you ask, yes, Lissa and I were there, along with Mr. Wakeman." I moved on quickly. "Rich, if you come across any references to the Garrett farm or Goshen among the Terwilliger stuff, please pass it on to Lissa. Oh, and I don't know if Latoya has told you yet, but we've filled the registrar position. Ben Hartley should be starting here tomorrow—I'll check with Latoya and let you know if that changes. I hope you'll help him out, because I don't think he's worked in a cultural institution before, although he knows computers and information management. But most of his experience is military." I debated about explaining more, like his accident, but decided to let Ben work things out for himself.

"Will I have some place to set up, or do you want me to work in the reading room?" Lissa asked.

I hadn't thought of that. "Normally I'd say you could snag a space in here, but as you can see it's kind of chaotic. Let me think about it. Anyway, this is where the photographic and scanning facilities are. You have a laptop you can use?"

"Of course. I'll figure something out."

"Are you familiar with our stacks? As an official researcher you'll have full access to them. I'll have to see that you get a key—ask Eric about that. You want a quick tour?" I was asking as much for myself as for her—I always welcomed the chance to prowl the stacks and marvel at the wealth of original materials we had at the Society, and I seldom had enough time to indulge myself.

"Sure," Lissa said promptly. "Rich, Alice, good to meet you. I'll probably see you tomorrow."

We spent a happy hour prowling the stacks. I have to admit I used the stacks tour as kind of a litmus test for new hires. If they wrinkled their noses at the scent of mildew and crumbling leather, I didn't think they'd last long here. I might not be a trained historian, but I loved old books and documents because of the window they gave us into the past. That's why I was willing to fight hard to preserve them and make them available to other people, so that they could share my love of them. An uphill battle, but one worth fighting, I thought. Lissa passed my test with flying colors.

By the time I had escorted Lissa to the front door and seen her off, after getting a key for her and starting her paperwork, it was almost the end of the day. I had promised James I'd be at his place to fix dinner. Somehow I couldn't bring myself to say "home for dinner," because his apartment wasn't home. This was the first day of the new "normal," with both of us working. And if things worked out, that normal would be changing pretty soon—as soon as we found a new place for the two of us. Something we still hadn't talked about in any detail. I found my cell phone in my bag and called him on his, since this wasn't official business.

"Hi," I said when he picked up. "What time will you be . . . back?"

"Sixish, I think—nothing urgent has come up. Why?"

"Just wanted to know what kind of cooking time I have. Maybe I'll stop at the market on the way." The Reading Terminal Market, that is—one of my favorite places in Philadelphia, and one that never failed to cheer me up, not to mention that it gave me great ideas for meals.

"Works for me. See you soon." He hung up. Not exactly warm and fuzzy, but he was in his office.

I left shortly after five, to Eric's surprise. "Both Ben and Lissa will be here tomorrow?" he asked.

"Looks like it. Fully staffed once again, and then some. See you in the morning, Eric."

I walked slowly over to the market. The streets were hot and steamy, although a breeze from the Delaware River blowing up Market Street helped a bit. I plunged into the market, struggling with myself about buying a Bassett's ice cream cone and resisted—which let me give myself permission to buy something luscious for dessert. I picked out meat and fish and a lot of fresh local vegetables, until I figured I couldn't carry any more home. Then I hopped on a Market-Frankford train, which brought me to James's neighborhood. I beat him home, so I started chopping and sautéing and so forth, aided by a glass of wine.

He walked in at six fifteen. "Hi, honey, I'm home."

And I melted into his arms. Playing house did have its moments.

CHAPTER 11

"This is great," James said, as he all but inhaled the dinner I had prepared. He must have been fully recuperated: his appetite was back. "You haven't said much."

I poked what was left of my dinner around the plate. "Just thinking. I'm still getting back into the swing of things at work, and it must be even harder for you. Look, there are some things we should talk about."

"That always sounds ominous," James said cheerfully, as he topped off my wine glass. "Such as?"

Brave man, to jump straight into the fray. I decided to start with a less-personal item. "This case you're on, for one thing. This is all kind of weird. Look, if I didn't happen to be standing in the middle of the crime scene when you arrived, would you have been able to share any information with me? Talk about it at all? I'm not sure what the guidelines are."

His expression turned serious. "That's a good question, Nell. Normally agents are discouraged from talking about

any open case. I'm not saying that agents don't go home and share with whomever they're with, but we aren't supposed to go blabbing at a bar, for instance, no matter how important it makes us feel to show off. But you're special."

"Thank you, I think. Are you talking from the FBI perspective?"

"Yes, for the moment." He smiled. "You have amply demonstrated that you are both trustworthy and discreet, so if there was an FBI seal of approval, you'd have it. And personally, I value your opinion. Particularly in matters—all right, crimes—that involve the cultural community."

"Which this one does, if one step removed. Look, I was there, and I've already got a public profile for finding myself in the middle of murder investigations, so de facto I am part of the cultural community and thus the cultural community is already involved. I should have stayed at work and sent Lissa to deal with it."

"No, you were doing your job, cultivating someone who could turn out to be a major supporter."

He was right, of course. I took another sip of wine. "You know, in the heat of the moment I didn't think about it, but how did you end up there so fast? I mean, aren't there procedures to be followed? Local police get first crack, and then they decide whether to ask anyone else for help?"

James looked pained. "You're right, in general, but Wakeman pulled rank. He was on the phone to the higher-ups before the first squad car arrived on the scene."

"That must make for a lot of unhappy campers among the police on the case."

"You've got that right. The FBI will assist any local force

that requests help, but nobody likes to have us jammed down their throats. The Chester County detectives were not pleased, so in addition to whatever investigating I'm doing, I have to smooth ruffled feathers and make nice."

"Welcome to my world. So Wakeman knows important people—no surprise there. Had you two ever met before?"

James shook his head. "No, not before yesterday. He's never been directly involved in any crime that I know of."

"Is that an evasive answer? Directly involved? That you know of?"

"I didn't mean it personally—I was just being careful. I have no reason to believe that he has ever been involved in anything that he shouldn't have. Of course, the construction industry isn't exactly as pure as the driven snow."

"Okay, you can stop waffling. What's your personal opinion of the man?"

James sat back in his chair and thought a moment. "Abrupt. Used to getting his own way. Doesn't play games. What about you?"

"I'd agree with what you said. But I'd add something: I spent a couple of hours with him on the site, before we found the body, and I think he really cares about this project. I know he's made a lot of money, but he's built some things that really made a difference, in a good way. And it's not all about ego, either—although I suppose that putting up tall buildings has a certain symbolic element. But I think he wants to do good, as opposed to doing well."

"How far would he go to eliminate anything or anyone who gets in his way?" James asked quietly.

I considered. "I don't know. Maybe I *should* know—after

all, what if poor Lissa finds something that the great man doesn't like, and he tries to suppress it? That's my responsibility, in a way."

"So she's going to be working on it?"

"He gave the go-ahead this morning. Has the crime scene been cleared?"

"Yes. Everybody's forensic people have crawled all over it. Not much to show for it, unfortunately."

"Has anybody figured out where the man died yet?"

"Nope. I think there was some talk of bringing dogs in to search the rest of the property. It's a pretty big parcel, and, I might mention, liberally sprinkled with cow pats."

"Oh, you city boys. In case you didn't notice, Wakeman loaned us some muck boots, in case of mud or more likely cow pats—he'd been there before so he would know. So the FBI has dogs?"

"We know people who have dogs. The local force knows more people who have dogs. So we can get into a dogfight about dogs." James stood up. "You want coffee?"

"If you make it. Oh, and you can do the dishes, too, since I cooked."

"Later." He went to the kitchen, or rather, the kitchen corner, all of five feet away, and put the coffee on.

"I assume there's more you want to talk about?" he said, keeping his eyes on the coffeemaker.

"Yes. How are we planning to go about finding a new place?" That large elephant in the room.

"How do *you* want to go about it?" he said cautiously.

This was not going anywhere fast. "I don't know. I haven't been in the market for a long time, and I'm sure things have changed. But don't we need to figure out our parameters?"

James waited until the coffee was done, then filled two cups and brought them to the table and sat down. "Such as?"

"Like how much we can afford. I have no idea how much money you make or how much you're willing to spend. How much does this place cost you?"

He named a number that was larger than my monthly mortgage payment, for a one-bedroom walk-up in a middle-aged building. I *had* been out of the market for a while. "Ouch."

"I can afford more, if you're worried. I've stayed here because it's convenient and there hasn't been any reason to move. Until now. Were you assuming that we'd split the cost of whatever we choose? Or pay proportionately to our respective incomes?"

I realized I hadn't even considered that. "I haven't even thought that far. I'm guessing that I don't make that much less than you do, since you're a government employee and I work for an impoverished nonprofit, and I'm sure we could adjust if we needed to. If we pooled what we're paying now"—I named an approximate figure—"what would that get us?"

"Where? City or suburbs?"

"I like the suburbs," I said, just a bit defensively. "Is that a problem for you?"

"I . . . don't know. I haven't given it much thought. But be warned: I'm not a mow-the-lawn, paint-the-house kind of guy."

"Noted. Rent or buy?" That was a big issue, since it was kind of symbolic about the level of commitment, and I sort of held my breath waiting to see how he responded.

James regarded me with an expression I couldn't read. "You really don't trust . . . us, do you?"

That hit me in the gut, but he was probably right. I took

a deep breath. "I . . . I don't trust anyone easily. Look, I've known you less than a year, and under some pretty strange circumstances. And the last month has been . . . really eye-opening. James, I trust you as much as I've ever trusted anyone. And I'm pretty sure I love you, although I haven't had a lot of practice. But this is a big step for me. No one would say that we're rushing into anything, and we're not young—or stupid, I hope. But I'm still feeling my way here. Look, we can say, let's find something we like, run the numbers, and make the decision based on the best financial outcome? But that's not what we're really talking about here, is it?"

"No." A long pause. "Look, Nell, if you're not ready to deal with this, I'll just renew my lease. No big deal."

I couldn't sit still any longer, so I got up and started pacing in the small space. "No, it is a big deal, because I *want* to make this decision. I just want to get it right."

He stood up and came over to me, and put his hands on my arms. "Nell, there are no guarantees. In some alternate universe, either one of us could have been killed one way or another in the past year. We weren't, and here we are. I know what I want: to live with you. But I don't want to make you miserable. It's your call."

Damn, why did I have to fall for a guy who was not only smart and good-looking, but also empathetic and patient? He made me feel small. "Where do we start?"

"Online Realtors," he said promptly, which led me to guess that he'd been looking already. "You can virtually walk through just about any place these days."

I leaned into him and laid my head on his chest. "You are unbelievable."

He tilted my head up. "No, I'm not—just practical. Saves time."

"And no doubt you want to show me six places you've already bookmarked?"

"Yup." He grinned.

"The coffee's getting cold."

"Let it. I have a microwave. And an idea . . ."

Which led to the bedroom. I went happily. Whatever our living arrangements, some things worked very well between us. Later, in the dark, I ran my hand lightly along the scar on his arm. It would take some time to fade; the memories of how he'd gotten it would take longer. I'd come so close to losing him, before I even knew what we had. "So, city or suburbs?" I murmured into his chest.

"Both? There are some pretty nice places on the periphery of the city. Old place or new?"

"That should be obvious: old. I work with history, remember? And I like old buildings."

"Fine. Nineteenth-century houses have a nice sense of scale—high ceilings, big rooms."

"No closets, though. You don't want a yard, so we don't need much land to go with it."

"Nope. Garage?"

"Shoot, we'll have two cars. We need a big garage with a small house? That could get complicated. Oh, and don't forget—near a train line. I do some of my best work on trains." I rolled over to face him. "Do you want me to look online? But not at work, I guess—bad example for the rest of the staff, and I've taken enough time off lately as it is."

"Maybe tomorrow, after work, we can look together. That way we'll both get a feel for what we like."

"Okay. Oh, Ben's starting tomorrow. Things are moving fast. I told the guys in the processing room to expect him, but I didn't say anything about . . . the wheelchair. Obviously they'll figure that out quickly."

"Yes. But as I told you, nobody has to coddle him. He doesn't want pity."

"I can understand that—I wouldn't, either. He should be judged on the quality of his work, period."

"Amen. Did you say something about dessert?"

"Ah, you know me too well. Yes, there's dessert, and I don't mean me."

Back in the kitchen, eating chocolate cake with an inch of mocha buttercream, washed down with lukewarm coffee, I said, "I don't know if we ever settled what we started out talking about. Your case, I mean. I'm not officially involved beyond being a peripheral witness. Of course I'm interested, but I don't feel I have the right to ask for day-by-day updates. And I don't want you to feel you have to report everything to me. So how do we work this out?"

"I'll tell you what I can. And you and Lissa should tell me whatever you find out, if you think it's relevant."

"Before we tell Wakeman?"

"How about at the same time? Unless you find a bloody weapon with the initials *MW* etched on it—then you should call me first. But he doesn't have to know you're reporting to me."

"It's not like we're going to come up with a lot of confidential information about a block of land."

"You never know. And, objectively, if you were to find something that threatened the project in any way and word got out, it could have a serious financial impact on Wakeman

et al., and you and the Society could be liable. So be careful. And remind Lissa, too."

"Got it. You finished with that?" I pointed toward his dessert plate, which looked polished. "And you're still doing the dishes."

CHAPTER 12

James and I carpooled to work the next morning. Would we do that when we lived together? Our schedules were so unpredictable and erratic that it probably wouldn't work, except on rare occasions like today. Did FBI agents ever go anywhere by train? That didn't really mesh with my mental image of them emerging from unmarked dark sedans with unusually powerful engines.

When I arrived at work, Latoya was waiting for me, as was a cup of coffee, thanks to Eric. I smiled at him as I led Latoya into my office.

"What's up?" I asked.

"As you know, Ben Hartley is starting this morning. I wondered if you'd like to show him around, introduce him to people."

I took a few seconds to think about that. Did Latoya just want Ben to get off to a good start, with my apparent blessing? Or did she want to make it clear to the rest of our staff

that Ben was my hire, not hers? "Why don't we just take him around together?"

"All right. I'll bring him up when he arrives."

I sat at my desk and sorted through papers and messages until I'd finished my coffee. Latoya arrived with Ben, who looked marginally less—what, hostile? Wary?—than he had the last time I'd seen him. He said quickly, "Thank you for this opportunity, Nell."

"Ben, we need someone with your skills, period. I'm glad you could join us. We're going to throw you straight into it, but first I'd like you to meet your colleagues. This way."

I led the way around the office, introducing Ben to our staff—Shelby in development; Felicity, our head librarian; even Front Desk Bob—then took him to the processing room, where Rich and Alice were already at work. I was surprised to see Lissa there, too, talking with Rich, who was explaining some document he had laid out on one of the work surfaces. "Hey, guys," I said, and waited until I had their attention. "I'd like you to meet our new registrar, Ben Hartley. He's starting today. I know you're all busy, but I'd appreciate it if you could show him how we do things here. Latoya, have you set him up with computer access?"

"Of course," Latoya said formally. "He'll be using that desk when he's working with physical objects in here, right?" She nodded toward the one in the corner that our former registrar had staked out, and I felt a pang—I had no idea if it would work with a wheelchair.

"If you need a different configuration, Ben, let us know," I said. I made the introductions. Lissa spoke up. "I'm short-term, Ben, but pleased to meet you. Uh, Nell, is it all right to talk about, you know . . . ? I haven't said much yet."

"It's already been in the news, and I mentioned it to Rich and Alice yesterday." I turned back to the others. "Lissa is working with Mitchell Wakeman on the historical background of a piece of land in Chester County, where he's planning a new development. She'll be here full-time for three months or so, unless she's out in Chester County. I know, this place just keeps getting more crowded all the time. Ben, you have any questions?"

"I need to familiarize myself with the computer and software setup. Latoya, you'll walk me through the computer procedures?" Ben asked.

"I will—as far as I understand them. I'm no computer expert myself, but I hope what you'll find in your space is current and clear."

"Great, thanks."

"Well, then, back to business. Ben, you want to have lunch today, sort of a welcome? Latoya, can you join us?"

Latoya shook her head. "I have a prior commitment, but I'll be spending time with Ben this morning. You two go ahead."

We all scattered to our respective workstations. Eric handed me a stack of papers and together we sorted through them, assigning priorities or handing them off to other staff members to deal with. It was a productive morning that passed quickly, and I was surprised when Ben appeared at my door. "We still on for lunch?"

I checked my watch: noon. "Sure. Any place around here you'd like to go?" I wondered if that was tactless. How many of my favorite restaurants would be hard for a guy in a wheelchair to access?

"I don't know the neighborhood. You can choose."

"There's a nice lunch place the next block down—nothing fancy, but good sandwiches."

"Sounds fine."

We made our way out the side entrance and to the restaurant, one where I ate (or got takeout) regularly. I'd remembered it as a place with widely spaced tables that I hoped would be easy to fit a wheelchair, and I was relieved to discover that I was right. I was going to have to rethink a lot of small things like this, if Ben stayed on. If? Well, the last registrar hadn't lasted long, and Ben faced special challenges working in our old building. Plus, who knew how well the job would suit him?

Once we were settled and had ordered the day's specials, Ben spoke quickly. "Look, if this doesn't work out, no hard feelings. I know you're taking a chance on me."

I admired his directness, even as I fumbled for an answer. "Heck, you're taking a chance on us, too. I don't know how much James has told you, but we've had some rather peculiar events happen recently."

Ben's mouth twisted in a reluctant smile. "So I've heard. But I don't know how much Morrison has told you about me, either. Look, here's the deal: I'm good with computers. I'm less good with people. That was true before this." He nodded toward his lap. "I have limited background in history, but I'm told I have a good eye and I can string together an accurate description. I'm assuming that describing something as 'old pink vase' is not going to cut it with you guys, but I can learn." Ben took a large bite of his sandwich and chewed and swallowed before continuing. "I like some aspects of history. I kind of got into military history when I was in the army—it's interesting to analyze where battles

went wrong and, in hindsight, how the commanders could have done things better. The analysis that goes into that is probably transferrable to dealing with your artifacts."

"What do you mean?"

"Well, you've got a building full of things. My job, as I understand it, is to define that stuff so that you and researchers can put it together in a meaningful and coherent way. I mean, take that pink vase I mentioned earlier. It's a lot more useful if I can describe it as 'nineteenth-century Chinese export blue willow,' isn't it?"

"Bingo. And don't be afraid to ask for help—Rich in particular knows his stuff," I said.

"Look, if I can lay my cards on the table—I don't want to be a pity hire. If I'm doing something wrong, I want to hear it. I won't fall apart or blow up at anyone. Morrison probably told you I have some issues with anger, about what happened, but I don't want people walking on eggshells around me."

"I would have anger issues, too, in your place. You got a lousy deal."

"But that's my problem to deal with, not yours. Let me do the job—that's all I want. If I can't hack it, you can get rid of me. But I appreciate the chance."

The waitress arrived with our sandwiches, which provided a welcome break from our rather heavy conversation. When she had retreated, I said, "Look, is this off the record? Because if whatever government agency is responsible for employer-employee relations hears us, I don't want to have problems."

"You mean, am I going to turn you in for being legally or politically incorrect? Don't worry."

"Good. If I ask you personal questions, it's not that I'm

prying, but if we're going to work together, I'd appreciate a few details. Look, the Society isn't a big place, so we all kind of know each other. Some people have been working there for years—far longer than I have. I got bumped into the president position through a strange series of events, and I'm still kind of feeling my way. Nobody makes a lot of money. Most people stay because they love history—their reward is getting to handle the real documents of our past. Carefully, of course. It's not just a nine-to-five job for most of them. Do you know what I'm saying?"

"Yeah, I get that."

"So, tell me something about yourself. Like, where are you living?"

"A few blocks from here. Ground-floor apartment."

"I thought you said you didn't know the neighborhood."

"I'm still learning how to get around in this thing." Ben slapped the arm of his wheelchair. "So I haven't done a lot of exploring."

"Do you drive?"

"Not yet. I'm told I could get a special vehicle, but I don't go far—I chose this neighborhood because it had everything I needed close by. I figured when I found a job, I could get there easily enough as long as it was in Center City."

"You live alone?" I wondered if I was pushing too far.

Ben didn't seem to mind. In fact, he grinned for the first time. "You asking if I'm a weirdo creep or if I'm available?"

"The former, I guess. As for the latter, I'm off the market."

"Yeah, I got that impression from Morrison. You know, this isn't exactly the conversation I expected to have with my new boss on my first day."

"Maybe not, but you know what? I think you'll fit in just fine."

We chatted amiably through the rest of lunch, then made our way back toward the Society. I set a slow pace because it was hot, not to accommodate Ben, who actually moved rather quickly. I followed him around to our handicap-access lift at the side of the building and rode up with him, then parted ways in front of my office, as he headed for his new work space.

I turned to find Eric frantically signaling to me. He threw a wary glance toward my office, then came around his desk, grabbed my arm, and dragged me down the hall the way I'd come.

"Eric, what's wrong?" I said quietly. I'd never seen him this upset.

"Mr. Wakeman is in your office," he whispered.

"Did we have an appointment? Did I miss something?" I asked.

Eric shook his head vehemently. "No. He just showed up and he said he had to talk to you, and I guess nobody knew how to stop him. So I parked him in your office. He's been there about fifteen minutes. I'm sorry."

"Don't worry about it, Eric," I reassured him. Stronger men than Eric had been cowed by Mitchell Wakeman, I suspected. "I've spent enough time around him already to know that he can kind of steamroll people to get his own way. I guess I'd better go see what he wants." I strode back down the hall and entered my office like I belonged there—which I did. He didn't, not right now. "Mr. Wakeman, what can I do for you today?"

Before he had a chance to answer, I noticed that Eric had left a message from James on my desk. No, two messages.

And then the phone rang, and two seconds later Eric stuck his head in, looking scared. "It's Agent Morrison—he says it's important."

Wakeman was glaring at me, but damn it, this was *my* office. "Excuse me," I said, "but I have to take this." I picked up the phone and turned my back on my fuming guest. "What's going on?"

James said abruptly, "The dogs found more bodies. Two."

I had not expected to hear that. "Wow. Uh, who knows about this?"

"Just the cops and the coroner. We've called in the FBI forensic team—there's something odd about these."

"What do you mean?"

"I'll explain later, when I'll probably know more. Oh, and by the way, it looks like Bowen was killed where the bodies were found."

I didn't have time to digest that information, not with Wakeman sitting across from me. "I see. You sure no one else has been informed? Because I have a guest in my office . . ."

James sighed in pure exasperation. "Wakeman?"

"Exactly."

"Does he know?"

"I can't say, but I'll find out."

"You do that. Call me after." He hung up.

I turned slowly to Mr. Wakeman, whose expression was a truly strange mix of sheepishness and belligerence.

"Why did you want to see me?" I asked him.

"Same reason that FBI guy just called you—those bodies. We need to talk."

I sat down slowly behind my desk and gestured toward the chair in front of it. "So talk."

CHAPTER 13

Much as I yearned to fill the silence with polite chatter, I clamped down hard on my tongue and waited for Mitchell Wakeman to explain. I had a sneaking suspicion that not many people successfully stared Wakeman down, but he had come to me, not the other way around. In the end he kind of wilted a bit, and said, "They found more bodies on the site this morning. The dogs were out early, before it got too hot."

I nodded but kept my mouth shut. I'd just heard the same news from James, but I had no idea how Wakeman could know so fast—or why he was coming to me with this information. So far, I didn't see why he was here. I waited.

Finally, he stopped waiting for a reaction from me. He added, "They're old."

Aha. I was beginning to see a glimmering of light.

He went on, "The thing is, nobody will say how long the bodies have been there. The science guys are gonna take a look at them. But best guess is a couple of hundred years."

Now he definitely had my attention. Centuries old? Really? That could put them in the Revolutionary War. Wow.

And had Mitchell Wakeman known or suspected they might be there? Was that why he had come to me and the Society?

"How did they happen to find them now, after all this time?" I said carefully.

"The dogs did. Looks like that Bowen guy had been poking around the place where they were buried. That's why the dogs found 'em. They were following Bowen's scent. Right to where they were buried."

This was one of the oddest conversations I'd ever had. "Excuse me, but why are you telling me this?"

He sighed. "If these bodies are as old as they say, they're *historic* old. I want you on top of this."

I suppressed a fleeting image of me lying on top of a few corpses—trying to protect them or to cover them up? "What do you mean?"

He leaned back in his chair and rubbed his face, then faced me again. "I told you, I came to you because I didn't want another Duffy's Cut mess. People in Malvern, even the college researchers, got pissed off because the railroad wouldn't let them take the time to excavate those graves properly. You've gotta know, there could be bodies and historic sites all over the place around here, including the land I now own. All I wanted was to be ready to handle it if and when something was found, just like this."

We studied each other silently for a few moments. Then he resumed: "Finding two old bodies can cut either way. They're a piece of history—and of course my people would treat that part of the site with respect, not just slap a café on

top of it. But I think we'd all be better off if we knew who those dead guys were and why they were there, and fast. And make sure we're not going to be stumbling over more. That's where you come in. I could tell you what I think the story is, or you can wait for that FBI agent guy to give you the official story. Either way, I'm betting the history angle just got a lot more important. I want you on it."

"We've hired Lissa to do the research . . ."

"Fine, keep her and let her do the book work. But I want your face out there when we talk about it for the press and the public. You're the chief here."

Maybe I was beginning to see his logic. I'd never claimed to be an expert on old bodies, but I *was* the official face of the Society. "Let me get this straight. You think the bodies they've just found on your development site are really old, and if that's true, you're afraid you're going to have issues with the local historical community unless you handle this problem carefully. So you want me to make sure we've done all the research we possibly can, and then explain it all to the public?" And, in addition to that, the evidence suggested that the dead man—the modern one—might have found them first, but that was not my problem, so I didn't bring it up.

He nodded. "Yeah, exactly. And I don't want some little part-timer trying to deal with the press and local groups and all that crap. I want you."

I was both flattered and horrified. Did he really see me as the spokesperson for Philadelphia regional history? When had *that* happened? Or maybe he saw me as the figurehead for historical crimes around here. Less good, but his position made a strange kind of sense either way. But did I want to get involved? I could still walk away, wash my hands of him

and the whole project. "If I may be blunt, Mr. Wakeman, what's in it for me?"

"What do you want?" he shot back, unfazed. I guess I was talking his language.

If we were horse-trading, that is. I wasn't about to sell him my carefully tailored opinion in exchange for, say, a new top-to-bottom security system or a modern HVAC for the stacks. Not that I wasn't tempted, if briefly. "Mr. Wakeman, let me tell you up front that I will not make false statements, nor will I spin whatever the findings are to make your problems go away. If this is in fact a historic site, there are protocols to be followed, and I have little or no control over those." Not exactly a direct response to his question, but at least I'd defined my position: I wasn't going to lie for him.

"Hell, I'm not asking you to fudge the facts. All I want is to be sure that whatever research is done on whatever they've found is rock solid and above criticism. I'm not knocking the kid you've hired, but her opinion doesn't carry any weight around here. I want you and your whole team here to vet whatever she comes up with. I'll make it worth your while."

Still vague, but I could live with that. From what I'd heard, Mitchell Wakeman kept his promises. "No matter what we find?"

"I want the truth, and I want it to be open and aboveboard. That's all."

Maybe he *was* one of the good guys. I'd have to wait and see. "All right. What's your time frame?"

"The news of these bodies is going to hit today's news cycle, and I can't do squat about that. Can you be ready with a statement today, or tomorrow? I want to set up a press conference."

Was he crazy? Lissa hadn't even started working on the research end of things. "Mr. Wakeman, that is unrealistic. If you'd like me to stand beside you and make a nonspecific statement that we are throwing all our resources at this and will have more detailed information shortly, I can put something together. But right now we have no facts."

"The FBI will, in a couple of hours—they're handling the autopsy. Tomorrow morning, then. I'll have my people call you." He stood up and stalked out of my office and down the hall, and Eric raced to catch up to activate the elevator for him. I was left sitting at my desk, stunned. What had just happened, and what had I agreed to?

I had to talk to Lissa, fast. No, wait—I'd promised to fill James in on whatever Wakeman had to say. I hit his speed dial.

"He gone?" James answered without preamble.

"Just left. How did he find out so fast?"

"He's probably got plenty of local people on his payroll. What did he tell you?"

"He knows the bodies are old. He wants the Society to do the historic research on the property ASAP. He wants to make it clear that he's not trying to cover anything up. He wants me to be the face for the cameras, starting tomorrow with a press conference. You have anything new?"

"Not yet. Our people have the bodies—I told you there were two, right? You have anything on the history of the place yet?"

"Good heavens, no! We only started yesterday. At least Lissa knows the area pretty well. I'll ask her what she can pull together quickly so I won't look like a dithering idiot in front of the cameras. You'll let me know if you learn anything else? Like from the autopsies? That could help."

"Of course. Nell, are you okay with all this? You can still say no to Wakeman."

I gave that idea about three seconds of thought. Saying no to Wakeman could make a significant enemy for the Society; saying yes but not coming up with anything that helped him could have risks of its own. But if these were historically old bodies, the Society had some sort of responsibility to at least look at them. Besides, I didn't want to bow to Penn or anyone else around here to do this kind of research. Wakeman had come to me first. "I don't think I can or should do that. Don't worry—I can handle it." I hoped. "See you later?"

"I'll call." He hung up, all business.

On to my next problem: talking to Lissa. Heck, now that the stakes were higher, maybe she'd bail out on the whole deal, leaving me worse off than I was now. At a minimum I had to put together a short-but-coherent statement for the press, but I didn't know anything, and I'd look stupid mumbling generalities for the news. "Protect our sacred heritage," "treasure the past," blah blah blah. Not my style. Maybe I could find something to say about the interesting intersection of history and forensics—assuming the forensics folk found anything worth talking about. I hoped James would let me know in time to use it.

I hauled myself out of my chair and went to the processing room, wondering if Lissa would still be there. Luckily she was, and I gestured her over. "We need to talk," I said, keeping my voice low so that Rich and Alice wouldn't hear. Not that they wouldn't know everything in short order, but I didn't have time to explain at the moment.

"Okay," Lissa said, looking mystified as she followed me back to my office.

When we were settled, I said, "Mitchell Wakeman was just here."

"What? Why?" Lissa asked quickly.

I explained what he had told me, and how he expected the Society to handle things. When I was done, I asked Lissa, "Is that a problem for you? You can still drop out of this if you want—I wouldn't hold it against you."

"No, I'm fine with it. In fact, it's kind of a cool challenge. I'm glad you'll be doing all the public speaking—I'm lousy at that. I'll just go do my research thing and tell you what I uncover."

"Thank you, Lissa," I said, feeling relieved. Things were happening fast, and I needed her *now*—there was nobody else to pass this off to. "Look, I expect to collect more information on the new—or rather, old—find later today or tonight, but that doesn't give us much time to whip it into shape to present publicly—Wakeman said he was going to set up a press conference tomorrow morning. Can you put something together from what you've got so far?"

"That should take about two minutes. I haven't had time to scratch the surface," she protested.

"I know, I know. But two minutes is probably the amount of face time I'll have on the news, if it comes to that, so we can keep this general until we know more." My brain was galloping ahead of my mouth at the moment. "Listen, maybe we should plan on going out to Chester County in the morning and paying a call on the historical society there. It would be good to have them on our side, and they should have useful information. You should come, since you'd be the one working with them. Can you do that?"

"Uh, yeah, I guess. Should I find my own way out there? Can you meet me somewhere?"

"You live near Penn, right?" When she nodded I said, "Catch a local train at Thirtieth Street Station. I can pick you up at the Paoli train station and we can drive from there. Okay?"

"Sounds good. Thanks for filling me in, Nell. This whole thing is crazy, isn't it?"

"That it is. Thanks for hanging in, Lissa."

Lissa's comment about transport made me realize I needed to touch base with James again. I picked up the phone.

"We're good but we're not that good," he said when he answered. "I don't have anything new since I talked to you fifteen minutes ago. What's up?"

"I talked to Lissa and she's going to do her best, but she doesn't have a whole lot to work with yet. Part of that involves whatever you guys find. *And* I think she and I need to be in Chester County in the morning, but I want to go over whatever your findings are with you before that."

Smart man: he went straight to the heart of the matter. "I'll take you home tonight."

"You are brilliant." Why hadn't I thought of that? Because I didn't want to ask for favors? "We can pick up dinner on the way."

"Great. I'll call when I can break free to pick you up."

"See you later."

James came by to collect me at the Society about six, and we fought commuter traffic all the way back to Bryn Mawr.

At least James could drive and talk and think all at the same time, a very useful skill set.

"Okay, what've you got?" I asked as I buckled my seat belt.

"Wait until I get onto the Schuylkill—I need to pay attention for that. So how was the rest of your day?"

"Ben started work, and we had lunch. I like him. I introduced him around and told him he could ask Rich and Alice if he needed any help with collections jargon. Latoya is reserving judgment, as far as I can tell, but since she hired the last one—and we know how well that turned out—I get a turn now."

We talked about minor stuff from our respective days until we were on the parking lot known as the rush hour Schuylkill Expressway, where there were few driving decisions to be made, and most of them occurred at about five miles per hour. "Okay, now talk," I said.

"I'll give you what I've got, which is more questions than answers. This morning about six, local handlers took their search dogs to go over the Garrett property to see if they could find any other locations the victim might have visited. They followed a scent that led to a wooded area on the east side of the property and stopped there. The handlers observed some recently disturbed soil and investigated further, and came upon a pair of skeletonized remains in a shallow grave."

"Okay, so based on that we now know that Bowen was there recently."

James smiled briefly at me before returning his gaze to the road. "Exactly. The handlers freaked, the dogs freaked, and they called for reinforcements—i.e., us. We arrived shortly

after eight thirty. After a couple of hours, our people determined that it was not a recent crime scene, so they packed up the skeletons and transported them back to the city for further study. As you've heard, the techs said the skeletons looked old, as in centuries. They're usually pretty accurate."

"Do you think George actually dug them up?"

"Not really. He was careful, but he uncovered enough to know what he was looking at. It didn't look like a formal burial—no evidence of coffins, and no stones."

"So it couldn't have been an old family plot?"

"Probably not. The bodies weren't neatly laid out, just kind of jumbled together. Didn't look as though that piece of land had been cultivated anytime recently. But a body is a body, so we are compelled to investigate."

"Wow again. From a historical viewpoint, this is cool. From a PR viewpoint, if you're Mitchell Wakeman, this is a nightmare. My conversation with him was, shall we say, elliptical. If I read the signals correctly, if I do right by him, then the Society could see a nice contribution. Of course, he didn't come out and *say* anything like that. He's not stupid." I filled James in on the rest of Wakeman's visit to my office, which lasted us most of the way to my house. As we drove through Bryn Mawr, debating what to pick up for dinner, James said, "So, let me get this straight. Wakeman wants you to take whatever historical straw we hand you and spin it into public relations gold?"

I turned to stare at him. "That may be the most muddled metaphor I have ever heard you utter. But the gist of it is correct."

"Did the man ask you to lie?" James said, expertly pulling into a small parking space.

"No, he did not. And I made it clear that I would not, either. He only wanted me to cast this most recent discovery in the best light, speaking for the collective local historical community. And to make sure we looked like we were concerned and acting promptly, with full disclosure of whatever we find out."

"I am honored to be in your presence—I didn't know you were an entire community."

"Oh, shut up," I said, swatting his arm. "I'm hungry."

Later, after we'd consumed our take-out dinners back at my place, I tried to think about the recently discovered skeletal remains—not easy with a full stomach and a glass of wine in me. Especially since we were sort of lying nestled on my couch. "So what does this mean, James? The bodies have been there beyond living memory, but our dead man had been poking around and found them very recently?"

"That's what the dogs would say, if they could speak."

"Let's say Bowen did find them, which seems likely. If he knew they were there, who would he tell?" I mused.

"If he told the wrong person, that could be why he's dead," James said.

That was a troubling idea. "And who would the wrong person be?"

"Ah, that's the question. I can think of several people who might have an interest in concealing the discovery, at least temporarily. Starting with your new friend Wakeman."

"Hardly *my* friend. Heck, I'm not sure what he is. A client?" I snuggled closer. "Do you think he's behind this? Because he did seem honestly upset, and I don't think he's a good actor."

"What? Oh, sorry—I'm drifting. You mean, is Wakeman

behind the new death? As in, he didn't want these new bodies to be found, so he had Bowen killed to keep him quiet? I can't say, not yet. He was the one who asked that the FBI be called in, which kind of argues against it. Unless he thinks we won't find anything and he'll come out looking like a hero for trying. But I don't pretend to know how a titan of industry thinks—he may be five steps ahead of us."

"Mmm. Well, come morning I'm going to pick up Lissa at the train station and then we're going to go talk to the folks at the Chester County Historical Society, and somewhere in between I've got to throw together a convincing speech that doesn't say anything important but will sound good on television."

"I have every faith that you can do this brilliantly. Can we go to bed now?"

"I thought you'd never ask."

CHAPTER 14

James got a very early call on his cell phone, and when he was finished he came back and kissed me behind my ear as I hid in the pillow. "Two males, in their twenties, evidence of trauma. Oh, and they have indeed been dead for a couple of centuries."

"You do say the sweetest things," I murmured. I rolled over. "Your forensic guys? They're in early."

"They finished up last night, but I turned my phone off." He smiled. "Remind me what you're doing today?"

I checked the clock. "Picking Lissa up at the Paoli station at eight"—I had texted her the night before with the right train to catch—"and then we've got an appointment at the Chester County Historical Society, before the doors open at nine thirty. I need to get up to speed on Chester County history, and I don't have time to read a book or twelve. And then we're supposed to meet with Wakeman and his band of merry men so we can look intelligent and informed for

his press conference, which is timed to catch the noon news. He's good at setting up that kind of thing."

"He seems pretty sure this project is going forward," James said.

"He's Mitchell Wakeman. He usually gets his way, I gather. You want the shower first? I'll go make coffee."

James and I left at the same time, headed in different directions. I arrived at the Paoli train station just as the train was unloading its passengers, and Lissa spotted me immediately. She opened the car door and slid into the passenger seat.

"Good morning," I said.

"Morning," she replied. "Any word on those skeletons?"

"The FBI says that they're definitely old, at least two hundred years. What do I need to know about Chester County and its history? And whatever you've got on the land Wakeman owns specifically."

"I'll give you what I can. What are we looking for from the historical society?"

"Mainly, I don't want to tick off the administrators there by tramping all over their territory without at least giving them fair warning. I can explain that it was Wakeman's idea to pull me in—and I have no idea why he didn't go to them first, or maybe he did and didn't think they were up to the job—but I'm sure we'll have to work with these people long after this particular project is done, and it helps to keep things collegial."

"That makes sense. Have you ever visited the place?" Lissa asked.

"A couple of times, but not recently. I know the president, Janet Butler, slightly from regional cultural events, but I

don't recall if I've ever had a real conversation with her. How about you?"

"I've checked out what they have, but the Society's resources are more comprehensive. They have a lot of good stuff from the Civil War in their collections, but not so much for the Revolution. They also have a separate genealogy library focusing on Chester County families."

I nodded. "That sounds useful. And you never know what you're going to find in unexpected places."

We followed the route we had taken before, driving past the Garrett farm on our way to West Chester. No sign of crime-scene tape or police guards; it looked idyllic, as if nothing unpleasant had happened there. I continued on into West Chester, just past the center of town, and pulled into a parking garage across from the historical society just as my phone started ringing. I looked to see who it was and was surprised to see the logo for the Wakeman Property Trust. I didn't recall giving anyone there my cell number.

"Hello?" I said when I connected.

"Where are you?" Mitchell Wakeman barked.

"In West Chester. I have a meeting."

"I need to talk with you—now."

I checked my watch. "I can meet you at eleven. Where?"

He was silent for a moment. I inferred that my not jumping at his *now* surprised him. "At the site, down by the pond," he finally said grudgingly. "Press conference starts at noon." He hung up.

I turned to look at Lissa. "Okay, we've got about two hours to learn everything we need to know about Chester County."

At the historical society we were greeted by a woman I

recognized vaguely, who must have been waiting for us, since she opened the door on my first ring. She held out her hand, "Hi, Nell, I'm Janet Butler—we met at one of those Philanthropy Network events in the past year, I think. Except you hadn't been elevated to upstairs then. You've had quite a year. And this is?" She looked at Lissa.

Lissa stepped forward. "I'm Lissa Penrose. I'm an intern working on a project . . . well, I'd better let Nell tell you about it."

Janet turned back to me. "All right. What's with all the rush-rush hush-hush? Is this about George Bowen?"

"Maybe. First, thanks for seeing us on such short notice, and under such vague circumstances. Is there somewhere we can talk? This may take a few minutes."

"My office is free. Coffee?"

"I don't think we have time," I said ruefully. Lissa and I followed her upstairs and to the back of the building. Janet settled herself behind her desk and pointed to the two guest chairs.

I cleared my throat. "Before I start, let me apologize up front and say that this whole approach was not my idea, and I'm in no way responsible for cutting you out of the loop. Mitchell Wakeman showed up at my office a couple of days ago and said he wanted the Society to do some research on a plot of land in Chester County, because he plans to build on it."

"The Garrett farm? No surprise there. There've been rumors floating around for months, although no public announcement. I gather that the great Wakeman likes to keep his cards close to his vest. If he has history questions, why didn't he come to us? We've got all the records here."

"I don't know, and I agree that he should have. But he is

who he is and I couldn't exactly tell him no thanks and send him to you."

Janet laughed. "I understand, believe me. So why are you here now?"

"Because we do need your help. I've been asked to act as figurehead for the press, but I don't know nearly enough about local history here, and I can't fake it. If you can help me out with a short course, I will be happy to share any credit that trickles down."

"Thanks, but don't worry about it," Janet said. "Will those other bodies turning up put a monkey wrench in his plans?"

"So you know about those?" Apparently there were no secrets in the suburbs.

"Of course. There's been a lot of traffic around the Garrett property these past few days, and I've got friends in Goshen. Although nobody's saying much about the details. What can you tell me?"

"They're not recent—more like a couple hundred years old. That comes from the FBI, not the local coroner, but don't spread it around."

I watched expressions flit across her face. The predominant one was excitement. "Wow! An old mystery!"

I had to smile at her enthusiasm. I resumed my spiel. "So you understand why this complicates things for Wakeman. I'll be the first to admit that the man probably has enough clout to sweep it all under the rug if those bodies turn out to be inconvenient for him, but he hasn't given me any indication that he plans to do that. I think he might have suspected that something like this would happen, and he wanted to be prepared. But since for the moment we're moving forward, and he brought us into the loop, Lissa and I can

also use your help to figure out who they are, or were, and why George Bowen was interested in them."

"George? How'd he get involved in that?"

I didn't answer her question immediately. "Did you know him well?"

Janet bobbed her head. "Not on a personal level, but George was a real history buff. He'd been a member here for years, and he'd done some volunteer stuff here. I know he'd done research using our collections, too."

That was encouraging to me: if he'd looked at research resources here recently, maybe we could figure out what those were and then follow in his footsteps and figure out how he found the bodies. "It looks like George was at the burial site in the recent past. The police sent in dogs to look for the actual crime scene where he was killed, and they found more than they were looking for."

"Are you asking me to participate in an investigation?" Janet looked at me. "Does this involve anything risky?"

"I don't think so, but I've learned never to say never. I am involved in this investigation, if only in a peripheral way, and in part because I was there—as was Lissa—when George Bowen's body was found. So by some sort of transitive property, you would be, too. You now know as much about the situation as anybody else around here, including the police. You've got to admit you have a better idea of the local history than they do. You might be able to help sort out the identity of the skeletons, and what their discovery might mean. Tell me, was George a treasure hunter, hoping to find artifacts and make a big score on eBay?"

Janet shook her head. "Nothing like that. He just liked history. He liked living in the middle of where it happened.

It was his hobby, after his kids moved out—that much he told me. Making money had nothing to do with it—which I think kind of annoyed his wife. In fact, she already brought over a couple of boxes of his artifacts. She wanted them out of the house."

"Could we see them?" I asked. In spite of the time pressure we were under, I was curious.

"I don't see why not. You know the drill—handle carefully, white gloves, etc. But from my first glance, I didn't see much that was very special. You want to see them now?"

Lissa spoke for the first time in quite a while. "Would you mind if I looked at your library and archives for a bit? We've got to leave soon, but it would really help if I could get an idea of what you have here."

"Sure, no problem. Nell will vouch for you, right? You won't be hiding valuable documents under your shirt?"

"Of course I'll vouch for her," I answered for Lissa. "But you should know that Lissa's technically working for Mitchell Wakeman."

Janet struck a dramatic pose. "Be gone, foul fiend of Satan!" Lissa looked startled, but Janet grinned. "Just kidding. Still, I don't want to see Wakeman plundering any historic sites under my watch."

A woman after my own heart. "Believe me, neither do I," I said firmly. "So it's okay if Lissa looks around?"

"Sure—Lissa, I'll take you down to the library, and then, Nell, I'll take you to where we stashed George's artifacts."

"Thank you. Let me know if there's anything I can do to thank you."

"I'll think of something," Janet said cheerfully, standing up. "Come on."

She pointed out the library as we passed it, and Lissa disappeared into it eagerly. I followed Janet down a hall and through a couple of doors, until we came to a crammed workroom. No one else was there, but there were several banker's boxes lined up on a rough table in the middle of the room. Janet pointed toward them. "That's what Pat, George's wife, brought. She said there might be more back at the house. Do you know what you're looking for?"

"Not really. This may be telling tales out of class, but it looks like George was not only at the site where the bodies were found, but he was also poking around—the earth was disturbed, enough that he would have known the bodies were there. He didn't do any harm to them, if you're worried."

"Oh my," Janet breathed. "He must have been thrilled."

"So he didn't come straight here and tell you?"

"No, this is news to me."

"Can you think of who he would have told? His wife?"

"Maybe, but I doubt that she'd have cared one way or the other."

"Was he a whistle-blower type? I mean, would he have gone to some authority or other and tried to stop Wakeman's building project until the site had been fully investigated?"

"Again, maybe. Probably. Like all of us here at the society, he took our local heritage seriously."

My phone buzzed: Wakeman. I checked the time: I wasn't due to meet him for at least a half an hour. Why was he calling?

"What's keeping you?" he said without any niceties.

This was starting to get on my nerves. "I told you, I'll be there at eleven," I said, managing not to add something like *Keep your shirt on.*

"Make it fast." He hung up again. What a charmer.

Janet and I were both startled when there was a pounding on a metal door at the back of the room, which I guessed led to the staff parking lot. We exchanged glances, and she went over to open it. Janet had barely pulled it open when a haggard-looking older woman shoved her way in, wrestling with a pair of stacked banker's boxes. After a brief glance at me, she addressed Janet.

"This is the last of them. I don't want them in the house. I don't want to see them again, ever. I've got people calling, and the kids are flying in, and there's a funeral to arrange, and I can't deal with any more of this. Do whatever you want with the stuff." She dumped the boxes on the table next to the others, and then, as if she had run out of steam, she dropped heavily into a folding chair. I realized there were tears running down her face. Obviously, this must be Mrs. George Bowen.

Janet took over immediately. "I'm so sorry, Pat. Of course we'll take care of it all—you have other things you need to worry about. Can I get you anything? Water? Coffee? Maybe you should just sit here a minute and catch your breath."

The woman just shook her head, but she made no move to get up. The tears kept trickling down her face.

I was torn. The woman was clearly grieving, and she faced a hellacious next few days. At the same time, I really wanted to ask if her late husband had said anything to her about a big discovery, and if not, who he might have told. But I didn't know the woman, and she didn't know me. I hadn't even known her husband.

"Pat, I know this must be hard for you, and you're under a lot of stress," Janet said to her, "but do you mind if I take

a peek in the boxes and make sure there's nothing you'll regret having gotten rid of?"

"I don't care. Go ahead. Just don't hand it back to me. You can keep it or sell it or pitch it—I don't care."

"Thank you. Nell, do you want to help?"

"I think I'll keep Mrs. Bowen company." I could ask her some questions, I rationalized, thinking that such things might be kinder coming from me than from the police or the FBI. I looked at Janet and tried to convey all this without saying anything, which was kind of absurd.

But somehow she got my message, for which I thanked the stars. I looked around until I found another folding chair, then pulled it close to Pat's. "Janet tells me your husband was really interested in local history?"

"Interested—ha!" Pat snorted, then rummaged in her pocket and pulled out a used tissue and blew her nose. "Obsessed is more like it. Why couldn't he have taken up something like golf or bridge? But no, he had to go poking around in the dirt looking for God knows what. And then he'd bring me home his new finds and expect me to *ooh* and *aah* over them. Pieces of trash, as far as I could see. Bits of this, shards of that. I wouldn't let him keep them in the house—made him stash them all in the garage. He built a whole wall of shelves for them. He never got tired of looking—even up to this week."

An opening? I seized it. "Had he found something new?"

"I'd never seen him so excited—I mean, he was practically hopping up and down. After all these years, he said, he'd finally found something big."

"Did he tell you what it was?"

"If he did, it didn't make an impression on me. There

was some dirty stuff spread out on his workbench in the garage. I just threw it all into one of those boxes. I don't know if it was what he was excited about, but it just looked like junk to me."

Janet and I exchanged another look, and Janet came over to join us, holding something small in her hand. "Is this what you're talking about?"

"Could be. I didn't look too closely."

Janet held out her hand toward me. "Does that soil look fresh to you?"

I saw some small round items encrusted in dirt in Janet's palm. I nodded. "What are they?"

"Metal buttons."

I peered more closely and made out something stamped on at least one of them. "Can you date them?"

"I'm pretty sure they're from the Revolutionary War. And if I'm not mistaken, they might be British."

We looked at each other for a long moment. "Oh my," I said intelligently. "A British soldier buried in Ezra Garrett's woods? This really is going to be a mess."

"Are you sure you don't want them, Pat?" Janet said gently.

Pat shook her head. "You keep them. George would probably want you to have them." She stood up abruptly, nearly knocking over the flimsy chair. "I've got to go." She was out the door before either Janet or I could protest.

CHAPTER 15

I was still struggling to make sense of what Janet—or rather, George—had found when my phone rang again. I walked a few feet away to answer it.

"You're late." The ever-charming Mitchell Wakeman: no hello or anything.

I knew I wasn't late, but there was no point in arguing with him. "I'm on my way." I hung up on him. If he could be abrupt, then so could I. I turned to Janet, who had come up beside me. "I'm sorry to bail on you like this, but I've got a press conference to attend, and Wakeman wants to talk with me before we go on the air."

"Are you going to talk about . . . these?" Janet asked, pointing to the dirt-encrusted artifacts.

"I don't know, but I think they're important—take good care of them, will you? And do you mind speaking to the FBI about them?" I wondered if I was supposed to worry

about chain of evidence or something like that, but I really didn't have time.

"Of course I don't mind. I'll see if I can find out anything else about them, maybe narrow down which group of soldiers they would have belonged to. And please let me know what's going on."

"Thanks, I will. I've got to go find Lissa and get over to the Garrett farm, like, immediately. I'll let myself out, okay?"

"Sure. Go."

I grabbed my bag and ran for the stairs. I located Lissa and all but dragged her out of the library and out to my car, and shoved her in, and we peeled out of the parking garage, heading for the farm.

"I know we're late, but what's the rush?" Lissa asked, after she had made sure her seat belt was buckled.

"George Bowen's wife Pat showed up with more artifacts. She said George came home all excited from one of his history hunts shortly before he died, but she had no idea why and really didn't care. She just dragged in everything he'd collected and dumped it on the historical society because she couldn't stand the sight of it. Janet found some bits and pieces that had fresh dirt on them, and it looks like they're Revolutionary War buttons, possibly British. I'm going to make a wild guess and say that they likely belonged to the bodies found up the hill, where we know the dead man had been poking around. Which means there's going to have to be a lot more investigation of the site. It could be those are the only bodies, or it could be the fields are full of them. Wakeman doesn't know about the buttons yet, but he's already called twice asking where we were. Which is why I'm in a hurry."

"Wow," Lissa said. "That's amazing."

"It would be if I didn't have to stand up at this press conference in about ten minutes and say something that won't tick off Mitchell Wakeman or the FBI and all the other cops."

"You think Wakeman won't be happy to learn that his new development property is an archeological site? In addition to being a crime scene?"

"What do you think?"

Lissa's mouth twitched into a half smile. "Can I stay in the car?"

We reached the Garrett farm in record time—good thing that most of the local cops were already there, or I'd probably have been busted for speeding on our way over. I pulled into the driveway near the old farmhouse and walked over to an unhappy-looking Mitchell Wakeman. "We need to talk," I said. I figured we had at least fifteen minutes before the newsies started tuning up their equipment.

"No time—I can't give you more than a few minutes," he replied curtly. He turned his back on me and resumed talking to someone I didn't recognize, alternating with a guy with a large camera hoisted on his shoulder. I recognized one of the daytime newscasters, a pretty youngish woman in heavy makeup, clutching a microphone. Once everyone was happy with the proposed camera angles, she said, "Let's get some background shots."

She and the cameraman stepped away and started panning the summer landscape. Wakeman turned his attention to me once again. "What took you so long?"

I swallowed a sharp retort. "You said the press conference was at noon. We've got plenty of time. And I've found some information that you need to know: those older bodies

they found are probably from the Revolution, and it's possible that at least one was British."

"Crap," he said eloquently. "Don't say anything about it on camera."

He left me gaping at his back. And fuming. I was not about to go public with what I'd just learned, not without making sure we all had the details right. Here was a scene of possible historic significance that might be connected to a recent murder, and he was telling me not to mention it? How dumb did he think I was? I reminded myself that I didn't work for him and we had no formal agreement, nor had any money changed hands. So I could damn well say what I wanted—but I knew better than to jeopardize this investigation, whether or not it involved Wakeman.

I checked my watch. Nearly twelve, and since this was a local event, I guessed it would come up somewhere in the middle of the broadcast rather than lead off, unless it was a really slow news day and the Phillies were slumping. I swallowed a smile. If the story led with "multiple bodies found in Chester County field" it might get moved up front, but Wakeman wouldn't be happy. If I were spiteful, I could probably ensure it went out like that on the five o'clock news, but that wouldn't be professional. I sighed. I knew I would wimp out and make nice for the cameras, because whatever my personal opinion of Mitchell Wakeman, he was still a major player in the region and it wouldn't be smart to antagonize him. I decided I would wait and see how he played it.

We assembled in a staggered row with Wakeman in front, flanked by people who seemed to be one of his employees and someone from the township, with me at the edge of the small group. Cameras came on, the news lady perked up and

raised her microphone, and we were off. I was no stranger to being on camera, so I smoothed whatever I could, stood up straighter, and waited for my turn. When it came, I was pleased that they got my name right, and my job title, and then the newscaster lobbed a softball at me: "I understand that the Wakeman Property Trust has invited you in to assess the historic importance of this site."

I smiled. "Yes, that's correct. This area is rich in history, and Mr. Wakeman wants to preserve the integrity of any historic structures, such as the old farmhouse. I hope the Society will be able to provide documentation for him."

"What about the body found here this week?"

Ulp. Why hadn't she asked anybody else? Did I look like a softy who would spill whatever I knew? "I can't comment on that."

"Weren't you present when the body was found?"

Double *ulp.* "Yes, because Mr. Wakeman was giving me a tour of the site at the time."

"And haven't you been involved in more than one Philadelphia-area homicide in the past?"

I could feel Wakeman glaring at me as I was apparently hijacking his moment in the press sun. I was trying to figure out how to answer her when someone else on her crew started making hand signals that I interpreted to mean something like "wrap it up." The woman looked frustrated, but turned back to the camera and made some chirpy noises tying up loose ends. She didn't look at me. Did she need my permission to quote me? Or was I now "news" myself? That was a depressing thought.

Wakeman stalked over to me. "What the hell was that about?"

I wasn't in a mood to make nice. "Hey, if you'd done your homework, you'd know what she said is true. And I hate to tell you, but this is probably going to get worse before it gets better. The dead man knew where those bodies were buried. And it's likely that he knew *what* they were. The question is; who did he tell? You?" I glared at him.

His complexion reddened and his jaw clenched, but he didn't speak for almost thirty seconds until he got himself under control. "Nobody told me anything about all that. You thinking that's what got him killed?"

"The FBI just figured it out this morning. It could be a motive. And the authorities may think the same thing. So you'd better be ready for more questions."

"Ah, crap," he muttered. His vocabulary was a bit limited; I had a feeling he'd had a stronger epithet in mind.

I wasn't interested in coddling him at the moment, if ever. "Who are all these other guys? Did you invite them?"

Wakeman looked around him. The television crew had packed up and vanished, but there was still a small crowd of others milling around in the field, apparently not sure if they had been dismissed. "Couple of guys who work for me. The others are from the township."

"Introduce me," I said. "They might be able to help with our report."

Wakeman nodded his head, then beckoned the group over. They came quickly, like well-trained dogs: Wakeman's project mattered to them. "Guys, this is Nell Pratt, from the historical society in the city. She's doing some research for me. You want to tell her who you all are? And answer whatever questions she's got. Thanks." He turned and strode off, followed by his own employees.

I turned my attention to the remaining people. "Sorry—I should have introduced myself sooner, but things have been kind of rushed. As Mr. Wakeman said, I'm Nell Pratt. And you are?"

One man stepped up first. "Ms. Pratt, good to meet you," he said eagerly. "I'm Mr. Wakeman's project manager, Scott Mason. We'll probably be seeing a lot more of each other. Let me introduce you to the team from the township here. Marv?"

A slightly portly middle-aged man wearing rumpled khakis held out his hand. "I'm Marvin Jackson, Goshen Township manager. This guy here is Joseph Dilworth, who heads up the Goshen historical commission. Oh, hi, Eddie—didn't see you arrive." That was addressed to a short stocky man who had hung back. "This is Eddie Garrett—Ezra was his father."

Ah, one of the offspring who had watched their father sell the farm. "Hello, Eddie." I extended my hand, and he took it unwillingly. His grip was strong, his skin surprisingly thick and rough, and I remembered that until fairly recently he had been a dairy farmer on the land where we now stood. What was he doing now? Or had he inherited enough from his father that he didn't need to work anymore? "I'm glad to meet you. I'd love to talk to you about your father and the farm, if you have the time."

Eddie mumbled something vague and backed off once again to hide behind the group—not exactly a sociable guy. I wondered briefly why he had been the only Garrett to show up today and why he had shown up at all, since he was so clearly uncomfortable. I suspected that Wakeman had ordered, er, asked him to be there to put a right spin on the family's participation.

Having struck out with Eddie Garrett, I turned to Joseph

Dilworth, a tall greying man in his early sixties. "Mr. Dilworth, you're head of the historical commission? Would you have time to speak with me?"

He glanced at his watch. "Want to grab a sandwich? And who's your colleague here?"

As Lissa slid up alongside me, I realized I hadn't even had time to introduce her. "This is Lissa Penrose. She's researching the history of Mr. Wakeman's property for us. But she's only just started, and I'm sure you could help point her in the right direction."

"No problem. The Salt Shaker up the road does good sandwiches. You want to follow my car? Marv, you want to come, too?"

"Can't do it, Joe," Marv said. "I've got budgets to go over. But if you want to talk with me, Ms. Pratt, give me a call. Happy to help." He held out a business card, and I took it.

"I'll do that, Marv. And we'd love to have lunch with you, Joe. Thank you." We all trudged up the hill to where the cars were parked, and I waited until Joe pulled out and turned down the hill, then followed.

"I hope you don't mind taking the time for lunch," I said to Lissa.

Lissa said, "Of course not. I'd be speaking with Joe Dilworth in any case, so it might be good to get to know him. That is, if I still have a job?"

"If Wakeman's smart he'll keep us on after this discovery, to make him look like a sensitive and responsible good citizen. But I'll let him work through that for himself. Actually, I'd be happy if you'd do at least a little more research anyway, to try to figure out who those skeletons are and what they were doing here. Because now I want to know. That's why we're

having lunch with the guy from the township. Feel free to ask him anything you want."

"Because he doesn't work for Wakeman?" Lissa asked promptly. "I'm curious myself, about all these bodies. And I think I've got some ideas where to start."

We parked next to Joseph Dilworth's car in front of the Salt Shaker, and he waited for us before entering the small building. Once we were inside, it was clear that it was a local place; at least three people waved or nodded at Dilworth as he made his way to a table. The waitress came over quickly, and we ordered sandwiches and iced tea.

Dilworth rubbed his hands together and smiled. "So what can I do for you two lovely ladies?"

"Mr. Dilworth, as you heard, Mr. Wakeman approached me to ask that the Society undertake a thorough investigation of the former Garrett property, which he now owns. Obviously things have gotten a bit more complicated over the past few days, particularly with the most recent find." I'd had little time to think about what I wanted to know from him and what he might be able to tell me. "Tell me about your town here, and about Ezra Garrett."

That seemed to be enough to get him started. He proceeded to outline for us the entire history of Goshen Township since its founding some three hundred years before; referred to every building within a several-mile radius that had been standing for a couple of centuries; and pointed with justifiable pride to the small historic district that the township had established under his watch. Apparently Goshen was truly invested in its history, which I found admirable. I waited until he paused long enough to take a drink of his tea before interrupting.

"Where does the Garrett farm fit in all this, Mr. Dilworth?" I asked

"Hey, call me Joe. Garretts are an old family around here—they go way back. There were Garretts back when the first meeting house was set up, back right after 1700."

"They were Quakers?"

"Were and are. Ezra was laid to rest in the cemetery there—right across the street."

I followed his gesture. I hadn't realized that there was a cemetery there, but I knew vaguely that the Quakers preferred low, simple stones, which weren't visible behind the stone wall that surrounded the site.

"I met Edward Garrett briefly after the press conference. Are there other family members?"

"He's got an older brother, William, but he couldn't be bothered to come. Eddie doesn't like public events, but I'll bet Wakeman pressured him to come, just to have a Garrett face in the pictures." Exactly as I had thought.

"Mr. Wakeman told me that he had arranged the purchase of the land before Ezra Garrett passed on, but he allowed the family to stay until Ezra's death. Did everyone know about that?"

Joe Dilworth cocked his head at me. "What's it to you? If you don't mind my asking."

I phrased my response carefully. "Mr. Dilworth—Joe—it was Mr. Wakeman who brought me into this and asked me to research the place. Because of that, I was there when George Bowen's body was found, so I guess you could say I feel a kind of personal interest in it now. You've told me that the land was in the Garrett family's hands for centuries.

Why did Ezra decide to sell? How did the rest of the family feel about that?"

"I'm sorry you had to see that. George was a good man, and he deserved better. As for what you're asking—William Garrett didn't want to have anything to do with dairy farming. What's more, he knew what the land would be worth, and I'm pretty sure Wakeman cut a fair deal."

"What about Eddie?"

Joe Dilworth signaled to the waitress that he wanted coffee; Lissa and I declined. He waited until the coffee arrived before answering. "Only thing Eddie ever wanted to do was raise dairy cattle. But he's not young, and he couldn't handle it by himself. I kind of guess Ezra overruled him, or Ezra and William together. Like I said, it was a good deal financially."

Poor Eddie. "What's he doing with himself these days?" I asked.

"I don't think he's settled on any one thing. He's kind of a lost soul."

Belatedly, I realized that Lissa had been shut out of most of our conversation. "Lissa, I'm sorry I haven't let you get a word in. Did you have any questions?"

Lissa addressed Joe Dilworth directly. "I do, but I think I should meet with Mr. Dilworth at another time. If that's all right with you?"

"I'm always happy to meet with nice young ladies who like history. Why don't you call my office, say, tomorrow, and we can set up a time?"

"I'll do that, thank you."

Dilworth looked at his watch again. "Shoot, I've got a meeting about ten minutes ago. Sorry to leave so fast, but

it's been a pleasure talking with you both. Lissa, I'll be talking with you again. Ms. Pratt, nice to meet you." And he was gone—leaving me with the check. At least it was fairly reasonable.

When I'd paid, I told Lissa, "I guess we'd better head back to the city. And on the way we can talk about what we've learned today."

CHAPTER 16

We drove into the city, making good time because it was mid-afternoon. We reviewed what we'd heard from Janet and Joe, and Lissa was already scribbling down a list of things to look up. I parked in the pay lot across from the Society, mentally planning to bill it to Wakeman. When I reached my desk, Eric handed me a sheaf of message slips. "Did you watch the news at noon?" I asked.

"I did, on the computer. Is something funny goin' on?"

"Is that how it looked to you? The problem is, we're not sure what yet. Stay tuned for further developments. Unless, of course, Mitchell Wakeman has called and told me that our services are no longer required." I wondered if I'd be happy to hear that.

Eric smiled. "Haven't heard from him. You know, nobody ever told me this job would be so exciting."

"I wouldn't have believed it myself, Eric." I went into my office and sorted through the slips. A couple of calls from

James. Since he'd called on my professional line, it was probably a professional question, and not urgent enough to use my cell. I called him back first.

"Nell," he said when he picked up.

"James. You called?"

"I saw the newscast. Your statement lacked a certain, uh, specificity."

"That was the plan. Look, I've got some new info for you. You want it over the phone?"

"No, I'll come by the Society. Half an hour?"

"Fine."

I returned a couple of more calls, then went looking for Lissa. I found her in the processing room talking with Ben, and they had some documents spread out in front of them.

"Hi, Ben," I said. "Lissa, Agent Morrison is on his way over here to talk about what we found out today in West Chester. I think you should sit in."

"Yes, I want to. I told you there were some things I wanted to check, and I asked Ben about one in particular. Turns out he knows a lot more than I do, and I'm guessing it may be relevant to the two bodies at the farm. I think he should join us—it might save time."

The more the merrier, apparently. Crime solving by committee. "Sure. Let's set up in the boardroom."

Ben rolled up a couple of the maps they had been looking at, then he and Lissa followed me to the boardroom. I kept going, so I could meet James downstairs. He was waiting in the lobby when I arrived.

"So, have you had any irate calls from Wakeman yet?" I asked, as we walked toward the elevator.

"Not that I'm aware of. I've kept Agent Cooper in the

loop, so if Wakeman reached out to him, Cooper would have shot him down. After all, Wakeman asked us in to look at Bowen's death, but he can't demand we drop it now that we're in it. Finding the other two bodies grew out of that, although strictly speaking they're not our problem. Why? Is he complaining about you? The investigation?"

We'd reached the elevator. As the doors slid shut behind us, I said, "No, I wouldn't say that. He seems to be on edge, but he's not interfering. In any case, you probably won't be surprised to hear that the two discoveries are kind of connected."

James smiled. "What else could I have expected?"

We'd reached the boardroom, where Ben and Lissa were busy studying one of the maps again. They looked up when James and I arrived. "Hey, Morrison," Ben said.

"Hey, Ben. What're you doing here?"

"Lissa thought we might have something useful. If you don't mind us sitting in? I mean, we're not talking super-secret stuff here, are we?"

James dropped into a chair. "Not if Wakeman keeps insisting on holding press conferences. What've you got, Nell?"

"You remember that Lissa and I met with Janet Butler at the Chester County Historical Society this morning, as a courtesy to her and to keep her informed, since Wakeman's project is in her backyard. I apologized to her that Wakeman hadn't included her, which seems kind of rude, professionally speaking."

"So?" James looked impatient.

"While I was talking with Janet, George Bowen's wife, Pat, came in, bringing with her all the artifacts and stuff

that her husband had collected over the years, saying she never wanted to see it again. Apparently she didn't share her husband's enthusiasm for local history. But she did say that he came home earlier in the week really excited about something he had found. Janet noticed that a couple of things still had damp soil on them, so we inferred that they were items George had found shortly before he died. It turns out that they were metal buttons that dated to the Revolutionary War, and Janet thinks they're British. I'd put money on it that they go with those skeletons, which mean they've been sitting there since the seventeen hundreds."

"I'd guess 1777," Ben spoke up for the first time. "Have you all heard of the Paoli Massacre? Also known as the Battle of Paoli? Because I think that's where they came from."

"That's what I wanted to check out," Lissa said triumphantly.

"The Paoli Massacre?" I asked Ben. "Shoot, I've been driving by that historical marker for years on the way to West Chester, but I don't know the details. The Garrett farm is only a couple of miles farther down the road."

"You have time for the full story?" Ben asked.

I glanced at James, who did not look relaxed. "Why don't you give us the high points?"

"Okay," he agreed. "You know the Battle of the Brandywine?"

"Uh, I know where it happened—I go by that all the time, too, when I go to the museum out that way. But I don't know the details of the battle itself. I guess my high school history class didn't include it." I was not covering myself with glory as the representative for local history. "How do you happen to know so much about a local battle?" I asked.

Ben shrugged. "I was in the military, remember? I always liked military history. So you know that the British took Philadelphia in 1777, right?"

"Yes, that much I knew."

Ben settled himself more comfortably in his wheelchair. "All right, so in September of 1777, Washington's troops faced off against British troops at the Brandywine Creek—yes, the one next to where that art museum is now." Ben grinned at me, teasing a little. "The thinking was that the patriot troops would have an advantage, because there were limited places where the British army could ford the creek. They lost anyway and were forced to retreat. It was disastrous—Washington's troops were outnumbered and outflanked. He lost a lot of men and eleven cannons, and opened up the way to Philadelphia. But he was also lucky—he got away with most of his army intact, and for a number of reasons the British forces didn't press their advantage.

"Washington was going to go toward Chester, but instead he decided to keep his army between the British and Philadelphia, and he laid out his troops in position both to block the access routes and to protect their supply centers. The next confrontation took place on September sixteenth near Malvern."

I was beginning to see where he was going with this. "Which is next to Paoli."

"Right. The American army got lucky again—it rained so hard it flooded the Schuylkill River, which kept the British troops from crossing. Could have been a major battle, if it weren't for the nor'easter. But the downside was, all their ammunition got wet, so Washington had to go restock."

James was looking at his watch. "Can we fast forward here?"

"Just setting the stage for you, pal. Don't you want to learn something?"

"I'd like to learn who killed George Bowen and what his death might have to do with those bodies he found."

"All right, all right. So Washington stationed some troops in Paoli to defend the rear, while the rest of them went to resupply. He left about fifteen hundred troops under General Anthony Wayne, who you might have heard of. Wayne was a local, so he knew the area well. But the British snuck up on their encampment in the middle of the night and attacked with sabers and bayonets. It was one of the more vicious battles of the war—there was a lot of blood shed by the Americans. In PR terms the British strategy turned out to be a mistake, because they were so brutal that public opinion rallied in the Americans' favor. The attack was thought to be ungentlemanly, if you will, and unnecessarily cruel. Anyway, Wayne lost a lot of people, with even more seriously wounded; the British lost all of four. Then Wayne gathered his troops as best he could and fled west."

I finally saw the connection. "You're saying Wayne's men headed west along what is now the Paoli Pike? Which would've taken at least some of them right past the Garrett farm."

"Exactly. Of course, the battle was chaotic, and to this day it's not one hundred percent certain who fought and what happened to them. Often local militia men would show up for a battle, but they wouldn't be recorded on any official rolls—they were just fighting in their backyards. And remember, there were Loyalists in that area, so who's to say some of them didn't throw on a red coat and join the British?"

"So," James said slowly, "one could hypothesize that

soldiers from both sides may have faced off on or near the Garrett farm during the retreat and died, and in the confusion nobody ever reported them as dead?"

"It could have happened," Ben said.

"Would this be important now, Ben?" Lissa asked.

"Depends on who got hold of that information—if it's true. It would make a good human interest story—you know, enemies lying together in a common grave for centuries, a footnote to a bloody battle. Which I guess might increase pressure to do a more thorough excavation, in case there're more bodies to be found. I mean, it would be a new story about an old event."

"But an excavation, if done right, would delay the development project." I said.

"Not my area of expertise," Ben said quickly. "And it wouldn't delay it forever—just slow it down a bit. If you're thinking about how Wakeman would react, he or his people might be able to spin it to his own advantage. You know, important historic site, treasured history, that kind of line—all very open and public. Just as long as he isn't viewed as bulldozing our sacred heritage—or building a condo over the grave."

"Got it," I said.

"You need anything else from me?" Ben asked.

"Could you write up a brief summary for us history-challenged types?"

"No problem," Ben said.

I turned to Lissa. "Lissa, you can probably guess what else we need. Would you look into land records and find out who lived where back then? Who was on which side in the war? Work with Chester County if you want—I'm sure

they've got plenty of local details. See if they have letters or family histories there. We should keep Janet in the loop. It would be great if we could identify who's who."

"Absolutely. Uh, maybe this is premature, but if I find anything worthwhile and put it together, would you mind if I published it?"

"I wouldn't mind, but we should run it by Wakeman, as a courtesy. I don't think he'd have any problem with it. Maybe the Society can help with publication. Great idea."

"I'll get right on it. Ben, you want to show me some more of your maps? Maybe we can pin down the path of the retreat more closely."

"Sure. Follow me." He wheeled his way out, followed closely by Lissa. I watched them go, and as they went down the hall, I said, "Is Ben involved with anyone?"

"What, you're playing matchmaker?" James said, with a laugh. "Not that I know of."

"Just checking." I turned to him. "So, what do we do now?"

"We?" He cocked an eyebrow at me.

I assumed he wasn't serious. "Hey, I brought you the details from the widow, didn't I? By the way, do you need anything more from her? You may not be able to interview her anytime soon—she's burying her husband this weekend, and the family is arriving. She seemed completely overwhelmed."

James thought for a moment. "Not right away. I need to know who George might have been close enough to on the township staff to tell about what he found. Any friends he might have shared this with, if he was really excited. His wife would know about either of those, but I agree—this is not the time to intrude on her with our questions. I wonder if your colleague Janet could help."

"How so?"

"Well, since she knew George, she has an entrée—maybe she could go by after the funeral and thank the widow for her generous contribution of some old buttons and whatever else was in the boxes. That would get her in the door, and then she could ask some questions, like: who did George share his love of artifacts with?" James sighed. "Of course, I can't ask her to do it any more than I can ask you. But you know as well as I do that the longer a murder goes unsolved, the less likely it ever will be solved."

"I'm pretty sure Pat Bowen doesn't want to hear anything relating to those artifacts she was in such a hurry to get rid of. She may even think that they're somehow related to George's death. Have you or the local police interviewed the people he worked with on the township staff?"

"The local police have, at least on a preliminary basis. But most of the cops have known those local government guys for years, so it's hard for me to know what questions they asked—or how hard they pushed. By the way, good work with the widow."

"I was lucky to be in the right place at the right time, that's all."

"Do you mind kicking some ideas around now?"

I looked at him incredulously; he was actually asking me? "About the murder? So now you're willing to share? Sure—I don't have any other commitments this afternoon." Not that there was much left of it.

"Thanks." He leaned back in his chair and studied the blank wall across the room. "Say you and Ben are right and the bodies in the copse were soldiers from the Revolution, at least one of them British, whose deaths were never recorded."

"That reminds me, do your guys want to look at the buttons? Janet still has them, but I told her you might want to see them."

"Eventually, yes. Anyway, George Bowen, amateur history enthusiast and artifact collector, stumbles on these bodies, maybe by accident or maybe because he's been prowling around the property for years."

"Janet did say he's been interested in local history for quite a while, and not because he wanted to sell his finds on eBay. He seems to have kept everything."

"Good. So Bowen finds the skeletons and he recognizes them for what they are, and he even brings back a button or two, just to confirm what he suspects or to try to look it up. He has to be excited, and he knows that his wife won't care. What does he do next?"

"Tell a friend? Janet says he didn't go to the historical society with his find, although he might have planned to soon."

James nodded. "Maybe. We'd need to find out who his friends were. And we need to know more about George. Option A: he tells someone he's close to, who shares his hobby or at least cares about it. Option B: he realizes the significance of his find and he runs to tell the township and/or the Wakeman Property Trust to tell them to hold their horses until the discovery can be evaluated."

"Okay, both make sense, and maybe he did both. But if it was someone at either the township or the trust, they haven't come forward about it. So, who did he talk to? And more important, who would have killed him because of what he found?"

James looked at me then. "That's the question. As we've

discussed before, *cui bono*? Who benefits from keeping this a secret? Is there a time value? Wakeman already owns the land. Is he expecting a change in state or local administration? Does something else come due or expire? Are there new regulations that are going to take effect at some point? And who would know about any of those and their potential impact?"

"I'm glad we're just spitballing, because I don't have an answer for any of these questions."

"But I'm not off base, am I?"

"No, I don't think so. The question is, what does the FBI do next? Who do you talk to? Do you hand this off to the local authorities? Do you pull rank and do it yourself? Do you go hand in hand with the police?"

He sighed. "All of the above? Or none? The local police resent the interference, and they kind of close ranks against an outsider. I understand that, and I'm not saying they aren't good at their jobs. And to be fair, the victim was one of their citizens. Wakeman has to tread lightly because he needs the goodwill of the township to make his project work—he doesn't want to fan any local resentment."

"He's the one who called you in, remember. He can't have it both ways. Do you know what approvals he needs, locally? Is there a single person who controls permits, like the zoning officer—and now they're going to need a new one—or if there's something that has to be approved by a committee, like the historical commission? Or, heck, if something this big has to be approved by local ballot."

James looked at me approvingly. "That's a good question, and I have no idea. But I can find out. Nell, why do you know about local government when I don't?"

"I live in the suburbs. I read the local paper, and I see notices like this all the time announcing zoning meetings or committee meetings or ballot initiatives."

"Good call. And I can delegate the task of finding all that out to someone junior in the office. Nobody's feathers will be ruffled if we're looking at zoning codes—that's public information."

"How much pull does Wakeman have at the FBI?"

"Officially? None, of course. We're a neutral government agency, and we aren't even dependent on keeping the local politicos happy, just the national ones. Off the record? It never hurts to have a friend in high places, so if we can accommodate someone like him without bending any rules, we will. Does that answer your question?"

"It's more or less what I expected."

He looked down at his hands. "Look, Nell, I've got some business to see to tomorrow morning, but maybe after that we could go over some property listings?"

It took me a moment to figure out what he mean by listings: a place to live. Together. Why was I avoiding thinking about that? "On paper or online? Or in person?"

He looked at me then. "Whichever you want. I think we need to move this forward. Don't you?"

Yes. Maybe. "Fine. Tomorrow is good for me."

I could swear he looked relieved. "That's great."

Maybe. I wasn't sure. Maybe if we looked at places that were neutral, new to us, with no history and no associations, it would be easier. I hoped. What was *wrong* with me?

"Where will you be tonight?" I asked.

"My place, I assumed. You want to join me there? Or,

no, I can meet you out at your place, since I've got some people to interview out that way."

I wasn't invited to that party. Of course, there was no reason why I should be; I was representing the historical community, not law enforcement. Still, I felt shut out, just a little. "Why don't we meet up at my place tomorrow?"

He stood up; I stood up. We were at my workplace, so no lingering good-bye kiss. And it looked like I'd be going home alone tonight. That was what I wanted, wasn't it? Some space? Some time to take a long hard look at my place and decide what I liked about it and what didn't work? That's what I told myself. "I'll walk you to the elevator."

After seeing James off, I went back to my office. I was surprised when Eric handed me a message slip from Janet Butler. "Did she say what she wanted, Eric?"

"No, just said she needed to talk with you."

"Nell, thanks for getting back to me," Janet said somewhat breathlessly when I called her back. "Look, this may sound really weird, but Pat Bowen wants to talk to us."

"Us? Did she say that?"

"Yes, she did—both of us."

"Isn't she in the middle of planning a funeral for her husband?"

"Yes, that's on Sunday. But she said it was important. Can you meet me here in West Chester tomorrow morning?"

"Sure, no problem. Nine?"

"Nine is great. See you then." Janet hung up, leaving me wondering what on earth Pat Bowen thought was so important that it couldn't wait until after the funeral.

CHAPTER 17

I went home—alone. I threw together a skimpy dinner and ate it—alone. Was this place more quiet than it used to be? As I ate I studied my onetime carriage house, with its tiny kitchen carved out of one corner, and the fireplace I had insisted on adding as a pure indulgence. I liked my fireplace. Its light and warmth struck some fundamental, even primitive, chord in me.

All right, I wanted a fireplace in our new place. But not some stark, architectural construct with lots of glass and angles or—heaven forbid—a switch to turn it on and off; I wanted a fireplace that belonged, that was integral to the structure of a building, inefficient and messy though it might be. Which, I reminded myself, wasn't likely to come with a modern apartment. Okay, back to the list. Fireplace. Closets. A bigger kitchen. A garden? No, neither of us seemed much interested in land or lawn. But definitely space for each of us to be alone, which meant at least three bedrooms, or at

least two plus a study. This hypothetical place was growing by the minute. And it looked like it would have to be a house. City row house? Something on the fringes of the city? I hadn't looked at real estate listings for years, but it seemed I was going to. That seemed like such a big leap forward. Living together—okay, I was getting used to the idea, sort of. But buying something together? That was—yes, I had to use the word—a big commitment. Financially it made sense, I had to admit: rents in or near the city were wicked, and a mortgage would probably be no higher. But whose name would go on the documents? I (and my bank) owned the little house where I sat. I liked that. I could call the shots, make any changes I wanted. I was responsible for it. I didn't have to negotiate everything with someone else. I felt I was in uncharted territory. James and I had seen each other under pretty much the worst possible circumstances and survived; handling day-to-day living should be a piece of cake, right?

Nell, what is your problem? Easy: I was scared. I'd been married once when I was young. It hadn't worked out and had just kind of ended, without recriminations or hurt feelings. I'd thought that it was good that we'd been so civil about it, but Marty had told me, not long ago, that I should be troubled by how the marriage had dissolved with so little pain. Had the marriage meant so little to me? I wasn't sure how to respond to that. I had long since chosen to see that split as specific, not symptomatic—but it was hard to hold to that rationalization when I hadn't managed to find another serious relationship since.

Until James. With James it was different. Of course, I was older, and James was older than my husband had been when we married. I had my own life and I had thought I was

happy, until we'd been thrown together. Now I had to rethink a lot of things. Why was I so reluctant to face this head-on? I loved him, he loved me. But where did that take us?

As I headed to West Chester the next morning, I struggled to understand why Pat Bowen would want to see me as well as Janet. She'd met me only the one time, and I didn't think we'd exactly bonded. Janet she knew only slightly better, and Pat had professed nothing but contempt for her late husband's historical interests. So why talk to either of us at all? At least I knew why I was headed to West Chester: it was possible that Pat held information that could point us toward who might have wanted her husband dead—information that both the police and James wanted. But if that was the case, why hadn't she simply told the police? Had they asked? Why call in the historical society and near-stranger me?

When I arrived and rang the doorbell at the CCHS, Janet pulled the door open immediately. "She's not here yet."

"I'm early," I replied. "I thought we should talk before Pat gets here. You still don't know why she's coming to see us? Or why she wanted me here?"

Janet shook her head. "Not really. It's not like we're close—I knew George better than I know her."

"Maybe she's got something she didn't feel comfortable telling the police," I speculated. "After all, she's almost too close to them, since they all live in the community here. We're more neutral."

"I can't believe she'd have anything worth hiding, although I suppose she might be feeling guilty about not sharing George's enthusiasms. Look, let me get right to it:

Do you think George was killed because of something he found? On the Garrett farm?"

"I think it's possible. George had been poking around here for a number of years, right? Nobody seemed to care. Suddenly he finds something that might actually be important, and he's killed pretty quickly after that. Maybe that's circumstantial, but I think it's suggestive."

Janet nodded. "I agree. Poor George—he finally found something and he never got to enjoy it. So who would care about two very old bodies enough to kill George?"

"Wakeman is the obvious suspect, because he wouldn't want his pet project to be derailed or held up. But I have trouble getting my head around that because, first, he came to me to ask to do a full historical analysis of the place. I told him up front that I wouldn't be party to any cover-up if we found something he didn't like. He said he was okay with that."

"Maybe he knew there was something to find and wanted to be prepared," Janet suggested.

"Maybe. But if he knew, and he suspected it would become public, why kill George? Plus, he's the one who called in the FBI from the start. If he'd wanted to hush things up, he'd have done better leaving the investigation to the local guys. Heck, he could have paid them off to keep quiet."

"So you think he's really not involved?" Janet asked.

"Based on what I know about him, and what he's done, I do. I don't think he had anything to do with George's death."

"Then who?" Janet asked.

We were interrupted by the ringing of the doorbell. "That'll be Pat—I'll go let her in. Why don't you wait here?"

I sat and thought about what I'd just said. I didn't believe

that Wakeman was implicated in this crime. Sure, he was rough around the edges, but he had a solid public reputation. He'd taken charge of more than one floundering local project and made it happen, usually on time and on budget. Would he sacrifice the reputation he'd built over the years for the sake of one small suburban development? Unlikely. I thought he was more of a realist than that.

Janet returned with Pat in tow. "Would anybody like coffee? Tea?"

"Can we just get this over with?" Pat said. "I know I'm the one who asked to meet you, but I've got a house full of relatives, and I've got to get back soon."

"Of course, no problem," Janet said. Janet's office was like mine in that it had a settee and a couple of chairs, so the three of us settled into a rough circle. Pat took a deep breath before jumping straight in.

"You must think I'm crazy, what with George's funeral tomorrow and all. But I had to get out of the house. It's bad enough having the kids and grandkids around, much as I love them, but then there are all the people in the neighborhood who keep showing up with casseroles, and then I have to repeat the same damn details, over and over. I mean, it's wonderful that he had so many friends, but I needed some space." She paused to collect herself. "I've been thinking of what we talked about before, about the stuff George liked to collect. I'm sorry I dumped it all on you and ran, Janet, but I wanted to get it out of my sight. I couldn't bear to see it sitting there in the garage."

She turned to me. "Ms. Pratt, I've read about you in the *Inquirer*, and I know your Society is one of the best of its kind in the country, and I want George to have the best. If

he found something important, I want him to get the recognition he deserves for it."

She shut her eyes for a moment, fighting for control, and when she opened them, she began again. "George always loved history. When the kids were little he dragged us on every tour within a hundred miles. We even took the kids to see Gettysburg, where they were bored silly. Williamsburg, one vacation. He'd always hoped to visit Monticello, but we never found the time. Then the kids grew up and left home, and I really didn't care about all that stuff, so the trips stopped. But George still cared. Don't get me wrong—we'd been married a long time, and I had my own interests and George had his. And one of his was roaming the countryside looking for bits and pieces of history. You know, foundations of old buildings he'd read about, or just tracing the paths of battles. He had plenty to keep him busy around here. I didn't pay much attention after a while, although he'd keep coming to me with his latest treasure, all excited. Even up to the end . . . He was so wound up, and I just ignored him."

She looked down at her lap, trying to hold back tears.

"And now you regret it?" I said gently.

"I do." Then Pat looked up again. "Was this obsession with collecting old stuff what got him killed?"

That seemed to be my territory. "It's . . . possible. It looks like George had been where those older bodies were found shortly before . . . we found him, so it's pretty likely he discovered the bodies, and took a couple of small items with him as proof. They were in those boxes you brought in. Do you know if George spent time on that farm?"

Pat nodded. "Oh, sure—he'd known the Garrett family all his life. It's kind of rare that you find a place that's been

in the family as long as that one had, until Ezra took it into his head to sell it."

"Why did he decide to sell?" I asked. "I mean, did he want the money, or did Wakeman sweet-talk him into it somehow?"

Pat shook her head. "George and I talked about it. It wasn't anything complicated. Ezra Garrett had two kids, and only Eddie—the younger one—wanted to stay on and keep the dairy business going. His brother, William, didn't want anything to do with it. Anyway, selling it made sense financially. Once Ezra decided to sell, he planned ahead. He didn't want to see a ticky-tacky housing development there—we've got enough of those already—so he decided he'd sell it before he died. He did his research. He didn't want another corporate park, either, but he saw something about Wakeman's plans for a structured community, and they got to talking, and he finally sold it to Wakeman's company for a nice piece of change. The kids got their share. And I'll give Wakeman and his people credit—he's been taking his time, getting to know people around here. He's smart. I think he'll make a good job of it. Of course, I may not stick around to see it. Now that George is gone, I'll probably sell the house and move closer to our kids. I'd hate to have to drive by that pond every time I want to get groceries."

"I can understand that," I said. I thought for a moment. "So, from what you're saying, it doesn't sound as though your husband posed any obstacle to Wakeman and his project, at least, not in the long run."

"Not to Wakeman, no. Maybe some of the guys who worked for him. Heck, you know what the economy's been like these past few years. People want jobs, sooner rather

than later. This is going to be a big project, spread over a couple of years. Maybe Wakeman's people didn't want to wait around while the boss admired the views and took the township people out to lunch."

"And someone thought George's discovery would interfere with their timetable? Janet, you'd know better than I would," I said, turning to her.

Janet answered quickly. "You know the whole Duffy's Cut mess?" When I nodded, she went on, "There was a lot of argument over that when it was found, like between the railroad and the archeologists and historians. The railroad wouldn't let the historians finish excavating the site because they had to keep the trains running, so who knows how many other bodies are buried there, really. So let's say those people who wanted to see the dig done right last time around and didn't get their way are all primed to fight now if somebody says, 'hey, there's a historic burial ground here,' what're they going to do? Shouldn't somebody check it out before this Philadelphia guy sticks a parking lot over it?"

Which was why I had been brought in, to provide at least a veneer of historical respectability to the project. "I can't say I blame them. Once history like that is lost, it's gone forever."

"Nell," Janet said, "you know the man. Would Wakeman condone a cover-up, literally in this case, to speed up the construction process? Or at least, look the other way?"

I shook my head. "As I said before, I can't see it. Of course, I haven't met any of the people who work for him. Look, Pat, there's something we need to know."

"What's that?" Pat asked, rousing herself from her misery.

"Who else besides you would George have told about what he found, or thought he found? He didn't bring it to

Janet here. Did he have friends who shared his interest? What about the township?"

"That's more than one question," Pat said. "Friends? Not so much. He was kind of a loner, liked to ramble around with a pocket full of maps, maybe a GPS locator so he could mark where the finds came from, maybe some binoculars and a camera. I don't think he knew anyone else who wanted to do that in all weather. Now, the township's another question. You see, George was zoning officer, so he would've had a legal and a moral obligation to inform them if he'd made a significant historical find."

"And had he told them, do you know?"

"I don't know. I mean, if he had found those bodies, it was pretty recently. And the lines of communication around here are kind of blurry, anyway. Like, there are official meetings, schedules, that kind of thing, and he would have had to submit something in writing. But that doesn't mean he didn't run into someone else from the township at the hardware store, and take him aside and give him a heads-up about what he'd found."

"Was he close to anyone in particular?"

"He wasn't exactly buddies with anyone. He got along okay with them. But he'd gone to work for the township because he thought it was his civic duty, not because he wanted to hang out with the guys."

"Who would he have had to report this to?" I asked.

"As far as official reporting, I think he'd have to tell Marvin Jackson—he's the township manager—and maybe the historic commission. Like I said, I don't know if he'd gotten around to it, or if he had time. He'd only just found . . .

the bodies, I guess." She stood up abruptly, her motions jerky. "I'd better get back before people worry."

Janet stood up as well and, after a moment's hesitation, gave her a quick hug, which surprised Pat. "Pat, thank you so much for coming to us with this," Janet said. "I know it can't be easy for you, especially right now."

Pat impatiently brushed away more tears. "I had to do something. I mean, I laughed at George's little hobby, but I never thought it'd get him killed. That's not right. He was a good man, a good father, a hard worker. He didn't deserve to die in that muddy puddle, so close to home. If I know something that can help you find whoever did this, I want to help." She glanced at her watch and stood up. "I've got to go. I'll be tied up for the next couple of days, as you can guess, but if you think of anything you need to know, call me, okay?"

"Of course. Thank you again." I wavered for a moment: I barely knew this woman, and I'm not a hugger by nature, but she'd just lost her husband and she wanted to make it right—and if anybody looked like they needed a hug, she did. So I reached out to her, and she leaned against me, just for a moment.

"Thank you," she said in a small voice. Then she turned and left quickly, with Janet trailing behind her to let her out.

Janet was back a minute later. "Well." She dropped back into her chair. "What do we do now?"

"I . . . I'm not sure. I suppose I'll start by telling the FBI what Pat told us about George and his relationship with the township, and who he might have told about his find."

Janet nodded, with a smile. "You're tight with that agent, right?"

There was no point in arguing. "Yes, and he'll want to know. I know it's not exactly evidence, but it gives us a clearer picture of what could have happened. I'll see him this afternoon. But I could use your insights about approaching the township."

"What do you mean?"

I tried to gather my thoughts. "I don't come from around here, so I don't know who's who or even what problems the township is facing. It would help to know things like who the players are, how they get along. Do they usually agree or are there a lot of battles? What kind of financial shape is the township in, and what would this development project mean to it, in terms of jobs and tax revenues and stuff like that? Who would think it's important that it go forward ASAP, and who would like to slow or stop it, see it go away completely?"

"You don't ask for much, do you?" Janet said in a sarcastic but not unkind tone. "I don't live in the township, so I can't answer you directly. But I can find out who does know, and who'd be willing to talk to you or your agent friend."

"That would be a start. How good are you at diplomacy? Subterfuge?"

She looked blankly at me for a moment, and then her face brightened. "Oh, you mean asking who knows what without being obvious about it?"

"Yes, sort of. Don't make it look like you're pumping them for information. We can't lose sight of the fact that somebody killed George, and it was probably over this. And it wasn't even in the heat of the moment, because that person moved George after he was dead, most likely to divert

attention from where it happened and what was there. I can't ask you to put yourself at risk."

"Message received, and I will be careful. But I guess I have to say that I want to help, too. I liked George. He was a decent guy, and made a point to chat with me for a minute when he visited here. I'm sure he never figured his hobby would be dangerous."

Now I was checking my watch. "I'd better go too. Take care, okay?"

"I will. Thanks, Nell. Good luck."

CHAPTER 18

James was sitting in his car reading something in a file when I pulled into my tiny driveway. "Am I late or are you early?" I asked when I climbed out of my car.

He smiled. "Neither. Both. No big deal. My interviews went more quickly than I expected."

I fished my keys out of my bag and headed toward my door, and he followed. "Are they something you can talk about?" I asked, opening the door—then crossing quickly to the other side of the room to open windows. It was getting stuffy in the August heat, but I didn't leave the air-conditioning on when I wasn't around.

"Maybe."

I waited for him to ask where I'd been, but he didn't, so I volunteered. "I may have something useful. Have you eaten? I think I have cold cuts and stuff. I haven't done much shopping lately." *Mostly because I've been spending a lot of time at your place.*

"Fine." He pulled off his jacket and draped it over a chair.

He came up behind me as I was peering into the rather empty depths of my refrigerator, and turned me around to face him. "I haven't said hello." He then kissed me thoroughly, and I wondered if we were going to skip lunch altogether. But he was the one to break it off. "We've got things to do, so let's eat."

"Right. Food. Bread, turkey, some kind of limp lettuce. There's beer." Which I kept only for him, since I didn't like the stuff much.

"Whatever," he said. "Mind if I plug in my laptop? I've bookmarked some sites."

"Sure, go ahead." I assembled a couple of sandwiches on bread that I didn't dare examine too closely, found a miraculously unopened bag of potato chips, and presented him with a loaded plate, then took my own and sat down next to him.

He pushed the laptop aside to focus on his sandwich. "You said you had something new?"

I chewed for a moment, then swallowed. "After I talked to you yesterday I got a call from Janet Butler at CCHS, and she said George Bowen's wife wanted to talk to us."

"The dead man's wife? I thought you said she'd be tied up with funeral arrangements and the like."

"That's what I'd figured, but I think she feels guilty about blowing off George's hobby and wanted to make it right." As we ate I proceeded to fill him in on what Pat Bowen had told Janet and me about who George might have told about his find. "So, in my humble opinion, you need to talk with Wakeman's senior staff, and as I've said before, with some of the guys at the township. And in the case of the township, maybe without the local police getting in the way."

"I do know how to do my job, Nell," he said.

"Of course you do, but you don't know local politics or who's buddies with who. I asked Janet to nose around and see if she could find someone you could talk to. You need someone who's willing to share the internal stuff."

"What, you'll actually let me take part in your investigation?"

I had to check to make sure he was joking. "Hey, I'm just trying to help. You're the one who can dig into phone records and financial backgrounds and all that stuff. I'm looking to work out the local dynamic and that takes some insider information. My big question now is, if George comes home all excited about his big find, who does he tell? You can ask everybody he's ever known, or everybody in his address book or on his Christmas list. I asked Pat directly, and she wasn't sure."

James held up both hands. "I surrender. You're right."

"Music to my ears." I grinned at him. "Look, I'll let you know if Janet comes up with a contact for you."

"Please do. So, are you ready to look for a place? Unless you'd rather not?" He looked at me as if challenging me to back off.

"No, no, we should do this." I stood up and took our few dishes into the tiny kitchen. "Do you want to lay out the basics? Size, location, number of bedrooms, all that stuff?"

He sat back in his chair. "You go first."

He wasn't going to make this easy, was he? "Okay. I don't think we'll find an apartment that would work. And there's something about the term *condo* that makes me think of plastic. I've told you before, I like living in the suburbs—it keeps work and home separate—but I can see that might be

difficult for you. I'm not wedded to the idea of a large house—a row house in a nice neighborhood would work. And I want a bigger kitchen and more closets. Your turn."

He was smiling. "So far we're pretty much on the same page. You're right about the burbs—I hate to waste time commuting, although keeping two cars in the city may be difficult, or at least expensive. What do you think of Marty's place?"

Marty lived in a nice, tree-lined neighborhood within walking distance of the Society. Her row house was narrow but had high ceilings. Still, from what I'd seen of it, I remembered it as cramped, and that was with only her living in it. "Why, is she selling it?"

"No, I'm just holding it up as a model."

"Not big enough for the two of us," I said firmly. "We'd be bumping into each other all the time." Neither of us was what you would call a small person.

"Okay. You want wider?"

"Yes. And maybe more windows, more light. I like it here because there are windows on all sides. And I want more elbow room if there are two of us. Don't you?"

"Yes. I wasn't sure if you would. More stuff to keep clean."

"We'll hire someone," I replied. "I hate housework. We're busy people, and we can afford it. What about condition? You into rehabbing a place?"

James skewered me with a look. "You seriously think either of us has the time to mess with woodwork and painting?"

Of course, older houses—which I preferred—always had something that needed fixing, but he was right. "Good point. So, how do we do this?"

"As I told you, you can take virtual tours of almost any place online these days. Of course, they're set up to make the place look good, so they don't show you the highway running right over the house, or tell you that you're in the airport flight path."

"I'm not going to decide on a place by looking at a two-inch picture."

"You don't have to. Tomorrow's Sunday—there should be plenty of open houses. Pick out some you like and we'll go look at them. I've already bookmarked a few."

We looked at the online listings. There were plenty to choose from, but many we easily eliminated for one reason or another. One looked too dark, even from the thumbnail pictures. Another had no parking. This one was too close to a major road; that one was too expensive, even with our combined incomes. After a while I was beginning to feel like Goldilocks, complaining that none of the porridge was "just right." "Am I being unreasonable, James?"

"I think we should walk through a few together. Things don't always look the same in reality."

"Okay. Maybe we should go through a house that we know we'll hate, too, just to get the patter right."

"Not a bad idea. Like a dry run. Are you into role-playing? Do you want to walk through and play happy home-maker and gush over the perfect cabinets and the cute bathroom tiles?"

"No. But if I did, you'd have to make manly noises about where you'd put your woodworking tools and the chain saw."

He shut his laptop with a snap. "I think we've passed the point of constructive virtual searching. We can put together a short list of three to five places to look at tomorrow. Deal?"

"Okay," I said hesitantly. "Can you take time off to go house hunting in the middle of a case?"

"Nell, I'm always in the middle of a case, usually more than one. But I'm allowed to have a life. Besides, half the people I need to talk to will be at George Bowen's funeral tomorrow. There's nothing that can't wait until Monday."

"All right then, we'll let it all wait." We passed the rest of the day in companionable fashion, doing nothing more significant than grocery shopping. It felt nice.

The next morning James pulled out a couple of maps of the city and its environs and spread them all out on my dining table, then booted up his laptop and started plotting. I left him alone because he seemed to be having so much fun. I was willing to go wherever he chose, since I had no idea where to start and I was trying to keep an open mind. I plied him with coffee and store-bought crumpets until he declared that he had a plan.

"I think I've got five that are worth a look. More than that and they'll start running together in your head."

"Okay," I said amiably, finishing my second cup of coffee.

He gave me a sharp look but didn't say anything. Was I not acting eager enough?

We set off on our house odyssey about eleven. James was a surprisingly patient driver and seldom got lost, so I felt free to watch the neighborhoods we passed through. It was interesting to see how quickly they could change, even within a block or two. I could also trace some of the city's history just by looking at the transitions, from sturdy rowhouses to modest individual homes to stately stone mansions or the other way around. I paid attention to where the public transit stops were and where the nearest amenities, like

grocery stores and pharmacies, were located. And I felt a little out of my depth; it was hard to imagine actually living in any of these areas. I kept reminding myself that even Bryn Mawr had been unfamiliar once.

We toured all five places. The Realtors burbled on about school districts and property taxes, and I nodded and smiled—and didn't fall in love with any of them. There was always something wrong: too small, too dark, too inconveniently located. Not that I'd expected to hit the ball out of the park on the first try. After all, this was just an exploratory trip. But I was finding far more elements I didn't like than those that I did.

At four we called it quits and found a quiet coffee shop to recharge our batteries.

"What did you think?" James said carefully.

"There was nothing that wowed me," I admitted, stirring the foam of my cappuccino. "This is harder than it looks. How about you?"

He shrugged. "About the same. But there's more out there, if we can find the time to look."

"When's your lease up again?"

"End of the month. I can always flash my badge and lean on the rental agency, but I'd hate to do that. They'd miss renting to the returning students."

Not a lot of time to make a big decision, although that didn't seem to be troubling James. "No pressure, right?"

"Nell, if you're having doubts . . ."

"No, it's not that. You know, something's been bothering me about Pat Bowen."

James seemed startled at my abrupt change of topic. "About the murder?"

"Not so much that. But she said that she and George had kind of grown apart. He had his interests—in this case, local history—and she had hers, and they didn't seem to have anything together. Now she feels bad because he's gone and there's nothing she can do about it, except try to find out what happened. It's like she's lost him twice. How do couples avoid that? The drifting apart?"

"Nell, I don't know. I don't have a lot of experience in this. But—what's the expression? Don't borrow trouble? The Bowens must have been married for thirty years or more. You and I, we've got a long way to go before we get bored. Don't we?"

"I hope so." I reached out for his hand across the table, and we gazed meaningfully into each other's eyes until the busboy came over and grabbed our empty cups. We weren't very good at mushy.

He finally said, "So what now? Are you going to see Wakeman anytime soon?"

"We don't have anything planned, but he kind of makes up his own rules. I've got Lissa looking at the early history of the area, so maybe she can figure out who the old bodies were. The FBI still has them, right?"

"We do. It's not quite clear what we're supposed to do with them. Bury them somewhere nearby, I suppose."

"It would help if we know who they were—there might even be family around here somewhere. Anything else you need me to look for?"

"Not that I can think of. Just stay safe, will you?"

"I try, honestly. Things keep happening."

He gave me a look but didn't say anything more on the topic, and our parting was sweet but short when he drove me home. I waved as he left and returned to my small, lonely home.

CHAPTER 19

Bright and early Monday morning I was seated at my desk at the Society with a steaming cup of coffee in front of me (on a coaster, of course, to protect the mahogany) when Eric answered the phone, and called out, "Mr. Wakeman is here."

Without an appointment. I sighed. So much for a quiet time to gather my thoughts for the coming week. "Can you bring him upstairs, please?"

"Will do." Eric headed quickly for the elevator, while I tried to figure out what Wakeman could want from me now. Maybe he wanted to end our informal agreement? I was starting to think that would be fine with me. I still believed he should have gone to Janet Butler first, and I was glad she didn't hold it against me that Wakeman had more or less ignored her and her institution and gone straight to me and the Society.

When Wakeman arrived, striding ahead of Eric, he was

not alone; he had with him a young man I thought I recognized from the press conference. I stood up to greet them.

"You've met Mason here?" Wakeman nodded toward the man next to him.

"You were at the press conference, weren't you?" I said to him.

"Scott Mason," he said, extending him hand and flashing a smile with a lot of white teeth, and we shook. "I'm the manager for the Paoli project."

I had to assume he liked saying that, because I'd heard it before. Of course, he had probably forgotten we'd already met. "Well, what do you need from me today? Do you want me to call Lissa in?" I wasn't sure she was in the building, but if it involved the history of the site, she should hear it from the horse's mouth.

"Nah, you can fill her in later," Wakeman said. "Listen, is that FBI agent any closer to solving this Bowen thing?" he asked bluntly. Not one to beat around the bush.

"No. Frankly, I'm not sure why you asked the FBI to participate. It only annoyed the local police, by implying that you didn't think they could do the job."

"Not sure they can," Wakeman answered. I wasn't going to comment, since I had no direct knowledge of that police force, but I was pretty sure having an FBI agent forced upon them by someone who didn't even live in the community did not sit well. He went on, "Look, I'm not here to argue police procedures. Mason here thinks we can move forward on schedule in spite of this murder problem. But we don't want to look like jerks, like that guy dying doesn't matter. It does, of course, and we want to get that message out. What I want from you is to get this story together fast. You know,

the history of the property, the history of the battle—real local color. Check with the township, find out what other historic projects they've supported—isn't there an old mill or something they restored? Or was it a blacksmith shop? Anyway, check those out. Make it clear that they're on board with us going ahead. If you find anything good, we can name a road after one of the dead guys or something."

I kept a smile plastered on my face and silently counted to ten. Wakeman was crude and rude, no question. But I had to add *shrewd* to that list. No matter what his real feelings were about history and the Revolutionary War, he was first and foremost a businessman, and he had a project to advance. Waiting cost money and momentum. He wanted me to put together a pretty story about the poor fallen dead, lying there in that field for a couple of centuries. I could do that, couldn't I?

"When do you want this, Mr. Wakeman?" I said sweetly.

"End of the week?" he said. He might have smiled, for maybe a tenth of a second. Had he expected me to refuse?

"I think that can be managed," I replied. It was Monday—that at least gave us a week. Then a thought occurred to me: here sat the project manager in front of me. I needed to talk to said project manager, and see if I could figure out if he had anything remotely resembling a motive for wanting to silence George Bowen. I turned to him. "Mr. Mason—" I began.

"Scott, please." He smiled eagerly. He didn't look much past thirty, but maybe that meant he was extra hungry to prove himself and impress his boss.

"Scott," I corrected myself. "Can I assume you've spent time on the site or in the township and you know the people involved there?"

"Of course. Why?"

"It might be helpful to us if you could fill me in on their personalities, their roles within the community. Then I'd be able to pitch what we write more accurately, to be more effective." That might be BS, but that didn't mean it wasn't true. "That is, if you can spare him for an hour, Mr. Wakeman?"

"Yeah, sure. Scott, you stay. But don't forget that meeting at eleven. Thanks, Ms. Pratt." He stood up and strode out the door, and Eric raced to catch up to escort him out.

Scott and I were left alone with each other. "I hope you don't mind, Scott," I said. "I live in Bryn Mawr, not that far from Paoli, but I won't pretend to know the local personalities in Goshen Township. Have you been involved in the negotiations with them from the start?"

"More or less. Well, Mitch has had his eye on that property for a long time, but he waited until he knew he had it locked in before starting any real planning. That's when he brought me on board. You know much about the town planning process?"

"I can't say that I do." I thought for a moment. "Listen, do you mind if I see if our researcher, Lissa Penrose, is in the building? I'd like her to hear what you have to say, and then you wouldn't have to repeat yourself. I'll have to go look for her, but if she's here, she should be right down the hall. Would you like some coffee while I go get her?"

"Uh, okay," he said.

"Great. Be right back." As I passed Eric's desk, I said, "I'm going to find Lissa. Could you get Mr. Mason some coffee?"

"Sure thing," Eric said.

I hurried down the hall, past the elevator, and into the processing room. Luckily Lissa was there, deep in conversation with Ben—again. "Lissa?" I called out.

She looked up, said something to Ben, then came over. "You need something, Nell?"

"Yes. Wakeman was just here again and he wants a historically accurate account about his project site—and the old bodies—by the end of the week. I've got the project manager in my office now, and I'd like you to sit in while we talk. And then you'll have to hit the ground running, I'm afraid."

"I can handle it," Lissa said calmly. "Ben's been filling me in on a lot of the details on the history and the battle, which will save me time."

"Great. Let's go. Oh, and if some of my questions seem a little, uh, oblique, just go with it, okay?"

"You're still looking at the murder?" she said, raising one eyebrow.

"Yes, kind of. I can't be too direct, but this man might know something that would help." Or he might be a killer, for all I knew, despite his fresh-faced appearance; he certainly had a strong motive for seeing this project continue. But I was on my own turf, surrounded by people, and I thought I could be tactful if I tried. I just didn't want Lissa to put her foot in anything by accident.

I led the way back to my office and introduced Lissa and Scott. We settled ourselves on the settee and flanking chairs, and I prompted Lissa to describe what she had done so far—in less than a week!—and what she planned to do next. Scott seemed pleased, nodding enthusiastically.

When Lissa had about wrapped up, I broke in. "Does that sound like the kind of material you had in mind, Scott?"

"It does, precisely. I have to say, this has been kind of an intriguing process. How much do you know about Mitchell Wakeman?" Scott asked.

I guessed he was itching to talk about his boss, who he obviously admired. "Mainly what I read in the papers. How long have you been working for him?"

"Since I graduated from college. I have a degree in architectural engineering, but Mitchell Wakeman likes everybody to get his hands dirty, so I've done a lot of things since I started working for him. This project is different, though."

"How do you mean?" I asked, honestly curious.

"Well, he's done a lot of big important buildings in the city, as I'm sure you know. He's made his name, and he's made a lot of money—he's not shy about either one. And he's given a lot back to the community, too."

"So what is special about this project?" I prompted.

"It's kind of like he wants to distill everything he's learned in his career and create this kind of ideal community, you know?"

I nodded. "I think so. The way he's described it to me, it would include homes for a range of lifestyles, from condos to fairly large freestanding houses, plus communal areas for the residents and basic amenities like shops. Have I got that right?"

"More or less. But he doesn't want it to be an insular community, closed off from the established local community. He wants it to be welcoming for area residents, too. Like with a small concert hall or movie theater, to draw other people in. It's not like a gated community, all closed in. He took a long time to pick his site, and he thought about it carefully. If you live in the suburbs, I'm sure you're aware of urban sprawl."

I had to laugh. "Yes, I've seen that even in the decade or so I've lived around here."

"It's certainly true in Chester County. Mitch wants to slow down that growth and create something that harmonizes with what's already there, while at the same time make it efficient, green—all that good stuff. It's a multiyear plan, and so far you've probably seen only the first phase."

"Wow," Lissa said. "This really sounds Utopian. And he thinks it can work? I mean, is it financially viable?"

"We think so." Scott nodded. "Again, he's been moving carefully. We've run the numbers, and we keep doing it as circumstances change. He's got enough contacts in and around Philadelphia—not to mention quite a few landmark projects that he's brought in on budget—that he was able to line up really solid funding. I know, it's rare, but if anyone can do it, Mitchell Wakeman can."

"I am impressed," I said, and I meant it. Now for my big question, for which Scott had given me a perfect opening: "So, tell me, Scott—does this discovery of these bodies, both new and old, throw a wrench into the project?"

"I'll be honest: I don't know. We have always intended to preserve the historic and physical integrity of the site to the greatest extent possible. I'm sure that there are many things yet to be discovered all around the area, and relics pop up all the time. Will it delay ground breaking? I don't think so, or if it does, not for long. Did Mitch show you the spot where they were found—before he knew they were there, of course?"

"I think we saw every square foot of the property, but I can't say I know where those men were buried," I replied.

"You probably went past it when you came in. It's a cluster of old-growth trees, on the side toward Paoli. Of course, we wouldn't be callous enough to build a home over that

particular place, but we never intended to. We always planned to retain that as a buffer or screen between the homes and the road. So, to get back to the point, what we want from you here at the Society is perhaps above and beyond what is necessary: we want to learn more about these poor soldiers, if that's what they were, not cover them up. If they were local we want to know it. If they were Hessians or something, we want to know that, too. I'm not a historian, but I don't believe we should ignore our history, especially when it's right under our noses like this."

I had to admit, Scott gave a good speech. I really wanted to believe Scott Mason. Was there any reason why I shouldn't have? "Will a historic discovery of this kind upset any of the funders?"

"I don't think so. We haven't spoken with them directly yet—we were waiting to see what you people found out first—but they take the long view, and they've seen things like this before."

Check that point off the list. "What's it been like, working with the township staff?"

"I'm not surprised you ask, Nell," Scott said. "Again, we approached this cautiously—we didn't just ride in roughshod and tell the local government that we were building a whole new development in the midst of their township whether they liked it or not. That's not the best way to get things done, and we do value their cooperation."

"I assume you need township approvals of some sort? Have you run into any opposition? Any naysayers?" I wondered what George had thought about the project.

"We are well on the path to obtaining all necessary permitting. We've met no substantial obstacles. After all, we're

becoming a part of their community. We need their infrastructure—water, sewer, power, schools, snowplowing. The whole range. And they need to know that those will not impose any new financial burden on the current citizens of the township. The tax revenues generated by this project will be far higher than they've been historically for the dairy farm. It's a win-win situation for everyone."

I was getting kind of overwhelmed. This sounded like the best of all possible worlds, a thoughtful and conscientious project intended to be fully integrated with the existing community and to actually improve the quality of life there. He almost had me sold.

"Scott, it all sounds wonderful, and I'm glad you came to us for help. Tell me, is there any township employee you've dealt with more than the others?"

"Well, the township manager, Marvin Jackson. He's a paid employee of the township. Then there was George Bowen—he was the zoning officer and also sat on the board of supervisors. That's an elected position. It's a small group, so there's a lot of overlap among the committees. Why do you ask?"

Because I'm investigating George's murder. I didn't say that. But now I knew that Scott had known George and had obviously worked with him to some extent. "I'd like to learn if there have been other historic discoveries within their boundaries and how they've handled them. Archeology has changed, and public opinion swings back and forth. If Mr. Wakeman wants us to make the strongest case for this project, then we need to know what's happened in the past."

"Of course. Was there anything else? Because I should leave for that meeting Mitch mentioned."

"Did you have any questions, Lissa?"

"I think you covered it, Nell. I really would like to see the details on how the township set up the historic district—it could be a good model."

"No problem." Scott beamed. "I'm sure the township sent us a copy for our files. I'll fax a copy over as soon as I get back to the office."

"Thank you, Scott," Lissa said. "That's all I need for now."

"So I think we've covered it," I said firmly. "We'll definitely have something for you by the end of the week. And thank you for taking the time to talk to us."

Scott stood up and smiled. "Nell, I really believe in this project, and I'm proud to be part of it. If you need anything else, just let me know. Lissa, it was nice to see you again."

"Same here," Lissa said.

"Let me walk you out." I escorted him downstairs and to the door, then made my way slowly back to my office. His story hung together, and I knew of nothing that contradicted it—but didn't explain why the body of George Bowen had ended up in the pond. James could look into the financial aspects of it, in case Scott had been lying when he said the funders weren't troubled by finding a few old skeletons. If it turned out that Mitchell Wakeman had strangled George himself and somebody had a video of it, it might be a different scenario, but that seemed more and more unlikely to me. Wakeman was a rare bird: exactly what he appeared to be, an honest businessman, even if he was a bit rough around the edges.

When I got back to the office, Lissa was chatting with Eric. "You were pretty quiet in there," I commented.

"I didn't think that township management was relevant to what I'm supposed to be looking for. I'd be happy to

explore any earlier historic projects in Goshen. I'm sorry if I misunderstood what you wanted."

"Don't worry about it—if Wakeman and his people keep dropping in unannounced, it's hard to plan. But if we get a meeting set up with the township officials, I'd like you there. Who knows—maybe there were historic projects they *didn't* pursue, for lack of funding or interest or whatever."

"I'd be happy to come, thanks. You know," she said, "I'm beginning to get really excited by this project, if it lives up to its own publicity. And of course, now it's personal—I really do want to know who the skeletons were. I'm glad Wakeman doesn't plan to mess with that part of the site."

"Me, too—and I'm glad he knows he shouldn't. Well, you've gotten a lot to get done in a short time. Let me know what you come up with and we can go over it before you put the final draft together. Okay?"

"Sure. I'm looking forward to it."

CHAPTER 20

No sooner had the dust settled from Wakeman's departure and that of his henchman Scott than Marty Terwilliger showed up. *So much for my getting anything done this morning*. "Hi, stranger!" I greeted her. "I haven't seen much of you lately."

Marty dropped into a chair in front of my desk. To my eye she was looking a bit sleeker than I'd seen her before.

"I've been, uh, busy," she said, trying to stifle a smile.

"With a certain professor?" I countered.

"Yup. I was going to tell you about it—since I guess I figure I owe you, what with James and all—but like I said, I've been busy."

"I'm glad," I said. Marty had been on her own for a while now, and I thought she deserved somebody in her life—other than her dead ancestors. And she needed to get out of the Society now and then, get some fresh air. "So, are you just touching base, or do you need me for something?"

"Both. Maybe. Let's start with this murder thing out your way, on that piece of land Wakeman owns."

I'd long since given up asking how Marty knew about everything that happened in Pennsylvania and half of New Jersey; the answer was usually from one of her relatives. "What about it?"

"Wakeman asked you to look at the history of the land, right?"

"Yes," I said slowly.

"And that's right down the road from the Paoli battle site, right?"

"Yes again. Look, is this a Terwilliger family thing?" Marty's ancestor John Terwilliger had played an important role in the Revolution in and around Philadelphia, and Marty had been sorting through his extensive family papers for years, only a small part of the Terwilliger Collection she had Rich working on.

"Sort of. Do I have to explain about General Wayne?"

I held up one hand. "No, I think I've got that covered. I've been doing a little research of my own on the battle, although Lissa's been handling the bulk of it. It seems like Wayne was not a happy camper after the battle and wanted to prove the dismal failure was not his fault. Right?"

"Close enough. It was one of the nastiest battles of the war, and Wayne was caught with his pants down in a place he knew well. He insisted on a court martial to prove he was right, and he was in fact cleared."

"So what's all this got to do with the murder? Wait—how much do you know about that?"

"Jimmy's filled me in on the bare outline. We'll come back to him. Anyway, you find a dead guy in the pond—you

know, you've got to cut that out, Nell—and it turns out he had found a couple of bodies himself not far away, except those were old enough that they could have been soldiers from that battle. Jimmy's people are running the forensics on that. Right so far?"

"I guess." I couldn't see where she was going with this, apart from her usual tendency to stick a finger in every pie she could.

Marty seemed to be enjoying herself. "You could count the Brits' casualties from that battle on one hand. They made sure everybody knew how well they'd done—although that kind of backfired on them, because the patriots got peeved that the redcoats had pulled off a sneak attack and gotten away unscathed. But anyway, if it turns out that there's a dead British soldier involved, and he was part of that battle, it would kind of change history, just a bit."

"And George Bowen, who was a history buff, would know that," I said, almost to myself. "Wait—why are you asking if there was a British soldier?"

"I heard about the buttons," she replied smugly. I didn't bother to ask how. "So if that's the case, it kind of ups the ante, doesn't it? So what would George do next?"

"That's what we've been trying to figure out. Quite possibly, if I were him, I'd do a little in-depth research on the battle, and then try to find out who the dead soldiers were. If that's even possible. Sounds like the records for that battle are a little sketchy."

"I agree. Have you talked to the Chester County Historical Society people?"

"Yes, of course I have. They knew George there, but he didn't bring this to them before he died."

"Huh. Maybe he didn't have time. But the logical conclusion is that he must have told somebody, and that somebody must have been pretty unhappy about it, and most likely that got him killed."

"Marty, James and I have already gotten that far. The question is, who would care enough to kill him? Who stood to gain anything? Wakeman's project doesn't sound like it's going to be affected, so I don't think it's related. Doesn't that more or less clear his people?"

Marty sagged just a little. "That's where I get stuck, too. You and Lissa come up with anything about the land?"

"Not yet, but we've barely had time to get started. Although Wakeman was here this morning, and he wants results by Friday, so I'm guessing we'll know a whole lot more by then."

"That'll be the old stuff. Bowen was killed last week, and not by a ghost. Who're you looking at for it?"

I tried not to laugh. "Marty, that's not my job, remember? That's the local detectives', and the FBI's, at least in part."

"Yeah, but you're the interface between the history of the place and the modern investigation. You're in a unique position. Tell me you haven't thought about it!"

"Of course I've thought about it."

"And?" she challenged.

I tried to line my thoughts up before I spoke. "I don't think the list of suspects is very long, since it's unlikely this is a random killing. Wakeman has a stake in it—he's been planning on developing this property for a while, and I will say his plans sound pretty impressive, from what I've heard. But he said to my face that he thinks things will go forward regardless."

"I've always heard that he's a straight shooter, and I can't see him killing anyone over this, even if it is his dream project. Next?"

"Unless George's wife, Pat, took out a large life insurance policy on him a couple of months ago, I'm inclined to think she's in the clear." James had no doubt already checked out things like insurance policies and the family's finances. "Of course, maybe George brought home one too many pieces of muddy junk that pushed her over the edge."

"Unless she's built like a linebacker, she couldn't have carried him and dumped him in the pond—that would have taken a man. Next?"

"Wakeman's project manager, Scott Mason, is young and eager. Maybe he saw George's discovery as a threat to the project and thought he'd do his boss a favor by covering it up and eliminating George?" Even if he was wrong, he might have believed it.

"Maybe. Keep him on the list. Who else?"

"There are the people at the township who could have a motive. I met a couple of them at that press conference the other day. It's their town, and I'm sure somebody there must have some negative feelings about Wakeman's plans."

"Anybody want to see this project shut down?"

I shook my head. "Marty, I don't know. I haven't talked to any of them, or at least, I haven't asked them that kind of question."

"Can you get to them?"

I was about to say no when I remembered that Scott had said he planned to meet with them. "The project manager said he'd be talking with them about past projects in the township that had historical significance. You know, see

how they presented the idea to the public, how they found the funding—that kind of thing. I'm sure he'd be willing to include me if I asked. It's no doubt in public records, but it would be easier to get it directly."

"So ask."

I was beginning to feel pressured. "Fine, I will. Marty, why does this matter so much to you?"

"Because I want you and Jimmy to get on with your lives."

"You think a murder investigation gets in the way of that? Heck, for us, that's business as usual. And what happened to your no-meddling policy?" This seemed to be a discussion we'd had before.

"I got tired of waiting. Are you even looking for a place?"

"Yes," I said, hating the defensive note in my voice. "We looked at a few places yesterday, but nothing's been right. Can't we get through this investigation first? With Wakeman pushing, it shouldn't be long."

Marty made a rude noise. "And then there'll be another investigation or something else in the way. Jimmy's a very patient guy, but you've got to move forward, Nell. He's not going to wait forever for you to figure things out."

"I know. I get it. Can we take this conversation in some other direction, please?"

She gave me one more searching look, then reverted to her favorite subject, the Terwilliger Collection and the status of its cataloging. It was nearly noon by the time she stood up, and said, "I'm going to go check on Rich in the processing room and see what's he's accomplished while I've been . . . busy. See you later." And she was gone, as abruptly as she'd arrived. Apparently her relationship with Ethan

hadn't mellowed her all that much, or maybe she was saving all her directness for me.

"Eric?" I called out.

"Yes, ma'am?" he responded quickly.

"Do I have any meetings scheduled for the rest of the week?"

"Nope, all clear."

"Then I'm going to try to set up a meeting in Goshen, so I'd be out of the office whenever I get it scheduled. I'll let you know." I picked up Scott Mason's card from my blotter and punched in his number. It went to voice mail, but I left a message saying I'd like to be included in any meeting he held with the Goshen township officials. Then I dug back into the pile of paperwork that seemed to multiply on my desk when I wasn't looking.

I had just pulled out my file on the Wakeman project and was searching for the phone numbers I needed when Shelby stuck her head in my door. "You busy?" she asked.

"Always." I smiled to soften the comment. "You need something?"

"I need lunch, and I feel like I haven't had a conversation with you for about a month. Wanna go get something to eat?"

"It couldn't have been that long," I protested, flipping through my daily calendar. No, not a month, only a week. And I was hungry. Dealing with Mitchell Wakeman was hard work. "Sure, as long as we don't take too long. Where?"

"The sandwich place down the street is fine. It's not the food, it's the company, right?"

I gathered up my bag and led the way out of the building. As we walked the block or so to the restaurant, I said, "You know, you're right—I haven't seen much of you for a couple

of weeks. It's this Wakeman project thing—you've heard the rumblings about that?" There was nothing secret about it anymore.

"Of course, but you can fill me in."

"Well, the result has been that I've been spending a lot of time out in Chester County rather than here at my office. I hope that won't last much longer."

"What's the man like?"

"I'll tell you over lunch." We entered the restaurant, ordered sandwiches, and settled in. As we ate I told her about Wakeman and Goshen and the recent murder (George) and the earlier, more mysterious deaths (soldiers?) and how the FBI had come to be involved, and suburban housing in general, and the state of the union, and . . . The next time I looked at my watch, an hour had passed. I couldn't remember if Shelby had said more than ten words. "I'm sorry, I've been babbling on. Everything okay with you?"

"No problems. Fundraising is always slow in summer, since all the people with money are out of town. I'll be busier by September. How's the house hunting going?"

I looked at her quizzically. "Did Marty put you up to asking? You're tag-teaming me now?"

"What? No, of course not! I haven't seen much of Marty, either—usually she pops in at least once a day. It's been a lonely few weeks. But from where I sit, it looks like you've been dragging your heels with Mr. Agent Man. He wants you to move in together. You don't want to?"

"No, it's not that." Was it? "But we've both been busy, and we haven't decided what we're looking for, and we've seen a couple of places but they just weren't right—"

Shelby cut me off. "Listen to yourself! I've never heard

such a lame string of excuses. The man's a catch and he's in love with you. What's your problem?"

I faced her squarely. "Shelby, I don't know. He's a terrific guy. We're good together. But I'm stuck. I mean, I've spent years building a nice life for myself, but it never included somebody else. It's kind of hard to turn my head around overnight."

"It's not overnight, lady—you've been seeing each other for months. It's a wonder he hasn't kicked you to the curb by now."

I sighed. "I know. What do you think I should do?"

"Bite the bullet. Buy a house. You can't get an insurance policy for Happily Ever After, but you've got to try. If it doesn't work, you'll be back to where you are now, only a couple of years older and with a few more wrinkles. And no James."

It was not a pretty picture. "I get it. And I appreciate your honesty. Don't hesitate to beat me up anytime you want to."

Shelby stuck out her tongue at me.

"I'd better get back—I've got calls to make. And I'll get the check, since you provided the free psychotherapy."

"Anytime."

CHAPTER 21

I settled back at my desk and started making phone calls. A couple of hours later, the office phone rang and Eric poked his head in the door. "A Ms. Butler on the phone for you?"

"Oh, right, from Chester County. I'll pick up."

When Janet came on the line, she said, "Hi, Nell. Are you going to be out this way anytime soon?"

"I'm trying to plan something out there for this week, actually. Why?"

"I've been going through some stuff, and I found a few things I think you ought to see. Nothing earthshaking, but they might be relevant. But you don't need to make a special trip just for those."

I trusted Janet's judgment on anything related to Chester County history. "I'd love to take a look at them. Let me see if I can get this other meeting scheduled and we'll firm up the date. And thanks for calling." After I'd rung off, I

reflected again how glad I was that Janet was willing to work with me rather than resenting my involvement. I resolved to make sure that Wakeman acknowledged her contribution to whatever solution we arrived at eventually.

Scott Mason returned my call after three. "Sorry it took me so long to get back to you, but that meeting ran on and on. I've got an appointment in Goshen tomorrow morning. Your message said you wanted to talk with the township people—you want to meet me at the township building at, say, ten?"

"That sounds fine. Who's the meeting with?"

"Marvin Jackson, the township manager, and Joseph Dilworth, who's on the historic commission."

"Sounds good. I've met both of them, but only briefly. Thanks for including me. I'll see you there." I debated a moment about involving Lissa, but decided that with a looming deadline she'd be more useful staying at the Society and pulling together the research on the Garrett farm. I could report back any important details, and she could talk with them at greater length later. If there was a later.

Then I hit the speed dial button for James's private line. He answered quickly. "What's up?"

"I'm meeting with Scott Mason at the Goshen township offices tomorrow morning to talk to Marvin Jackson and Joseph Dilworth about their past historic projects. So I should probably head home again after work tonight." I realized I wasn't sure what message I was sending him: did I want him to join me there or not?

There was an infinitesimal hesitation before he answered. "All right. Dinner tomorrow?"

"Sounds good. I should get to the office sometime in the

afternoon." I debated briefly about mentioning Marty's lecture, and decided that would be better handled in person. "Oh, by the way—have you FBI types looked at the backgrounds for the township employees?"

"I can't talk about that, Nell."

Another topic for tomorrow night. At least then I'd know something more about the people involved, face-to-face. "Okay. I'll call you tomorrow when I get here and you can let me know where you want to meet."

"I will. Take care." He hung up first. I'd driven in, and I arrived home while it was still daylight and grabbed my mail on the way in. Maybe most of the commuters were down at the shore—I wasn't going to complain. I dumped the mail on the dining table, where it joined at lot of other unsorted stuff, and went upstairs to change into something grubby and comfortable. Back downstairs I wandered aimlessly to the kitchen. Spending so much time in the city with James had wrought havoc with my grocery shopping, and I didn't feel like getting in the car and going out to find food. I petulantly told myself that if I lived alone I could eat cereal and ice cream for dinner whenever I wanted, so there. Very mature.

Instead of cereal I made myself some marginally more grown-up scrambled eggs, and sat at my table and looked through the mail while I ate. Mostly junk mail and solicitations—as a former fundraiser I sympathized with the senders, but I didn't write checks to them—but one letter caught my eye: it was from the group of psychologists who owned the "big house" for which my little building had once been the carriage house. I opened the letter with some trepidation. Was the group telling me that they had sold the front property to someone else? I wasn't sure what that would

mean, but the area was kind of transitional. The grand old houses now held a shifting mix of multifamily residences and discreet commercial offices such as those of "my" psychologists. I didn't see whoever handled zoning in Bryn Mawr loosening the restrictions anytime soon, but odd things could happen.

The letter was a preliminary offer to buy my little property. It seemed that the practice was prospering and they wanted more space, and had decided that my ex–carriage house would make an excellent site for group sessions. The price they preemptively offered made me blink and look again: it was more than twice what I had paid for the place a decade ago, admittedly before a lot of fixing up, and it was more than fair by current market standards.

Was this a sign from above? Had James somehow exerted pressure on the group to buy me out? I smiled at that paranoid thought. My first impulse was to call him and tell him about the very nice offer, but after a moment of consideration I decided to sit on it overnight and see how I felt about it in the morning. I could talk to James about it at dinner tomorrow. At the rate that list of topics was growing, it was going to be a very long dinner.

The next morning I slept in, since I didn't need to be in Goshen until ten and it was a relatively short drive away; I'd even scheduled lunch with Janet. But I found I was restless. After I'd washed up my few breakfast dishes, I kind of drifted around my small home, looking at it with a new eye. A decade ago I'd transformed it from a badly renovated rental unit to a comfortable home—for one. I'd been happy here, though—or had I just been kidding myself? What did it mean, that I'd built myself a home with room for only one person?

Finally, I couldn't stand fidgeting any longer and decided to leave early. I could sit in my car in the parking lot and make notes of the questions I wanted to ask, if I arrived with time to spare. Since I was driving against traffic headed toward Philadelphia, I took Route 30 to Paoli and then turned onto the Paoli Pike, following it to the Goshen township building, a sturdy, modern brick structure. Scott Mason was already waiting, ever the eager beaver.

"Good morning," I called out as I got out of my car. The air still felt pleasantly cool, although it promised to be hot later. "Are you an early bird, or do you live near here?"

"Hi, Nell. I live in the city, but I thought I'd allow myself plenty of time for traffic. I forgot it would all be going the other direction, so here I am. You have any questions before we go in and meet with the guys?"

"Tell me about who we're seeing?"

"The township manager, Marvin Jackson—he's an outside hire, but he's been here for a while—and the head of the historical commission, Joe Dilworth. He's local. That's a seven-member board, and advisory only, but they do carry some weight in decision making. Other people said they might drop by—like the township engineer and the township solicitor, but they've already been involved in plenty of meetings, and they're on board with the project going forward. Nobody's raised any new issues. So my main goal today is to touch base with the manager, bring him up to speed on what impact the death might have on the plans, and talk about strategy with the historical commission. As you may know, not too many years ago the township did a thorough renovation of the old blacksmith shop not far from here, and there's also a small historic district—I sent Lissa

the details on all that before the end of the day yesterday. Both have been well handled and the community has responded positively to them. You may have noticed as you drove over here that even the corporate park you passed maintains a lot of green space and a couple of the old stone buildings. That's the feeling Mr. Wakeman is aiming for, maybe even a little more private with the addition of some more greenery over time."

"It sounds lovely. So you've been working with the township staff from the beginning?"

"I have. They're a good bunch. And what's more, old Ezra laid the groundwork well. He made his plans known to the township well before he passed on, so everybody had time to get used to the idea. He was a supervisor for the township for decades and was always respected, so people listened to him. It's been a pleasure to work on this, and everything has gone really well—at least, up until George Bowen's unfortunate death." He looked quickly at his watch. "We should go in now."

I followed him into the building, where a pleasant receptionist escorted us to a well-lit conference room. Three men were already there. They greeted Scott, and then he introduced me—again, as it turned out, since we all recognized each other from the press conference. Coffee was offered and accepted. While we poured from the carafe on the table, Scott handed out copies of stapled documents.

"As you can see, this is simply an update on documents you already have," he explained. "The numbers have held remarkably steady, and we're ready to proceed along the lines of the original schedule."

"What about the murder?" The township manager,

Marvin Jackson, said bluntly. "You going to wait until the cops have figured that out?"

"We're hoping that won't take long, Marv. After all, we have the best minds of the local police working on it, plus FBI assistance. You knew George, didn't you?"

"Sure did. Good guy, did his job well. He really cared about Goshen." The men observed an awkward moment of silence.

"How did George feel about this project?" I asked.

The township men exchanged a glance. "I think it made him sad to see one more parcel lost—we've already got that corporate park up the road. But he knew what it would mean for the township."

"What exactly was his job?" I went on.

"Zoning officer. He made sure local codes were enforced. We're not that big a township, so people who work here kind of wear different hats. George kept an eye on most building projects, even things like rebuilding a chimney or installing lawn sprinklers. Anything that needed a permit, really. He liked it—he enjoyed talking to people, and he wasn't hard-nosed about it. If somebody was having problems getting a home repair project done, he'd cut them some slack. But he didn't forget about it, either—he'd nudge people gently until it was finished and he could sign off on it."

"People must have liked him."

"Yeah, they did. Last person I would have expected to be murdered. I don't know anybody who ever said a bad word about him."

Scott seemed to be fidgeting, no doubt impatient to move the meeting along and get back to the city. "Joe, tell Nell about the historic district."

Joe smiled at me, then sat back in his chair and proceeded to outline the entire forty-year history of the Goshen historic district, now a national historic district. A variety of buildings had been moved there from different parts of the township, but had been carefully integrated so they looked as though they had always been there. It had proved a mildly popular local attraction over the past decade or so.

"Upkeep comes out of the township budget, right?" I finally said, when Joe seemed to be winding down.

"Sure does." He nodded. "We contribute some basic maintenance for the buildings, but there's always more. You should know all about that."

I smiled at him. "I sure do. Did the township make any effort to acquire the Garrett property?"

Marvin addressed that question. "Unless Ezra had decided to give it to us free and clear, there was no way we could have afforded it. He'd cut a deal with Wakeman before we even thought about it, but he made sure there were some restrictions about what could and couldn't be done on it. He brought it to the township as a courtesy, since he had every right to sell, but we couldn't find anything to object to."

I filed that away for future thought. "Mr. Dilworth—Joe—you said that the Garrett land had been in the family for a long time?"

"Since Goshen was first settled," Dilworth replied. "That's why we were so glad that the land wouldn't be chopped up. There's a lot of history there."

"I look forward to learning more about it. It sounds as though Ezra Garrett was an impressive man."

"That he was. He's been gone for a while now, but he's still missed."

"What about his sons? How did they feel about their dad selling the place?"

"Will and Eddie? Heck, there was no future in a rundown dairy farming operation, and they weren't about to hold on to a prime piece of real estate out of sentiment, even if it has been in the family for centuries. Wakeman gave Ezra a fair price, and the kids inherited the proceeds. To be honest, I'm kinda glad Ezra handled it the way he did—at least Wakeman is keeping the parcel intact, and he's promised to make this a classy development, not a bunch of ticky-tacky houses. Right, Scott?"

"Exactly," Scott agreed. "Mr. Wakeman knew and liked Ezra, and they worked it out between them. We intend to follow through in that spirit." He hesitated a moment. "Look, would it be in bad taste if we named something after George Bowen? A street, or maybe a community center? You know the people around here better than I do."

The township men were nodding thoughtfully. "Might be a nice idea. Let us think about it, okay? Nobody has to decide this right now."

Scott looked relieved. "Of course not. You can ask around, see what the response is."

Marvin rubbed his hands together; he looked like he was eager to end the meeting. "Anything else we can help you with today? Ms. Pratt, you and your people are looking at the history of the place, right?"

"We are. Does anyone here know anything about those older bodies found on the land?" I asked, curious to see how they would respond.

Marvin deferred to Joseph, who seemed happy to answer. "Ms. Pratt, we're sitting on a lot of history here. We turn up

musket balls and old tools and bottles all the time. No bodies until now, but it's not really surprising. If you know anything about the Paoli Massacre, you know it was a mess. Who knows how many other bodies might have met the same fate?"

"I've read a little, and I can see your point." I didn't mention that the timing of the discovery seemed a bit odd. "In any case, we aren't planning a scholarly study. More likely we'll give Mr. Wakeman something that he can use to help promote his development to prospective buyers. You know, 'live in the midst of history,' and so on. I hope he'll share it with you."

Scott bounced to his feet. "Well, gentlemen, I'll let you review the handouts when you have time, but I think it's safe to say there are no surprises. We hope to break ground in the fall, as planned. Please call me if you have any questions or concerns."

I seemed to have no option but to follow Scott's lead, but I couldn't think of any more questions myself. "Thank you for seeing me. May I get in touch with you if I have any questions about the history of the town?" I handed each man one of my business cards.

"Sure, no problem," Marvin said. "But Janet Butler over in West Chester probably knows as much as we do."

I laughed. "And I'm meeting her for lunch today."

"Thanks again, guys," Scott said, shaking hands and all but pushing me out the door.

I followed meekly, but once in the parking lot, I asked, "Are you in a hurry?"

"What? No. But this was mainly a courtesy call—there really wasn't much new. Did you get what you needed?"

"I think so," I said, although I wasn't sure what I had

hoped for. I'd confirmed that everybody had liked George, but that wasn't a surprise. Nobody seemed to want to stop the project from going forward. So why was George dead? Maybe he'd found something more than a few old buttons when he was snooping around. Maybe the bodies had been buried with a carefully wrapped diary written by George Washington, or General Wayne's battle plan, and George Bowen's killer had snatched it from him. "You're headed back to the city now?"

"Yup. You said you were meeting Janet Butler at the historical society?"

"Yes." I stopped short of telling him that Janet thought she had found something I needed to see. It could be nothing or it could be important, but Scott didn't need to know about it. "I assume I'll be talking with you later in the week, when the Society puts that report together for you."

"Great, thanks, Nell. See you!"

I watched him pull away, and then I got into my car and headed in the opposite direction, toward West Chester—a route that took me by the Garrett farm yet again. It still looked green and peaceful; there were a few ducks bobbing on the small pond by the road. It seemed an unlikely place for a murder. Or two, or three.

CHAPTER 22

I arrived at the Chester County Historical Society a few minutes early, but Janet was free, and came down from her office to meet me. She looked excited.

"Thanks for coming on such short notice, Nell. I know you must be busy."

"I'm happy to be here, especially since this Wakeman thing has leapfrogged to the top of my priority list—not by my own choosing, may I add."

Janet's eyes twinkled. "The man can be a bit, uh, peremptory, can't he?"

I laughed. "That's putting it kindly! Did you want to show me what you've found, or should we get something to eat first?"

"Are you hungry?"

"I'm always hungry. Is there someplace nearby we could walk to?"

"Sure—right around the corner. Follow me."

I didn't need much encouragement. It was a lovely day, and I liked West Chester—it felt about the right size, and it had a real center, not just shops flanking a too-busy local highway. High trees arched over the street, keeping the downtown cool. We strolled without hurrying, arriving at a corner brewpub on the nearest corner in a few minutes. Once seated inside, we each ordered the brew of the day and sandwiches, and settled in to talk.

"I am so glad you brought me in on this," Janet began. "This is really exciting, especially since I think I can help."

"I'm glad to hear it. And I'll do my best to make sure your participation is recognized somewhere, and not just in a footnote. After all, you're putting a lot of time into this. Do you have any staff who can help?"

Janet waved her hand dismissively. "Sure there's staff, but I knew George, and I find this whole thing with the old bodies fascinating. Why should I hand the research off and miss all the fun?"

We talked about professional matters through our sandwiches, and I noted that we shared a lot of the same problems, setting aside the difference in the respective sizes of our institutions. The sandwiches were generously sized and tasty, and the local brew was good. If I hadn't had to go into the city later, I might have been tempted to play hooky and get to know West Chester a little better. But now was not the time.

"Let me pick up the tab," I volunteered. "I'm pretty sure I can pass it on to the Wakeman Trust, or whoever he decides is paying the bills."

"I'm not going to argue with you."

With the bill settled, Janet and I emerged from the

restaurant and walked the few blocks back to her society. "You know," I began tentatively, "I feel like I'm here on false pretenses. I'm not really a historian—I started out as an English major and then ended up as a fundraiser. I'm president of the Society kind of by default. So I'm willing to bet you know a whole lot more about the history of this area than I do."

"I suppose I do," Janet replied. "I've lived here most of my life. I started out as a docent at the society, leading tours, which kind of shifted into researching the collections, and things kind of happened from there. As I'm sure you know quite well."

"I do. It's been a strange trip, and nothing that I'd planned."

"Are you enjoying it?"

"I am. I won't say it's always a pleasure to be an administrator, but I do believe in the institution and what we're doing, and if I can keep it moving forward in this increasingly digital world, I'll be satisfied." *I'd like it even better if I could concentrate on the job and stop finding crimes under my nose*, I reflected silently.

"There's still nothing like the real thing," Janet said firmly. "I love being able to handle the original documents."

"Amen to that!" We'd reached her building, and she held open the door for me to enter. "So, what've you got to show me?"

"Follow me." Instead of leading me to her office, we went back to the shabby working area at the rear of the building, where several archival boxes sat on the long table, along with a few pairs of white cotton gloves lying beside them.

I looked at Janet and waited for her to explain.

"Have a seat," she said, waving at one of the folding

chairs next to the table. I sat, and she took another chair opposite and pulled on a pair of the gloves. "When Ezra Garrett reached ninety years old—still in full possession of his faculties, let me add—he decided to go through all the family documents. That must have been about the same time he started talking to the Wakeman people. Since the Garretts had been living on the farm for over two hundred years, and since they seem to have had a gene for hoarding, if there is such a thing, you can imagine the scope of what Ezra and the family had assembled over the years. Well, maybe that's not overstating it: his ancestors hadn't gone in much for papers. They were farmers from the beginning, and Ezra and his son Eddie were the last of them, once William washed his hands of the place. Let's say that what was preserved was very succinct, but valuable to any social historian. And to anyone interested in the history of Chester County, like me."

"Believe me, I understand. What did you find?"

"I'm getting there. Ezra got started, but his energy wasn't what it used to be, so after a bit he turned it all over to us."

"As a gift, or only for processing?"

"He gave it all to us, with the provision that we make it accessible to any of his family members who wanted to see it, and eventually to the public, once we'd cataloged and conserved it. And, yes—I can see you thinking—he left money to cover that work. But as you might guess, we don't have a lot of staff, and there was no apparent rush to get the processing done. Ezra had made a first pass and seen whatever he wanted to see, so he wasn't pressuring us to hurry. And then he died, and since nobody had requested access to the documents, we've been taking our time with the

cataloging, kind of dipping into it a little at a time whenever somebody was interested. We've had a couple of interns from the university here, but most of them don't know anything about local history, so they're just going through the mechanics of cataloging."

I understood what she was telling me, but I wondered when she was going to get to the point. Here we were sitting in front of Ezra Garrett's family's historical collection of documents. I guessed that she had found something that she wanted to share with me, and I hated to begrudge her the pleasure of telling her tale, but I still had to get into the city sometime today. "Did the Wakeman deal prompt you to work any faster?"

"To be honest, no. You've got to remember that a lot of the discussion about the disposition of the land went on behind the scenes, and nobody came to us for anything. It was really only when you were called in that I sat up and took notice. That's when I hauled out these boxes and took stock of where we were in the cataloging."

"And?"

"I know, you're getting impatient." Janet grinned at me. "Okay, I checked our rough list, and then I focused on the Revolutionary War period, say, 1770 to 1790. There wasn't a lot, as you might guess, but I was lucky to find that Edward Garrett, the owner back then, had kept sort of a daybook. He mainly kept notes about farm issues, like the weather and which cows had calved, and major expenses, like replacing the roof or adding on to the house. But he did mention the battle."

Aha, now we had finally gotten down to it. "What did he say?"

"Not as much as I'm sure you'd like. He was a Quaker, which was a difficult thing to be during the Revolution because nobody really trusted a group of people who refused to fight, or even to pick sides. I'd guess the family kept pretty quiet about it, but that's only by inference, since they held on to their land and there were no public complaints about them."

"I assume that means they didn't take part in the local militia?" I asked.

"Not officially, at least. Anyway, as you must know by now, the Battle of Paoli took place just up the road from the farm, so it would have been hard to ignore it entirely. Then these two bodies turn up now, and evidence suggests that they died somewhere around the same time, and at least one of them must have been wearing a British uniform, because of the buttons that George found. Anyway, long story short, Edward makes a rather cryptic mention of the event. Here, it's easier to show you. But please, put on gloves first!"

I had already reached for the cotton gloves. I took the small volume Janet offered me from her hand and studied it briefly: worn leather binding, pages in surprisingly good condition, ink browned by age but still legible. I leafed through it carefully, noting the intermingling of financial notations, comments on planting cycles, even the occasional note of someone's death.

"I marked the pages," Janet said, watching me.

I turned to the place she had marked, and read. Edward, if he was indeed the writer, had summed up the battle in two lines, but had given a little more space to the chaos of the retreat. There must have been people milling around all over the roads that dawn, the American soldiers torn between rallying to defend themselves and retreating as fast

as possible to regroup and assess what they had left. And Garrett's farm had been smack in the middle of the path. I looked up at Janet. "This is fascinating from a historical point of view, but what's it got to do with the bodies?"

"Look at the next page."

I turned the page, and read, " 'We laid the two dead men to rest where they fell. God grant them peace.' " The handwriting was the same, but shakier, as if the writer were upset; it returned to normal by the next page, where the entry was about shoeing a horse.

"So you're assuming that those are the two bodies that George Bowen found?"

"Wouldn't you? It's not a burial ground—all the Garretts are buried behind the meeting house nearby. But the conditions at that moment must have been awful, and I've read that most of the casualties during that war were buried where they fell. But there's another possibility—and this is pure speculation on my part, mind you: What if the two dead men were indeed from different sides? How were the Garretts supposed to return them to the right people? Think about it—no matter which way they turned, somebody would have been angry at them, and might possibly have taken it out on good Quaker Edward. Maybe it wasn't right to simply bury them and say nothing, but in the heat of the moment it was the easiest thing to do, and safest for the Garretts. And things in the region stayed pretty unsettled for a while—maybe there never was a good opportunity to fix things. Does that make sense to you?"

I nodded slowly. "I think it does. Tell me, did George Bowen ever look at the Garrett papers?"

Janet tilted her head. "He may have. He's someone who

would've had an interest, out of sheer curiosity. He was in and out over the past few years, not that he always stopped to chat with anyone. We probably don't keep track as scrupulously as you do, and he may not have filled out a request. He had kind of free rein with the collections, because everyone knew him and trusted him."

"I was wondering if he knew he was looking for bodies, or if he just happened to stumble on them. I don't suppose it matters, since it's pretty clear that he found them. Who would George have talked to first?"

"I'm still not sure. I think he would have told us, sooner rather than later, but he might have gone to the township first."

"Somebody on the historical commission, maybe?"

Janet considered that. "Like Joe Dilworth? I . . . don't know. I'd like to say that George's commitment to history outweighed his sense of duty to the township, but he was a conscientious man, and it could have gone either way. I really can't say. Poor George. He must have been torn."

And now he was dead. Had he picked the wrong person to tell?

"Does this help anything?" Janet asked.

I sighed. "Janet, I don't know. I think there could be a great story in there to give to Wakeman, and I'll tell Lissa about it, because I'm sure she'll want to see the book. Whether it tells us anything about who killed George, it's not clear. I need to think about this, maybe share it with someone." Like James, for instance. "Take good care of this book, though. Is there anything else in there that you think I should see? Or anything else about the farm in that era that may tie in?"

"I'll go through it more carefully, particularly the part that comes right after the war. I can't believe they just left those poor men in the field there, but I guess I can understand their thinking. Where are the bodies now?"

"The FBI took custody of them—they have the best forensics lab around. I'm not sure what they can tell us, but at least they're looking at them carefully. Listen, I've got to get into the city this afternoon, but thank you for sharing this. Wakeman wants a short report by the end of the week, and if we find anything that either corroborates or contradicts your theory, I'll let you know."

"Thank you—I'd appreciate it." She stood up. "Let me see you out."

Stepping out into the bright sunshine after being closeted in a dim room with documents from another century was a bit of a shock. "I'll be in touch," I told Janet, then walked over to the parking garage where I'd left my car. It was early enough in the day that I didn't have to contend with traffic as I drove toward Philadelphia, but I still had time to think about what Janet had shown me. Had Edward Garrett had mixed loyalties? Shouldn't he have told either the patriots or the redcoats, or both, about the two dead men, if in fact they had fought on different sides? Telling no one sounded politically expedient but not exactly honorable. I decided that I needed to know more about Edward Garrett before I made a final judgment.

And I wondered if the FBI forensic team could tell me any more about the bodies. I would have to ask James, over dinner. Another romantic conversation: *What's new with those skeletal corpses we found?*

CHAPTER 23

I arrived in Philadelphia about three and was lucky to find a space in the lot across from the Society. Not much was left of the workday, but I was looking forward to seeing James later.

On my way upstairs I made a detour to look for Lissa. I found her in the third-floor stacks, sitting cross-legged on the floor reading an old book, so completely absorbed that she was startled when I spoke. "Hey, Lissa. No, don't get up." I paused by a sturdy bookshelf and listened for a moment but didn't hear any other human sounds near us. I leaned down toward her. "Listen, I found out something today from Janet. Edward Garrett kept a daybook during the Revolution, and he mentions burying two bodies on his land after the battle at Paoli."

Lissa sat up straighter, her eyes bright. "Really? Did he say who they were?"

"Nothing like that. In fact, it's barely more than a

sentence, but I think it corroborates our guess about how those bodies came to be there."

"It's too bad that Edward Garrett didn't identify who he buried."

I smiled. "That would've been too easy, eh? He might honestly not have known them—after all, there were soldiers from all over the place running around in that battle. Or, since they may have fought for different sides, maybe he simply didn't want trouble, and burying them was the easiest solution." I straightened up. "I want you to check everything about Edward Garrett and the farm around the time of the Revolution, please. I'm sure you're itching to get a look at that daybook, but you probably won't have time before Wakeman wants his report."

"I was hoping to look into the Garrett family in more depth a bit later. I'm not a genealogist, and since the land stayed in the family all along, there wasn't a lot of reason to look at all the wills or deeds."

"Could you do that now? We may not need to give all that information to Wakeman, but I'm curious about a couple of things." I stopped her before she could ask for particulars. "No, I don't want to give you any hints—just assemble the basic facts and give them to me tomorrow sometime. How's the rest of it coming?"

"Good, I think. You had lunch with Janet today, right?" I nodded, and she went on. "Did she find that reference to the bodies while you were there?"

"No. She told me that Ezra Garrett gave the Chester County society a big batch of family papers before he died, and they're not fully cataloged, so she's been slowly going through them and came across this. If you exhaust what we

have here at the Society, you might want to take a run out there and look. Of course, all this has to be in presentable form by Friday."

"That's barely three days!"

"I know, I know," I replied, laughing. "Do what you can, and we'll see where that takes us."

"Gotcha," Lissa said. "I'll get back to you."

With only a couple of hours of the working day left, I hesitated to start anything new. I called James to confirm our date, then took care of the messages from the day and signed a few papers that Eric had left neatly stacked on my desk for me. Then, feeling restless, I got up and wandered down the hall. I hadn't talked to Ben recently, and I felt badly about that, since he'd kind of been thrown directly into the deep end. I saw that Latoya was in her office and went over and knocked on the doorframe.

She looked up, startled. "Nell? What can I do for you?"

"I wanted to see if you've been keeping an eye on Ben Hartley. You know, giving him a helping hand when he needs it."

"I have made sure to speak with him at least daily. He does not appear to acknowledge that he might need help. I only hope that he doesn't assume that to ask for help is a sign of weakness."

"Duly noted. He has a lot to prove, to himself at least, but he still doesn't know collections management. What do you think we need to do to modify his physical space appropriately?" There, I was asking her opinion.

"He seems to have settled into the processing room. It may be that's a better location than in the cubicle outside this office that has been used by prior registrars."

We talked about furniture options for a few minutes, and in the end, I stood up, and said, "Why not just ask him what he wants? If he's touchy, he's going to have to get over it, here or at any other workplace."

"A good point, Nell. We are all trying so hard to be politically correct that we miss the obvious."

We parted ways amicably.

I didn't mean to invade Latoya's turf, but since I was close by I decided to drop in on Ben and make sure he was doing all right. I felt guilty for not thinking of what he might need. Of course, I often felt guilty that most of the staff had to make do with elderly desks and rickety chairs; and then I felt guilty because I had the nicest furniture in the building. But that was for impressing important people, not to keep me happy.

I located Ben in front of a computer in the processing room.

"Hey, Ben, how's it going?"

"All right, I guess. I'm somewhere halfway up the slope of the learning curve, maybe."

"Don't worry. That's to be expected."

"Hey, can I ask you something?" he said.

"Sure, go ahead."

"You think I can find a better desk, or modify this one? It's not exactly wheelchair-friendly."

Just what I'd feared. "I'm sorry. Tell me what you'd prefer and we'll see what we can do about getting it."

Ben actually laughed. "Hey, don't get bent out of shape about it. If you're okay with it, though, I may know some people I can ask to help. I assume the budget is nonexistent?"

"Close to. But we'll work it out. Does that mean you're

thinking about sticking around long enough to use the new-and-improved furniture?"

"Yeah, I think so. I'm enjoying it. Nice place, nice people. Why would I leave?"

"Dusty history isn't for everyone. Oh, and thanks for your insights on the Battle of Paoli. I look at that site in a whole new way now, every time I drive by it. Of course, it's always amazed me that anybody managed to conduct a battle in those days. How did the military communicate with each other on the field? And if the original plan fell apart, did all the commanders have a plan B, or did everything just fall into chaos?"

"Some of each. That particular battle is a good example. And add to the mix that any local militia that took part had precious little military training, and not necessarily with large units. The Brits really did have the advantage there—they were better organized and equipped, and they had more experience."

"Well, I have to say it becomes a lot more real when you're standing on the spot where it took place. I'll let you get back to work. Contact whoever you want about the desk and let me know what you come up with."

As I left I reflected that I hadn't asked him anything about the technical aspects of what he was supposed to be doing, but at least he was proving to be a true history enthusiast, and that counted for a lot.

I left the office at six thirty, assuming—correctly—that I'd run into city traffic on my way to James's neighborhood. I was lucky that it was still summer, which meant I found parking easily, since the Penn students hadn't yet returned to the nearby campus. I let myself into the building and into

James's apartment to find he hadn't arrived home. That gave me time to look critically at the place—and at what it said about him. Sure, I'd spent plenty of time in it, especially over the past month, but I'd never really paid attention to it. Actually, the simplicity of the place had made the caretaking part of the job easier: I could concentrate on nursing rather than housekeeping, not that I ever gave much energy to the latter in any case. But once James was on the road to recovery, we kept colliding with each other. The space had worked for him; it did not work for the two of us.

I heard his key in the lock, and James walked in with a couple of bags that smelled wonderful. He dropped them on the kitchen counter quickly, then turned and kissed me. "I missed you."

"Me, too," I said. "I keep thinking of things I want to tell you. I should start keeping a list."

He finally let me go and started pulling containers out of the bags. "I got Greek for a change. What sort of things were you thinking about? Houses or dead bodies?"

"Both, I guess. How much of the case can you talk about?"

"Depends." He pulled plates out of a cabinet. "Wine?"

Did I plan to go back to my place later? No, I decided quickly. "Sure."

He handed me the plates and I took them to the small round dining table while he filled two wine glasses, then joined me. "Business before pleasure?"

"The case, you mean? Let me go first. Today Scott Mason and I met with Marvin Jackson and Joe Dilworth and the other Goshen Township people. Have you talked to them?"

He shrugged, chewing, then said, "Not yet, or not personally. What did you make of them?"

I looked at him curiously. Was he fishing for something? Was there something I should have noticed? "They seemed nice enough. They said the right things about George Bowen and his death. Joe told me all about the local historic district and how it came about. What are you looking for?"

"Just between us, Nell, Marvin Jackson's bank accounts show that he's stretched very thin."

"Why does that matter?"

"Because it's possible he's been dipping into township funds to cover his personal debts. Wakeman's project would help him refill the coffers before anybody had to take notice officially at the end of the fiscal year. Bowen's discovery might have delayed things enough to make that an issue."

"Huh." Funny how little we know about what goes on behind the scenes in any community, large or small. "Would that give him enough of a motive for silencing George? Even if George told him about finding the bodies right away, Marvin should have known that George would talk to someone else, like the county historical society."

"But did he?"

"Not that I know of, actually. I had lunch with Janet in West Chester today, and she said George hadn't gotten around to telling her people about it. But that's not to say he didn't tell *someone* at the township. Can you tell me anything significant about Joseph Dilworth?"

"Dilworth's been having an affair with George's wife," James said bluntly.

I gaped at him. "How do you find out these things? And this is just scratching the surface for you guys at the FBI? You scare me."

"Phone records, mostly. Let's not get into that. But it does

mean that, while Dilworth might not have any reason to interfere with the historical aspects of this project, he might well have had a personal reason to want George out of the way."

I tried to remember what Pat Bowen had said when I'd talked to her. "Pat hates history. Or maybe it was only how much of George's attention it consumed. Joseph isn't a burly guy—heck, Marvin is beefier—but could he and Pat together have hauled George's body to where it was found?"

"Possibly."

"Great. So you haven't eliminated anyone? What about Scott Mason, the eager young assistant?"

"He has no alibis for the relevant time periods. Nor does Wakeman, officially, for that matter—he volunteered that he was home with his wife of thirty-five years and whichever of his eight kids are still living at home. I haven't confirmed that with any of them, but I'm inclined to believe Wakeman and leave it at that."

"What about phone records? Did Scott and Wakeman exchange any calls at the right times?"

"Nell, we don't have enough evidence to request a subpoena for Wakeman's records. I don't supposed you 'borrowed' Scott's phone to check his call list?" He hurried to add, "Just kidding." He took a sip of wine. "Was there anything else?"

"Well, as a matter of fact, Janet did show me something interesting. Ezra Garrett left all his family papers to the county society before he died—I guess he wanted to be sure they stayed together and were well looked after—but Janet and her staff hadn't gotten around the cataloging them yet when all this started. They have even less staff than we do,

so recently Janet took a look at them herself. She found a daybook kept by Edward Garrett—that's Ezra's Quaker ancestor who owned the farm at the time of the Revolution."

James interrupted me. "What's a daybook?"

"Kind of a daily journal that covers administrative and financial things about running the farm. Not a personal diary, mostly business details. Anyway, there's a short entry right after the battle, where he mentions burying two bodies where they fell. What're the odds that those are the same two bodies that George found?"

"I'd say it's pretty likely. I'd hate to think there were more bodies scattered around the place—or anywhere else for that matter, but from what Ben told us about the battle, it wouldn't surprise me. I don't suppose that book mentioned who they were?"

"No. It was a very terse entry. I got the impression that Edward would rather not have mentioned it at all, but maybe he thought it was important to leave some kind of record. It does seem to be the only mention of bodies we've found so far."

"Did Ezra know about them?"

"How am I supposed to know that? From what Janet said, he just showed up one day with several boxes full of family books and papers. Who knows if anybody in his family ever read them? Janet said no one has shown any interest in them since Ezra dropped them off—that's partially why they haven't exactly rushed to sort through the contents. Maybe some of Edward's offspring, if they were still involved in running the farm—they might have looked back to see how he had done things. Or—" I stopped myself and realized what had been percolating in the back of my consciousness, and what had

prompted me to ask Lissa to look more closely at Edward Garrett and his family. "What if the family *did* know?"

"Know what? That there were two bodies on their land?"

"Well, maybe they kept quiet about it. Maybe Edward hid the book—he couldn't bring himself to destroy it because it was the only evidence of those two bodies, vague though it is. How do we figure that out now?" And then another thought hit me. "James," I said slowly, "have you done a DNA analysis on the bodies?"

"Looking for what?"

"Maybe Edward Garrett did know who the dead men were. And maybe one of them was related to him."

James sat back in his chair. "I never thought of that. It's not standard operating procedure for an FBI investigation, but I can get a quick-and-dirty DNA test done, for a price. I suppose Wakeman would foot the bill. But who am I comparing it to?"

"Ezra's two sons, William and Eddie, still live in Chester County. I'm sure you could persuade one of them to provide a DNA sample."

"Wait a minute—you're suggesting that one or both of the dead men are related to the Garrett family? That's a heck of a big jump."

"I know that. But it might explain why that first Edward never said anything about the bodies."

James thought for a moment, staring into space. "I'll look into getting the DNA work done. But even in the unlikely case that it was a Garrett who killed the soldier, how do you get from there to killing George Bowen now?"

"Maybe if you keep a secret that long, it becomes a force of its own. Maybe somebody didn't want it to go public."

"Maybe. I'd still be more comfortable with finding someone with a financial motive, like Jackson, or a personal motive, like Joseph Dilworth and Pat Bowen."

"Well, it would certainly be easier to make a case."

We'd finished eating without my even noticing. "So," James began, "I've got some more listings for us to check out." He looked at me expectantly.

"I, uh," I fumbled, then raised my chin, determined to feign enthusiasm if I needed to. "Okay, show me."

He permitted himself a small smile, and it hurt—I'd made him happy, and it had taken so little. He stood up to fetch a slim stack of printouts, and snagged the bottle of wine on the way back, refilling both our glasses before sitting down. He took the chair next to me, rather than sit across the table. "I kind of like this one," he said, shuffling the stack and handing me a page.

I barely glanced at it. "Mmm, nice. Where is it?"

As we went through the stack, I made polite noises. But it's hard to fool a trained FBI agent. After a while James backed up his chair and looked at me. "What's wrong, Nell?"

"Nothing. Well, not nothing, but I don't know what it is."

"You don't want to move in together."

"I do. Really. But . . ." There was nothing to come after the *but*. Either I did or I didn't, and if I didn't know by now, when would I? I took another sip of wine, stalling. "James, you know I love you. I want to be with you. I hate not knowing from day to day if I'll see you, or where we'll be. But something is holding me back, and I don't even know what it is. And I can't seem to get past it." He started to speak, and I raised a hand. "It's not that I'm afraid it won't work out. I know the statistics. I know we're both reasonable,

intelligent people, and we should be able to talk about this. I know we're not young, and if this is going to happen we don't have the luxury of drifting along for years. We've even had a sort of trial run these last few weeks, under challenging conditions, and we came through it with flying colors. So I don't understand why I can't seem to move forward." His gaze had never left my face, and I wanted to cry. How could I be doing this to him?

Then his expression changed, just a bit. "Nell, I have an idea. No, don't say anything—I've got a few details to work out. But will you hold tomorrow night for me? Or, no, better make it Thursday, in case something comes up."

"You mean, like finding another corpse or two?" I pulled together a wavering smile. "Thursday sounds good for me."

"All right, then. Are you staying, tonight?"

"I've had a few glasses of wine—I shouldn't drive. So, yes."

He gave me a quizzical look, no doubt questioning my lukewarm response. We really did need to work this out—just as soon as I figured out what my problem was.

CHAPTER 24

The next morning, I woke up early and studied still-sleeping James. He still looked a bit thinner since he'd been attacked, but he claimed there were no aftereffects from the concussion, no more headaches or dizziness. The long scar on his arm was fading slowly, but it would always be with him. He didn't remember those awful minutes when I was trying to stop the bleeding and wondering if I could—and wondering if he was going to die under my hands. *Cheerful thoughts for an early morning, Nell!* He'd survived, I'd survived, and the whole thing had shoved our relationship to this new level—where it had stalled. Now he was back at work and ready to resume a normal life, and here I was dragging my feet. Clearly I was an idiot, as my friends kept telling me.

I slid carefully out of bed and went to the kitchen—more like a kitchenette—to make coffee. What was on my calendar for today? No board meeting looming yet, and the next major social event at the Society was still a few months

away. Shelby had the planning for that well in hand, and it promised to be fun: we were celebrating the life of the great nineteenth-century actor Edwin Forrest, whose larger-than-life personality lent itself to over-the-top festivities. New registrar Ben seemed to be getting a handle on his job, and despite, or maybe because of, the limitations to his mobility, he appeared to be a calm, stable presence—exactly what we needed. I was looking forward to seeing how he interacted with Latoya once he got his bearings.

Lissa, with a little help from me, would be cobbling together a report on the history of the Garrett site in Goshen to present to Wakeman by Friday, a deadline barreling toward us way too fast. I believed that if we made him happy, it could mean good things for the Society, maybe in the form of money, or maybe as some in-kind contributions for the building, like an updated HVAC system, or even a new roof. That would be a trifle to the Wakeman Property Trust, but it would mean a lot to us. If we disappointed him . . . no, I wasn't going to think about that. The Society had one of the best collections of historical material in the country, particularly on Pennsylvania history, and with Janet's help we could fill in whatever gaps there were. And I had enough experience with fine-tuning pitches to present a streamlined and concise story that would appeal to the public and the press alike. All good.

The coffee was ready when James emerged from the bedroom freshly showered. I handed him a cup and, said, "Want an English muffin?"

"Sure." He sat down at the table and watched me exercise my expert toaster skills.

When I'd set a plate in front of him and brought mine

over to the table, I said, "What's next on your plate with the Wakeman—or should I say Bowen?—investigation?"

James sighed and sipped his coffee. "I really don't know. We're waiting for the final forensic details on the old bodies. The local police have interviewed everyone with a connection to George Bowen and they've sent on the reports to us. But in reading through them, it's clear that their prior knowledge of the people and the situation interferes with their objectivity to some extent. And maybe they haven't asked the right questions. But the FBI can't muscle in and redo everything."

That made sense to me. "Wakeman's not getting in your way?"

"Nope. He's getting the investigation he asked for. You have any suggestions?"

"You're asking me?" I thought for a moment. "James, we've worked together on a few cases now, and I think what I bring to the table is a different perspective. I know more about the people involved, and you deal with the facts. And I can ask questions that you can't, because I'm not official. Does that sound about right?"

"It does," he said. "And don't think I don't appreciate it."

"Thank you. To get back to the point, I think it still comes back to those two Revolutionary War bodies. We do agree that that's what they are?" When James nodded, I went on, "George Bowen found them, whether or not he was looking specifically for them. George told somebody about them, although we still aren't sure who. That person had what he—or she—thought was a motive to silence George. Does that sum it up?"

"It does. That's why I'm glad you're on this with me. And as you were saying, it may be that some of us don't appreciate

that something that happened over two hundred years ago can matter so much to someone today."

"But you *can* work your forensic magic on the old bodies," I pointed out.

"We're working on it."

"Are you going to talk to anyone in Goshen today?"

"Maybe. I'd like a word with Jackson, and maybe Pat Bowen. What about you?"

"What am I doing? Going to work. Lissa's only got two days to put together that preliminary report for Wakeman, and I need to vet it first."

"How's she working out?"

"Very well. She's smart and she knows quite a bit about local history. Too bad the Society can't hire her, but it's not in the budget. Maybe I can talk Wakeman into endowing a position for a project historian, assuming he's pleased with what we give him. And then she can keep seeing Ben."

James smiled. "I'm not taking that bait. You aren't going to interfere, are you?"

"Why would I do that? My only concern is that Ben is now my employee, so I have some responsibility for him. Latoya and I haven't really had time to assess his professional capabilities. I was just wondering, in case I should say something to Lissa."

"They're both adults—let them work things out." He stood up and carried his dishes to the sink. "I'd better get going. Don't forget, we've got a date tomorrow night," he said.

"Oh, right. I might have to make another run out to Chester County, either today or tomorrow, so I'll check in with you later. And I'll have to see how much progress Lissa has made on that report for Wakeman."

"Tomorrow." His tone didn't permit any argument. He gave me a serious kiss and headed out the door.

It didn't take me long to dress; the scant closet space didn't allow me to keep much at James's place, so I had few choices for work clothing. Then I drove into Center City and parked across from the Society. The day promised to be a warm one, but as usual the interior of my building was cool and serene. "Hi, Bob," I greeted our gatekeeper.

"Mornin', Nell. Busy day yesterday, and looks like it might be busy again today."

"All those summer genealogists, right? But that's what keeps us in business." I headed for the elevator and my office.

Eric had already arrived. "I'll get your coffee, Nell," he said as soon as he saw me, and went down the hall to the break room. He returned a minute later. "There you go."

"Thank you, Eric. I promise I'll start getting in earlier soon, so we can share coffee duty. How're things going? What with all this running back and forth to Goshen, I feel kind of left out of the loop. Any crises? Excitements?"

"Things've been pretty smooth this week. How's it going with your bodies?"

"The new one or the old ones? I think they're connected, but I still don't know how. We haven't heard from Mr. Wakeman yet today, have we?" I knew Wakeman had my cell phone number and wouldn't have hesitated to use it if he'd really wanted to reach me.

"No, ma'am. A couple of calls from his project manager."

"Scott?"

"That's the one. I don't think it was urgent."

"As long as Mr. Wakeman can find me, I think we're okay. Have you seen Lissa this morning?"

"Sure have. She came in real early."

Even as Eric spoke, Lissa appeared in the doorway behind him. "Hey, Nell. I've got some stuff I want to show you. Oh, hi, Eric."

"Hey, Lissa. You want some coffee?"

"Already helped myself, thanks. You make good coffee, Eric."

"Thank you! Then I'll let you all get down to business." Eric retreated gracefully to his desk.

When he was gone, I gestured toward a chair. "Sit down. You look excited—you've found something?"

"Maybe. Hey, don't worry, I'll have a draft of that Wakeman report for you by tomorrow afternoon at the latest, so you can review it. But you asked me to look more closely at the genealogy of the family, right? Edward, the one who owned the land during the Revolution, and the rest of his family?"

"I did. What've you learned?" She must have thought it was significant, because she was almost bubbling with excitement.

"Well, as I'm sure you know, records are a little patchy back then. We've got the 1790 census, after the dust from the war had settled, and there's a 1774 list of taxable inhabitants in Goshen, and Edward's on it. If you're interested, he had two horses, three cattle, and three sheep at the time. Married to Hannah, and they had seven kids, four daughters and three sons, Charles, William, and Thomas. Thomas was the youngest boy. Edward left a will, and Thomas inherited the property when Edward died. So that made me wonder—what must've happened to Charles and William?"

CHAPTER 25

It took me a moment to grasp what Lissa was suggesting, and then another moment to see the connection she had made. "You're saying that you think that either or both of the two bodies found on the property were Edward's sons? That's a pretty huge leap of logic. Tell me why."

"Okay." Lissa picked up the thread dimpled, her enthusiasm undimmed. "It's kind of hard to prove a negative, but hear me out. When I started digging into the sources from after the war, I couldn't find any mention of Charles or William Garrett anywhere, not near Goshen or even in the commonwealth. Not in Edward's will, as I've just said, and no marriage or death records anywhere. They didn't leave wills, at least not in Pennsylvania, although I can't say I've looked beyond the state. No mention of widows or offspring for either of the sons. What is interesting is that William shows up in the Goshen militia company—there are some Sons of the American Revolution applications that refer to him."

"But wasn't he a Quaker? I thought they were pacifists."

"Yes and no. Quakers are basically Christians but historically they've been very tolerant of individual beliefs. George Fox, who founded the Religious Society of Friends in England back in the mid 1600s, said that Quakers should refuse to bear arms or use deadly force against other humans or participate in any wars, but there have been Quakers who've fought. They were and are willing to fight for peace and freedom, if that makes sense to you, but mostly they're a very quiet group that avoids violence. The Goshen Meeting was founded in 1702 or 1703—"

"And is close to the Garrett farm. I know. You've looked at their records?"

"Not yet. They're in the Friends Historical Library at Swarthmore College and in the Haverford College Quaker Collection. They're available for research, but I haven't had the time to get there, and only the catalog is online, not the documents themselves."

I sat back in my chair and thought. "So how do you get from there to two dead men buried secretly on the Garrett farm, one with a British uniform?"

"I'm getting there. You might guess that being pacifists put a lot of Quakers in difficult positions during the Revolution, because they weren't supposed to officially swear loyalty to either side, much less fight. Some remained Loyalists, and others sided with the patriots—and they could be disowned by their meeting for either. In Pennsylvania almost a thousand Quakers were disowned for bearing arms. Anyway, the result was that *nobody* trusted the Quakers around here."

I was beginning to see her logic. "And you're guessing

that the Garrett family, in the confusion after the battle, found the bodies and buried them quickly, to avoid any problems?"

"It's possible, isn't it?" Lissa nodded eagerly. "The local Quakers had very mixed feelings about which side to choose and whether or not to fight, and besides, tempers run high in any war. Maybe Edward just wanted to avoid any difficulties."

I was intrigued, but she was really going out on a limb with her theory. I played devil's advocate. "If that was the case, why would anyone want to silence George Bowen? If anything, it would be kind of an intriguing archeological find, wouldn't it?"

Lissa's face clouded. "That's where I hit a wall. And that's why the missing heirs are important. What if one of them killed the British soldier? Or was killed by him? And maybe his brother helped cover that up, and then left, so no one would ask him about it?"

"It's possible, maybe. But why wouldn't Edward have resurrected his son, so to speak, when the war was over, and had him buried properly at the meeting?"

"That's why I'd really like to take a look at the original records at Swarthmore. Maybe the brothers are mentioned there, but I haven't had time to check, and we're running out of time if we're going to meet Wakeman's deadline."

Lissa fell silent while I digested what she'd told me. Finally, I said, "I guess the question is, if it's true—and that's still very much an *if*—then how did the family manage to keep the secret for all this time?"

Lissa shrugged. "You told me that Ezra Garrett made a point of giving the family documents to the historical

society before he died. I wonder: do you think he knew?" Lissa said.

Something I couldn't answer. "Well, either he wanted to make sure the documents stayed together and were well cared for, or he knew there was something in there that probably would or should come out sometime. Maybe he didn't trust his own family to preserve them. I think maybe we need to know a bit more about family relations there, and I'll bet Janet can fill in some of the blanks. I wish we had more time to figure this out. How much can we take to Wakeman?"

"You're asking me?" Lissa laughed. "From what I understand, he wants a nice report to help sell his homes and condos. We don't have any proof about these conjectures, no matter how interesting a story it might make for him. I suppose we could say something like 'The Garrett family had a long and troubled history on their homestead . . .' And the bodies would be quietly reburied somewhere and never identified."

I shot upright in my chair. "But there is a way we can prove it!" While she looked at me, bewildered, I picked up my office phone and hit James's number.

"Morrison," he said automatically, then, "Nell? Why are you calling on this line?"

"Because this is official business. I'll be quick. Do you remember that we talked about DNA profiles for the old bodies from the Garrett property? How long would it take to get them done? Remember, this is for Wakeman. Money is no object." I hoped that was true. If we got the story right, he might have something really interesting to include in his promotional material. It seemed worth trying.

"If our lab does it, you might see results in a couple of

weeks. But I know the guys at the Jersey lab that takes our overflow. They can probably have something for you tomorrow—for a price. Why the hurry?"

I smiled to myself. "I'm working on a theory, but I don't want to prejudice you. I'll tell you when we get the results."

"All right. I'll call if there's any problem with getting the lab work done."

We hung up at the same time. I looked up to see Lissa grinning at me. "DNA tests, huh? Like, overnight? So we'll know if one of the bodies was related to the Garretts?"

"Only if we get a sample from a living Garrett. So we have to figure out how to get a sample from one of the surviving ones."

"Can you ask?"

"They might want to know why we're asking."

"Why can't we just tell them the truth? If you say it's to help with the murder investigation, won't they be willing?"

"Maybe. I don't really know any of them. And, as far as I know, neither William nor Eddie has shown much interest in this investigation. Of course, they don't own the land anymore. I think we need to talk to Janet again. Do you have time today, or should I go alone?"

"If I can take my laptop along, I'd love to go. I can work on the report in the car. Maybe I can even get some pictures while we're out that way."

"Deal. I'll call Janet and see if she's free this afternoon."

"Great. I'll check back with you later."

Lissa left, and I spent a few minutes gathering my thoughts. Two dead men in the woods; two corpses in a copse. The buttons pointed to the Revolutionary War; a major battle in that war had taken place only a short distance

away from the farm. The land had been held continuously by the same family since before that battle, up until Ezra Garrett had sold it to Mitch Wakeman. Had Ezra known about the bodies? If so, he must have realized that Wakeman would most likely discover them in the course of construction. If there had been no dark secret, any member of the Garrett family could have reported the bodies at any time over the past two centuries; ergo, there had to be a dark secret. What was it, and who had known?

Or maybe the Garrett family had simply forgotten about the bodies; the story had not been passed down. The fact that the copse had never been disturbed was merely a coincidence. And George had been killed by a crazed stranger in the dark.

Which was more likely? Too many coincidences. My vote was for the first option.

I picked up the phone to call Janet Butler and luckily found her in her office. "Hey, Janet," I said. "It's Nell. Look, Lissa and I have some more questions about the whole Garrett history, and you know we've got a Friday deadline. Would you mind terribly if we came out and talked to you this afternoon?"

"Uh, sure, I guess. Does two o'clock work for you?"

"Fine. And thank you. I promise we'll stop bothering you soon."

Janet laughed. "Hey, this is more excitement than we usually get here. I'll see you at two."

Lissa and I left the city at one, and as I drove she read out loud pieces of the text she had assembled for the Wakeman report. I was pleased to find that she wrote well,

striking a nice balance between accurate historical fact and readable, entertaining style. Since traffic was light at mid-day, we arrived slightly early.

Janet was waiting for us in the lobby. "Welcome back, you two. Come on up to the office and we can talk." She led the way to her office, and I made sure the door was shut. As I did that, she gave me a curious look. "What do you need?"

I took a deep breath and started in. "Lissa has been doing some basic genealogy research on Edward Garrett and his family, and she turned up something odd. Edward had three sons, and the youngest one inherited the farm. The other two vanished from any records, just about the time of the Battle of Paoli."

Janet was quick to arrive at the same conclusion we had. "And you think they're connected to the two bodies that George found in the woods?"

"That's our working theory at the moment, but we need some help to flesh it out, if you'll pardon a bad pun. We know that Edward Garrett knew about the bodies, from his daybook, but he didn't identify them there, or anywhere else, as far as we know."

"But I still need to look at the Quaker records," Lissa said, then went quiet again.

I went on, "We been kicking around a theory that one of them was Edward's son. Would Edward have had reason to hide the death?"

"What an interesting idea. I can't say for sure. If I'm not mistaken, the records for the Goshen Meeting can be found in the Friends Library at Swarthmore College."

"Lissa will follow through on that, of course," I added.

"She did find a record that says that one of the sons was listed as a member of the Goshen militia, which you know would have been relatively unusual. Add to that the buttons that George found, and it suggests that one of Edward's sons may have killed a British soldier on the family property, and then they died together and were buried right there, without ceremony or recognition. And then nobody said anything about them until Wakeman showed up."

"This is amazing!" Janet said. "Sounds like a soap opera."

"It does, but it's a strong possibility that George Bowen died because he found the bodies. At least, that's the only explanation that makes sense. Tell me, what was the timing of Ezra Garrett's gift of the family papers in relation to the start of the Wakeman project?"

"As I told you, about the same time. Of course, the announcement of the Wakeman project didn't go public right away, but there were hints coming from the township guys. Obviously Ezra and Wakeman had been talking about it for a while before that. I just figured Ezra handed over the papers because he was settling his affairs. He must have known he didn't have much time left. He was already ninety."

"What if he was worried that someone else would find the papers? Maybe even destroy them?"

Janet looked bewildered. "His family must have known about them, and they'd probably had access to them all along."

"What if the family didn't know?" I pressed. "Or what if it didn't matter until it became public that Wakeman was going to develop the site and would probably find those bodies?"

"I'm still not following," Janet said. "Why would anyone care now? Whatever happened, happened a long time ago. What's it got to do with the present?"

"That's what we don't know. As I'm sure you've seen, family traditions have a way of hanging on long after the people involved are gone. Like 'We don't talk about Aunt Hattie's first husband,' because he turned out to be a swindler—things like that. It's only when there's an outside eye looking at these things that the family members are kind of jolted out of their rut and take a different view. Say Edward did not want it known that his son was buried there, and swore the son who inherited to secrecy, and that information got passed down from generation to generation. So nobody touched that piece of land. They couldn't have known that the bodies and other bits and pieces would be so well-preserved."

"All this is kind of built on straw, isn't it? It could have been two strangers fleeing from the battle who happened to cross paths right there and died."

"Of course it could. That's why I've asked the FBI to do a DNA analysis of the remains."

"Oh-ho!" Janet replied, nodding. "So you'll know if one of them was a Garrett. But you still need a sample from a living Garrett, don't you?"

"That's where you come in."

CHAPTER 26

"Janet, is there some way to get a sample from the two sons?"

Janet smiled. "You mean, without asking them?"

I almost laughed. "That would be too easy. Do you know either of them well enough to ask? Where do they live?"

"Huh—let me think. I think both of them are still around West Chester, or at least in Pennsylvania. The younger son, Eddie—yes, the name has been passed down—lived on the farm until his father died and Wakeman took over the property. He never married, and he must be sixty now. He's a member here, but only because his father gave so much that we made him an honorary one. So I guess I know him, but he's not exactly a regular customer here. I do know him better than his brother, William, but that's not saying much. I don't think I've ever seen William in here."

"I met Eddie at that press conference," I said, "but he left as fast as he could. I had the impression he wasn't

comfortable with that kind of attention. I'm sure the brothers have been interviewed about George's death and the bodies and the whole history of the farm." But who had interviewed them? I wondered. Odds were that the interviewers were local good ole boys who'd known the Garretts all their lives. Had the interviewer asked the right questions? Would that person have known if he was being lied to by one or another or even all of the Garretts? "It might look odd if someone came around now asking for a cheek swab."

"You want to break into their houses and steal a toothbrush?" Janet said, with a glint in her eye.

"That only happens on television. Look, if we want to prove our theory, we need to get serious. Janet, do you think you could ask them to come here?"

"I could come up with an excuse, I guess, at least for Eddie, since he's a member. Maybe a question about the family papers?"

"Has Eddie shown any interest in the past?"

"Not really, but he has to know that we're looking at the papers now, given everything that's been happening."

"But we don't have much time," Lissa said. "Even if Eddie comes in right away and you get DNA from him, it'll take a couple of days to process that to compare to the other samples. So the whole investigation has slopped over into next week already."

"At least it would be progress," I said. "No other agency has come up with anything. We ought to have preliminary DNA results for the bodies by tomorrow, and if we have to wait for a sample from Eddie to compare to, so be it."

Suddenly I really wanted to talk to James. I was out of my depth here. I had no idea what constituted evidence of

anything or how to go about getting it even if I knew. I could end up doing more harm to the investigation than good. Heck, Eddie could probably sue someone if we tricked him into giving a sample.

Lissa's voice interrupted my thoughts. "Nell, how do you want me to spin all this for Wakeman's report?"

"I don't think he'll want wild speculation. If it turns out to be a good story, we can add it later, but I'd rather have the basic story of the land in his hands than give unsupported guesses about possible murders."

"So, what do you want me to do, Nell?" Janet asked.

"Call Eddie Garrett and ask him if he can come in to talk about the family papers. That's an innocent and appropriate request. Don't make it sound urgent—tomorrow would be fine. Then if he shows up, offer him a cup of coffee or tea or whatever then make sure you save whatever he drank out of."

Janet laughed. "Okay, I can do that. But I think you've been watching too much *CSI*."

"Probably." I stood up. "We've already taken too much of your time. Let me know if you reach Eddie and if he'll talk to you."

"You want to sit in, if I do talk to him?"

"If it seems natural. It might look odd if I was there. You know the Garrett material well. Oh, you are taking good care of the daybook, aren't you?"

"Yes, I put it in the safe. And I won't mention it unless Eddie brings it up."

"Good. Who knows, it may turn out to be crucial. Lissa, you ready to go?"

Janet escorted us to the front door. Outside it was still hot, even on the tree-shaded street. I dropped Lissa off at

the Paoli train station and headed back to Bryn Mawr. We had cobbled together some shaky theories with very little to back them up, and if we told someone and we were wrong, we'd look very foolish. I parked behind my house and let myself in, then I went upstairs to change into something cool. Downstairs again, I checked the time: only four thirty, so James would still be at work. Well, I had work-related things to discuss with him, so I called him.

"Again?" he answered, but with a hint of humor.

"Yes, again. I wanted to report on my meeting with Janet Butler. That's business related, right?"

I could hear his sigh. "Before you ask, I don't have the DNA results yet."

"I didn't think you would. But Janet and Lissa and I talked about our theory." I decided not to mention that we were going to try to get yet another DNA sample for him to run. I wasn't sure how legal or ethical it would be if we tricked either Garrett male to obtain the sample. And it was a pretty weak theory to begin with.

"Who've you got?" he said, all business.

"Both of Ezra Garrett's sons still live in the immediate area. Both are members of the historical society in West Chester but spend very little time there, if any. Janet is going to call and ask Eddie Garrett if he could come in to discuss the family papers that his father left to the society. And then maybe she can segue into asking him if he knew about the buried bodies on the land, since it was recorded in the family records." *And somehow get a DNA sample.*

"You think he's involved?"

"I have no idea. I barely know the man—I shook hands with him at Wakeman's press conference and that's it—and

Janet knows him only slightly better because he's used the historical society's resources. I'm sure the local detectives have interviewed him, but they don't know as much about the family history as we do now. Besides, if something has been a closely guarded secret for two centuries plus, then it's likely to stay a secret, right? He may know something he hasn't told."

"Pretty thin stuff, Nell."

"You have anything better?"

"No. Where are you?"

"Home. But we're getting together tomorrow night, right?"

"Yes, we have plans for tomorrow night," he finally said enigmatically. "I'll meet you at the Society, unless something else breaks. Six?"

"Good. And then we'll have the whole weekend to look at places, right?"

"Yes. I'll hold you to it. See you tomorrow." He hung up, endearments conspicuously missing. I knew he was at work, but still. Why was I doing this to him? *Well, free single woman with no strings, what are you going to do with yourself tonight?*

I ended up playing on the computer, trolling through search engines, sticking in the name *Ezra Garrett* just to see what came up. Bits and pieces, including a nice obituary. Ezra sounded like he'd been a great all-around guy, a solid member of his meeting, an elected township official for decades, a supporter of worthy causes, a former school bus driver and a fox hunter—how did those last two go together? He'd been a good custodian of his land and his history. Had he known about the bodies? Had he handed over the family documents knowing that eventually the daybook would send someone looking for them? Who in Goshen would have

pointed a finger at a pillar of the local community like Ezra in any event?

I kept searching idly, coming up with different versions of the same information. But then I found something new: a small news article from a local newspaper a few decades back reporting the death of a *third* son of Ezra Garrett's, who had died at the age of twelve in an unfortunate accident involving one of his father's guns. Details were vague, probably to protect the one who had pulled the trigger, but I thought I could read between the lines.

I felt chilled. I had my own history with weapons, one that I tried my best to avoid thinking about. Generally that worked, but what had happened when James was injured and nearly died had brought it barreling to the forefront again. I was still processing my own feelings about that, and I hadn't even told James the whole story, although I knew he needed to know. Add one more item to the list for dinner tomorrow. But at the very least, I could empathize with the family's tragic loss—I knew all too well how much pain that could cause. So now I knew that Ezra's long and productive life had not been without tragedy. It made me sad. Or maybe I was just sad in general: if I was honest with myself, I would have rather have been with James tonight. What would it be like to come home to each other in the same place every night? I was used to being alone; could I adapt to being half a couple all the time?

With a man who people shot at?

With a man who I loved?

Fish or cut bait, Nell. Get off the fence and commit to one side or the other. All you're doing now is making the two of you miserable.

CHAPTER 27

I woke up early, feeling anxious even before I opened my eyes. Today was Thursday, and Wakeman wanted his report tomorrow. I was confident that Lissa could put together something appropriate, but George Bowen's unsolved murder nagged at me. It had to be connected to those older bodies, didn't it? My mind wandering, I pondered what to wear. James and I hadn't made detailed plans for the evening, but I assumed I'd be staying over, which suited me fine, even if we spent the night looking at property listings.

It was only when I went downstairs to make breakfast that I noticed that the light on my landline phone was blinking. I didn't check it often because few people called me on that line, and most of those were telemarketers or people asking for money, and I preferred to not answer rather than try to come up with yet another polite way to say no. I punched in numbers and retrieved my message, which turned out to be from Eric, informing me that Janet Butler

had managed to set up a meeting with Eddie Garrett for ten o'clock this morning and he hoped I'd get the message before I came all the way into the city.

Why hadn't he called me on my cell phone? I checked it and realized I'd turned the sound off. Had I been subconsciously trying to avoid talking to James? During our last conversation, at the end of the workday, he'd sounded a bit cool, and I hadn't wanted to make things worse. But I scrolled through the messages and there were none from him last night, although I did find one from Eric, which was identical to the one he'd left on my home phone.

I thought for a moment, and then I realized I was tired of tiptoeing around the murder. I wanted some answers, and Eddie Garrett might have them. If he didn't, I'd rather know now so we could move in another direction.

So it looked like I was going to West Chester rather than to Philadelphia this morning.

It wasn't even eight o'clock yet, so I decided I'd wait until nine to call Janet to strategize. If she wasn't answering by then, I'd just go over and sit on her steps and wait for her. That would still give us a little time to figure out how we should approach Eddie at ten.

In the end, that's what I did, and I was sitting in the shade enjoying watching the morning bustle of the town when Janet walked up to the building. "I take it you got my message!" she said. "But I didn't expect you in person."

"I decided I'd rather sit in on it than not. My presence won't intimidate Eddie, will it? We've already met, so he knows who I am. I thought you and I should talk before Eddie arrives. Did he think there was anything strange about you inviting him over?"

Janet was working her key into the front door. "No, or not that I could tell, but he's not one to waste words. Come on in." She led the way through the cool interior, flipping on a few lights along the way, and into her office. "You want coffee?"

"Always, but I'll come along with you so we can talk."

"Great."

I followed her to a space barely bigger than a closet, which held a single-cup coffeemaker and a sink and a small fridge and little more. "I should have given you my home number or my cell number yesterday," I said. "I guess I figured it would take you longer to set up something with Eddie."

"He more or less retired when the farm was sold, so he has plenty of time on his hands. How do you suggest we approach him?" Janet handed me a cup of coffee and then started one for herself.

"You've had conversations with him in the past, haven't you?" When Janet nodded, I went on, "You can start with telling him about how you've been going through Ezra's bequest since all the attention on the Wakeman project started up, asking him if he could tell us more about the family papers. That should give an opening to talk about the daybook, if he's seen it. Then see how he reacts. If he knows about the bodies, he should show *some* sort of reaction. But be tactful, of course."

Her coffee made, Janet turned to me and leaned against the mini fridge. "Nell, what do you really think we're going to find out?"

I thought I owed her an honest answer. "I don't know for sure. Let's just talk to him and see where it goes—he's one more piece of this puzzle. If you're okay with that?"

"That I can do. I really do think we need to get to the bottom of this. I know a little about Eddie, and I have a hard time visualizing him harming anyone. But I'm glad you're here, anyway—I'd probably put my foot in my mouth without you for backup. Let's leave the coffee in my office and go down and meet him in the lobby."

The building was slowly coming alive as staff came in and turned on more lights. Janet and I stood chatting in the lobby until Eddie Garrett walked in. I paid more attention that I had the last time I'd seen him: he looked older than what I knew to be his sixty-plus years, his face weathered, his hands still rough from many years of manual work; he was also taller and broader than I recalled. Dairy farming must be hard, and he'd put in a lifetime doing it. He hovered hesitantly, looking from one of us to the other.

Janet stepped forward with a warm smile. "Welcome, Eddie! I'm so glad you could make it on such short notice. You remember Nell Pratt, right? I asked her to join us because she's the local expert on historical documents, and I'm sure she'll be interested in your family's records. Please, come upstairs where we can be comfortable."

"Hello, Miss Pratt. Yeah, I remember you from that press conference." We followed Janet back to her office in silence.

"Would you like some coffee?" Janet asked.

"Don't trouble yourself," Eddie said.

"Oh, it's no trouble with these modern machines. Won't take a minute." Janet darted down the hall, leaving Eddie and me to sit in awkward silence.

I fought to break it. "We didn't have a chance to talk much at the press conference. From all that I've read or

heard, your father was quite a noteworthy figure in Goshen. He was involved in a lot of different things, wasn't he?"

"Yeah. He liked to keep busy. Course, he had me to look after the farmwork."

Did I detect a hint of bitterness in his tone? "Did you handle it all on your own?"

"We had some hired help. Herd was too big for one man, even with the fancy modern machines. And there was always some new regulation coming along. Hard work. Then he sold the place to that damn developer. Oh, sorry." Yes, definitely bitter.

Janet returned and set a mug filled with coffee in front of Eddie. "I didn't know how you liked it, so I brought sugar and creamer."

"Black's fine." Eddie picked up the mug and sipped once, then set it down again, looking at us expectantly. Time to talk: I sat back and let Janet take the lead.

Janet gave him a smile that didn't betray any nervousness. "Eddie, I can't tell you how happy we are that your father entrusted us with his papers. Since all this recent trouble, I thought we should go through them sooner rather later, so I pulled out the boxes and I've been doing some preliminary sorting. Awful thing about George Bowen, wasn't it? Did you know him?"

I wondered if Eddie would notice the abrupt change of subject, but all he said was, "Met him now and then at the township. Wouldn't say we were friends."

"He was a member here, too—really took an interest in local history." Janet's glance darted briefly toward me, but I didn't interrupt her.

"Plenty of that to go around," Eddie said. "What do you want from me?"

"I thought you might be familiar with the papers that your father donated, since they involve many generations of your family, and maybe you could give me some guidance about where to start? You know, which documents might be the most interesting? Maybe we could put together a small exhibit, timed to coincide with the opening of the Wakeman development."

Eddie's expression didn't change. "Not much to tell. Family settled on the place seventeen-something, and we were still there until Pa sold it to that Wakeman guy."

"Kind of an unusual transaction, wasn't it?" I asked. "Did all the family agree to that? Or would you rather have stayed and kept the dairy farm going?" I wondered if he would think I was being rude, asking such a personal question.

Apparently not. Eddie shrugged. "Pa had his mind made up. My brother, William, went along with it, so I didn't have much choice. The money offered was good, and the dairy business isn't what it once was. It seemed for the best."

Given what I'd seen of him so far, I had to wonder if Eddie had put up much of a fight, no matter what his preferences had been. "It must be hard to leave a place where you and your family had so much personal history."

"I've moved on." Eddie didn't add anything else. I wondered where he was living now.

I heard my cell phone ringing in the depths of my bag. When I looked at it, I saw it was James. "Excuse me—I have to take this." I walked out of the office and into the hall before I answered.

"Where are you?" James said.

"In West Chester, talking to Eddie Garrett. Why?"

"The DNA results are in."

"And?"

"I don't know what you were expecting, but it turns out that the two dead men were closely related, probably brothers. You're betting they were also both Garretts?"

I was stunned into silence for a moment; that was one item I had not been expecting. "You are very good at your job. Yes, I am." More so than ever.

"And you're going to ask Eddie Garrett for a sample?"

"I . . . don't know. Depends on what he says. It may not be necessary."

James was silent for a couple of seconds. "Do you think he had anything to do with George Bowen's murder?"

"Maybe. It makes sense, in a way."

"Nell, be careful. Tell Janet Butler to be careful. You're interfering in a police investigation."

Not for the first time, I wanted to say, but didn't. "I will. See you later." I hung up before he could lecture me any more. And turned off the ringer.

"I apologize," I said as I returned to Janet's office. She raised an eyebrow a discreet eighth of an inch, and I nodded, just a bit. I hoped she had gotten the message, that there was more to tell. "Did I miss anything?"

"Eddie was just telling me about how proud his father was of the history of the farm."

"Do you share his enthusiasm, Eddie?" I asked, hoping it sounded like an innocent question.

"About history? Not much. There was always too much to do around the place—I didn't have time to mess around with old stories and papers and stuff. My brother went to

college, got a job where he wears a suit. I ended up looking after the farm with Pa."

I nodded, mainly to encourage him to talk. "Let me tell you, people like Janet and me, who work at institutions like this, we're always thrilled to find original documents. It makes history seem so much more real, and then we get to share that feeling with the public. What did you think when those two older bodies were found? Obviously they'd been there for a long time."

His expression hardened. "I was as surprised as the next man," he said.

"Do you know, there's something in one of the documents that suggests that those bodies had been there since the Revolution," Janet said brightly.

Eddie's gaze swiveled slowly from me to Janet. "Is that so."

"We think they might have taken part in the Battle of Paoli," I added. He didn't rise to the bait, so I went on. "I thought it was curious that the part of the farm where they were found was never used as pasture."

"Pa never wanted to—said he liked to keep some trees around the place. Cattle need shade now and then." Eddie's tone was neutral, giving nothing away.

"Still, it's surprising that nobody found the bodies before now," I said, watching him.

"Like I said, lots of history around here." If he'd been a cat, I thought his tail would be twitching by now.

Time to lob my little bomb. "There's something even more interesting about those bodies, Eddie. It turns out they were brothers."

Eddie's head whipped back toward me. "How would anybody know that?"

"DNA," I said. We held each other's eyes for several beats.

He stood up suddenly. "Janet, I've got a . . . an appointment I've got to be at. Can we pick this up some other time?"

Janet had come to her feet when he stood. "Of course, whenever you like. I really appreciate your help on this, Eddie."

"Yeah." He turned and left abruptly, too quickly for Janet to follow.

She sat down again slowly. "Well, that was interesting. I take it that call was from the FBI, about the DNA test?"

"Yes. I certainly didn't expect that result. We have to rethink our theory, if it was brother against brother." And only one of them in a British uniform. "What an awful thing."

"It is," Janet said softly.

We were silent for a few beats, and then I said, "And if you handle that carefully"—I nodded toward Eddie's coffee mug—"you'll have a Garrett sample to compare it to. He was definitely spooked we knew that the bodies were related, which makes me think he must have known."

"But why would he care so much?"

It was all coming together. That so-polite article I'd read the night before? The boy with the gun had to have been Eddie, even though he wasn't named. "I think it's something personal." I described the old news article to Janet. "I think it's possible that Eddie was involved in the shooting accident that killed his older brother, even though the article didn't say so outright, since they were both children and the family

was respected in the community. If that's true, then the idea of brother killing brother would have a lot more meaning to him. He might think that if it came out, the old story would be dredged up again and people would know what he'd done all those years ago. But of course, that would also mean he knew who the bodies were."

"Oh God, how sad. Poor Eddie."

"Poor Eddie may have killed a man to keep his secret," I reminded her. "The article I saw online was pretty vague, and Eddie would've been young at the time, so the reporter was probably protecting him. But I'd guess Eddie didn't want the story of how his brother died to become common knowledge, which is in fact what is probably going to happen now that the old bodies have been discovered. News coverage has changed a lot, and I don't think they'd respect his privacy now."

"What the heck do we do now?" Janet asked.

"I really don't know. All we've done is establish a potential motive for George's murder: Eddie wanted the bodies to stay buried, and he knew George would talk. That makes Eddie the most likely suspect. We don't know if George went to Eddie to tell him, or if Eddie just happened to cross paths with George right after he'd made his big find. But there's nothing remotely resembling proof of any of this. Still, you should be careful. If we're right, he's already killed one person."

"But he has to realize he can't keep a lid on this now."

"Still, just watch out. And don't tell anyone else what we suspect for the moment."

"I'll stick close to my husband—that should make him happy. What about you?"

"I'll be in the city, so I'm not worried." Not with my own personal FBI bodyguard. "I'll take that mug with me and give it to the FBI." I stood up, retrieved the mug with a tissue, and retraced my steps to the break closet, where I carefully poured out the coffee, then slipped the mug into a large clean envelope I'd gotten from Janet—feeling absurdly foolish all the way—then stuffed the mug into my bag.

Janet walked me downstairs. "Well, this has been interesting. Is your job normally like this?"

I laughed. "More often than you might guess. I hope this will all be wrapped up soon. I think your cover story about a small exhibit was a good one, by the way. We should talk more about it, when all this is settled."

"I'd like that. Thanks for everything—let me know if you need anything else."

"I will, Janet. Take care."

I retrieved my car and set off for Philadelphia with my bag of evidence.

CHAPTER 28

I arrived in the city not long after noon. The drive gave me time to think—always risky. I had to wonder how I kept finding myself in the middle of situations that involved murder and mayhem—and now I was dragging other people, like Janet, into them as well. It wasn't that I went looking for trouble, or that I thought I was some super sleuth, wiser than the police, the FBI, and anybody else who might be looking at a crime. What I did bring to the table was a different perspective: I knew history. I'd be a fish out of water in the investigation of a domestic killing or a street-corner drug shooting, but anything that had deep roots in the greater Philadelphia area and its history was my turf. Sure, I would have said it was unlikely that the discovery of the remains of two men who had fought and died in the Revolution—and oddly, I could name the precise day they had died—could point to the culprit in a killing that had taken place only a

week or two earlier, but there it was. I'd be happy to be proved wrong. Maybe George Bowen had been killed by his wife's lover or a random stranger.

But I doubted it. In any case, my heart ached for Eddie Garrett.

Once I was back in my office, Lissa appeared promptly and handed me a sheaf of papers. "This is the draft. You want me to go away while you read it?" she asked anxiously.

"In a minute. First, come in and close the door, will you?" When she had, I said, "I met with Janet Butler and Eddie Garrett this morning in West Chester. While I was there, I got a call from James, who said that the DNA samples from the two bodies shows that they were brothers. So I think you got it right: they were the first Edward Garrett's sons and died in the aftermath of the Battle of Paoli. I've got a sample of Eddie's DNA in my purse. But I think Janet and I more or less showed our hand when we were talking to Eddie."

Lissa seemed to take my statements in stride. "So he knows what you know?"

"Sort of. We didn't spell it out, but I think he knew what we were saying."

"But why on earth would he kill anybody?"

"I think I can guess. I was doing some research on the Garrett family online last night, and I found an article about the death of a third Garrett brother, when he was a child. Apparently it was an accident involving a gun. Back then reporters were pretty discreet, but it seems all too likely that somehow Eddie was responsible for his brother's death, or at least believes he was. And if that's true, then finding the two bodies now must have brought it all back. He probably

couldn't face having all of his own family history dragged out and examined, so he lashed out to silence George. But remember, this is still just a theory. We don't have proof."

"That poor man," Lissa said softly. "No wonder it was such a sloppy murder. And he must have moved the body to draw attention away from that burial, but he didn't count on the police bringing dogs in."

"Criminals are not always smart people, and Eddie may have panicked, believed that silencing George would be enough to keep all of it quiet. George could have come to him first with his discovery, out of courtesy, since it had been his family's farm. Maybe he hoped Eddie would know something more. Poor George."

"Wow," Lissa said. "I never thought historical research could be so dramatic. What do I do with the report?"

"Hang on a moment." I went around my desk and opened the door, then asked Eric, "Have Wakeman's people called?"

"Sure have," Eric replied. "About four times. You're on for two o'clock tomorrow."

"Thanks, Eric." I went back into the office, shutting the door carefully behind me. "We have until two tomorrow to sort things out. I'll read what you've put together, and then I'll see James tonight, and I'll let you know in the morning if I think we need to make any changes. But we may not have enough information to include the full story of the two dead soldiers. Maybe you could include a brief discussion of that in your final draft, and we can decide tomorrow whether to present it to Wakeman. Sound OK?"

"That's fine. I'll get out of your hair now."

After she'd left I read through what she'd given me. It was good, and I had few suggestions for changes. As it was

currently structured, we could either skirt around the Revolutionary War graves entirely, or we had the option of making them a prominent talking point. That decision was up to Wakeman and his crew, though I had a feeling the timing would depend on whether any arrest was imminent.

I threw myself back into the ordinary business of running the Society for the rest of the day. It was a good distraction. Signing begging letters was seldom a life-or-death issue. It was close to six when I went downstairs to the lobby to find James already there, deep in conversation with Front Desk Bob. I tended to forget that Bob was a retired police officer, which is what gave his quiet presence such authority when it came to arguing with cranky patrons. That made him a colleague of James's, sort of.

"Am I the last one to leave?" I asked Bob.

"Just about. I'll do a check after you go, and lock up."

"Thanks, Bob. Good night."

Out on the front steps, I looked up at James. "Where to?"

"We walk."

"We're going out for dinner?"

"Yes." He didn't elaborate. I didn't press.

We strolled amiably for a few blocks. A public sidewalk was not the place to discuss a murder investigation—or anything else of substance, for that matter—so we made chitchat in a desultory fashion. It was warm and humid, but occasionally we caught a breeze from the Delaware River.

After several blocks we stopped in front of a restaurant I had walked by countless times but had never been in. "This is where we're going?" I asked.

"It is. Have you been here?"

"No, but it smells wonderful." Behind a high iron fence

I could see tables scattered around a courtyard surrounded by nineteenth—or even eighteenth?—century buildings. Tea lights flickered on the tables, illuminating the small vases filled with fresh flowers. It looked lovely—and I was reminded that I'd never eaten lunch.

We went through the gate, and James had a quiet word with the maître d', who nodded and escorted us to a table in a corner with an ivy-covered brick wall behind us. He held my chair for me, and I glared at him when he made a move toward my napkin; I was perfectly capable of unfolding a napkin for my lap, thank you. "Something to drink, perhaps?" he said.

James looked at me. "Wine?"

"Fine."

James conferred with the maître d', who nodded and retreated quickly toward the kitchen.

When he was gone, I said, "Don't let me forget that I have a DNA sample for you in my bag."

James cocked an eyebrow at me for a moment, then burst out laughing. "Here I try to create a lovely romantic evening, and this is what you say?"

He had a point, and I backtracked quickly. "I apologize. This is delightful, and I was hoping to get business out of the way so I could enjoy it." *Good save, Nell.*

"All right, I will remind you later. And before you ask, I have no new information on that case to offer. Do you?"

"No, not since I talked to you this morning. Although I think we spooked Eddie Garrett."

"What was your impression of him?"

"Sad. Taciturn. Bitter. Physically strong, since he's done farmwork his whole life. Do I think he's a killer? I'm not sure."

The maître d' reappeared with a bottle of wine in an ice bucket, and he and James went through the ritual of opening and tasting. Ultimately the waiter was allowed to pour us two glasses, then he distributed menus. Poring over the menus took another two minutes and some consultation, but finally we conveyed our orders and were left in peace.

I distracted myself with carefully buttering a roll (warm from the oven, and the butter was unsalted), because I had no idea what to say. I had the strong feeling that he'd set up this lovely dinner with a purpose in mind. I knew there were things I *didn't* want to say, but I also knew that at some point I had to say them. I loved James—that much I knew. But I still wasn't sure how much I wanted to change my life for him. I knew he wanted more, and a part of me did, too. So what was my problem? I looked up to find him watching me, and his expression broke my heart; it was so vulnerable, so uncertain. I wanted to fall back on a challenging *What?* but I knew what.

"I'm sorry," I said softly. "I'm not being fair to you. About us, I mean."

"So you're not apologizing for inserting yourself in the middle of yet another criminal investigation?" His mouth twitched, so I knew he wasn't serious.

"I don't go looking for them, and you know it. But I'll concede that they're a distraction."

"That they are."

A waitperson appeared and silently slid our appetizers before us. They looked too pretty to eat, but that didn't stop me.

Between bites I said, "You aren't going to go all macho on me and tell me to tend to my knitting and stay out of police and FBI business, are you?"

"Heaven forbid. I know it wouldn't work anyway. And I acknowledge that you do bring a unique perspective to certain cases."

"Thank you. I'm glad you feel that way. I'm also glad I can help—I couldn't just sit by when I thought I knew something that might make a difference."

"And I wouldn't ask you to. But know that I worry about you, about your safety."

"And you don't think I worry about yours? Your job is a heck of a lot more dangerous than mine."

"Most of the time, anyway," he agreed.

The appetizer plates were whisked away, to be replaced by our entrees. I took one look at my plate, and said, "Can we table this discussion until we've finished eating? This looks incredible, and I'd hate to waste it."

"I agree. And there's no hurry."

We ate. No, we more than ate: We savored. Reveled. Wallowed. Gorged. I ran out of verbs. How had I never known about this little gem of a restaurant, mere blocks from where I'd worked for years?

"How did you ever find this place?" I asked James, all but licking the plate to capture the last few smears of an exquisite sauce.

"Marty."

"Marty doesn't do food."

"But she knows about it."

"Marty apparently knows about everything in a two-hundred-mile radius. But I'll thank her for this. Did Marty know we were coming here?"

"Yes."

I pondered that for a moment. Maybe Marty was trying

to nudge—or given Marty's lack of subtlety, shove—our relationship forward. I opened my mouth to speak, and the server appeared again. "Dessert?"

I looked at James, and he looked at the server. "Espresso. Two."

The server collected our plates and disappeared. I love dessert; I always order dessert. James knew that. But tonight I *didn't* want dessert—and James knew that, too. I looked around the charming courtyard, filled with happy couples enjoying the food and one another's company. The sun had sunk low, although it was still light, and there were shadows in the corners. I felt tears pricking my eyes.

I turned to face James squarely. "Are you ending things with me?"

He looked shocked. "What? No! Of course not. Why the hell would you think that?" His vehemence attracted a few curious looks from people at nearby tables.

"Because this would be the perfect setting. You know I wouldn't make a scene. You've softened me up with good food and fine wine. Now you're supposed to say something like 'Nell, I don't think this is going to work.' "

"How could you think such a thing? Nell, I love you. Maybe we've hit a couple of speed bumps, but nothing serious. I brought you here because I thought you'd like it. And . . ."

"I do like it, very much. What's the *and*?"

"This restaurant is attached to the hotel there. I took a room for the night."

That I had not expected. "Why?"

"Because I thought we needed neutral ground—not your place, not my place—if we're going to make some serious

decisions. We have things to talk about, yes, but it's not about ending this, it's about moving forward."

"Oh. Well, then. Good idea." James was one smart man.

The server appeared with our espressos. We finished off the last of the wine in the bottle, then drank our coffee silently. But it was not an ominous silence.

No bill appeared, so James must have arranged to have it added to the hotel bill. "Are you ready to go?" he asked.

"I am." And I followed him into the building.

CHAPTER 29

Worried though I was about whatever was to come, I was impressed by the boutique hotel. I guessed that it had been built as an elegant home for a prominent family in the eighteenth century, and any changes made since were discreet. The rooms were scattered over three floors above the ground floor, one or two rooms off each landing with a curving stairway connecting the floors.

Clearly James had taken care of all the details earlier. He nodded toward the concierge at a desk in the small lobby, then pointed me toward the stairway and guided me to a door on the third floor, which he opened with a key he pulled from his pocket. I walked in to find, first, a miniature sitting room with a short settee and a small desk, on which were a vase of flowers and an ice bucket with another bottle of chilled wine. Beyond that lay the bedroom, with a small bathroom—obviously a later addition, but nicely done—shoehorned into the corner adjacent to the sitting room. The

windows overlooked the restaurant courtyard, but they were well insulated and I couldn't hear anything from below.

My mind was working slowly, and eventually it occurred to me that I didn't have any night things or clothes. "I don't have . . ." I began.

"Yes, you do," James said, nodding toward a bag tucked in a corner.

"Marty?" I guessed. He nodded.

"So, what now?"

James took off his jacket and hung it neatly over the back of a chair. And then he took off his holster and his gun. No matter how often I saw James armed, it still threw me. After what had happened earlier this year, I was grateful for his weapon, but it was still unsettling.

"Is that . . . ?" I pointed. I hadn't actually looked at his gun since he'd gone back to work. The sight, the presence of that weapon, disturbed me, made me edgy. And it looked especially incongruous in this lovely antique room.

"The same weapon? Yes, it was returned to me." Then he looked at me more closely. "Yes, that's the one you fired. You know, we never talked about that."

I quailed inwardly. "Well, there really wasn't a good time right after, and then things just moved on . . . Are you going to open the wine?"

Yes, it was a distraction, but I needed it. I followed James into the front room, where he was filling two glasses. He handed me one. "What's wrong?"

A good observer was Special Agent James Morrison of the FBI. "I owe you that explanation. Can we sit?"

He sat on the mini settee. I sat on the stiff side chair by the small window, not touching him.

I hesitated, unsure of how to begin; I knew this would be hard for me, but it had to be said. "About the gun thing—there are some things you need to know. I've been handling weapons—handguns, shotguns, the whole gamut—since I was in high school. My father taught me. It was one of the bonding things we did—I was an only child, and I think he would have preferred a boy, but he took me along to the range one day, and when I turned out to be a pretty good shot, it helped. We used to go regularly on Sundays, just the two of us."

James was watching me intently, but he made no effort to interrupt. I took a deep breath and went on. "When I realized that I could get my hands on your Glock that day, I acted without even thinking."

"So it wasn't just a lucky shot?"

I nodded. "No, it wasn't. I hit what I was aiming for. Besides, it would have been hard to miss at that distance."

"Thank you," James said. "Your father would be proud of you. He taught you well."

I looked away, fighting to get the next words out. "There's more. Have you ever wondered why I never talk about my family?"

"I hadn't really thought about it. There's a reason?"

"Yes." There was no pretty way to put this, so I just stated it bluntly. "My father killed himself when I was seventeen, with one of his handguns. My mother didn't take it too well, and more or less drank herself to death, although it took her five years to destroy her liver. She wouldn't let me get rid of the gun collection, even though she hated it. I didn't tell her, but I made sure the guns were disabled, so she wouldn't be able to do what my father had done. As soon as she was

gone, I sold the lot of them. I never wanted to see them again. I never wanted to touch a gun again."

Wisely James made no move toward me. I was afraid I would fall apart if he touched me. "Nell, I'm so sorry. I'm sorry it had to happen to you. I'm sorry that this thing brought it all back."

"It's not your fault. Part of me was glad I knew what to do—to save you."

James nodded once, acknowledging what I'd said. "Is it a problem for you that I carry a gun?"

"To be honest, I never really gave it much thought. I mean, I know you do, but . . ." I couldn't seem to find words that made sense. I knew James was not my father, and in his hands a gun was not an evil thing. Or maybe I cared enough about him that it didn't matter. ". . . I can handle it," I finished. "It's part of who you are and what you do. Maybe what happened was some kind of cosmic balancing act, good compensating for evil."

But somehow that didn't seem to be the whole story . . . until at last the pieces fell into place and I saw what had been holding me back—not just with James but with so many other things in my life. "Oh God," I whispered, more to myself than to him.

Now he made a move to get up, to reach out to me, but I stopped him with a gesture. "No, wait, please . . . I have to work this out." I took a swallow of wine, then another, mostly as a stalling tactic—and to keep me from hyperventilating. How could I have been so stupid for so long?

And James watched and waited, his concern etched on his face. He knew, he had always known, that I had to be ready.

Another deep breath helped. "I know what the problem

is, but I never saw it before. I guess I never had a reason to look too hard before now." *Before you.* "I loved my father, and I worked hard to get close to him. He was a complicated man, I can see that now. And then he killed himself, with no warning, and I was shocked, and hurt. He left my mother, and he left me, with no explanation. Maybe there was a reason, or maybe he was just depressed, but to me he was simply . . . gone. And then because of that my mother withdrew from me, too, although it took longer. But somewhere inside, I felt like they'd left because I wasn't good enough for either of them. That I didn't matter enough to stick around for. I know, it's not rational, but I think that's why I've never really committed to anyone since. Because it would hurt too much when they left me."

I took another sip of wine, and I noticed that my glass was empty. I reached out to retrieve the bottle and refilled it. "You know I was married once before?"

"Yes."

"And it ended. Not badly, but there just wasn't a lot holding us together. He was a good guy, and after we split up, he married someone else and had a couple of kids. He's happy. But the worst part was, I really didn't miss him. We'd been married for three years, and when he was gone, I felt . . . relieved, I guess. I didn't have to worry anymore about making him happy or wonder why things weren't working and if it was my fault. It seemed like the right thing to do at the time, but we never should have gotten married at all. I couldn't let him in. I couldn't let myself care about him too much. And there hasn't been anyone since, not anyone that mattered. Until you."

"And that's why you've been pushing me away?" James asked quietly. "Because you do care? Too much?"

"But I didn't want to push you away! I didn't mean to. It's just that this whole thing between us has me scared."

"And my getting injured didn't help."

"Weirdly enough, it did. Not because I got to play heroine and save you, but because it forced me to recognize how much I cared about you and that I didn't want to lose you. But as soon as you started talking about moving in together, I started backing away."

"I noticed," James said wryly. Then he turned serious again. "Nell, I could say something trite here like 'You're never going to lose me,' but you're an intelligent woman and you know I can't promise that. My job can be dangerous, as you know all too well. When I joined the Bureau, I had only myself to consider, and it didn't make a difference to me. Now it does. I don't want to inflict that on you. I can quit, find something else to do."

"No!" I stood up abruptly, unable to sit still like a calm, rational person, which at the moment I wasn't. "I don't want that. I mean, I don't want that for *you*. It's an important job, you like it, and you're good at it. I don't want to be responsible for telling you to change your life, not because I have baggage. I don't have the right to do that, and I don't want to."

Now he stood up, too. "What about what *I* want? What if you're more important to me than any job?"

"How can I be?" I whispered. He was standing close, so close . . .

"You are."

We stopped talking for a while. A long while.

Later, we lay in the dark, propped up by a dozen or so pillows—this was a *nice* little hotel—finishing up the last of the wine, now room temperature. "Thank you," I said.

"For what? This?"

"Yes, this, but mainly for not giving up on me. First Marty, and now you—you keep telling me how to fix my life, and I can't even resent it because I know you're both right, in your own ways. I'm getting a little old to be scared of messing things up. It's time I figured out how to commit." I pulled myself up and rolled onto my side to look at James, or at as much of him as I could see in the light that trickled in from the courtyard below. "Don't quit your job. What you do matters. I know that. I understand that because I've had a little taste of it myself."

"And given me palpitations when you do," he grumbled.

"Look, there are idiots who go skydiving or swimming with sharks, looking for danger. You risk your life because you're helping someone else. And that's all I'm trying to do. If I have knowledge that matters, I'm going to act on it. And pass it on to you."

"Does it have to be in that order?"

"We'll see. And I'm sorry I've been dragging my feet about finding a place—I just needed time to process the idea. You gave me time. So let's do this thing."

"What are you doing tomorrow? Or I guess I mean later today."

"The only thing on my schedule is meeting with Mitchell Wakeman to present Lissa's report, at two."

"Will that include what you guess about Eddie Garrett?"

"It doesn't have to. We can simply call the bodies two unknown Revolutionary War soldiers from opposing sides, lying side by side through the centuries."

"Good spin. What about George Bowen's death?"

"That might be trickier, but it doesn't have to go into the

Society's report. If anyone asks, I'll just refer them to the police, or you."

We drifted into sleep, entangled, and woke up the same way. "What time is it?" I asked, not that I was in a hurry. After all, I was only a few blocks from work.

James rolled over. "Looks like . . . seven something. There's a buffet breakfast downstairs—part of the package."

"Sounds good. Can I have the first shower?"

"Go for it."

I rolled out of bed and realized I hadn't even checked what Marty had included in the overnight bag she had so thoughtfully provided—I'd never gotten around to opening it. I assumed she'd raided what I kept at James's place and knew what was appropriate for a day at work. She had included one new item, a slithery silk nightgown—that we hadn't had a chance to try out.

We did the normal morning things, and Marty's choices were fine. I hated to leave our little universe—James's brilliant idea to get us out of our respective nests and into a place where we were on equal footing had paid off.

Downstairs, breakfast was served in a large, brightly lit room lined with bookshelves, its tall windows facing the street. A diverse array of hot and cold foods was laid out in silver-plated dishes, and we served ourselves and found a table a comfortable distance from the few other people in the room.

"Maybe we could just move in here," I joked. "The food is good, someone else does all the cleaning, and we could both walk to work."

"It might be a bit beyond our combined budget," James said.

"Oh, pooh—you're no fun. Maybe you could moonlight as their in-house security and get a discount."

"I'll take it under advisement." I didn't hear a phone ring, but James must have set his on vibrate, because he reached into his jacket pocket and pulled out his cell phone. He looked at it, then stood up, and said, "I need to take this," and walked into the adjoining room. He was back in under two minutes, his expression somber.

"What?" I asked.

"Eddie Garrett was found dead in his home this morning when police went to question him. He committed suicide with an old shotgun. He left a note, confessing to George Bowen's murder."

I couldn't speak for a long moment, buffeted once again by memories of my father. But then I realized they didn't hurt as much as they had—before I'd told James the story. "Poor Eddie," I whispered, fighting tears once again.

James reached across the table and took my hand. "Don't blame yourself, Nell. It would have come out one way or another."

"That doesn't make it hurt less. I feel responsible."

"I know. There's something else."

I wiped my eyes and faced him. "What?"

"You were right—he was the one who'd been holding the gun that killed his brother. He never really got over it, and dealing with the exposure of those two early Garrett brothers was too much for him. He said all that in the note. It's not your fault, Nell."

"I know, or at least the rational part of me does. But it still hurts. Funny how history comes back to haunt us, isn't it?"

CHAPTER 30

Even the sad news about Eddie Garrett couldn't dampen my spirits altogether. After talking things through with James, I felt like a huge burden had been lifted from my shoulders—one I hadn't even recognized I was carrying. For years I'd done a good job of *not* thinking about a lot of things, like what had happened with my family and my marriage, and I hadn't realized how much it was dragging me down. And it had taken a catastrophic event to make me understand it. And James.

I still wasn't entirely sure I deserved James. He was smart and good at a job he liked and nice to his extended family and honest and brave and true and all that good stuff—and he loved me. Of that I had no doubt, for how else could anyone have put up with my vacillating?

We finished up our breakfast quickly and packed up what little we had, and then strolled out onto the street, side by side. The sun was shining, there was a cool breeze, and all

that was missing were a few bluebirds and butterflies and maybe a rainbow. At the corner I turned toward the Society, and James followed. "Wait, don't you work in the other direction?" I teased.

"I'm escorting you home—figuratively, at least."

"Oh. Thank you." We took our time covering the few blocks to the Society building, enjoying the moment. When we arrived, I said, "Will there be more fallout from . . . Eddie's death?"

"For me, possibly. I can keep you out of it."

"I'm already in it—I just want to figure out what to say to Wakeman. I bet he thought the whole deal would be easy when Ezra agreed to the sale, and now all this happens. Oh, and I should talk to Janet, too—I don't know if she'll have heard the news. Will I see you tonight?"

"I hope so. I'll call you during the day if there are any new developments."

"Let me know where we're going to be, okay?" If I recalled, my car was still parked across the street, with a whopping bill, no doubt. But, oh, last night had been worth it!

I let myself into the building and went upstairs to find that Eric had beaten me to the office yet again. "Hey, Eric. Can we use the conference room for our meeting with Wakeman? He may decide to bring his staff." Or he might not bring anyone at all, if he was discouraged by the events that kept springing up like mushrooms around his beloved project.

"Already booked," he said.

"I should have guessed. Have you by any chance seen Lissa yet?"

"She's in your office. You want coffee?"

"Sure."

When I walked into my office, Lissa was sitting on the settee, scribbling edits on printed pages. "Did you ever go home last night?" I asked.

She looked up, dazed. "What time is it? No. I figured I'd go over this with you, then run home for a quick shower and change before our meeting at two. It is still at two, right?"

"Yes, but I have some new details and you may have to make a few changes." Eric appeared with a mug of steaming coffee, and I waited until he'd returned to his desk before resuming, glad of the delay. "You know about my meeting with Janet Butler and Eddie Garrett yesterday. This morning James got a call that Eddie Garrett killed himself sometime during the night. He left a note confessing to the murder of George Bowen." It still hurt me to say that. Although I know it wasn't rational, I felt responsible for pushing Eddie to such a drastic solution. The fact that the whole story was likely to have come out eventually was little comfort.

"Oh my God," Lissa said, trying to process the new information. "Oh, wow. Do we assume Wakeman will know about this?"

"Probably somebody on one or more police forces will tell him, right?"

"Yeah, sure. He's got friends everywhere, doesn't he? So what do we put in the report?"

Based on my half hour of absorbing the news and its ramifications, I said, "I think we go with the straight history part of it—who owned the land over the centuries. I think you can put together a separate appendix about the dead soldiers and Eddie Garrett's connection to them, for Wakeman's eyes only, and let him decide what he wants to do

with it. I don't think it's our place to tell the world, no matter how juicy a story it might be. Wakeman asked for a simple report on the history of the farm, and that's what we'll give him. If he wants more, let him ask."

Lissa thought hard for a moment, her fatigue clear on her face. "I think I agree. And it makes my job easier, because the core stuff is done. You want to see another draft?"

"No, I think what you've already done is great. Make those last few changes, print me out a copy, give one to Eric to make copies for the meeting, and go home and take a nap. Well, once you add that other bit, just for Wakeman's copy."

"Thanks, Nell. You want me at the meeting, right?"

"Of course I do. You did all the work."

"Then I'll see you later."

After she had left, I checked the time. It was still early, but maybe Janet would already be in her office. I'd rather she heard the news from me than from a cop or not at all.

She picked up after the first ring. "Nell?"

From the tone of her voice I could tell she knew. "You heard?"

"I did. A friend who works for the township called me. What an awful thing. I feel so guilty. And so bad for Eddie."

"I know what you mean. Maybe no one could have accused him of killing George Bowen, but I guess he couldn't handle having everyone know about his role in his brother's death, which was bound to come out once the dead soldiers had been found. There was no putting the genie back in the bottle."

"Poor Eddie," Janet echoed my comment. "What are you going to tell the Wakeman people?"

"I told Lissa just now that we should stick with the simple

history. I'll let him know the rest of the story, but privately. If he wants to use the information, it's up to him."

"Fair enough. Thanks for calling, Nell. Despite everything, I enjoyed working with you."

"Me, too. And I was serious about that idea for an exhibit. Let's talk about it later, when the dust settles. Keep in touch." As I hung up I wondered if Wakeman would go as far as to shut down the project, but somehow I doubted it. From what I'd learned, he'd had his heart set on this for a long time.

I muddled through the next few hours. I made a few phone calls, including one I'd been putting off for a while. But my mind was somewhere else, or rather several somewheres, bouncing from yesterday's conversation with Eddie Garrett and the way his face changed when he realized I knew the story, to several memorable moments last night with James. For all that he was a government agent, he was an extraordinarily kind and patient man. I was staring into space, no doubt with a small smile on my face, when Eric, followed by Lissa, came in to announce that Mitchell Wakeman was waiting downstairs.

I brought my wandering attention back to the present. "Thank you, Eric. Will you go down and get him, and escort him up to the conference room?"

"Sure thing. Everything's set up in there."

When Eric had left, I asked Lissa, "Are you ready?"

"I hope so. No matter how it goes, Nell, thanks for this opportunity. I think we academic types tend to forget that history is still very much with us, and we've seen that this week."

"I know what you mean. Well, let's do this thing."

We were waiting in the conference room when Mitchell Wakeman stalked in—alone. I wasn't sure whether this was a good or bad sign.

"You heard about Garrett?" he demanded.

"I did."

"You know why he did it?"

"I do. Why don't we sit down and talk about it? Will Scott or anyone else from your team be joining us?"

"Nope. I wanted to get the facts first. I'll pass along whatever I think they need to know."

He dropped into a chair. I handed him one of the copies of the reports. "We decided to break this up into two parts. The first is the history of the farm and its place in the community. The second is about those two soldiers—for your eyes only, if you choose, and there's more I can add that we didn't write down."

"Let me read 'em first." He took them both, then started leafing through the first report. I glanced briefly at Lissa, and then we sat in silence while Wakeman read. Thank goodness he was a fast reader, and it didn't take long. When he was finished, he put the papers down, sat back in his chair, and rubbed his hands over his face. "You said there's more?"

"Yes. We know the dead soldiers were brothers, and we suspect that they were members of the Garrett family, fighting for opposite sides, and that the family passed down the story. And that's why Eddie killed George Bowen, and then himself. He was involved in the shooting death of his brother when they were both children, and he couldn't face it all coming out again."

"You got proof?"

"We can compare Eddie's DNA with the others, if it's necessary."

"Who else knows?"

"Apart from Lissa and me? James Morrison, the FBI agent you called in, and Janet Butler in West Chester. No one else."

"Will it come out?"

"Do you want it to?" I parried. "Odds are high it will reach the press eventually, since there's already been coverage about the bodies' discovery. If you want to put your own spin on it, now's the time. Do you plan to move forward with the project?"

"Hell, yes. I've got too much invested in this to walk away now. And I don't mean just money. Let me think."

He thought. Lissa and I waited. I wasn't even sure what outcome to hope for.

Finally he sat up again and slapped both hands on the table. "First, I've got to thank you for finding all this out and then for keeping it quiet. I think you're right—it's too good a story for the press to ignore, and there's probably somebody nosy enough to keep digging, so I'll turn it over to my people and let them work out how we can use it. But I owe you—both of you here—and you'll get what's coming to you. And I guess I owe that lady in West Chester, too. Look, I'm going to put together another press conference, and I want you on the podium."

"I won't sugarcoat it."

"I didn't ask you to. You can't mess with history, and I wouldn't want to."

"I'm glad to hear that."

Wakeman stood up abruptly. "I gotta get this thing rolling. Thanks for everything. We'll be in touch." He strode out of the room, and I rushed to catch up so I could take him downstairs.

In the poky elevator, I asked him. "Why is this project so important to you?"

Wakeman sighed. "I've built a lot of things around here. I'm proud of them, and I've made a lot of money. This one, though—it's not about the money, it's about what's the best way to live in the world today. I wanted to make a model for the future. And then the past popped up in the middle of it. Maybe there's a lesson in that. But the idea is still good. It'll work."

"I hope it does." I let him out of the elevator and watched him head toward the front door, and then the elevator doors closed and I pressed the button for the third floor again.

Upstairs, Lissa was still hovering anxiously outside my office. "Everything okay?" she asked.

"You know, I think it is. When I first met the man, I hoped he was basically a decent guy, and I haven't seen anything to change my mind. Don't worry. If he doesn't come up with a check soon, I'll make it right with you and then I can hound him so you won't have to. But it occurs to me that the Society could probably use you for other assignments like this, as a contractor. You know, the genealogy of building sites or houses or the like? On a project-by-project basis. If Wakeman puts in a good word for you, more people might be interested."

"That sounds great, Nell! And I could fit it in around my graduate course work. Thanks a lot!"

"Hey, we all win—you did a great job on this, with too little time and a few unexpected distractions. Now take the rest of the day off and have some fun."

"I'll do that." She left my office with a smile on her face, but I noticed that instead of heading toward the elevator she went down the hall toward Ben's cubicle. Interesting.

Eric came in and handed me a few message slips. "Agent Morrison called while you were in your meeting. He said I didn't need to interrupt you, but he'll stop by at five and pick you up."

"Did he say anything else?"

"Nope. Just to meet him outside—he'll be driving."

CHAPTER 31

I was on the sidewalk outside the Society waiting for James when he pulled up. He opened the door for me. "Get in."

"You do remember I have a car parked across the street?" I said, climbing in anyway.

"We'll deal with that later. Buckle up."

"Where are we going?" I said as I complied.

"You'll see."

The man was full of surprises these days. I wondered if Marty had had a hand in this one, too, or if she'd just given him instructions on how to woo reluctant me. I wasn't going to complain. Besides, James looked like he was enjoying himself.

I was mildly curious when he took the Schuylkill Expressway heading west, which meant we were actually going north. I made a point of studying his profile as we passed the Fairmount Water Works on the other side of the river. That was the site where James had been injured, and it

was going to be a while before I could look on that view without feeling a pang. The traffic was surprisingly light, given that it was a sunny Friday, one of the last of the summer, although generally most of the traffic escaping the city was heading east for the shore.

After a few miles, he asked, "How was your meeting with Wakeman?"

"Surprising. He came alone—no entourage. I think he was expecting bad news and wanted time to digest it before he shared it."

"So he wasn't surprised by what you told him?"

"Not entirely. He read through our report, and he took it well, though—kind of sad, and quiet. I guess I expected more bluster. He thanked us, and he said we'd get something for our efforts, although he didn't say what, and I didn't ask. By the way, I think I'm going to try to keep Lissa on at the Society as a researcher for hire. She did a good job, and her specialty is local history, so maybe we can create a new niche for her—building historian or something like that. Do you think Ben will be happy about that?"

"Ask him. Or Lissa. I told you, I don't mess with other people's romantic lives."

"Ha! So you're saying they might have one."

"No, I'm not. But if they do, I wouldn't mess with it."

"Obviously you're much too busy managing your own romantic life, right?"

We talked happy nonsense for a few more miles as we wended our way around the western edge of the city. Then he veered off on Wissahickon Avenue, still traveling west, away from the city. I knew the area, but not well. James

seemed to know exactly where he was going. The farther we went, the greener the streets became, and the larger the houses, with more space between. Chestnut Hill, I guessed, a beautiful—and pricey—neighborhood.

A few more turns, and then he pulled into a driveway that led up a hill. There was a house sitting on a rise in the middle of a surprisingly large expanse of lawn. He stopped in front of a set of steps and parked.

"Are we meeting someone here?" I asked.

"We're meeting a house. Come on."

He climbed out of the car and came around to my side and politely opened my door. I closed it behind me and looked up at the house. Late Victorian, I guessed, fieldstone, its trim painted a rich, dark red. Three stories with a mansard roof and a porch running across the front, with what looked like original gingerbread woodwork. I looked at James, who was watching me with a peculiar expression that seemed to combine excitement and apprehension.

"Are we going in?"

"Yes." He let me precede him up the steps, and then pulled a key from his pocket and unlocked the door. He held the door open for me to enter.

I stepped inside and stopped in my tracks. *Oh my.* My first impression was that the interior was largely untouched: no idiotic remuddling or well-intentioned "improvements." The second was that it had been lovingly maintained. All the woodwork was gleaming with varnish but looked as though it had never been painted. The ornate door and window moldings had to be nearly a foot wide.

I stepped tentatively forward. Living room—no,

parlor—on the right, running the full depth of the house, with a glorious bay window at the back and an original fireplace with an elaborate overmantel and tiled surround that had me salivating. I hated to tear myself away from it, but I knew there was more to see. I crossed the hall to a narrow dining room, and behind that was a fully remodeled modern kitchen with a huge refrigerator and tiers of cabinets. Back stairs led upward, and beyond the kitchen I could see a wall of windows suggesting a sunroom.

I turned to James, who had followed me like an eager puppy. "Okay, what are we doing here?"

"Do you like it?"

"I think it's spectacular."

"Five bedrooms, three baths, over half an acre of land, and parking for three cars," he recited. "Oh, and it's three blocks from the train line."

"James, what are you saying? You're seriously considering this place? For us?"

"Yes for us, but only if you like it."

I couldn't imagine living in such a splendid place, but I knew I wanted to. "Can we possibly afford it?"

James named a figure that made me gulp. "What's that come out to in real-world terms? Like how much we would pay a month?" I wasn't good at calculating mortgage payments in my head. The answer he gave meant it would be tight, but between us it was doable . . . particularly if we could pay a good chunk up front. Like the kind of money the psychiatrists were offering for my carriage house.

"Okay," I said.

He stared at me. "You mean, yes, you like it? Yes, let's do it?"

Poor man, he was almost quivering with eagerness. "There's something I've been meaning to tell you." I fished around in my bag and pulled out the offer letter—I'd brought it with me that morning. I pulled the letter out of its envelope and handed it to James.

He scanned it quickly, then looked at me. "They're serious?"

"They are. I told them yes this morning."

"We're buying this house?" he said, just to be sure.

"Yes. We are."

He let out a long sigh. "Good, because I made an offer for it this morning."

"Smart man."

I caught a glimpse of the happy, boyish James—the one the Bureau had never met—when he grabbed me up then and swung me around, right in the kitchen.

"Now that I've already agreed, you might as well show me the rest of the house now."

"That's right, I can't believe you said yes before you even looked upstairs."

"You had me at the fireplace," I said cheerfully. "Let's go on up. And can we take the back stairs? I've always loved back stairs—they're like one step above a secret passage."

After we looked around from the attic to the basement and back again, we circled the spacious yet private yard. I said, "I thought you said you weren't going to mow lawns. There's a lot of lawn out here."

"With what we'll be paying monthly, we can afford to hire someone. You're sure?"

"Yes, I'm sure. Oh, wait—did Marty have anything to do with finding this place?"

"She did not. She hasn't seen it. I found this one all by myself, thanks to all that online research."

"You are brilliant. When are we going to tell her?"

"I'm guessing in about an hour—we made plans to meet for dinner. She's bringing Ethan along."

"Have you met him?"

"Nope, not yet. You?"

"No. She's been very secretive about him. I'm glad she's got someone, though. She wasn't just feeling competitive, was she, now that she's got us settled?"

"Hey, Marty does what Marty wants to do."

Since we had time to spare, I had to go back and study the fireplace again. It looked even better the second time around. Then I drifted back to the ornate window overlooking the lawn. James came up behind me and folded his arms around me.

"Happy?" he said into my hair.

"Very. You are an extraordinary man, and I love you. When can we move in?"

"I think the paperwork may take a month. We can stay at your place until then. Or we might have to stay at a hotel . . . I think I know a nice one."

We beat Marty and the mysterious Ethan Miller to the restaurant and ordered a bottle of champagne, because I was certainly ready to celebrate. And we could surprise Marty, which was a rare occurrence.

But in the end, Marty surprised us first. She grinned at us as she made introductions. "Ethan, this is my cousin Jimmy, and my friend and colleague and sometimes partner in crime Nell Pratt."

We shook all around. Then Ethan said, "Marty didn't tell

you, did she? My mother was a Korean war bride, and my father was a GI Mayflower descendant—the best of two worlds, I always thought."

I decided I liked Ethan. Before we could all sit down again, I had to tell Marty. "We bought a house!"

"Without consulting me?" Marty said in mock dismay. "Where is it?"

And we opened the champagne and described our new home in glowing terms, I realized that I was as happy as I could ever remember being.

And we were going to need a lot more furniture to fill all those rooms.

FROM *NEW YORK TIMES* BESTSELLING AUTHOR

SHEILA CONNOLLY

Scandal in Skibbereen

A County Cork Mystery

As the new owner of Sullivan's Pub in County Cork, Ireland, Maura Donovan gets an earful of all the village gossip. But uncovering the truth about some local rumors may close her down for good. . .

"An exceptional read! Sheila Connolly has done it again with this outstanding book . . . [A] must read for those who have ever wanted to visit Ireland."

—*Shelley's Book Case* on *Buried in a Bog*

sheilaconnolly.com
facebook.com/TheCrimeSceneBooks
penguin.com

M1424T0114

Berkley Prime Crime titles by Sheila Connolly

Orchard Mysteries

ONE BAD APPLE
ROTTEN TO THE CORE
RED DELICIOUS DEATH
A KILLER CROP
BITTER HARVEST
SOUR APPLES
GOLDEN MALICIOUS

Museum Mysteries

FUNDRAISING THE DEAD
LET'S PLAY DEAD
FIRE ENGINE DEAD
MONUMENT TO THE DEAD
RAZING THE DEAD

County Cork Mysteries

BURIED IN A BOG
SCANDAL IN SKIBBEREEN

Specials

DEAD LETTERS
AN OPEN BOOK

"The mystery is great, and will have readers guessing all the way until the end." —*RT Book Reviews*

"[An] engaging amateur sleuth filled with fascinating characters, interesting museum information, plenty of action including a nice twist, and a bit of romance."

—*Genre Go Round Reviews*

"Skillfully executed . . . It's a pleasure to accompany Nell on her quest." —*Mystery Scene*

"A terrific new cozy museum mystery series with a dynamic accidental sleuth . . . Nell's strong, smart, and sassy—the kind of person you wish lived next door." —AnnArbor.com

"*National Treasure* meets *The Philadelphia Story* . . . Secrets, lies, and a delightful revenge conspiracy make this a real page-turner!"

—Hank Phillippi Ryan, Agatha, Anthony, and Macavity award–winning author of *The Other Woman*

Praise for the Museum Mysteries

"Sheila Connolly has written another winner in her Museum Mystery series . . . The facts and history that Ms. Connolly provides certainly adds to the charm of the story . . . [A] real page-turner."

—MyShelf.com

"A witty, engaging blend of history and mystery with a smart sleuth who already feels like a good friend . . . [Connolly's] stories always keep me turning pages—often well past my bedtime."

—Julie Hyzy, *New York Times* bestselling author of the White House Chef Mysteries

"The archival milieu and the foibles of the characters are intriguing, and it's refreshing to encounter an FBI man who is human, competent, and essential to the plot."

—*Publishers Weekly*

"Nell is a mature and intelligent sleuth, who works with historic treasures and takes her responsibilities seriously. Great pacing and placement of clues build tension as Nell uncovers the truth in this enjoyable and sophisticated mystery."

—*RT Book Reviews*

"The practical and confident Nell Pratt is exactly the kind of sleuth you want in your corner when the going gets tough. Sheila Connelly serves up a snappy and sophisticated mystery that leaves you lusting for the next witty installment."

—Mary Jane Maffini, author of the Charlotte Adams Mysteries

"[The] mystery intrigues . . . The best is the relationship between Nell and James, two people who thoroughly enjoy each other's company day and night."

—*Kings River Life Magazine*

continued . . .

Melanie Milburne

THE VENETIAN ONE-NIGHT BABY

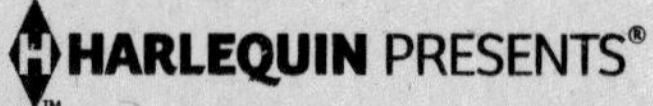

Recycling programs for this product may not exist in your area.

ISBN-13: 978-1-335-53805-5

The Venetian One-Night Baby

First North American publication 2019

This edition published by arrangement with Harlequin Books S.A.

For questions and comments about the quality of this book, please contact us at CustomerService@Harlequin.com.

Printed in U.S.A.

Melanie Milburne read her first Harlequin novel at the age of seventeen, in between studying for her final exams. After completing a master's degree in education, she decided to write a novel, and thus her career as a romance author was born. Melanie is an ambassador for the Australian Childhood Foundation and a keen dog lover and trainer. She enjoys long walks in the Tasmanian bush. In 2015 Melanie won the HOLT Medallion, a prestigious award honoring outstanding literary talent.

Books by Melanie Milburne

Harlequin Presents

The Tycoon's Marriage Deal
A Virgin for a Vow
Blackmailed into the Marriage Bed
Tycoon's Forbidden Cinderella

Conveniently Wed!

Bound by a One-Night Vow

One Night With Consequences

A Ring for the Greek's Baby

The Ravensdale Scandals

Ravensdale's Defiant Captive
Awakening the Ravensdale Heiress
Engaged to Her Ravensdale Enemy
The Most Scandalous Ravensdale

The Scandal Before the Wedding

Claimed for the Billionaire's Convenience

Visit the Author Profile page
at Harlequin.com for more titles.

To Mallory (Mal) and Mike Tuffy. It was so lovely to meet you on the European river cruise a few years ago—it must be time for another one! It's wonderful to continue our friendship since. We always look forward to seeing you in Tasmania.

Xxx

CHAPTER ONE

SABRINA WAS HOPING she wouldn't run into Max Firbank again after The Kiss. He wasn't an easy man to avoid since he was her parents' favourite godson and was invited to just about every Midhurst family gathering. Birthdays, Christmas, New Year's Eve, parties and anniversaries he would spend on the fringes of the room, a twenty-first-century reincarnation of Jane Austen's taciturn Mr Darcy. He'd look down his aristocratic nose at everyone else having fun.

Sabrina made sure she had extra fun just to annoy him. She danced with everyone who asked her, chatting and working the room like she was the star student from Social Butterfly School. Max occasionally wouldn't show, and then she would spend the whole evening wondering why the energy in the room wasn't the same. But she refused to acknowledge it had anything to do with his absence.

This weekend she was in Venice to exhibit two of her designs at her first wedding expo. She felt safe from running into him—or she would have if the hotel receptionist could find her booking.

Sabrina leaned closer to the hotel reception counter. 'I can assure you the reservation was made weeks ago.'

'What name did you say it was booked under?' the young male receptionist asked.

'Midhurst, Sabrina Jane. My assistant booked it for me.'

'Do you have any documentation with you? The confirmation email?'

Had her new assistant Harriet forwarded it to her? Sabrina remembered printing out the wedding expo programme but had she printed out the accommodation details? She searched for it in her tote bag, sweat beading between her breasts, her stomach pitching with panic. She couldn't turn up flustered to her first wedding expo as an exhibitor. That's why she'd recently employed an assistant to help her with this sort of stuff. Booking flights and accommodation, sorting out her diary, making sure she didn't double book or miss appointments.

Sabrina put her lipgloss, paper diary, passport and phone on the counter, plus three pens, a small packet of tissues, some breath mints and her brand-new business cards. She left her tampons in the side pocket of her bag—there was only so much embarrassment she could handle at any one time. The only bits of paper she found were a shopping list and a receipt from her favourite shoe store.

She began to put all the items back in her bag, but her lipgloss fell off the counter, dropped to the floor, rolled across the lobby and was stopped by a large Italian-leather-clad foot.

Sabrina's gaze travelled up the long length of the expertly tailored charcoal-grey trousers and finally came to rest on Max Firbank's smoky grey-blue gaze.

'Sabrina.' His tone was less of a greeting and more of a grim *not you again.*

Sabrina gave him a tight, no-teeth-showing smile. 'Fancy seeing you here. I wouldn't have thought wedding expos were your thing.'

His eyes glanced at her mouth and something in her stomach dropped like a book tumbling off a shelf. *Kerplunk*. He blinked as if to clear his vision and bent down to pick up her lipgloss. He handed it to her, his expression as unreadable as cryptic code. 'I'm seeing a client about a project. I always stay at this hotel when I come to Venice.'

Sabrina took the lipgloss and slipped it into her bag, trying to ignore the tingling in her fingers where his had touched hers. She could feel the heat storming into her cheeks in a hot crimson tide. What sort of weird coincidence was *this*? Of all the hotels in Venice why did he have to be at *this* one? And on *this* weekend? She narrowed her gaze to the size of buttonholes. 'Did my parents tell you I was going to be here this weekend?'

Nothing on his face changed except for a brief elevation of one of his dark eyebrows. 'No. Did mine tell you I was going to be in Venice?'

Sabrina raised her chin. 'Oh, didn't you know? I zone out when your parents tell me things about you. I mentally plug my ears and sing *la-de-da* in my head until they change the subject of how amazingly brilliant you are.'

There was a flicker of movement across his

lips that could have been loosely described as a smile. 'I'll have to remember to do that next time your parents bang on about you to me.'

Sabrina flicked a wayward strand of hair out of her face. Why did she always have to look like she'd been through a wind tunnel whenever she saw him? She dared not look at his mouth but kept her eyes trained on his inscrutable gaze. Was he thinking about The Kiss? The clashing of mouths that had morphed into a passionate explosion that had made a mockery of every other kiss she'd ever received? Could he still recall the taste and texture of her mouth? Did he lie in bed at night and fantasise about kissing her again?

And not just kissing, but…

'Signorina?' The hotel receptionist jolted Sabrina out of her reverie. 'We have no booking under the name Midhurst. Could it have been another hotel you selected online?'

Sabrina suppressed a frustrated sigh. 'No. I asked my assistant to book me into this one. This is where the fashion show is being held. I have to stay here.'

'What's the problem?' Max asked in a calm, *leave it to me* tone.

Sabrina turned to face him. 'I've got a new

assistant and somehow she must've got the booking wrong or it didn't process or something.' She bit her lip, trying to stem the panic punching against her heart. *Poomf. Poomf. Poomf.*

'I can put you on the cancellation list, but we're busy at this time of year so I can't guarantee anything,' the receptionist said.

Sabrina's hand crept up to her mouth and she started nibbling on her thumbnail. Too bad about her new manicure. A bit of nail chewing was all she had to soothe her rising dread. She wanted to be settled into her hotel, not left waiting on stand-by. What if no other hotel could take her? She needed to be close to the convention venue because she had two dresses in the fashion parade. This was her big break to get her designs on the international stage.

She. Could. Not. Fail.

'Miss Midhurst will be joining me,' Max said. 'Have the concierge bring her luggage to my room. Thank you.'

Sabrina's gaze flew to his. 'What?'

Max handed her a card key, his expression still as inscrutable as that of an MI5 spy. 'I checked in this morning. There are two beds in my suite. I only need one.'

She did *not* want to think about him and a bed in the same sentence. She'd spent the last three weeks thinking about him in a bed with her in a tangle of sweaty sex-sated limbs. Which was frankly kind of weird because she'd spent most of her life deliberately *not* thinking about him. Max was her parents' godson and almost from the moment when she'd been born six years later and become his parents' adored goddaughter, both sets of parents had decided how perfect they were for each other. It was the long-wished-for dream of both families that Max and Sabrina would fall in love, get married and have gorgeous babies together.

As if. In spite of both families' hopes, Sabrina had never got on with Max. She found him brooding and distant and arrogant. And he made it no secret he found her equally annoying...which kind of made her wonder why he'd kissed her...

But she was *not* going to think about The Kiss.

She glanced at the clock over Reception, another fist of panic pummelling her heart. She needed to shower and change and do her hair and makeup. She needed to get her head in order. It wouldn't do to turn up flustered and nervous. What sort of impression would she make?

Sabrina took the key from him but her fingers brushed his and a tingle travelled from her fingers to her armpit. 'Maybe I should try and see if I can get in somewhere else...'

'What time does your convention start?'

'There's a cocktail party at six-thirty.'

Max led the way to the bank of lifts. 'I'll take you up to settle you in before I meet my client for a drink.'

Sabrina entered the brass embossed lift with him and the doors whispered shut behind them. The mirrored interior reflected Max's features from every angle. His tall and lean and athletic build. The well-cut dark brown hair with a hint of a wave. The generously lashed eyes the colour of storm clouds. The faint hollow below the cheekbones that gave him a chiselled-from-marble look that was far more attractive than it had any right to be. The aristocratic cut of nostril and upper lip, the small cleft in his chin, the square jaw that hinted at arrogance and a tendency to insist on his own way.

'Is your client female?' The question was

out before Sabrina could monitor her wayward tongue.

'Yes.' His brusque one-word answer was a verbal Keep Out sign.

Sabrina had always been a little intrigued by his love life. He had been jilted by his fiancée Lydia a few days before their wedding six years ago. He had never spoken of why his fiancée had called off the wedding but Sabrina had heard a whisper that it had been because Lydia had wanted children and he didn't. Max wasn't one to brandish his subsequent lovers about in public but she knew he had them from time to time. Now thirty-four, he was a virile man in his sexual prime. And she had tasted a hint of that potency when his mouth had come down on hers and sent her senses into a tailspin from which they had not yet recovered—if they ever would.

The lift stopped on Max's floor and he indicated for her to alight before him. She moved past him and breathed in the sharp citrus scent of his aftershave—lemon and lime and something else that was as mysterious and unknowable as his personality.

He led the way along the carpeted corridor and came to a suite that overlooked the Grand

Canal. Sabrina stepped over the threshold and, pointedly ignoring the twin king-sized beds, went straight to the windows to check out the magnificent view. Even if her booking had been processed correctly, she would never have been able to afford a room such as this.

'Wow…' She breathed out a sigh of wonder. 'Venice never fails to take my breath away. The light. The colours. The history.' She turned to face him, doing her best to not glance at the beds that dominated the room. He still had his spy face on but she could sense an inner tension in the way he held himself. 'Erm… I'd appreciate it if you didn't tell anyone about this…'

The mocking arch of his eyebrow made her cheeks burn. 'This?'

At this rate, she'd have to ramp up the air-conditioning to counter the heat she was giving off from her burning cheeks. 'Me… sharing your room.'

'I wouldn't dream of it.'

'I mean, it could get really embarrassing if either of our parents thought we were—'

'We're not.' The blunt edge to his voice was a slap down to her ego.

There was a knock at the door.

Max opened the door and stepped aside as the hotel employee brought in Sabrina's luggage. Max gave the young man a tip and closed the door, locking his gaze on hers. 'Don't even think about it.'

Sabrina raised her eyebrows so high she thought they would fly off her face. 'You think I'm attracted to *you*? Dream on, buddy.'

The edge of his mouth lifted—the closest he got to a smile, or at least one he'd ever sent her way. 'I could have had you that night three weeks ago and you damn well know it.'

'*Had* me?' She glared at him. 'That kiss was…was a knee-jerk thing. It just…erm… happened. And you gave me stubble rash. I had to put on cover-up for a week.'

His eyes went to her mouth as if he was remembering the explosive passion they'd shared. He drew in an uneven breath and sent a hand through the thick pelt of his hair, a frown pulling at his forehead. 'I'm sorry. It wasn't my intention to hurt you.' His voice had a deep gravelly edge she'd never heard in it before.

Sabrina folded her arms. She wasn't ready to forgive him. She wasn't ready to forgive herself for responding to him. She wasn't ready to admit how much she'd enjoyed that kiss and how she had encouraged it by grabbing the front of his shirt and pulling his head down. Argh. Why had she done that? Neither was she ready to admit how much she wanted him to kiss her again. 'I can think of no one I would less like to "have me".'

Even repeating the coarse words he'd used turned her on. Damn him. She couldn't stop thinking about what it would be like to be *had by him.* Her sex life was practically non-existent. The only sex she'd had in the last few years had been with herself and even that hadn't been all that spectacular. She kept hoping she'd find the perfect partner to help her with her issues with physical intimacy but so far no such luck. She rarely dated anyone more than two or three times before she decided having sex with them was out of the question. Her first and only experience of sex at the age of eighteen—*had it really been ten years ago?*—had been an ego-smashing disappointment, one she was in no hurry to repeat.

'Good. Because we're not going there,' Max said.

Sabrina inched up her chin. 'You were the one who kissed me first that night. I might have returned the kiss but only because I got caught off guard.' It was big fat lie but no way was she going to admit it. Every non-verbal signal in her repertoire had been on duty that night all but begging him to kiss her. And when he finally had, she even recalled moaning at one point. Yes, moaning with pleasure as his lips and tongue had worked their magic. *Geez*. How was she going to live *that* down?

His eyes pulsed with something she couldn't quite identify. Suppressed anger or locked-down lust or both? 'You were spoiling for a fight all through that dinner party and during the trip when I gave you a lift home.'

'So? We always argue. It doesn't mean I want you to kiss me.'

His eyes held hers in a smouldering lock that made the backs of her knees fizz. 'Are we arguing now?' His tone had a silky edge that played havoc with her senses.

Sabrina took a step back, one of her hands coming up her neck where her heart was beating like a panicked pigeon stuck in a pipe. 'I need to get ready for the c-cocktail party…' Why, oh, why did she have to sound so breathless?

He gave a soft rumble of a laugh. 'Your virtue is safe, Sabrina.' He walked to the door of the suite and turned to look at her again. 'Don't wait up. I'll be late.'

Sabrina gave him a haughty look that would have done a Regency spinster proud. 'Going to *have* your client, are you?'

He left without another word, which, annoyingly, left her with the painful echo of hers.

Max closed the door of his suite and let out a breath. Why had he done the knight in shining armour thing? Why should he care if she couldn't get herself organised enough to book a damn hotel? She would have found somewhere to stay, surely. But no. He had to do the decent thing. Nothing about how he felt about Sabrina was decent—especially after that kiss. He'd lost count of how many women he'd kissed. He wasn't a man whore, but he enjoyed sex for the physical release it gave.

But he couldn't get *that* kiss out of his mind.

Max had always avoided Sabrina in the past. He hadn't wanted to encourage his and her parents from their sick little fantasy of them getting it on. He got it on with women he chose and he made sure his choices were simple and straightforward—sex without strings.

Sabrina was off limits because she was the poster girl for the happily-ever-after fairytale. She was looking for Mr Right to sweep her off her feet and park her behind a white picket fence with a double pram with a couple of chubby-cheeked progeny tucked inside.

Max had nothing against marriage, but he no longer wanted it for himself. Six years ago, his fiancée had called off their wedding, informing him she had fallen in love with someone else, with someone who wanted children—the children Max refused to give her. Prior to that, Lydia had been adamant she was fine with his decision not to have kids. He'd thought everything was ticking along well enough in their relationship. He'd been more annoyed than upset at Lydia calling off their relationship. It had irritated him that he hadn't seen it coming.

But it had taught him a valuable lesson. A lesson he was determined he would never have to learn again. He wasn't cut out for long-term relationships. He didn't have what it took to handle commitment and all its responsibilities.

He knew marriage worked for some people—his parents and Sabrina's had solid relationships that had been tried and tested and triumphed over tragedy, especially his parents. The loss of his baby brother Daniel at the age of four months had devastated them, of course.

Max had been seven years old and while his parents had done all they could to shield him from the tragedy, he still carried his share of guilt. In spite of the coroner's verdict of Sudden Infant Death Syndrome, Max could never get it out of his mind that he had been the last person to see his baby brother alive. There wasn't a day that went by when he didn't think of his brother, of all the years Daniel had missed out on. The milestones he would never meet.

Max walked out of his hotel and followed the Grand Canal, almost oblivious to the crowds of tourists that flocked to Venice at this time of year. Whenever he thought of Daniel, a tiny worm of guilt burrowed its way into his mind. Was there something he could have done to save his brother? Why hadn't he noticed something? Why hadn't he checked him more thoroughly? The lingering guilt he felt about Daniel was something he was almost used to now. He was almost used to feeling the lurch of dread in his gut whenever he saw a small baby. Almost.

Max stepped out of the way of a laughing couple that were walking arm in arm, carrying the colourful Venetian masks they'd bought from one of the many vendors along the canal. Why hadn't he thought to book a room at another hotel for Sabrina? It wasn't as if he couldn't afford it. He'd made plenty of money as a world-acclaimed architect, and he knew things were a little tight with her financially as she was still building up her wedding-dress design business and stubbornly refusing any help from her doctor parents, who had made it no secret that they would have preferred her to study medicine like them and Sabrina's two older brothers.

Had he *wanted* her in his room? Had he instinctively seized at the chance to have her to himself so he could kiss her again?

Maybe do more than kiss her?

Max pulled away from the thought like he was stepping back from a too-hot fire. But that's exactly what Sabrina was—hot. Too hot. She made him hot and bothered and horny as hell. The way she picked fights with him just to get under his skin never failed to get his blood pumping. Her cornflower-blue eyes would flash and sparkle, and her soft and supple mouth would fling cutting retorts his way, and it would make him feel alive in a way he hadn't in years.

Alive and energised.

But no. No. No. No. No.

He must *not* think about Sabrina like that. He had to keep his distance. He had to. She wasn't the sex without strings type. She wasn't a fling girl; she was a fairytale girl. And she was his parents' idea of his ideal match—his soul mate or something. Nothing against his parents, but they were wrong. Dead wrong. Sabrina was spontaneous and creative and disorganised. He was logical, responsible and organised to the point of pedantic. How could anyone think they were an ideal couple? It was crazy. He only had to spend a few minutes with her and she drove him nuts.

How was he going to get through a whole weekend with her?

CHAPTER TWO

SABRINA WAS A little late getting to the cocktail party, which was being held in a private room at the hotel. Only the designers and models and their agents and select members of the press were invited. She entered the party room with her stomach in a squirming nest of nibbling and nipping nerves. Everyone looked glamorous and sophisticated. She was wearing a velvet dress she'd made herself the same shade of blue as her eyes and had scooped her hair up into a bun and paid extra attention to her makeup—hence why she was late to the party.

A waiter came past with a tray of drinks and Sabrina took a glass of champagne and took a generous sip to settle her nerves. She wasn't good at networking...well, not unless she was showing off in front of Max. She always worried she might say the wrong thing or make a social faux pas that would make everyone snigger at her.

Large gatherings reminded her of the school formal the day after she'd slept with her boyfriend for the first time. The rumourmongers had been at work, fuelled by the soul-destroying text messages her boyfriend had sent to all his mates. Sabrina had heard each cruelly taunting comment, seen every mocking look cast in her direction from people she had thought were her friends.

She had stood behind a column in the venue to try and escape the shameful whispers and had heard her boyfriend tell a couple of his mates what a frigid lay she had been. The overwhelming sense of shame had been crippling. Crucifying.

Sabrina sipped some more champagne and fixed a smile on her face. She had to keep her head and not time-travel. She wasn't eighteen any more. She was twenty-eight and ran her own business, for pity's sake. She. Could. Do. This.

'You're Sabrina Midhurst, aren't you?' a female member of the press said, smiling. 'I recognised you from the expo programme photo. You did a friend's wedding dress. It was stunning.'

'Yes, that's me,' Sabrina said, smiling back. 'And I'm glad you liked your friend's dress.'

'I'd like to do a feature article on you.' The woman handed Sabrina a card with her name and contact details on it. 'I'm Naomi Nettleton, I'm a freelancer but I've done articles for some big-name fashion magazines. There's a lot of interest in your work. Would you be interested in giving me an interview? Maybe we could grab a few minutes after this?'

Sabrina could barely believe her ears. An interview in a glossy magazine? That sort of exposure was gold dust. Her Love Is in the Care boutique in London was small and she'd always dreamed of expanding. She and her best friend Holly Frost, who was a wedding florist, hoped to set up their shops side by side in Bloomsbury in order to boost each other's trade. At the moment, they were blocks away from each other but Sabrina knew it would be a brilliant business move if they could pull it off.

She wanted to prove to her doctor parents the creative path she'd chosen to follow wasn't just a whim but a viable business venture. She came from a long line of medicos. Her parents, her grandparents and both her brothers were all in the medical profession. But she had never wanted that for herself. She would much rather have a tape measure around her neck than a stethoscope.

She had been drawing wedding gowns since she was five years old. All through her childhood she had made dresses out of scraps of fabric. She had dressed every doll and teddy bear or soft toy she'd possessed in wedding finery. All through her teens she had collected scrapbooks with hundreds of sketches and cuttings from magazines. She'd had to withstand considerable family pressure in order to pursue her dream and success was her way of proving she had made the right choice.

Sabrina arranged to meet the journalist in the bar downstairs after the party. She continued to circulate, speaking with the models who had been chosen to wear her designs and also with the fashion parade manager who had personally invited her to the event after her daughter had bought one of Sabrina's designs.

She took another glass of champagne off a passing waiter.

Who said word of mouth didn't still work?

* * *

Max came back to the hotel after the dinner with his client had gone on much later than he'd originally planned. He hadn't intended having more than a drink with Loretta Barossi but had ended up lingering over a meal with her because he hadn't wanted to come back to his room before Sabrina was safely tucked up and, hopefully, asleep in bed. Unfortunately, he'd somehow given the thirty-six-year-old recently divorced woman the impression he'd been enjoying her company far more than he had, and then had to find a way to politely reject her broadly hinted invitation to spend the night with her. But that was another line he never crossed—mixing business with pleasure.

He was walking past the bar situated off the lobby when he saw Sabrina sitting on one of the plush sofas talking to a woman and a man who was holding a camera in his lap. As if she sensed his presence, Sabrina turned her glossy honey-brown head and saw him looking at her. She raised her hand and gave him a surreptitious fingertip wave and the woman with her glanced to see to whom she was waving. The woman leaned forward to say something to Sabrina, and even from this distance Max could see the rush of a blush flooding Sabrina's creamy cheeks.

He figured the less people who saw him with Sabrina the better, but somehow he found himself walking towards her before he could stop himself. What had the other woman said to make Sabrina colour up like that?

Sabrina's eyes widened when he approached their little party and she reached for her glass of champagne and promptly knocked it over. 'Oops. Sorry. I—'

'You're Max Firbank, the award-winning architect,' the young woman said, rising to offer her hand. 'I've seen an article about your work in one of the magazines I worked for a couple of years ago. When Sabrina said she was sharing a room with a friend, I didn't realise she was referring to you.' Her eyebrows suggestively rose over the word *friend.*

Sabrina had stopped trying to mop up her drink with a paper napkin and stood, clutching the wet and screwed-up napkin in her hand. 'Oh, he's not *that* sort of friend,' she said with a choked little laugh. 'I had a problem with my booking and Max offered me his bed, I mean *a* bed. He has two. Two big ones—they look bigger than king-sized, you could fit a dozen people in each. It's a huge room, so much space we hardly know the other is there, isn't that right, Max?' She turned her head to look at him and he almost had to call for a fire extinguisher because her cheeks were so fiery red.

Max wasn't sure why he slipped his arm around her slim waist and drew her to his body. Maybe it was because she was kind of cute when she got flustered and he liked being able to get under her skin for a change, the way she got under his. Besides, he didn't know any other woman he could make blush more than her. And, yes, he got a kick out of touching her, especially after That Kiss, which she enjoyed as much as he had, even though she was intent on denying it. 'You don't have to be shy about our relationship, baby.' He flashed one of his rare smiles. 'We're both consenting adults.'

'Aw, don't you make a gorgeous couple?' the woman said. 'Tim, get a photo of them,' she said to the man holding the camera. 'I'll include it in the article about Sabrina's designs. That is, if you don't have any objection?'

Hell, yeah. He had one big objection. He didn't mind teasing a blush or two out of Sabrina but if his family got a whiff of him sharing a room with her in Venice they would be measuring him for a morning suit and booking the church. Max held up his hand like a stop sign. 'Sorry. I don't make a habit of broadcasting my private life in the press.'

The woman sighed and handed him a business card. 'Here are my details if you change your mind.'

'I won't.' He gave both the journalist and the photographer a polite nod and added, 'It was nice meeting you. If you'll excuse us? It's been a big day for Sabrina. She needs her beauty sleep.'

Sabrina followed Max to the lift but there were other people waiting to use it as well so she wasn't able to vent her spleen. What was he thinking? She'd been trying to play down her relationship with Max to the journalist, but he'd given Naomi Nettleton the impression they were an item. She stood beside him in the lift as it stopped and started as it delivered guests to their floors.

Max stood calmly beside her with his expression in its customary inscrutable lines, although she sensed there was a mocking smile lurking behind the screen of his gaze. She moved closer to him to allow another guest into the lift on level ten and placed her high heel on Max's foot and pressed down with all her weight. He made a grunting sound that sounded far sexier than she'd expected and he placed the iron band of his arm around her middle and drew her back against him so her back was flush against his pelvis.

Her mind swam with images of them locked together in a tangle of sweaty limbs, his body driving into hers. Even now she could feel the swell of his body, the rush of blood that told her he was as aroused as she was. Her breathing quickened, her legs weakened, her heart rate rocketed. The steely strength of his arm lying across her stomach was burning a brand into her flesh. Her inner core tensed, the electric heat of awakened desire coursing through her in pulses and flickers.

The mirrors surrounding them reflected their intimate clinch from a thousand angles but Sabrina wasn't prepared to make a scene in front of the other guests, one of whom she had seen at the cocktail party. After all, she had a professional image to uphold and slapping Max's face—if indeed she was the sort of person to inflict violence on another person—was not the best way to maintain it.

But, oh, how she longed to slap both his cheeks until they were as red as hers. Then she would elbow him in the ribs and stomp on his toes. Then she would rip the clothes from his body, score her fingernails down his chest and down his back until he begged for mercy. But wait…why was she thinking of ripping his clothes off his body? No. No. No. She must not think about Max without clothes. She must not think about him naked.

She. Must. Not.

Max unlocked the door and she brushed past him and almost before he had time to close it she let fly. 'What the hell were you playing at down there? You gave the impression we were sleeping together. What's *wrong* with you? You know how much I hate you. Why did you—?'

'You don't hate me.' His voice was so calm it made hers sound all the more irrational and childish.

'If I didn't before, I do now.' Sabrina poked

him in the chest. 'What was all that about in the lift?'

He captured her by the waist and brought her closer, hip to hip, his eyes more blue than grey and glinting with something that made her belly turn over. 'You know exactly what it was about. And just like that kiss, you enjoyed every second of it. Deny it if you dare.'

Sabrina intended to push away from him but somehow her hands grabbed the front of his jacket instead. He smelt like sun-warmed lemons and her senses were as intoxicated as if she had breathed in a potent aroma. An aroma that made her forget how much she hated him and instead made her want him with every throbbing traitorous cell of her body. Or maybe she was tipsy from all the champagne she'd had downstairs at the party and in the bar. It was making her drop her inhibitions. Sabotaging her already flagging self-control. Her head was spinning a little but didn't it always when he looked at her like that?

His mouth was tilted in a cynical slant, the dark stubble around his nose and mouth more obvious now than earlier that evening. It gave him a rakish air that was strangely attractive.

Dangerously, deliciously attractive. She was acutely aware of every point of contact with his body: her hips, her breasts and her belly where his belt buckle was pressing.

And not just his belt buckle, but the proud surge of his male flesh—a heady reminder of the lust that simmered and boiled and blistered between them.

The floor began to shift beneath her feet and Sabrina's hands tightened on his jacket. The room was moving, pitching like a boat tossed about on a turbulent ocean. Her head felt woolly, her thoughts trying to push through the fog like a hand fumbling for a light switch in the dark. But then a sudden wave of nausea assailed her and she swayed and would have toppled backwards if Max hadn't countered it with a firm hand at her back.

'Are you okay?' His voice had a note of concern but it came from a long way off as if he was speaking to her through a long vacuum.

She was vaguely aware of his other hand coming to grasp her by the shoulder to stabilise her, but then her vision blurred and her stomach contents threatened mutiny. She made a choking sound and pushed Max back and stumbled towards the bathroom.

To her mortifying shame, Max witnessed the whole of the undignified episode. But she was beyond caring. And besides, it had been quite comforting to have her hair held back from her face and to have the soft press of a cool facecloth on the back of her neck.

Sabrina sat back on her heels when the worst of it was over. Her head was pounding and her stomach felt as it if had been scraped with a sharp-edged spoon and then rinsed out with hydrochloric acid.

He handed her a fresh facecloth, his expression wry. 'Clearly I need some work on my seduction routine.'

Sabrina managed a fleeting smile. 'Funny ha-ha.' She dragged herself up from the floor with considerable help from him, his hands warm and steady and impossibly strong. 'Argh. I should never drink on an empty stomach.'

'Wasn't there any food at the cocktail party?'

'I got there late.' She turned to inspect her reflection in the bathroom mirror and then wished she hadn't. Could she look any worse?

She could almost guarantee none of the super-sophisticated women he dated ever disgraced themselves by heaving over the toilet bowl. She turned back around. 'Sorry you had to witness that.'

'You need to drink some water. Lots of it, otherwise you're going to have one hell of a hangover in the morning.' His frown and stern tone reminded her of a parent lecturing a binge-drinking teenager.

'I don't normally drink much but I was nervous.'

His frown deepened and he reached for a glass on the bathroom counter and filled it from the tap and then handed it to her. 'Is this a big deal for you? This wedding expo?'

Sabrina took the glass from him and took a couple of sips to see how her stomach coped. 'It's the first time I've been invited to exhibit some of my designs. It's huge for me. It can take new designers years to get noticed but luckily the fashion show floor manager's daughter bought one of my dresses and she liked it so much she invited me along. And then Naomi, the journalist in the bar, asked for an interview for a feature article. It's a big opportunity for me to get my name out there, especially in Europe.' She drained the glass of water and handed it back to him.

He dutifully refilled it and handed it back, his frown still carving a trench between his brows. 'What did you tell her about us?'

'Nothing. I didn't even mention your name. I just said I was sharing a room with a friend.'

'Are you sure you didn't mention me?'

Sabrina frowned. 'Why would I link my name with yours? Do you think I want anyone back home to know we're sharing a room? Give me a break. I'm not *that* stupid. If I let that become common knowledge our parents will have wedding invitations in the post before you can blink.' She took a breath and continued, 'Anyway, you were the one who made it look like we were having a dirty weekend. You called me "baby", for God's sake.'

'Drink your water,' he said as if she hadn't spoken. 'You need to get some rest if you want to look your best for tomorrow.'

Sabrina scowled at him over the top of her glass. 'Do you have to remind me I look a frightful mess?'

He released a slow breath. 'I'll see you in the morning. Goodnight.'

When Sabrina came out of the bathroom

after a shower there was no sign of him in the suite. She wondered if he'd left to give her some privacy or whether he had other plans. Why should she care if he hooked up with someone for a night of unbridled passion? She pulled down the covers on one of the beds and slipped between the cool and silky sheets and closed her eyes…

Max went for a long walk through the streets and alleys of Venice to clear his head. He could still feel the imprint of Sabrina's body pressing against him in the lift. He'd been hard within seconds. His fault for holding her like that, but the temptation had caught him off guard. Had it been his imagination or had she leaned back into him?

He wanted her.

He hated admitting it. Loathed admitting it but there it was. He was in lust with her. He couldn't remember when he'd started noticing her in that way. It had crept up on him over the last few months. The way his body responded when she looked at him in a certain way. The way his blood surged when she stood up to him and flashed her blue eyes at him in defiance. The way she moved her dancer-slim body making him fantasise about how she would look naked.

He had to get over it. Ignore it or something. Having a fling with Sabrina would hurt too many people. Hadn't he hurt his parents enough? If he started a fling with her everyone would get their hopes up that it would become permanent.

He didn't do permanent.

He would get his self-control back in line and get through the weekend without touching her. He opened and closed his hands, trying to rid himself of the feeling of her soft skin. Trying to remove the sensation of her touch. What was wrong with him? Why couldn't he just ignore her the way he had for most of his adult life? He'd always kept his distance. Always. He avoided speaking with her. He had watched from the sidelines as she'd spoken to everyone at the various gatherings they'd both attended.

There was no way a relationship between them would work. Not even a short-term one. She had fairytale written all over her. She came from a family of doctors and yet she had resisted following the tradition and become a wedding-dress designer instead.

Didn't that prove how obsessed with the fairytale she was?

His mistake had been kissing her three weeks ago. He didn't understand how he had gone from arguing with her over something to finding her pulling his head down and then his mouth coming down on hers and… He let out a shuddering breath. Why was he *still* thinking about that damn kiss? The heat of their mouths connecting had tilted the world on its axis, or at least it had felt like it at the time. He could have sworn the floor had shifted beneath his feet. If he closed his eyes he could still taste her sweetness, could still feel the soft pliable texture of her lips moving against his, could still feel the sexy dart of her tongue.

The worst of it was he had lost control. Desire had swept through him and he still didn't know how he'd stopped himself from taking her then and there. And *that* scared the hell of out him.

It would not—*could* not—happen again.

When Max entered the suite in the early hours of the morning, Sabrina was sound asleep, curled up like a kitten, her brown hair spilling over the pillow. One of her hands was tucked under the cheek; the other was lying on the top of the covers. She was wearing a cream satin nightie for he could see the delicate lace trim across her décolletage peeking out from where the sheet was lying across her chest.

The desire to slip into that bed and pull her into his arms was so strong he had to clench his hands into fists. He clearly had to do something about his sex life if he was ogling the one woman he wanted to avoid. When was the last time he'd been with someone? A month? Two…or was it three? He'd been busy working on multiple projects, which hadn't left much time for a social life. Not that he had a much of a social life. He preferred his own company so he could get on with his work.

Work. That's what he needed to concentrate on. He moved past the bed to go to the desk where he had set up his laptop the day before. He opened one of the accounts he was working on and started tinkering.

There was a rustle from the bed behind him and Sabrina's drowsy voice said, 'Do you have to do that now?'

Max turned around to look at her in the muted light coming off his laptop screen. Her hair was a cloud of tangles and one of her cheeks had a linen crease and one spaghetti-thin strap of her nightie had slipped off her shoulder, revealing the upper curve of her left breast. She looked sleepy, sexy and sensual and lust hit him like a sucker punch. 'Sorry. Did I wake you?'

She pushed back some of her hair with her hand. 'Don't you *ever* sleep?'

I would if there wasn't a gorgeously sexy woman lying in the bed next to mine.

Max kept his features neutral but his body was thrumming, hardening, aching. 'How's your head? Have the construction workers started yet?'

Her mouth flickered with a sheepish smile. 'Not yet. The water helped.'

He pushed a hand through his hair and suppressed a yawn. 'Can I get you anything?'

'You don't have to wait on me, Max.' She peeled back the bed covers and swung her slim legs over the edge of the bed. She padded over to the bar fridge and opened it, the light spilling from inside a golden shaft against her long shapely legs.

'Hair of the dog?' Max injected a cautionary note in his tone.

She closed the fridge and held up a chocolate bar. 'Nope. Chocolate is the best hangover cure.'

He shrugged and turned back to his laptop. 'Whatever works, I guess.'

The sound of her unwrapping the chocolate bar was loud in the silence. Then he heard her approaching from behind, the soft *pffft, pffft, pffft* of her footsteps on the carpet reminding him of a stealthy cat. He smelt the fragrance of her perfume dance around his nostrils, the sweet peas and lilacs with an understory of honeysuckle—or was it jasmine?

'Is that one of your designs?' She was standing so close behind him every hair on the back of his neck lifted. Tensed. Tickled. Tightened.

'Yeah.'

She leaned over his shoulder, some of her hair brushing his face, and he had to call on every bit of self-control he possessed not to touch her. Her breath smelt of chocolate and temptation. In the soft light her skin had a luminous glow, the creamy perfection of her skin making him ache to run his finger down the slope of her cheek. He let out the breath he hadn't realised he'd been holding and clicked the computer mouse. 'Here. I'll give you a virtual tour.' He showed her the presentation he'd been working on for a client, trying to ignore the closeness of her body.

'Wow…' She smiled and glanced at him, her head still bent close to his. 'It's amazing.'

Max couldn't tear his eyes away from the curve of her mouth. Its plump ripeness, the top lip just as full as the lower one and the neat definition of the philtrum ridge below her nose. He met her gaze and something in the atmosphere changed. The silence so intense he was sure he could hear his blood pounding. He could certainly feel it—it was swelling his groin to a painful tightness. He put his hand down on hers where it was resting on the desk, holding it beneath the gentle but firm pressure of his. He felt her flinch as if his touch electrified her and her eyes widened into shimmering pools of cornflower blue.

The tip of her tongue swept over her lips, her breath coming out in a jagged stream. 'Max…' Her voice was whisper soft, tentative and uncertain.

He lifted her hand from the desk and toyed with her fingers, watching every micro-expression on her face. Her skin was velvet soft and he was getting off thinking about her hands stroking his body. Stroking *him*. Was she thinking about it? About the heat they generated? About the lust that swirled and simmered and sizzled between them? She kept glancing at his mouth, her throat rising and falling over a series of delicate swallows. Her breathing was uneven. He was still seated and she was standing, but because of the height ratio, he was just about at eye level with her breasts.

But the less he thought about her breasts the better.

Max released her hand and rose from the desk chair in an abrupt movement. 'Go back to bed, Sabrina.' He knew he sounded as stern as a schoolmaster but he had to get the damn genie back in the lamp. The genie of lust. The wicked genie that had been torturing him since he'd foolishly kissed Sabrina three weeks ago.

'I was sound asleep in bed before you started tapping away at your computer.' Sabrina's tone was tinged with resentment.

Max let out a long slow breath. 'I don't want to argue with you. Now go to—'

'Why don't you want to argue with me?'

Her eyes flashed blue sparks. 'Because you might be tempted to kiss me again?'

He kept his expression under lockdown. 'We're not doing this, Sabrina.'

'Not doing what?' Her mouth was curved in a mocking manner. 'You were going to kiss me again, weren't you? Go on. Admit it.'

Max gave his own version of a smile and shook his head as if he was dealing with a misguided child. 'No. I was not going to kiss you.'

She straightened her shoulders and folded her arms. 'Liar.'

Max held her gaze, his body throbbing with need. No one could get him as worked up as her. No one. Their verbal banter was a type of foreplay. When had it started to become like that? For years, their arguments had just been arguments—the clash of two strong-willed personalities. But over the last few months something had changed. Was that why he'd gone to the dinner party of a mutual friend because he'd known she'd be there? Was that why he'd offered to drive her home because her car was being serviced? There had been other people at the dinner who could have taken her but, no, he'd insisted.

He couldn't even recall what they'd been arguing about on the way home or who had started it. But he remembered all too well how it had ended and he had to do everything in his power to make sure it never happened again.

'Why would I kiss you again? You don't want another dose of stubble rash, do you?'

Her combative expression floundered for a moment and her teeth snagged her lower lip. 'Okay…so I might have been lying about that…'

Max kept his gaze trained on hers. 'You're not asking me to kiss you, are you?'

The sparkling light of defiance was back in her eyes. 'Of course not.' She gave a spluttering laugh as if the idea was ludicrous. 'I would rather kiss a cane toad.'

'Good.' He slammed his lips shut on the word. 'Better keep it that way.'

CHAPTER THREE

SABRINA STALKED BACK to her bed, climbed in and pulled the covers up to her chin. Of course she'd wanted Max to kiss her. And she was positive he'd wanted to kiss her too. It secretly thrilled her that he found her so attractive. Why wouldn't it thrill her? She had all the usual female needs and she hadn't made love with a man since she was eighteen.

Not that what had happened back then could be called, by any stretch of the imagination, making love. It had been selfish one-sided sex. She had been little more than a vessel for her boyfriend to use to satisfy his base needs. She'd naively thought their relationship had been more than that. Much more. She had thought herself in love. She hadn't wanted her first time to be with someone who didn't care about her. She had been so sure Brad loved her. He'd even told her he loved her. But as soon as the deed was done he was gone. He'd dumped her and called her horrible names to his friends that still made her cringe and curl up in shame.

Sabrina heard Max preparing for bed. He went into the bathroom and brushed his teeth, coming out a few minutes later dressed in one of the hotel bathrobes. Was he naked under that robe? Her mind raced with images of his tanned and toned flesh, her body tingling at the thought of lying pinned beneath him in the throes of sizzling hot sex.

She couldn't imagine Max ever leaving a lover unsatisfied. He only had to look at her and she was halfway to an orgasm. It was embarrassing how much she wanted him. It was like lust had hijacked her body, turning her into a wanton woman who could think of nothing but earthly pleasures. Even now her body felt restless, every nerve taut with the need for touch. *His* touch. Was it possible to hate someone and want them at the same time? Or was there something wrong with her? Why was she so fiercely attracted to someone she could barely conduct a civil conversation with without it turning into a blistering argument?

But why *did* they always argue?

And why did she find it so…so stimulating?

It was a little lowering to realise how much she enjoyed their verbal spats. She looked forward to them. She got secretly excited when she knew he was going to be at a function she would be attending, even though she pretended otherwise to her family. No wonder she found joint family functions deadly boring if he didn't show up. Did she have some sort of disorder? Did she crave negative interaction with him because it was the only way she could get him to notice her?

Sabrina closed her eyes when Max walked past her bed, every pore of her body aware of him. She heard the sheets being pulled back and the sound of him slipping between them. She heard the click of the bedside lamp being switched off and then he let out a sigh that sounded bone-weary.

'I hope you don't snore.' The comment was out before she could stop herself.

He gave a sound that might have been a muttered curse but she couldn't quite tell. 'No one's complained so far.'

A silence ticked, ticked, ticked like an invisible clock.

'I probably should warn you I've been known to sleepwalk,' Sabrina said.

'I knew that. Your mother told me.'

She turned over so she was facing his bed. There was enough soft light coming in through the gap in the curtains for her to see him. He was lying on his back with his eyes closed, the sheets pulled to the level of his waist, the gloriously naked musculature of his chest making her mouth water. He looked like a sexy advertisement for luxury bed linen. His tanned skin a stark contrast to the white sheets. 'When did she tell you?'

'Years ago.'

Sabrina propped herself up on one elbow. 'How many years ago?'

He turned his head in her direction and opened one eye. 'I don't remember. What does it matter?'

She plucked at the sheet covering her breasts. What else had her mother told him about her? 'I don't like the thought of her discussing my private details with you.'

He closed his eye and turned his head back to lie flat on the pillow. 'Bit late for that, sweetheart.' His tone was so dry it could have soaked up an oil spill. 'Your parents have been citing your considerable assets to me ever since you hit puberty.'

Sabrina could feel her cheeks heating. She knew exactly how pushy her parents had been. But so too had his parents. Both families had engineered situations where she and Max would be forced together, especially since his fiancée Lydia had broken up with him just before their wedding six years ago. She even wondered if the family pressure had actually scared poor Lydia off. What woman wanted to marry a man whose parents staunchly believed she wasn't the right one for him? His parents had hardly been subtle about their hopes. It had been mildly embarrassing at first, but over the years it had become annoying. So annoying that Sabrina had stubbornly refused to acknowledge any of Max's good qualities.

And he had many now that she thought about it. He was steady in a crisis. He thought before he spoke. He was hard working and responsible and organised. He was a supremely talented architect and had won numerous awards for his designs. But she had never heard him boast about his achievements. She had only heard about them via his parents.

Sabrina lay back down with a sigh. 'Yeah, well, hate to tell you but your parents have been doing the same about you.' She kicked out the rumples in her bed linen with her feet and added, 'Anyone would think you were a saint.'

'I'm hardly that.'

There was another silence.

'Thanks for letting me share your room,' she said. 'I don't know what I would have done if you hadn't offered. I heard from other people at the cocktail party that just about everywhere else is full.'

'It's fine. Glad to help.'

She propped herself back on her elbow to look at him. 'Max?'

He made a sound that sounded like a *God, give me strength* groan. 'Mmm?'

'Why did you and Lydia break up?' Sabrina wasn't sure why she'd asked the question other than she had always wondered what had caused his fiancée to cancel their wedding at short notice. She'd heard the gossip over the children issue but she wanted to hear the truth from him.

The movement of his body against the bed linen sounded angry. And the air seemed to tighten in the room as if the walls and ceiling and the furniture had collectively taken a breath.

'Go to sleep, Sabrina.' His tone had an intractable *don't push it* edge.

Sabrina wanted to push it. She wanted to push him into revealing more about himself. There was so much she didn't know about him. There were things he never spoke about—like the death of his baby brother. But then neither did his parents speak about Daniel. The tragic loss of an infant was always devastating and even though Max had been only seven years old at the time, he too would have felt the loss, especially with his parents so distraught with grief. Sometimes she saw glimpses of his parents' grief even now. A certain look would be exchanged between Gillian and Bryce Firbank and their gazes would shadow as if they were remembering their baby boy. 'Someone told me it was because she wanted kids and you didn't. Is that true?'

He didn't answer for such a long moment she thought he must have fallen asleep. But then she heard the sound of the sheets rustling and his voice broke through the silence. 'That and other reasons.'

'Such as?'

He released a frustrated-sounding sigh. 'She fell in love with someone else.'

'Did you love her?'

'I was going to marry her, wasn't I?' His tone had an edge of impatience that made her wonder if he had been truly in love with his ex-fiancée. He had never seemed to her to be the falling-in-love type. He was too self-contained. Too private with his emotions. Sabrina remembered meeting Lydia a couple of times and feeling a little surprised she and Max were a couple about to be married. The chemistry between them had been on the mild instead of the wild side.

'Lydia's divorced now, isn't she?' Sabrina continued after a long moment. 'I wonder if she ever thinks she made the wrong decision.'

He didn't answer but she could tell from his breathing he wasn't asleep.

Sabrina closed her eyes, willing herself to relax, but sleep was frustratingly elusive. Her body was too strung out, too aware of Max lying so close by. She listened to the sound of him breathing and the slight rustle of the sheets when he changed position. After a while his breathing slowed and the rustling stopped and she realised he was finally asleep.

She settled back down against the pillows with a sigh…

Max could hear a baby crying…the sound making his skin prickle with cold dread. Where was the baby? What was wrong with it? Why was it crying? Why wasn't anyone going to it? Should he try and settle it? Then he saw the cot, his baby brother's cot…it was empty… Then he saw the tiny white coffin with the teddy bear perched on top. *No. No. No.*

'Max. Max.' Sabrina's voice broke through the nightmare. 'You're having a bad dream. Wake up, Max. Wake up.'

Max opened his eyes and realised with a shock he was holding her upper arms in a deathly grip. She was practically straddling him, her hair tousled from being in bed or from him manhandling her. He released her and let out a juddering breath, shame and guilt coursing through him like a rush of ice water. 'I'm sorry. Did I hurt you?' He winced when he saw the full set of his fingerprints on her arms.

She rubbed her hands up and down her

arms, her cheeks flushed. 'I'm okay. But you scared the hell out of me.'

Max pushed back the sheets and swung his legs over the edge of the bed, his back facing her. He rested his hands on his thighs, trying to get his heart rate back to normal. Trying not to look at those marks on her arms. Trying not to reach for her.

Desperately trying not to reach for her.

'Max?' Her voice was as soft as the hand she laid on his shoulder.

'Go back to sleep.'

She was so close to him he could feel her breath on the back of his neck. He could feel her hair tickling his shoulder and he knew if he so much as turned his head to look at her he would be lost. It had been years since he'd had a nightmare. They weren't as frequent as in the early days but they still occasionally occurred. Catching him off guard, reminding him he would never be free from the pain of knowing he had failed his baby brother.

'Do you want to talk about your nightmare?' Sabrina said. 'It might help you to—'

'No.'

Sabrina's soft hand was moving up and down between his shoulder blades in soothing strokes. His skin lifted in a shiver, his blood surging to his groin. Her hand came up and began to massage the tight muscles of his neck and he suppressed a groan of pleasure. Why couldn't he be immune to her touch? Why couldn't he ignore the way she was leaning against him, one of her satin-covered breasts brushing against his left shoulder blade? He could smell her flowery fragrance; it teased and tantalised his senses. He felt drugged. Stoned by her closeness.

He drew in a breath and placed his hands on either side of his thighs, his fingers digging into the mattress. He would *not* touch her.

He. Would. Not.

Sabrina could feel the tension in his body. The muscles in his back and shoulders were set like concrete, even the muscles in his arms were bunched and the tendons of his hands white and prominent where he was gripping the mattress. His thrashing about his bed had woken her from a fitful sleep. She had been shocked at the sound of his anguish, his cries hadn't been all that loud but they had been raw and desperate and somehow that made them seem all the more tragic. What had he been dreaming about? And why wouldn't he talk about it? Or it had it just been one of those horrible dreams everyone had from time to time?

Sabrina moved her hand from massaging his neck to trail it through the thickness of his hair. 'You should try and get some sleep.'

'You're not helping.' His voice was hard bitten like he was spitting out each word.

She kept playing with his hair, somehow realising he was like a wounded dog, snipping and snarling at anyone who got too close. She was close. So close one of her breasts was pressing against the rock-hard plane of his shoulder blade. The contact, even through the satin of her nightie, made her breast tingle and her nipple tighten. 'Do you have nightmares often?'

'Sabrina, please…' He turned and looked at her, his eyes haunted.

She touched his jaw with the palm of her hand, gliding it down the rough stubble until she got to the cleft in his chin. She traced it with her finger and then did the same to the tight line of his mouth, exploring it in intimate detail, recalling how it felt clamped to hers. 'Do you ever think about that night?

The night we kissed?' Her voice was barely more than a whisper.

He opened and closed his mouth, the lips pressing together as if he didn't trust himself to use them against hers. 'Kissing you was a mistake. I won't be repeating it.'

Sabrina frowned. 'It didn't feel like a mistake to me… It felt…amazing. The best kiss I've ever had, in fact.'

Something passed through his gaze—a flicker of heat, of longing, of self-control wavering. Then he raised a hand and gently cupped her cheek, his eyes dipping to her mouth, a shudder going through him like an aftershock. 'We shouldn't be doing this.' His voice was so gruff it sounded like he'd been gargling gravel.

'Why shouldn't we?' Sabrina leaned closer, drawn to him as if pulled by an invisible force.

He swallowed and slid his hand to the sensitive skin of her nape, his fingers tangling into her hair, sending her scalp into a tingling torrent of pleasure. 'Because it can't go anywhere.'

'Who said I wanted it to go anywhere?' Sabrina asked. 'I'm just asking you to kiss me, not marry me. You kiss other women, don't you?'

His breath came out and sent a tickling waft of air across the surface of her lips. 'The thing is… I'm not sure I can *just* kiss you.'

She stared at him in pleasant surprise. So pleasant her ego got out of the foetal position and did a victory dance. 'What are you saying?' She couldn't seem to speak louder than a whispery husk.

His eyes had a dark pulsing intensity that made her inner core contract. 'I want you. But I—'

'Can we skip the but?' Sabrina said. 'Let's go back to the *I want you* bit. Thing is, I want you too. So, what are we going to do about it?'

His gaze drifted to her mouth and then back to her eyes, his eyes hardening as if he had called on some inner strength to keep his self-control in check. 'We're going to ignore it, that's what.' His tone had the same determined edge as his gaze.

Sabrina moistened her lips, watching as his gaze followed the movement of her tongue. 'What if I don't want to ignore it? What if I want you to kiss me? What if I want you to make love to me just this once? No one needs to know about it. It's just between us. It will get it out of our system once and for all and then we can go back to normal.'

She could hardly believe she had been so upfront. She had never been so brazen, so bold about her needs. But she could no longer ignore the pulsing ache of her body. The need that clawed and clenched. The need that only *he* triggered. Was that why she hadn't made love with anyone for all these years? No one made her feel this level of desire. No one even came close to stirring her flesh into a heated rush of longing.

'Sabrina...please...' His voice had a scraped-raw quality as if his throat had been scoured with a bristled brush.

'Please what? Don't tell it like it is?' Sabrina placed her hand on his chest where his heart was thud, thud, thudding so similar to her own. 'You want me. You said so. I felt it when you kissed me three weeks ago. And I know you want me now.'

Max took her by the hands, his fingers almost overlapping around her wrists. At first, she thought he was going to put her from him, but then his fingers tightened and he drew her closer. 'This is madness...' His smoky grey-blue gaze became hooded as it focussed on her mouth as if drawn to it by a magnetic force too powerful for his willpower.

'What is mad about two consenting adults having a one-night stand?' There she went again—such brazen words spilling out of her mouth, as if she'd swallowed the bad girl's guide to hook-up sex. Who was this person she had suddenly become since entering his hotel room? It wasn't anyone Sabrina recognised. But she wasn't going to stop now. She couldn't. If she didn't have sex with Max, someone she knew and trusted to take care of her, who else would she get to do the deed? No one, that's who.

Ten years had already passed and her confidence around men had gone backwards, not forwards. It was do or die—of sexual frustration. She wanted Max to cure her of her of her hang-ups...not that she was going to tell him about her lack of a love life. No flipping way. He'd get all knight-in-shining-armour about it and refuse to make love to her.

Max brushed the pad of his thumb over her bottom lip, pressing and then releasing until her senses were singing like the Philharmonic choir. 'A one-night stand? Is that really what you want?'

Sabrina fisted her hands into the thickness of his dark brown hair, the colour so similar to her own. She fixed her gaze on his troubled one. 'Make love to me, Max. Please?' *Gah.* Was she begging now? Was that how desperate she had become?

Yep. That desperate.

Max tipped up her chin, his eyes locking on hers. 'One night? No repeats? No happy ever after, right?'

Sabrina licked her lips—a mixture of nerves and feverish excitement. 'I want no one and I mean no one to find out about this. It will be our little secret. Agreed?'

One of his dark brows lifted above his sceptical gaze. But then his gaze flicked back to her mouth and he gave a shuddery sigh, as if the final restraint on his self-control had popped its bolts. 'Madness,' he said, so low she almost couldn't hear it. 'This is madness.' And then his mouth came down and set fire to hers.

CHAPTER FOUR

Six weeks later...

'SO, ARE YOU still keeping mum about what happened between you and Max in Venice?' Holly asked when she came into Sabrina's studio for a wedding-dress fitting.

Sabrina made a zipping-the-lips motion. 'Yep. I promised.'

Holly's eyes were twinkling so much they rivalled the sparkly bridal tiaras in the display cabinet. 'You can't fool me. I know you slept with him. What I don't understand is why you haven't continued sleeping with him. Was he that bad a lover?'

Sabrina pressed her lips together to stop herself from spilling all. So many times over the last six weeks she'd longed to tell Holly about that amazing night. About Max's amazing lovemaking. How he had made her feel. Her body hadn't felt the same since. She couldn't even think of him without having a fluttery sensation in her stomach. She had relived every touch of his hands and lips and tongue. She had repeatedly, obsessively dreamed about his possession, the way his body had moved within hers with such intense passion and purpose.

She picked up the bolt of French lace her friend had chosen and unrolled it over the cutting table. 'I'm not going to kiss and tell. It's…demeaning.'

'You kiss and told when he kissed you after he drove you home that night a few weeks back. Why not now?'

'Because I made a promise.'

'What?' Holly's smiling expression was exchanged for a frown. 'You don't trust me to keep it a secret? I'm your best friend. I wouldn't tell a soul.'

Sabrina glanced across the table at her friend. 'What about Zack? You guys share everything, right?'

Holly gnawed at her lip. 'Yeah, well, that's what people in love do.'

She tried to ignore the little dart of jealousy she felt at Holly's happiness. Her friend was preparing for her wedding to Zack Knight in a matter of weeks and what did Sabrina have on her love radar? Nothing. *Nada.* Zilch.

A mild wave of nausea assailed her. Was it possible to be lovesick without actually being in love? Okay. She was in love. In love with Max's lovemaking. Deeply in love. She couldn't stop thinking about him and the things he had done to her. The things they had done together. The things she had done to him. She placed a hand on her squeamish tummy and swallowed. She had to get a grip. She couldn't be bitter and sick to her stomach about her best friend's joy at marrying the man she loved. So what if Holly was having the most amazing sex with Zack while all Sabrina had was memories of one night with Max?

Holly leaned across the worktable. 'Hey, are you okay? You've gone as white as that French lace.'

Sabrina grimaced as her stomach contents swished and swirled and soured. 'I'm just feeling a little…off.'

Holly did a double blink. 'Off? As in nauseous?'

She opened her mouth to answer but had

to clamp her hand over it because a surge of sickness rose up from her stomach. 'Excuse me…' Her hand muffled her choked apology and she bolted to the bathroom, not even stopping to close the door.

Holly came in behind her and handed her some paper towels from the dispenser on the wall. 'Is that a dodgy curry or too much champagne?'

Sabrina looked up from the toilet bowl. 'Ack. Don't mention food.'

Holly bent down beside her and placed a hand on Sabrina's shoulder. 'How long have you been feeling unwell?'

'Just today…' Sabrina swallowed against another tide of excessive saliva. 'I must have a stomach bug…or something…'

'Would the "or something" have anything to do with your weekend in Venice with Max, which you, obstinately and totally out of character, refuse to discuss?'

Sabrina's scalp prickled like army ants on a military parade. Max had used a condom. He'd used three over the course of the night. She was taking the lowest dose of the Pill to regulate her cycle because the others she'd tried had messed with her mood. 'I can't possibly be pregnant…'

Holly helped her to her feet. 'Are you saying you didn't sleep with him?'

Sabrina pulled her hair back from her face and sighed. 'Okay, so I did sleep with him. But you have to promise you won't tell anyone. Not even Zack.'

'Honey, I can trust Zack to keep it quiet.' Holly stroked Sabrina's arm. 'Did Max use a condom?'

Sabrina nodded. 'Three.'

Holly's eyes bulged. 'At a time?'

'No, we made love three times.' She closed the toilet seat and pressed the flush button. 'We made a promise not to talk about it. To anyone. Ever.'

'But why?'

Sabrina turned to wash her hands and face at the basin. 'We both agreed it was the best thing considering how our families go on and on about us getting together. We had a one-night stand to get it out of our system. End of story. Neither of us wants be involved with the other.'

'Or so *you* say.' Holly's tone was so sceptical she could have moonlighted as a detective.

Sabrina made a business of drying her face and hands. 'It's true. We would be hopeless as a couple. We fight all the time.'

Holly leaned against the door jamb, arms folded. 'Clearly not all the time if you had sex three times. Unless it was combative sex?'

Sabrina glanced at her friend in the reflection of the mirror. 'No…it wasn't combative sex. It was…amazing sex.' She had to stop speaking as the tiny frisson of remembered delight trickled over her flesh.

'Have you seen Max since that weekend?'

'No. We agreed to keep our distance as if nothing happened.' Sabrina sighed. 'He even checked out early from the hotel after our night together. He wasn't there when I woke up. He sent me a text from the airport to say he'd covered the bill for the suite and that's the last time I heard from him.' It had hurt to find the suite empty the next morning. Hurt badly. So much for her following the Fling Handbook guidelines. She'd foolishly expected a good morning kiss or two…or more.

'If you're not suffering from a stomach bug, then you'll have to see him sooner or later,' Holly said.

Sabrina put her hand on her abdomen, her

heart beginning to pound with an echo of dread. She couldn't possibly be pregnant… *Could she?* What on earth would she say to Max? Max, who had already made it known he didn't want children. How could she announce *he* was the father of her child?

But wait, women had pregnancy scares all the time. Her cycle was crazy in any case. She had always planned to have kids, but not yet. She was still building up her business. Still trying to prove to her family her career choice was as viable, rewarding and fulfilling as theirs.

She'd had it all planned: get her business well established, hopefully one day fall in love with a man who would treat her the way she had always longed to be treated. Not that she had actively gone looking for the love of her life. She had been too worried about a repeat of her embarrassing falling-in-love episode during her teens. But getting married and having babies was what she wanted. One day. How could she have got it so messed up by falling pregnant? Now? While being on the Pill and using condoms? She was still living in a poky little bedsit, for God's sake.

Sabrina moved past Holly to get out of the

bathroom. 'I can't tell him until I know for sure. I need to get a test kit. I have to do it today because there's a Midhurst and Firbank family gathering tomorrow night and I can't do a no-show. It's Max's mother's birthday. She'd be hurt if I didn't go.'

'You could say you've got a stomach bug.'

Sabrina gave her a side-eye. 'My parents and brothers will be there and once they hear I've got a stomach bug, one or all of them will be on my doorstep with their doctor's bag.' She clutched two handfuls of her hair with her hands. 'Argh. Why am I such a disaster? This wasn't meant to happen. Not *no-o-o-w*.' To her shame, her last word came as a childish wail.

'Oh, sweetie, you're not a disaster. Falling pregnant to a guy you love is not a catastrophe. Not in this day and age in any case.'

Sabrina dropped her hands from her head and glared at her friend. 'Who said I was in love with Max? Why do you keep going on about it?'

Holly placed her hands on her hips in an *I know you better than you do yourself* pose. 'Hello? You haven't slept with anyone for ten years, and then you spend a night in bed with a man you've known since you were in nappies? You wouldn't have slept with him if you didn't feel something for him.'

Sabrina rolled her lips together and turned away to smooth the fabric out on the worktable. 'Okay, so maybe I don't hate him as much as I used to, but I'm not in love with him. I wouldn't be so…so…stupid.' *Would she?* She had promised herself she would never find herself in that situation again. Fancying herself in love with someone who might reject her in the end like her teenage boyfriend had. Falling in love with Max would be asking for the sort of trouble she could do without. More trouble, that was, because finding herself pregnant to him was surely trouble enough.

Holly touched Sabrina on the arm. 'Do you want me to stay with you while you do the test?'

Sabrina gulped back a sob. 'Oh…would you?'

Holly smiled. 'That's what best friends are for—through thick and thin, and sick and sin, right?'

If it hadn't been his mother's birthday Max would have found some excuse to not show up. Not that he didn't want to see Sabrina. He did, which was The Problem. Wanting to see her, wanting to touch her, wanting to kiss her, wanting, wanting, wanting to make love to her again. He had told himself one night and one night only and here he was six weeks later still replaying every minute of that stolen night of seriously hot sex. Sex so amazing he could still feel aftershocks when he so much as pictured her lying in his arms. Sex so planet-dislodging he hadn't bothered hooking up with anyone else and wondered in his darkest moments if he ever would.

He couldn't imagine touching another woman after making love with Sabrina. How could he kiss another mouth as sweet and responsive as hers? How could he slide his hands down a body so lush and ripe and feminine if it didn't belong to Sabrina?

Max arrived at his parents' gracious home in Hampton Court, and after greeting his mother and father took up his usual place at the back of the crowded room to do his people-watching thing. He searched the sea of faces to see if Sabrina was among them, more than a little shocked at how disappointed he was not to find her. But then a thought shot like a stray dart into his brain. What if she brought someone with her? Another man? A new date? A man she was now sleeping with and doing all the sexy red-hot things she had done with him?

Max took a tumbler of spirits off the tray of a passing waiter and downed it in one swallow. He had to get a hold of himself. He was thirty-four years old, not some hormone-driven teenager suffering his first crush. So what if Sabrina slept with someone else? What business was it of his? They'd made an agreement of one night to get the lust bug out of the way.

No repeats.

No replays.

No sequel.

No happy-ever-after.

Max turned to put his empty glass down on a table next to him and saw Sabrina greeting his mother on the other side of the room. The way his parents adored her was understandable given they hadn't had any children after the loss of Daniel. Sabrina, as their only godchild, had been lavished with love and attention. Max knew their affection for her had helped them to heal as much as was possible after the tragic loss of an infant. Not that his parents hadn't adored him too. They had been fabulous parents trying to do their best after such sad circumstances, which, in an ill-advised but no less understandable way, had fed their little fantasy of him and Sabrina one day getting together and playing happy families.

But it was a step too far.

Way, way too far.

Sabrina finally stepped out of his mother's bone-crushing hug and met his gaze. Her eyes widened and then flicked away, her cheeks going an intense shade of pink. She turned and hurriedly made her way through the knot of guests and disappeared through the door that led out to the gallery-wide corridor.

Max followed her, weaving his way through the crowd just in time to see Sabrina scuttling into the library further down the corridor, like a terrified mouse trying to escape a notoriously cruel cat. In spite of the background noise of the party, the sound of the key turning in the lock was like a rifle shot. Or a slap on the face.

Okay, so he had left her in Venice without saying goodbye in person but surely that didn't warrant *this* type of reaction?

Max knocked on the library door. 'Sabrina? Let me in.'

He could hear the sound of her breathing on the other side of the door—hectic and panicked as if she really was trying to avoid someone menacing. But after a moment the key turned in the lock and the door creaked open.

'Are you alone?' Sabrina's voice sounded as creaky as the door, her eyes wide and bluer than he had ever seen them. And, he realised with a jolt, reddened as if she'd been recently crying. A lot.

'Yes, but what's going on?' He stepped into the room before she could stop him and closed the door behind him.

Sabrina took a few steps back and hugged her arms around her middle, her eyes skittering away from his. 'I have something to tell you…'

Here we go. Max had been here so many times before. The *I want more than a one-night stand* speech. But this time he was okay with it. More than okay. He could think of nothing he wanted more than to have a longer fling with her. Longer than one night, that was. A week or two, a month or three.

Long enough to scratch the itch but not long enough for her to get silly ideas about it being for ever. 'It's okay, Sabrina. You don't have to look so scared. I've been thinking along the same lines.'

Her smooth brow crinkled into a frown. 'The same…lines?'

Max gave a soft laugh, his blood already pumping at the thought of taking her in his arms. Maybe even here in the quiet of the library while the guests were partying in the ballroom. What could be sexier than a clandestine affair? 'We'd have to keep it a secret, of course. But a month or two would be fun.' He took a step towards her but she backed away as if he was carrying the Black Plague.

'No.' She held up her hands like stop signs, her expression couldn't have looked more horrified than if he'd drawn a gun.

No? Max hadn't heard that word from a woman for a long time. Weird, but hearing it from Sabrina was unusually disappointing. 'Okay. That's fine. We'll stick to the original agreement.'

She gave an audible swallow and her arms went back around her middle. 'Max…' She slowly lifted her gaze back to his, hers still wide as Christmas baubles. 'I don't know how to tell you this…'

His gut suddenly seized and he tried to control his breathing. So she'd found someone else. No wonder his offer of a temporary fling had been turned down. She was sleeping with someone else. Someone else was kissing that beautiful mouth, someone else was holding her gorgeous body in their arms.

'It's okay, Sabrina.' How had he got his voice to sound so level? So damn normal when his insides were churning with jealousy? Yes, jealousy—that thing he never felt. Ever. Not for anyone. The big green-eyed monster was having a pity party in his gut and there was nothing he could do about it.

One of Sabrina's hands crept to press against her stomach. She licked her lips and opened her mouth to speak but couldn't seem to get her voice to work.

Max called on every bit of willpower he possessed to stop himself from reaching for her and showing her why a temporary fling with him was much a better idea than her getting involved permanently with someone else. A hard sell to a fairytale girl, but still. His hands stayed resolutely by his sides, but his fingers were clenching and unclenching like his jaw. 'Who is it?' There. He'd asked the question his pride had forbidden him to ask.

Sabrina's brow creased into another puzzled frown. 'I… You think there's someone… *else*?'

Max shrugged as if it meant nothing to him what she did and whom she did it with. But on the inside he was slamming his fist into the wall in frustration. Bam. Bam. Bam. The imaginary punches were in time with the thud, thud, thud of his heart. 'That's what this is about, isn't it?'

'Have *you* found someone else?' Her voice was faint and hesitant as if it was struggling to get past a stricture in her throat.

'Not yet.'

She closed her eyes in a tight squint as if his answer had pained her. She opened her eyes again and took a deep breath. 'In a way, this is about someone else…' She laced her fingers together in front of her stomach, then released them and did it again like a nervous tic. 'Someone neither of us has met…yet…'

Max wanted to wring his own hands. He wanted to turn back time and go back to Venice and do things differently. He had to get control of himself. He couldn't allow his jealousy over a man who may or may not exist to mess with his head. He took a calming breath, released it slowly. They would both eventually find someone else. He would have to get used to seeing her with a husband one day. A man who would give her the family she wanted. The commitment and the love she wanted. And Max would move from woman to woman just as he had been doing for the last six years. 'So, you're saying you're not actually seeing someone else right at this moment?'

'No.' Her face screwed up in distaste. 'How could you think I would want to after what we shared?'

'It was just sex, Sabrina.' He kept his tone neutral even though his male ego was doing fist pumps. Damn good sex. Amazing sex. Awesome sex he wanted to repeat. Then a victory chant sounded in his head. *There isn't anyone else. There isn't anyone else*. The big green monster slunk away and relief flooded Max's system.

'Yeah, well, if only it had been just sex…' Something about her tone and her posture made the hairs of the back of his neck stand up. Her hand kept creeping over the flat plane of her belly, her throat rising and falling over a swallow that sounded more like a gulp.

Max was finding it hard to make sense of what she was saying. And why was she looking so flustered? 'I'm not sure where this conversation is heading, but how about you say what you want to say, okay? I promise I won't interrupt. Just spit it out, for God's sake.'

Her eyes came back to his and she straightened her spine as if girding herself for a firing squad. 'Max… I'm pregnant.'

CHAPTER FIVE

MAX STEPPED BACK as if she had stabbed him. His gut even clenched as if a dagger had gone through to his backbone. *Pregnant?* The word was like a poison spreading through his blood, leaving a trail of catastrophic destruction in its wake. His heart stopped and started in a sickening boom-skip-boom-skip-boom-skip rhythm, his lungs almost collapsing as he fought to take a breath. His skin went hot, then cold, and his scalp prickled and tightened as if every hair was shrinking away in dread.

'You're…pregnant?' His voice cracked like an egg thrown on concrete, his mind splintering into a thousand panicked thoughts. A baby. They had made a baby. Somehow, in spite of all the protection he had used, they had made a baby. 'Are you sure?'

She pressed her lips together and nodded,

her chin wobbling. 'I've done a test. Actually, I've done five. They were all positive.'

Max scraped a hand through his hair so roughly he nearly scalped himself. 'Oh, God…' He turned away, a part of him vainly hoping that when he turned back he wouldn't find himself in the library of his parents' mansion with Sabrina telling him he was to be a father. It was like a bad dream. A nightmare.

His. Personal. Nightmare.

'Thanks for not asking if it's yours.' Sabrina's soft voice broke through his tortured reverie.

He swung back to face her; suddenly conscious of how appallingly he was taking her announcement. But nothing could have prepared him for this moment. He had never in his wildest imaginings ever thought he would be standing in front of a woman—any woman—bearing this bombshell news. Pregnant. A baby. *His* baby. 'I'm sorry, but it's such a shock.' Understatement. His heart was pounding so hard he wouldn't have been out of place on a critical care cardiac ward. Sweat was pouring down between his shoulder blades. Something was scrabbling and scratching like there was a frantic animal trapped in his guts.

He stepped towards her and held out his hands but she stepped back again. His hands fell back by his sides. 'So…what have you decided to do?'

Her small neat chin came up and her cornflower-blue eyes hardened with determination. 'I'm not having a termination. Please don't ask me to.'

Max flinched. 'Do you really think I'm the sort of man to do something like that? I'm firmly of the opinion that it's solely a woman's choice whether she continues with a pregnancy or not.'

Relief washed over her pinched features but there was still a cloud of worry in her gaze. 'I'm not against someone else making that difficult choice but I can't bring myself to do it. Not under these circumstances. I don't expect you to be involved if that's not what you want. I know this is a terrible shock and not something you want, but I thought you should know about the pregnancy first, before it becomes obvious, I mean.' Her hand went protectively to her belly again. 'I won't even tell people it's yours if you'd rather not have them know.'

Max was ashamed that for a nanosecond he considered that as an option. But how could he call himself a man and ignore his own flesh and blood? It wasn't the child's fault so why should it be robbed of a relationship with its father? He had grown up with a loving and involved father and couldn't imagine how different his life might have been without the solid and dependable support of his dad.

No. He would do the right thing by Sabrina and the baby. He would try his hardest not to fail them like he had failed his baby brother and his parents. He stepped forward and captured her hands before she could escape. 'I want my child to have my name. We'll marry as soon as I can arrange it.'

Sabrina pulled out of his hold as if his hands had burned her. 'You don't have to be so old-fashioned about it, Max. I'm not asking you to marry me.'

'I'm not asking you. I'm telling you what's going to happen.' As proposals went, Max knew it wasn't flash. But he'd proposed in a past life and he had sworn he would never do it again. But this was different. This was about duty and responsibility, not foolish, fleeting, fickle feelings. 'We will marry next month.'

'Next month?' Her eyes went round in shock. 'Are you crazy? This is the twenty-first century. Couples don't have to marry because they happened to get pregnant. No one is holding a gun to your head.'

'Do you really think I would walk away from the responsibility to my own flesh and blood? We will marry and that's final.'

Sabrina's eyes flashed blue sparks of defiance and her hands clenched into fists. 'You could do with some work on your proposal, buddy. No way am I marrying you. You don't love me.'

'So? You don't love me either,' Max said. 'This is not about us. This is about the baby we've made. You need someone to support you and that someone is me. I won't take no for an answer.'

Her chin came up so high she could have given a herd of mules a master class in stubbornness. 'Then we're at an impasse because no way am I marrying a man who didn't even have the decency to say goodbye in person the night we...had sex.'

Max blew out a breath and shoved a hand back through his hair again. 'Okay, so my exit might have lacked a little finesse, but I didn't want you to get any crazy ideas about our one night turning into something else.'

'Oh, yeah? Well, because of the quality of your stupid condoms, our one-night has turned into something else—a damn baby!' She buried her face in her hands and promptly burst into tears.

Max winced and stepped towards her, gathering her close against his body. This time she didn't resist, and he wrapped his arms around her as the sobs racked her slim frame. He stroked the back of her silky head, his mind whirling with emotions he had no idea how to handle. Regret, shame and blistering anger at himself. He had done this to her. He had got her pregnant. Had the condoms failed? He was always so careful. He always wore one. No exceptions. Had he left it on too long? At one point he had fallen asleep with her wrapped in his arms, his body still encased in the warm wet velvet of hers.

Was that when it had happened? He should never have given in to the temptation of touching her. He had acted on primal instinct, ruled by his hormones instead of his head. 'I'm sorry. So sorry. But I thought you said you were on the Pill?'

She eased away from his chest to look up at him through tear-washed eyes. 'I'm on a low dose one but I was so caught up with nerves about the expo, I had an upset tummy the day before I left for Venice. Plus, I was sick after having that champagne at the cocktail party.' She tried to suppress a hiccup but didn't quite manage it.

Max brushed the hair back from her face. 'Look, no one is to blame for this other than me. I shouldn't have touched you. I shouldn't have kissed you that first time and I definitely shouldn't have booked you into my room and—'

'Do you really regret what happened between us that night?' Her expression reminded him of a wounded puppy—big eyes, long face, fragile hope.

He cradled her face in his hands. 'That's the whole trouble. I don't regret it. Not a minute of it. I've thought of that night thousands of times since then.' He brushed his thumbs over her cheeks while still cupping her face. 'We'll make this work, Sabrina. We might not love each other in the traditional way, but we can make do.'

She tugged his hands away from her face and stepped a metre away to stand in front of the floor-to-ceiling bookshelves. 'Make do? Is that all you want out of life? To...' she waved her hand in a sweeping gesture '...*make do*? What about love? Isn't that an essential ingredient of a good marriage?'

'I'm not offering you that sort of marriage.'

Her eyes flashed and she planted her hands on her hips. 'Well, guess what? I'm not accepting *that* sort of proposal.'

'Would you prefer me to lie to you?' Max tried to keep his voice steady but he could feel ridges of anger lining his throat. 'To get down on bended knee and say a whole lot of flowery words we both know I don't mean?'

'Did you say them to Lydia?'

'Let's keep Lydia out of this.' This time the anger nearly choked him. He hated thinking about his proposal six years ago to his ex-fiancée. He hated thinking about his failure to see the relationship for what it had been—a mistake from start to finish. It had occurred to him only recently that he had asked Lydia to marry him so his parents would back off about Sabrina. Not the best reas one's measure.

'You still have feelings for her, d That's why you can't commit to anyo

Max rolled his eyes and gave a shor of a laugh. 'Oh, please spare me the pop choanalysis. No, I do not still love Lydia. fact, I never loved her.'

Sabrina blinked rapidly. 'Then why did yo ask her to marry you?'

He walked over to the leather-topped mahogany desk and picked up the paperweight he had given his father when he was ten. He passed it from hand to hand, wondering how to answer. 'Good question,' he said, putting the paperweight down and turning to look at her. 'When we first dated, she seemed fine with my decision not to have kids. We had stuff in common, books, movies, that sort of thing.' He gave a quick open-close movement of his lips. 'But clearly it wasn't enough for her.'

'It might not have been about the kid thing. It might have been because she knew you didn't love her. I never thought your chemistry with her was all that good.'

Max moved closer to her, drawn by a force

he couldn't resist. 'Unlike ours, you mean?' He traced a line from below her ear to her chin with his finger, watching as her pupils darkened and her breath hitched. Her spring flowers perfume danced around his nostrils, her warm womanly body making his blood thrum and hum and drum with lust. *Don't touch her.* His conscience pinged with a reminder but he ignored it.

Her hands came up to rest against his chest, the tip of her tongue sweeping over her rosebud lips. But then her eyes hardened and she pushed back from him and put some distance between them. 'I know what you're trying to do but it won't work. I will not be seduced into marrying you.'

'For God's sake, Sabrina,' Max said. 'This is not about seducing you into changing your mind. You're having my baby. I would never leave you to fend for yourself. That's not the sort of man I am.'

'Look, I know you mean well, but I can't marry you. I'm only just pregnant. I can't bear the thought of everyone talking about me, judging me for falling pregnant after a one-night stand, especially to you when I've done nothing but criticise you for years. Anyway, what if I were to have a miscarriage or something before the twelve-week mark? Then you'd hate me for sure for trapping you in a marriage neither of us wanted in the first place.'

The mention of miscarriage gave him pause. He had seen his mother go through several of them before and after the death of Daniel. It had been torture to watch her suffer not just physically but emotionally. The endless tears, the longing looks at passing prams or pregnant women. He had been young, but not too young to notice the despair on his mother's face. 'Okay. So we will wait until the twelve-week mark. But I'm only compromising because it makes sense to keep this news to ourselves until then.'

Sabrina bit her lower lip and it made him want to kiss away the indentation her teeth made when she released it. 'I've kind of told Holly. She was with me when I did the test.'

'Can you trust her to keep it to herself?'

'She'll probably tell Zack, but she assures me he won't blab either.'

Max stepped closer again and took her hands, stroking the backs of them with his thumbs. 'How are you feeling? I'm sorry I didn't ask earlier. Not just about how you're feeling about being pregnant but are you sick? Is there anything you need?'

Fresh tears pooled in her eyes and she swallowed a couple of times. 'I'm a bit sick and my breasts are a little tender.'

'Is it too early to have a scan?'

'I'm not sure, I haven't been to see the doctor yet.'

'I'll go with you to all of your appointments, that is, if you want me there?' Who knew he could be such a model father-to-be? But, then, he figured he'd had a great role model in his own dad. Even so, he wanted to be involved for the child's sake.

'Do you want to be there or would you only be doing it out of duty?'

'I want to be there to see our baby for the first time.' Max was a little surprised to realise how much he meant it. But he needed to see the baby to believe this pregnancy had really happened. He still felt as if he'd stepped into a parallel universe. Could his and Sabrina's DNAs really be getting it on inside her womb? A baby. A little person who would look like one or the other, or a combination of both of them. A child who would grow up and look to him for protection and nurturing. Did he trust himself to do a good job? How could he when he had let his baby brother down so badly?

The door suddenly opened behind them and Max glanced over his shoulder to see his mother standing there. 'Oh, there you two are.' Her warm brown eyes sparkled with fairy godmother delight.

Sabrina sprang away from Max but she bumped into the mahogany desk behind her and yelped. 'Ouch!'

Max reached for Sabrina, steadying her by bringing her close to his side. 'Are you okay?'

She rubbed her left hip, her cheeks a vivid shade of pink. 'Yes…'

'Did I startle you?' Max's mother asked. 'Sorry, darling, but I was wondering where you'd gone. You seemed a little upset earlier.'

'I'm not upset,' Sabrina said, biting her lip.

His mother raised her eyebrows and then glanced at Max. 'I hope you two aren't fighting again? No wonder the poor girl gets upset with you glaring at her all the time. I don't want my party spoilt by your boorish behaviour. Why can't you just kiss and make up for a change?'

Max could have laughed at the irony of the situation if his sense of humour hadn't already been on life support. He'd done way more than kiss Sabrina and now there were consequences he would be dealing with for the rest of his life. But there was no way he could tell his mother what had gone on between them. No way he could say anything until she was through the first trimester of her pregnancy. It would get everybody's hopes up and the pressure would be unbearable—even more unbearable than it already was.

'It's fine, Aunty Gillian. Max is being perfectly civil to me,' Sabrina said, carefully avoiding his gaze.

Max's mother shifted her lips from side to side. 'Mmm, I'm not sure it's safe to leave you two alone for more than five minutes. Who knows what might happen?'

Who knew, indeed?

As soon as the door closed behind Gillian Firbank, Sabrina swung her gaze to Max. 'Do you think she suspects anything?'

'I don't think so. But we have to keep our relationship quiet until you get through the first trimester. Then we can tell everyone we're marrying.'

She stared at him, still not sure how to handle this change in him. So much for the one night and one night only stance he'd taken before. Now he was insisting on marrying her and wouldn't take no for an answer.

She blew out a breath, whirled away and crossed her arms over her middle. 'You're being ridiculous, Max. We can't do this. We can't get married just because I'm pregnant. We'd end up hating each other even more than we do now.'

'When have I ever said I hated you?' Max's jaw looked like it was set in stone. A muscle moved in and out next to his flattened mouth as if he was mentally counting to ten. And his smoky blue eyes smouldered, making something fizz at the back of her knees like sherbet.

'You don't have to say it. It's in your actions. You can barely speak to me without criticising something about me.'

He came to her and before she could move away he took her by the upper arms in a gentle but firm hold. Deep down, Sabrina knew she'd had plenty of time to escape those warm strong fingers, but right then her body was craving his touch. Six long weeks had passed since their stolen night of passion and now she was alone with him, her senses were firing, her needs clamouring, her resolve to resist him faltering. 'I don't hate you, Sabrina.'

But you don't love me either.

She didn't say the words out loud but the silence seemed to ring with their echo. 'We'd better get back to the party otherwise people will start talking.'

His hands tightened. 'Not yet.' His voice was low and deep and husky, his eyes flicking to her mouth as if drawn by a force he couldn't counteract.

Sabrina breathed in the clean male scent of him, the hint of musk, the base note of bergamot and a top note of lemon. She leaned towards him, pushed by the need to feel him close against her, to feel his body respond to hers. He stirred against her, the tempting hardness of his body reminding hers of everything that had passed between them six weeks ago. 'Max… I can't think straight when you touch me.'

'Then don't think.'

She stepped out of his hold with a willpower she hadn't known she possessed. 'I need a couple of weeks to get my head around this…situation. It's been such a shock and I don't want to rush into anything I might later regret.'

She didn't want to think about all the madly-in-love brides who came to her for their wedding dresses. She didn't want to think about Max's offer, which had come out of a sense of duty instead of love. But she didn't want to think about bringing up a baby on her own either. She walked to the library door, knowing that if she stayed a minute longer she would end up in his arms.

'Where are you going?' Max asked.

She glanced over her shoulder. 'The party, remember?'

He dragged a hand over his face and scowled. 'I hate parties.'

CHAPTER SIX

BY THE TIME Max dragged himself out of the library to re-join the party there was no sign of Sabrina. He moved through the house, pretending an interest in the other guests he was nowhere near feeling, surreptitiously sweeping his gaze through the crowd to catch a glimpse of her. He didn't want to make it too obvious he was looking for her, but he didn't want her to leave his parents' house until he was sure she was okay.

He was having enough trouble dealing with the shock news of her pregnancy, so he could only imagine how it was impacting on her. Even though he knew she had always wanted children, she wanted them at the right time with the right guy. He wasn't that guy. But it was too late to turn back the clock. He was the father of her child and there was no way he was going to abandon her, even if he had to drag her kicking, screaming and swearing to the altar.

Max wandered out into the garden where large scented candles were burning in stands next to the formal garden beds. There was no silky honey-brown head in the crowd gathered outside. The sting of disappointment soured his mood even further. The only way to survive one of his parents' parties was to spar with Sabrina. He hadn't realised until then how much he looked forward to it. Was he weird or what? Looking forward to their unfriendly fire was not healthy. It was sick.

And so too was wanting to make love to a woman you got pregnant six weeks ago. But he couldn't deny the longing that was pounding through him. He'd wanted to kiss her so badly back in the library. Kiss her and hold her and remind her of the chemistry they shared. Hadn't it always been there? The tension that vibrated between them whenever their gazes locked. How the slightest touch of her hand sent a rocket charge through his flesh. That first kiss all those weeks ago had set in motion a ferocious longing that refused to be suppressed.

But it *had* to be suppressed. It *must* be suppressed. He was no expert on pregnancy, having avoided the topic for most of his adult life, but wasn't sex between the parents dangerous to the baby under some circumstances? Particularly if the pregnancy was a high-risk one? How could he live with himself if he harmed the baby before it even got a chance to be born? Besides, he didn't want their families to get too excited about him and Sabrina seeing each other. He could only imagine his mother's disappointment if she thought she was going to be a grandmother only to have it snatched away from her if Sabrina's pregnancy failed.

No. He would do the noble thing. He would resist the temptation and get her safely through to the twelve-week mark. Even if it damn near killed him.

Max's mother came towards him with half a glass of champagne in her hand. 'Are you looking for Sabrina?'

'No.' *Shoot*. He'd delivered his flat denial far too quickly.

'Well, if you are, then you're wasting your time. She went home half an hour ago. Said she wasn't feeling well. I hope it wasn't your fault?' The accusatory note in his mother's voice grated along his already frayed nerves.

Yep, it was definitely his fault.

Big time.

Sabrina managed to make it back to her tiny flat without being sick. The nausea kept coming and going in waves and she'd been worried it might grip her in the middle of the party celebrations. She had decided it was safer to make her excuses and leave. Besides, it might have looked suspicious if her mother or Max's noticed she wasn't drinking the champagne. After all, the party girl with a glass of bubbles in her hand and a dazzling smile on her face whilst working the room was her signature style.

But it seemed Sabrina had left one party to come home to another. The loud music coming from the upstairs flat was making the walls shake. How would she ever get to sleep with that atrocious racket going on? She only hoped the party wouldn't go on past midnight. Last time the neighbours had held a party the police had been called because a scuffle had broken out on the street as some of the guests had been leaving.

It wasn't the nicest neighbourhood to live in—certainly nowhere as genteel as the suburbs where her parents and two older brothers lived and where she had spent her childhood. But until she felt more financially stable she didn't feel she had a choice. Rents in London were continually on the rise, and with the sharing economy going from strength to strength, it meant there was a reduced number of properties available for mid-to long-term rent.

She peeled off her clothes and slipped her nightgown over her head. She went to the bathroom and took off her makeup but then wished she hadn't. Was it possible to look that pale whilst still having a functioning pulse?

Sabrina went back to her bedroom and climbed into bed and pulled the covers over her head, but the sound of heavy footsteps clattering up and down the stairs would have made a herd of elephants sound like fairies' feet. Then, to add insult to injury, someone began to pound on her front door.

'Argh.' She threw off the covers and grabbed her wrap to cover her satin nightgown and padded out to check who was there through the peephole. No way was she going to open the door if it was a drunken stranger. But a familiar tall figure stood there with a brooding expression. 'Max?'

'Let me in.' His voice contained the thread of steel she had come to always associate with him.

She unlocked the door and he was inside her flat almost before she could step out of the way. 'What are you doing here?'

He glanced around the front room of her flat like a construction official inspecting a condemned building. 'I'm not letting you stay here. There isn't even an intercom on this place. It's not safe.'

Pride stiffened her spine and she folded her arms across her middle. 'I don't plan to stay here for ever but it's all I can afford. Anyway, you didn't seem to think it was too unsafe when you kissed me that time you brought me home.'

'My mind was on other things that night.' There was the sound of a bottle breaking in the stairwell and he winced. 'Right. That settles it. Get dressed and pack a bag. You're coming with me.'

Sabrina unfolded her arms and placed them on her hips. 'You can't just barge into my home and tell me what to do.'

'Watch me, sweetheart.' He moved past her and went to her bedroom, opening drawers and cupboards and throwing a collection of clothes on the bed.

Sabrina followed him into her bedroom. ‘Hey, what the hell do you think you’re doing?’

‘If you won’t pack, then I’ll do it for you.’ He opened another cupboard and found her overnight bag and, placing it on the bed, began stuffing her clothes into it.

Sabrina grabbed at the sweater he’d picked up and pulled on it like a dog playing tug-of-war. ‘Give it back.’ *Tug. Tug. Tug.* ‘You’re stretching it out of shape.’

He whipped it out of her hands and tossed it in the bag on the bed. ‘I’ll buy you a new one.’ He slammed the lid of the bag down and zipped it up with a savage movement. ‘I’m not letting you stay another minute in this hovel.’

‘Hovel?’ Sabrina snorted. ‘Did you hear that clanging noise? Oh, yes, that must be the noise of all those silver spoons hanging out of your mouth.’

His grey-blue eyes were as dark as storm clouds with lightning flashes of anger. ‘Why do you live like this when you could live with your parents until you get on your feet?’

‘Hello? I’m twenty-eight years old,’ Sabrina said. ‘I haven’t lived with my parents for a decade. And nor would I want to. They'd bombard me constantly with all of your amazingly wonderful assets until I went stark certifiably crazy.'

There was the sound of someone shouting and swearing in the stairwell and Max's jaw turned to marble. 'I can't let you stay here, Sabrina. Surely you can understand that?'

She sent him a glare. 'I understand you want to take control.'

'This is not about control. This is about your safety.' He scraped a hand through his hair. 'And the baby's safety too.'

Sabrina was becoming too tired to argue. The noise from upstairs was getting worse and there would be no hope of sleeping even if by some remote chance she convinced Max to leave her be. Besides, she secretly hated living here. The landlord was a creep and kept threatening to put up the rent.

Sabrina was too proud, too determined to prove to her parents she didn't need their help. But it wasn't just herself she had to think about now. She had to take care of the baby. She'd read how important it was for mothers-to-be to keep stress levels down and get plenty of rest for the sake of the developing foetus. Was

Max thinking along the same lines? 'Why did you come here tonight?' she asked.

'I was worried about you. You left the party early and I worried you might be sick or faint whilst driving home. I'm sorry. I should have offered to drive you but I was still reeling from your news and—'

'It's okay.' She tossed her hair back over one shoulder. 'As you see, I managed to get home in one piece.'

He stepped closer and took her hands in his. His touch made every nerve in her skin fizz, his concerned gaze striking a lethal blow to her stubborn pride. 'Let me look after you, Sabrina. Come home with me.'

Her insides quivered, her inner core recalling his intimate presence. The memories of that night seemed to be swirling in the air they shared. Her body was so aware of his proximity she could feel every fibre of her satin nightgown against her flesh. Was he remembering every moment of that night? Was his body undergoing the same little pulses and flickers of remembered pleasure? 'Live with you, you mean?'

'We'll have separate rooms.'

She frowned. 'You don't want to...?'

'I don't think it's a good idea.' He released her hands and stepped back. 'Not until you get through the first trimester. Then we'll reassess.' His tone was so matter-of-fact he could have been reading a financial report.

Sabrina couldn't quell her acute sense of disappointment. He didn't want her any more? Or maybe he did but he was denying himself because he'd set conditions on their relationship. 'But how will we keep our…erm…relationship or whatever we're now calling it a secret from our families if we're living under the same roof?'

'In some ways, it'll make it easier. We won't be seen out and about together in public. And I travel a lot for work so we won't be on top of each other.'

Doubts flitted through her mind like frenzied moths. Sharing a house with him was potentially dangerous. Her body was aflame with lust as soon as he came near, living with him would only make it a thousand times worse. She ached to feel his arms around her, his kiss on her mouth, his body buried within hers. What if she made a fool of herself? Wanting him so badly she begged him to make love to her?

What if she fell in love with him?

He wasn't offering her love, only his protection. Food and shelter and a roof over her head. And a stable but loveless marriage if the pregnancy continued. But wasn't that a pathway to heartbreak? How could she short-change herself by marrying someone who wasn't truly in love with her?

Max came closer again and took her hands. 'This is the best way forward. It will ensure your safety and my peace of mind.'

She looked down at their joined hands, his skin so tanned compared to the creamy whiteness of hers. It reminded her of the miracle occurring inside her body, the cells dividing, DNA being exchanged, traits and features from them both being switched on or off to make a whole new little person. A little person she was already starting to love. 'I don't know…'

His hands gave hers a small squeeze. 'Let's give it a try for the next few weeks, okay?'

Sabrina let out a sigh and gave him a wry glance. 'You know, you're kind of scaring me at how convincing you can be when you put your mind to it.'

He released her hands and stepped back

with an unreadable expression. 'I'll wait for you out here while you get changed out of your nightgown. Any toiletries you need from the bathroom before we get going?'

She sighed and turned back for the bedroom. 'I'll get them once I've got changed.'

Max waited for Sabrina while she gathered her makeup and skincare products from the bathroom. He would have paced the floor but there wasn't the space for it. He would have taken out a window with his elbow each time he turned. It was true that he hadn't noticed how appalling her flat was when he'd brought her home that night all those weeks ago. The flat wasn't so bad inside—she had done her best to tart things up with brightly coloured scatter cushions and throw rugs over the cheap sofa, cute little knick-knacks positioned here and there and prints of artwork on the walls. There was even a bunch of fresh flowers, presumably supplied by her best friend Holly, who was a florist.

But it was what was on the outside of Sabrina's front door that worried him. Apart from the stale cooking smells, there were no security cameras, no intercom to screen the people coming in and out of the building. How could he sleep at night if he left her here with who knew what type of people milling past? Criminals? Drug dealers? Violent thugs?

No. It was safer for her at his house. Well, safe in one sense, dangerous in another. He had made a promise to himself that he would keep his hands off her. He knew he was locking the stable door even though the horse was well on its way to the maternity ward, but he had to be sensible about this. Sleeping with her before the three-month mark would make it even harder to end their relationship if the pregnancy failed.

Something tightened in his gut at the thought of her losing that baby. *His* baby. He had never imagined himself as a father. For most of his life he had blocked it out of his mind. He wasn't the type of man who was comfortable around kids. He actively avoided babies. One of his friends from university had asked him to be godfather to his firstborn son. Max had almost had a panic attack at the church when his friend's wife had handed him the baby to hold.

But now *he* was going to be a father.

Sabrina came out after a few minutes

dressed in skinny jeans and a dove-grey boyfriend sweater that draped sensually over her bra-less breasts. On her feet she was wearing ballet slippers, and on her face an expression that was one part resignation and one part defiance. He tore his gaze away from the tempting globes of her breasts, remembering how soft they had felt in his hands, how tightly her nipples had peaked when he'd sucked on them. In a few months her body would be ripe with his child.

A child *he* had planted in her womb.

He had never considered pregnancy to be sexy but somehow with Sabrina it was. Damn it, everything about her was sexy. Wasn't that why he'd crossed the line and made love to her last month in Venice?

But now he had drawn a new line and there was no way he was stepping over it.

No. Freaking. Way.

Sabrina hadn't realised she had slept during the drive from her flat to Max's house in Notting Hill. She woke up when the car stopped and straightened from her slumped position in the passenger seat. She hadn't been to this new house of his before—but not for want of trying by his and her parents. She had walked past it once or twice but was always so keen to avoid him that she had stopped coming to the Portobello Road markets for fear of running into him.

The house was one in a long row of grand four-storey white terrace houses. Each one had a black wrought-iron balustrade on the second-floor balcony and the same glossy black decorative fencing at street level.

When Max led the way inside, she got a sense of what Lizzie Bennet in *Pride and Prejudice* had felt when seeing Pemberley, Mr Darcy's estate, for the first time. *This could be your home if you marry him.*

She turned in a circle in the black and white tiled foyer, marvelling at the décor that was stylish and elegant without being over the top. The walls and ceiling were a bone white but the chandelier overhead was a black one with sparkling crystal pendants that tinkled with the movement of air. There was a staircase leading to the upper floors, carpeted with a classic Persian runner with brass rods running along the back of each step to hold it in place. Works of art hung at various points, which she could only presume were originals. He didn't strike her as the sort of man to be content with a couple of cheap knock-offs to adorn his walls, like she had done at her flat.

'I'll show you to your room,' Max said. 'Or would you like something to eat and drink first?'

Sabrina tried to smother a yawn. 'No, I think I'll go straight to bed. I'm exhausted.'

He carried her small bag and led the way up the stairs, glancing back at her every few steps to make sure she was managing okay. It would have been touching if it hadn't been for how awkward the situation between them was. She was very much aware of how she had rocked his neat and ordered life with her bombshell news. She was still trying to come to terms with it herself. How was she going to run her business and look after a baby? What was she going to say to her parents and brothers?

Oh, by the way, I got myself knocked up by my mortal enemy Max Firbank.

'I'll show you around tomorrow, but the main bathroom is on the ground floor, along with the kitchen and living areas,' Max said. 'On this floor there's my study, second door on the left, and the guest bedrooms, each with its own bathroom. My room is on the third floor. There's a gym on the top floor.'

Sabrina stopped on the second-floor landing to catch her breath. 'Who needs a gym with all these stairs?'

He frowned and touched her on the arm. 'Are you okay?'

'Max, I'm fine. Please stop fussing.'

He drew in a breath and released it in a whoosh, his hand falling away from her forearm. 'Tomorrow I'll have the rest of your things brought over from your flat.'

'How am I going to explain why I'm not at home if my parents or brothers drop by? Where will I say I'm staying?'

'Tell them you're staying with a friend.'

Sabrina arched her eyebrows. 'Is that what you are now? My…friend?'

He glanced at her mouth before meeting her gaze with his inscrutable one. 'If we're going to be bringing up a child together then we'd damn well better not be enemies.'

She had a feeling he was fighting hard not to touch her. One of his hands was clenching and unclenching and his chiselled jaw was set in a taut line. 'This is your worst nightmare, isn't it? Having me here, pregnant with a baby you didn't want.'

'Let's not talk any more tonight. We're both tired and—'

'I'm not so tired that I can't see how much you're hating this. Hating *me*.' She banged her fist against her chest for emphasis. 'I didn't do it deliberately, you know.'

'I never said you did.'

Sabrina was struggling to contain her overwrought emotions. Her life was spiralling out of her control and there was nothing she could do about it. She swallowed a sob but another one followed it. She turned away and squeezed her eyes shut to stop the sting of tears.

Max put the bag down and placed his hands on her shoulders, gently turning her to face him, his expression etched with concern. 'Hey…' His finger lifted her face so her eyes met his. 'Listen to me, Sabrina. I do not hate you. Neither do I blame you for what's happened. I take full responsibility. And because of that, I want to take care of you in whatever way you need.'

But I need you. The words stayed silent on her tongue. She would not beg him to make love to her again. She wanted him to own his desire for her. To own it instead of denying it. She blinked the moisture away from her eyes. 'I'm worried about how I'll cope with my work and a baby. What if I lose my business? I've worked so hard to get it to this stage.'

His hands tightened on her shoulders. 'You will not lose your business. You can appoint a manager or outsource some work. The golden rule in running a business is only to do the stuff that only you can do.'

'I've been trying to do that by hiring a part-time assistant but she messed up my booking for Venice,' Sabrina said.

'It takes time to build up your confidence in your staff but if you train them to do things the way you want them done, and check in occasionally to see if they're on track, then things will eventually run the way you want them to.' He removed his hands from her shoulders and picked up her bag again. 'Now, young lady, it's time for you to get some shut-eye.'

He led her to one of the guest bedrooms further down the corridor. It was beautifully decorated in cream and white with touches of gold. The queen-sized bed was made up with snowy white bedlinen, the collection of standard and European pillows looking as soft as clouds. The cream carpet threatened to swallow her feet up to the ankle and she slipped off her shoes and sighed as her toes curled against the exquisite comfort of luxury fibres.

Max put Sabrina's bag on a knee-high chest near the built-in wardrobes. 'I'll leave you to settle in. The bathroom is through there. I'll see you in the morning.' His tone was so clipped he could have trimmed a hedge. He walked the door to leave and she wondered if he was thinking about the last time they had been alone together in a room with a bed. Did he regret their lovemaking so much that he couldn't bear the thought of repeating it? It felt uncomfortably like her boyfriend walking away, rejecting her. Hurting her.

'Max?'

He turned back to face her. 'Yes?'

Sabrina had to interlace her fingers in front of her body to keep from reaching out to him. She couldn't beg him to stay with her. Wouldn't beg him. The risk of him rejecting her would be too painful. 'Nothing…' A weak smile flickered across her lips. 'Goodnight.'

''Night.' And then he left and closed the door with a firm click.

CHAPTER SEVEN

MAX WENT DOWNSTAIRS before he was tempted to join Sabrina in that damn bed. What was wrong with him? Hadn't he done enough damage? He wanted slip in between those sheets with her, even if just to hold her against his body. He hadn't forgotten how it felt to have her satin-soft skin against his. He hadn't forgotten how it felt to glide his hands over her gorgeous breasts or how it felt to bury himself deep into her velvet warmth.

But he must *not* think about her like that. He had to keep his distance otherwise things could get even more complicated than they already were. Relationships got complicated when feelings were involved and he was already fighting more feelings than he wanted to admit. Everything was different about his relationship with Sabrina. Everything. And if that wasn't enough of a warning for him to back off in the feelings department, he didn't know what was.

He couldn't remember the last time he'd had a sleepover with a lover. It hadn't been in this house as he'd only moved in a few months ago once the renovations had been completed. He hadn't even shared his previous house with Lydia in spite of her broad hints to move in with him.

Max sat at his desk in his study and sighed. For the next six weeks he would have to make sure he kept his relationship with Sabrina completely platonic. Since when had he found it sexy to make love to a pregnant woman? But now he couldn't stop thinking about the changes her body was undergoing.

Changes *he* had caused.

His gaze went to the framed photograph of his family on his desk. It had been taken just days before Daniel had died. His mother and father were sitting either side of him and he was holding his brother across his lap. Everyone was smiling, even Daniel.

Max wondered if he would ever be able to look at that photograph without regret and guilt gnawing at his insides. Regret and guilt and anger at himself for not doing more to help his little brother. It had taken many years for his parents to smile again, especially his mother.

Would the birth of his parents' first grandchild heal some of the pain of the past?

When Sabrina woke the next morning, it took her a moment to realise where she was. The room was bathed in golden sunlight, and she stretched like a lazy cat against the marshmallow-soft pillows. It was a Sunday so there was no rush to get out of bed…although staying in bed would be a whole lot more tempting if Max was lying here beside her. She'd heard him come up the stairs to his room on the floor above hers in the early hours of the morning. Didn't the man need more than three or four hours of sleep?

There was a tap at the door and she sat up in the bed. 'Come in.'

Max opened the door, deftly balancing a tray on one hand as he came in. 'Good morning. I thought you might like some tea and toast.'

'Oh, lovely, I haven't had breakfast in bed in ages.'

He came over to the bed and placed the

tray, which had fold-down legs, across her lap. This close she could smell his freshly shampooed hair and the citrus fragrance of his aftershave. He straightened and gave his version of a smile. 'How are you feeling?'

'So far, so good,' Sabrina said. 'Sometimes the nausea hits when I first stand up.'

'Good reason to stay where you are, then.'

She picked up the steaming cup of tea and took a sip. 'Mmm…perfect. How did you know I take it black?'

His expression was wry. 'I think it's safe to say your parents have told me just about everything there is to know about you over the years.'

Not quite everything.

Sabrina had never told her parents about her first sexual experience. The only person she'd told was Holly. It was too embarrassing, too painful to recall the shame she'd felt to hear such horrible rumours spread about her after giving herself to her boyfriend. 'Seriously, they told you how I take my tea?'

He gave a half smile. 'Only joking. No, I've been observing you myself.'

She put her tea back on the tray and picked

up a slice of toast and peeped at him from half-lowered lashes. 'I've noticed.'

'Oh?'

'Yep. You got really annoyed when I danced with one of the guys at that party at my parents' house a few months back.' She nibbled on the toast and watched his expression go from that mercurial smile to a brooding frown. She pointed the toast at him. 'There. That's exactly how you looked that night.'

He rearranged his features back into a smile but it didn't involve his eyes. 'You imagined it. I was probably frowning about something else entirely.'

Sabrina examined her slice of toast as if it were the most interesting thing in the world. 'Thing is… I've never been all that comfortable with the dating scene.'

'But you're always going on dates.' Max's frown was one of confusion. 'You've nearly always got someone with you when you go to family gatherings.'

So, he'd noticed that too, had he? Interesting. Sabrina shrugged. 'So? I didn't want everyone to think I was a freak.' She hadn't intended to tell him about her past. It hadn't seemed necessary the night they'd made love. Max's magical touch had dissolved all of her fears of physical intimacy. Well, most of them. But it wasn't physical intimacy that was her problem now. Emotional intimacy was the issue. What if she developed feelings for him that weren't reciprocated? Real feelings. Lasting feelings. *Love* feelings.

'When was the last time you had sex with a guy?' His voice had a raw quality to it.

She looked at the toast in her hand rather than meet his gaze. 'Other than with you? Ten years.'

'Ten years?' The words all but exploded from his mouth.

Sabrina could feel her colour rising. 'I'm sure that seems like a long time to someone like you, who has sex every ten minutes, but I had a bad experience and it put me off.'

He took the toast out of her hand and held her hand in both of his. 'Sabrina…' His thumbs began a gentle stroking of her wrist, his eyes meshing with hers. 'The bad experience you mentioned…' His throat rose and fell as if he was trying to swallow a boulder. 'Were you—?'

'No, it was completely consensual,' Sabrina

said. 'I was eighteen and fancied myself in love and felt ready to have sex for the first time. I never wanted my first time to be outside the context of a loving relationship. But my so-called boyfriend had another agenda. He just wanted to crow to his friends about getting it on with me. I overheard him telling his friends I was hopeless in bed. The gossip and rumours did the rounds of my friendship group. It was humiliating and I wanted to die from shame. Up until you, I hadn't been brave enough to sleep with anyone else.' She chanced a glance at him from beneath her lowered lashes. 'Go on, say it. Tell me I'm a frigid freak.'

His frown carved a deep V into his forehead, his hands so soft around hers it was as if he were cradling a baby bird. 'No...' His voice had that raw edge again. 'You're no such thing. That guy was a jerk to do that to you. You're gorgeous, sensual and so responsive I can barely keep my hands off you.'

His words were like a healing balm to her wounded self-esteem. So what if he didn't love her? He desired her and that would have to be enough for now. His gentle touch made her body ache to have him even closer, skin on skin. She leaned in and pressed a soft-as-air kiss to his mouth, just a brush of her lips against his. 'Thank you…'

His mouth flickered as if her light kiss had set off an electric current in his lips. He drew her closer, one of his hands going to the back of her head, the other to glide along the curve of her cheek, his mouth coming down to within a breath of hers. But then he suddenly pulled back to frown at her again. 'But that night we made love… My God, I probably hurt you. Did I?'

Sabrina wound her arms around his neck, sending her fingers into the thickness of his hair. 'Of course you didn't. You were amazingly gentle.'

'But you were practically a virgin.' His expression was etched with tension. 'I should have taken more time. I shouldn't have made love to you more than once. Were you sore? Did I do anything you didn't like?'

She shook her head. 'No, Max. I enjoyed every second of our lovemaking. I just wish…' She bit her lip and lowered her gaze.

'Wish what?'

'Nothing. I'm being silly.'

Max inched up her chin with the end of his finger. 'Tell me.'

Sabrina took a breath. 'I've only had sex four times in my life, one time I don't want to even think about any more. The other three times were so amazing that I sometimes wonder if I imagined how amazing they were.'

'What are you saying?'

'I'm asking you to make love to me again.'

His eyes searched hers. 'Is that really what you want?'

She looked into his smouldering eyes. 'I want you. You want me too…don't you?'

His hand slid under the curtain of her hair. 'It scares me how much I want you. But I don't want to complicate things between us.'

'How will it complicate things if we sleep together? It's not as if I'm going to get pregnant.' Her attempt at humour fell flat if his reaction was anything to go by.

He closed his eyes in a slow blink, then he removed her hand from him and stood up. 'I'm sorry, Sabrina, but I can't. It wouldn't be fair to you.' He scraped a hand through his still-damp-from-a-shower hair. 'You're not thinking straight. It's probably baby brain or something.'

'Baby brain?' Sabrina choked out a humourless laugh. 'Is that what you think? Really? Don't you remember how amazing that night in Venice was?'

'Sabrina.' His stern schoolmaster tone was another blow to her flagging self-esteem.

She pushed the tea tray off her legs and set it on the other side of the bed. 'Or maybe sex is always that amazing for you. Maybe you can't even distinguish that night from the numerous other hook-ups you've had since.' She threw him a glance. 'How many have there been, Max?' Tears smarted in her eyes but she couldn't seem to stop herself from throwing the questions at him, questions she didn't really want answered. 'Is that why you've refused to sleep me with since that night? How many have you had since then? One or two a week? More?'

He drew in a long breath and then released it. 'None.'

'None?'

He came and sat beside her legs on the bed and took her hand again, his fingers warm and strong around hers. 'None.'

Sabrina used the back of her free hand to

swipe at her tears. 'Are you just saying that to make me feel better?'

'It's the truth. There hasn't been anyone because…' He looked down at her hand in the cage of his, a frown pulling at his forehead.

'Because?'

His gaze met hers and a wry smile flickered across his mouth. 'I'm not sure.'

Sabrina moistened her dry lips. 'Was it… amazing for you too? That night in Venice, I mean?'

He gave her hand a squeeze. 'How can you doubt it? You were there. You saw what you did to me.'

She lowered her gaze and looked at their joined hands, thinking of their joined bodies and the sounds of their cries of pleasure that night. His deep groans and whole-body shudders. 'It's not like I have much experience to draw on…'

He brought up her chin with the end of his finger. 'It was amazing for me, sweetheart. You were everything a man could ask for in a lover.' His frown came back, deeper than before. 'I just wish I'd known you were so inexperienced. Are you sure I didn't hurt you?'

Sabrina placed her other hand on top of his. 'Max, listen to me. You didn't hurt me.'

He brought her hand up to his mouth, pressing his lips against the back of her knuckles, his gaze locked on hers. 'When I saw you at my mother's party last night I was considering offering you more than a one-night fling.' He lowered her hand to rest it against his chest. 'I would've been breaking all of my rules about relationships in doing so, but I couldn't get you out of my mind. Or stop thinking about how good we were together.'

'Then why won't you make love to me again?'

His irises were a deep smoky grey, his pupils wide and ink black, and they flicked to her mouth and back to her gaze. 'You're making this so difficult for me.' His voice was gravel rough and he leaned closer until his lips were just above hers. 'So very difficult...' And then his mouth came down and set hers aflame.

It was a soft kiss at first, slow and languorous, his lips rediscovering the contours of her mouth. But it soon changed when his tongue stroked across her bottom lip. She opened to him and his tongue met hers, his groan of satisfaction as breathless as her own. His hands came up to cradle her face, his fingers splaying across her cheeks, his mouth working its mesmerising magic on hers. The movement of his tongue against hers set off fireworks in her blood. Her pulse raced, her heart thumped, her need for him rising in a hot tide of longing that left no part of her body unaffected. Her breasts tingled at the close contact as he drew her closer, the satin of her nightgown sliding sensually over her flesh.

He lifted his mouth to blaze a hot trail of kisses along her neck to the scaffold of her left clavicle. 'God, I want you so damn much…' His voice came out as a growl, the warmth in his lips as hot as fire. He was making her burn for him. She could feel it smouldering between her legs, the slow burn of lust that he had awakened in her.

'I want you too.' She breathed the words against his lips, her tongue stroking his lower lip, tasting him, teasing him.

He sealed her mouth with his, massaging her lips in a tantalising motion that made her pulse and ache with feverish desire. His tongue danced with hers, an erotic choreography that made her senses sing. One of his hands slipped the shoestring strap of her nightgown down her shoulder, uncovering her right breast. He brought his mouth down to its rosy peak, his caress so gentle it made her shiver with delight. His teeth lightly grazed her nipple, his tongue rolling over and around it until she gave a gasp of pleasure. He lowered the other strap off her left shoulder, the satin nightgown slithering down to her waist, revealing her body to his feasting gaze.

'You are so damn beautiful.'

Sabrina began to lift his T-shirt, desperate to touch his warm male skin. 'I want to touch you.'

He pulled back to haul his T-shirt over his head, tossing it to the floor. He stood and came over to remove the tea tray from the bed and set it on top of a chest of drawers. He came back to her. 'Are you sure about this?'

'Never surer.' Sabrina wriggled out of her nightgown, a part of her a little shocked at her lack of shyness. But hadn't he already seen all there was to see? She loved the way he looked at her with eyes blazing with lust. It was the most ego-boosting thing to see him struggle to keep control. No one had ever made her feel as beautiful as he did. No one had ever made her feel proud to be a woman, proud of her curves, proud of her sounds as desire shuddered through her.

Max swallowed and stared at her for a long moment, seemingly still struggling with the tug-of-war between his body and his brain. Sabrina drank in the sight of him naked, his taut and tanned torso cut and carved with well-defined muscles that would have made Michelangelo drool and sharpen his chisel. She had never thought of a man as being beautiful before—it was a term usually applied to women. But in Max's case it was entirely appropriate. There was a classical beauty about the structure of his face and body, the aristocratic lines and planes and contours reminding her of heroes—both fictional and historical—from times past.

Max gathered her close, his touch as gentle as if he were handling priceless porcelain. It made her skin lift and shiver in a shower of goose-bumps. 'Are you cold?' He frowned and glided his hand over her thigh.

Sabrina smiled and brushed her hand down the wall of his chest, suddenly feeling shy about touching him. But she ached to touch him. To caress him. 'I'm not cold. I'm just enjoying being touched. You have such incredible hands.'

He brought his mouth back to hers in a lingering kiss that made her need of him throb deep in her core. Every movement of his lips, every touch of his tongue, every contact point of his body with hers made her desire build to the point of pain. There was a storm gathering in her feminine flesh, a tight turbulence that spread from her core to each of her limbs like all her nerves were on fire. There was a deep throbbing ache between her legs and every time his tongue flicked against hers, it triggered another pulse of lust that made it throb all the more. She moved against him restively, wanting more but not sure how to ask for it.

Perhaps he sensed her shyness, for he took one of her hands and brought it down between their bodies. 'You can touch me.' His voice was so deep and husky it made her skin tingle to think she was having such an effect on him.

Sabrina stroked him with her fingers, enjoying the satin-wrapped steel of his male flesh. He drew in a sharp breath as if her touch thrilled him as much as his thrilled her. 'Am I doing it right?'

'Everything you're doing is perfect.' His breathing increased its pace, his eyes dark and glittering with need.

She moved her hand up and down his shaft, enjoying the feel of him without the barrier of a condom. Skin on skin. The smoothness and strength of him making everything that was female in her do cartwheels of delight.

After a moment, he removed her hand and pressed her down so he was balanced above her on his elbows. 'I don't want to rush you.'

'Rush me?' Sabrina gave a soft laugh. 'I'm practically dying here I want you so much.'

His slow smile made her heart trip and kick. 'Slow is better. It makes it more enjoyable for both of us.'

She reached down to stroke him again. 'Isn't it killing you to hold on so long?'

His jaw worked as if he was reining in his response to her touch. 'I want this to be good for you. Better than good.'

Sabrina's heart was asking for more room inside her chest. He was the dream lover, the lover she had fantasised about for most of her adult life. A lover who put her needs ahead of his own. A lover who respected her and made sure she enjoyed every second of their lovemaking.

But she wanted more. More of him. All of him. He moved over her, gathering her close, nudging her entrance with his erection, taking his time to move, waiting for her to get used to him before going further.

It was so different from her first time as a teenager. So very different it made her chest tighten with emotion. If only *he* had been her first lover. Her body responded to him like fuel to fire. It erupted into sensations, fiery, pulsating sensations that rippled through her entire body. She welcomed him into her with a breathless gasp of pleasure, her inner muscles wrapping tightly around him, moving with him as he began to slowly thrust. Her need built and built within her, his rhythmic movements triggering electrifying sensations that made every cell of her body vibrate. Tension gathered again in her core, a teasing tantalising tension that was more powerful than before. It was taking over her body, taking over her mind, pulling her into one point of exquisite feeling…

But she couldn't quite complete the journey. Her body was poised on a vertiginous precipice, needing, *aching* to fall but unable to fly.

Max brought his hand down to her tender flesh, caressing, providing that blessed friction she needed to finally break free. And fly she did, in waves and ripples and pulses that left no part of her body unaffected. It was like being tossed into a whirlpool, her senses scattering as shockwave after shockwave rocketed through her. Sabrina heard someone gasping and crying in a breathless voice and realised with a jolt that those primal and earthy sounds had come from her.

Max waited until her storm had eased before he increased his pace, bringing himself to his own release with a series of shuddering movements that made her wonder if he had been as affected by their lovemaking as she. Or was this normal for him? Was sex simply sex for him and nothing else? The physical satiation of primal needs that could be met with any willing female? Or had he been as moved as she had been by the flow and ebb of sensations that were still lingering in her body like waves gently washing against a shore?

He began to play with her hair, running his fingers through the tousled strands, the slight pull on her scalp sending a frisson down her spine. How could one person's touch be so powerful? Evoke such incredible sensations in her body?

After a long moment, he raised his head to look down at her, his hand now cradling the back of her head. His expression was confusing to read, it was as if he had pulled down an emotional screen on his face but it hadn't gone all the way down, leaving a gap where a narrow beam of light shone through. The contours of his mouth that hinted at a smile, the smoky grey-blue of his eyes, the pleated brow that wasn't quite a frown made her wonder if he—like her—was privately a little shocked at how good they were together. 'You were wonderful.' His voice had that gravel and honey thing going on. 'Truly wonderful.'

Sabrina let out a shuddery sigh—just thinking about the sensations he had caused made her shiver in delight. 'Is it like that for you all the time?'

He didn't answer for a moment and she wished she hadn't gone fishing for compliments. Stupid. Stupid. Stupid. Of course it wasn't different for him. Of course it wasn't special. Of course it wasn't unique.

She wasn't special.

She wasn't unique.

Max's hand cupped the side of her face, his gaze more blue than grey—a dark, intense blue that made her think of a midnight sky. 'It's not often as good as that. Rarely, in fact.'

Sabrina's heart lifted like it was attached to helium balloons. 'But it sometimes is?' Why couldn't she just let it drop? But she had to know. She longed to know if he felt even a portion of what she'd felt. Her body would never be the same. How could it? It had experienced a maelstrom of sensations that even now were lingering in her flesh in tiny tingles and fizzes.

A small frown appeared on his brow and his eyes moved between each of hers in a back and forth motion as if he were searching for something he didn't really want to find. 'Sabrina…' He released a short sigh. 'Let's not make this any more complicated than it already is.'

Sabrina knew she was wading into the deep end but couldn't seem to stop herself.

'What's complicated about asking you if the sex we just had was run-of-the-mill for you?'

He held her gaze for a beat and then pushed himself away. He got off the bed and rubbed a hand over the back of his neck, tilting his head from side to side as if to ease a knot of tension.

He let out another sigh and turned back to face her, a twisted smile ghosting his mouth. 'Okay, you win. It was great sex. Awesome. The best I've had in years, which was why I was going to offer you a longer fling yesterday at my mother's party.'

Sabrina searched his expression, wondering whether to believe him or not. How silly was she to push for a confession from him only to doubt it when he gave it to her? 'Do you mean it?' Her voice was as soft as a whispered secret, uncertain and desperately seeking reassurance.

Max came back to sit on the bed beside her. He took one of her hands and brought it up to his mouth, kissing each of her fingertips in turn, his eyes holding hers. 'You're a beautiful and sexy woman. I can't remember a time when I've enjoyed sex more.' He gave another rueful twist of his mouth. 'Maybe I've been dating the wrong type of woman.'

Sabrina lowered her gaze and chewed one side of her mouth. 'Better than not dating at all, I suppose…' She didn't want to think about him dating other women. Now that they'd made love again, it made her sick to think of him kissing and caressing someone else. Thank God he hadn't been with anyone since their night in Venice, but how would she feel if he had? But if she didn't marry him, he would be at liberty to sleep with whomever he wished.

It was her call.

Max tipped up her chin with his finger, meshing his gaze with hers. 'What happened to you when you were eighteen would be enough to put most people off dating for a decade. But you have no need to feel insecure. You're one hell of a sexy partner, sweetheart. That night we first kissed? I wanted you so badly it was all I could do to tear myself away.'

'Really?'

His smile made something in her chest ping. He leaned down to press a soft kiss to her mouth. 'Couldn't you tell?'

Sabrina smiled against his mouth. 'It was kind of an enthusiastic kiss now that I think about it.'

He kissed her again, a longer kiss this time, the movement of his lips stirring her senses into overdrive. He lifted his mouth just above hers, his eyes sexily hooded. 'Is that enthusiastic enough for you?'

She traced the line of his mouth with her finger, her body tingling with excitement at the way his hard body was pressing against her. 'Getting there.'

He captured her finger with his teeth, holding it in a soft bite, his eyes pulsating with lust. 'I want you.'

Sabrina shivered in anticipation and looped her arms around his neck. 'I want you too.'

He brought his mouth back down to hers, kissing her long and deep, his tongue gliding into her mouth with a slow thrust that made her body tremble. His hands cradled her face, his upper body pressing down on her breasts, the skin-on-skin contact thrilling her senses all over again. She could feel the swollen ridge of his erection against her lower body, and her inner core responding with tight contractions and clenches. The sweet tension was building, all her pleasure points in heightened awareness of his touch. One of his hands went to her breast in a slow caress that made her skin tighten and tingle. His thumb rolled over her nipple, back and forth until it was a hard pebble of pleasure. The sensations travelled from her breasts to her belly and below as if transmitted by a sensual network of nerves, each one triggered and tantalised by his spine-tingling touch. He went lower to caress her intimately, his clever fingers wreaking havoc on her senses, driving up her need until she was breathless with it.

But he coaxed her only so far, leaving her hanging in that torturous zone that made her wild with longing. Wild and wanton and racked with primitive urges she'd had no idea she possessed. She felt like she would *die* if he didn't let her come. The need was like a pressure cooker inside her flesh. Building. Building. Building.

He gently pressed her down with his weight, his body entering hers with a smooth deep thrust that made her gasp and groan in delight. Her body welcomed him, worshipped him, wrapped around him in tight coils of need that sent pulses of pleasure ricocheting through her flesh.

He set a slow rhythm at first, but then he gradually increased his pace and she went with him, holding him, stroking his back and shoulders, her body so finely tuned to his that she was aware of every breath he took, every sound he made, every movement of his body within hers.

He rolled her so she was lying on top of him, his hands gripping her hips, encouraging her to move with him in an erotic rhythm that intensified her pleasure. She should have felt exposed and vulnerable but she didn't, instead she felt sexy and desirable. His eyes gleamed with delight as she rode him, naked flesh to naked flesh, hers soft and yielding, his hard and commanding.

Sabrina could feel the tight tingle in the core of her being; the slow build was now a rush of heady sensation threatening to consume her like a swamping wave. It was terrifying and yet tantalising as her body swept her up into a tumult of powerful pulses of pleasure, blissful, frightening pleasure that stole her breath and blanked out her thoughts. She heard herself cry out, a high wail that sounded almost primitive, but she was beyond caring. Her body was riding out a cataclysmic storm that made every pore of her skin tingle and tighten as the waves of orgasm washed over her.

Max continued to move within her, his hands holding her by the hips now, his face screwed up in intense pleasure as he pumped his way to paradise. It was as thrilling as the orgasm she'd just had to watch him shudder through his. The way his hands tightened on her almost to the point of pain, the clench of the toned muscles of his abdomen, the momentary pause before he allowed himself to fly. The raw sexiness of his response made her feel proud of her femininity in a way she had never before.

He arched his head back on the pillow and let out a ragged-sounding sigh as his whole body relaxed. He ran a light hand up and down her right arm, his touch like an electrical current on her sensitised-by-sex skin.

His eyes meshed with hers, holding them in a lock that communicated on another level—a level she could feel deep in her flesh. Their bodies were still connected, neither of them had moved. She hadn't been able to. Hadn't wanted to.

He gave a crooked smile and gathered her close so she was sprawled across his chest. She laid her head against the thud of his heart, and sighed as his hand went to the back of her head in a slow-moving caress that made every hair on her scalp shiver at the roots.

Words didn't seem necessary, although Sabrina had plenty she wanted to say. But she kept her mouth closed. He might hold her like a romantic lover but this was not a love match. She had to keep her head. She had to keep her heart out of this. She closed her eyes and nestled against him, breathing in the musky scent of their coupling. For so long Max had been her enemy. The man she actively avoided or if she couldn't avoid him, she fought with him. But how would she be able to conceal her body's involuntary response to him? How would she stop herself from betraying how he made her feel?

Max wasn't her ideal husband. How could he be when he'd always made it clear he didn't want children? He'd been prepared to marry his ex-fiancée but only on the proviso that the marriage would be childless. He didn't want the things Sabrina wanted, the things she'd wanted since she was a little girl. But now circumstances had forced them together because he refused to walk away from her and their child.

Max moved so he was lying beside her and leaning on one elbow. His free hand moved from her face in a slow caress down between her breasts to rest against the flat plane of her belly. There was a faintly disturbing gravitas about his expression that made her wonder if he was already regretting making love to her. Regretting the child they had made.

Sabrina searched his tense features, noted the shadows behind his eyes. 'Does your decision never to have children have something to do with what happened to your brother Daniel?' She knew she was crossing a line by bringing up the subject of his baby brother. Some of the tiny muscles on his face flinched as if she'd slapped him with the pain of the past.

His hand fell away from her belly and he rolled away and got off the bed, his back turned towards her. 'I was the last person to see him alive.' The words were delivered in a hollow tone that echoed with sadness. 'You didn't know that, did you?' His glance over his shoulder was almost accusing.

Sabrina pressed her lips together and shook her head. 'No…no, I didn't…'

He turned back around and drew in a savage-sounding breath, releasing it in a gust. 'No. Because my parents wanted to protect me from blame.' Guilt was etched on his features and shadowing his gaze in smoky clouds.

She frowned in confusion. Why was he blaming himself for his baby brother's death? 'But Daniel died of SIDS, didn't he?'

'Yes, but I can't help blaming myself.' His throat rose and fell. 'I was seven years old. Surely that's old enough to know if something was wrong with my baby brother? But I must have missed it. I thought he was asleep. If only I had acted earlier, called Mum to check on him or something.'

Sabrina thought of Max as a young child, confused and distraught by the death of his baby brother. Even adults blamed themselves, particularly mothers, when a baby tragically died of Sudden Infant Death Syndrome, so how much more would Max shoulder the blame from his immature and somewhat ignorant perspective as a young child?

'But, Max, you were so young. You shouldn't be blaming yourself for Daniel's death. It was a tragic thing but no way was it your fault. Your parents don't blame you, surely?' She had heard nothing of this from his parents or her own, who were such close friends of Gillian and Bryce Firbank.

'No, of course they don't,' Max said in the same grim tone. 'They were in shock and grieving terribly at the time but they were always careful to make sure I was shielded from any sense of responsibility for Daniel's death. But I couldn't stop blaming myself. Still can't, to be perfectly honest.' He gave a twisted movement of his mouth that was as sad to see as the shadows in his eyes.

'Oh, Max…' Sabrina got off the bed and went to him, put her arms around him and hugged him close. After a moment, she leaned back to look up into his eyes. 'I don't know what to say… I can't bear the thought of you blaming yourself all this time. Have you talked to your parents about it?'

He shook his head, his shoulders going down on a sigh. 'We hardly ever mention Daniel's name now. It upsets Mum too much.'

'Understandable, I guess.'

Max's arms fell away from around her body and he stepped back, his expression difficult to read. 'My mother had several miscarriages before and after Daniel died. That's why there was such a gap between Daniel and me. She desperately wanted another child after he died, but each time another pregnancy ended, I saw another piece of her fade away.' Something flickered in his gaze. 'I've always felt guilty about my decision not to have children. My parents would love grandchildren. But I realised I can't tell them about this baby of ours until we're through the danger period. It would destroy them to have their hopes raised and then dashed.'

'Your poor mum. I'm not sure I knew about the miscarriages,' Sabrina said. 'Mum's never mentioned it. Neither has your mum.'

'She doesn't talk about it. Hasn't for decades. She's always so upbeat and positive but I know she must still think about it.' He sighed again. 'And that's another thing I blame myself for. My parents' marriage has been tested way too much because of my failure to protect my brother.'

'But your parents are happy together, aren't they? I mean, they always look like they are. Your dad adores your mum and she adores him.'

His mouth gave a twisted movement, his eyes shadowed. 'But how much happier would they have been if I hadn't let them down?'

Sabrina placed her hand on his arm. 'Max, you haven't let them down. It's not your fault. They're amazingly proud of you. They love you.'

He covered her hand with his and attempted a smile. 'You're a sweet girl, Sabrina. But I have a habit of letting people down in the end. That's why I keep my relationships simple. But nothing about us is simple now, is it? We've made a baby.'

Sabrina hadn't realised until now how deeply sensitive Max was. He was aware of the pain his mother had suffered and was doing all he could to protect Sabrina during the early days of her pregnancy. But marrying him was a big step. Sleeping with him six weeks ago had changed her life in more ways than she had thought possible. 'Max… this offer of yours to marry me…'

His hands came up to cradle her face, his eyes moving back and forth from her gaze to her mouth. His breathing had altered, so too had hers. Their breaths mingled in the small space between their mouths, weaving an intoxicating spell on her senses. 'Maybe I need to work a little harder to convince you, hmm?'

His mouth came down and covered hers, his lips moving in soft massaging movements that made every bone in her body feel like it had been dissolved. She swayed against him, dizzy with need, her body on fire with every spine-tingling stroke and glide of his tongue. The dance of their mouths was like sophisticated choreography, no one else could have kissed her with such exquisite expertise. No one else could have made her mouth feel so alive, so vibrantly, feverishly alive. Her heart picked up its pace, sending blood in a fiery rush to all the erogenous zones of her body, making her acutely aware of pleasure spots that ached to be touched, longed to be caressed. Longed to be filled with his intimate invasion.

Max lifted his mouth off hers, his eyes still gleaming with arousal. 'That one night was never going to be enough. We both know that.'

'Then why didn't you contact me afterwards?'

His mouth shifted in a rueful manner. 'We agreed to stay clear of each other but there wasn't a day that went past that I didn't regret agreeing to that rule.'

Sabrina hadn't been too enamoured with that rule either. Every day of those six weeks she'd ached to see him. Ached to touch him. Ached to give herself to him. But that was how she'd got in to this mess in the first place. Max and she had made a child together from their one night of passion.

Passion but not love.

Max didn't love her and was only offering to marry her because of their child. Her dreams of a romantic happily ever after with a man who adored her were fast disappearing.

'Do you regret this?' Sabrina couldn't hold back the question. 'Taking our relationship to this level?'

His frown deepened and his hand stilled on her hair. 'No.' He released a jagged sigh and added, 'But I don't want you to get hurt. I'm offering you marriage. Not quite the sort you're after but it's all I can offer.'

Sabrina aimed her gaze at his Adam's apple. 'I know what you're offering, Max… I'm just not sure I can accept it…'

He brought her chin up with his finger and did that back and forth thing again with his eyes, searching hers for any trace of ambiguity. 'We're good together, Sabrina. You know that. We can make a go of this. We've both come from stable backgrounds so we know it'll be the best thing for our child to have both its parents together.'

She felt torn because there was nothing she wanted more than to give her baby a stable upbringing like the ones she and Max had experienced. Didn't every mother want that for her baby? But would marrying a man who didn't love her be enough in the long run? He might come to love their child, but would he ever come to love her as well? And why was she even asking such a question? She wasn't in love with Max. *Was she?* She had to keep her feelings out of it. If she fell for him it would make her even more vulnerable than she already was.

But she couldn't ignore the chemistry between them when her body was still tingling from head to foot from his lovemaking. Neither could she ignore the dread that if she refused to marry him, he would be free to go back to his playboy life. Sure, he would be an involved father but not permanently on site like hers had been. Sabrina released a sigh and rested her hand against his thudding heart.

'Okay, I will marry you, but we can't tell anyone until after the twelve-week mark. We'll have to keep our relationship secret from our families until then, because no way am I going to be subject to pressure and well-meaning but unsolicited advice from our families.'

The frown relaxed slightly on his forehead but it seemed to lurk in the grey shadows of his eyes. He brushed back her hair from her face and pressed a soft kiss to her lips. 'They won't hear about it from me.'

CHAPTER EIGHT

TWO WEEKS PASSED and Sabrina's noisy and cramped flat became a distant memory. All of her things had now been moved and were either in storage or at Max's house. She was touched by his attention to detail, the way he made sure everything was perfectly set up for her. Nothing seemed too much trouble for him, but she couldn't help wondering if he was finding the rapid change in his neat and ordered life a little confronting.

But for her, living with him showed her how seriously she had misjudged him in the past. It made it harder and harder to remember exactly why she had hated him so much. Or had that been a defence mechanism on her part? Somehow her heart had recognised that he was the one man who could make her fall for him and fall hard.

Each time Holly came in for a fitting, Sabrina had to quell her own feelings of disappointment that her wedding wasn't going to be as she had dreamed and planned for most of her life.

But Holly wasn't Sabrina's best friend for nothing and it didn't take her long to pick up on Sabrina's mood at her fitting that afternoon. 'You don't seem yourself today, Sabrina. Is something wrong?'

Sabrina placed another pin in the skirt of Holly's gown to mark where she needed to take it in. 'Other than my husband-to-be is only marrying me out of duty because I'm pregnant with his baby?'

'Oh, honey,' Holly sighed. 'Do you really think Max doesn't care about you? Personally, I think he's been in love with you for months.'

Sabrina sat back on her heels and looked up at her friend. 'What makes you think that?'

Holly lifted one shoulder. 'It's just a vibe I got when I saw him at that party a few months ago. He was acting all dog-in-the-manger when you were dancing with that other guy.'

'So? He was probably just annoyed with me for drawing attention to myself.' Sabrina picked up another pin. 'Turn a little to the left. That's it.' She inserted the pin at Holly's waistline. 'Have you been dieting? This is the third time I've had to take this dress in.'

Holly laughed. 'Wedding nerves. Or excitement more like.'

There was a silence broken only by the rustle of fabric as Sabrina fiddled with the alterations on the dress.

'Have you and Max set a date for the wedding?' Holly asked.

Sabrina scrambled to her feet and stabbed the pins back in her pincushion. 'Not yet…' she sighed. 'I can't see him wanting a big one. He's never been one for large gatherings. He missed out on the Firbank party animal gene.'

Holly's look was as probing as a spotlight. 'Have you decided what you feel about him?'

Sabrina made a business of tidying up her dressmaking tools. She had been deliberately avoiding thinking about her feelings for Max. They were confusing and bewildering, to say the least. He was the last person she had thought she would fall in love with, but how could she not lose her heart to such a wonderful man? He was everything she wanted in a life partner. He was stable and strong and dependable. He had good family values, he was hard working and supportive.

Yes, he was nervous about becoming a father, which was understandable given what had happened to his baby brother. But she wished he would open up more to her about his concerns. To let her in to his innermost doubts and fears. She had hated him for so long, loathed and resented him, and yet these days she only had to think of him and her heart would flutter and a warm feeling spread through her body. 'It's complicated…' She glanced at her friend. 'I used to think I hated him but now I wonder if I ever did. Was it like that for you with Zack?'

Holly's toffee-brown eyes melted at the sound of her fiancé's name. 'It was exactly like that. I hated him when I first met him but as soon as he kissed me…' she gave a dreamy smile '… I think that's when I fell completely and hopelessly in love.'

Sabrina knew from earlier conversations with Holly that handsome playboy Zack Knight had fallen in love with Holly the moment he'd met her. With Zack's reputation as a celebrity divorce lawyer and Holly a twice-jilted wedding florist, their romance had been the talk of London. And while Sabrina was thrilled Holly and Zack were so in love and looking forward to their wedding in a few weeks' time, it made her situation all the more heart-wrenching. She longed for Max to love her the way she had come to love him. Her feelings for him—now that she'd acknowledged them—were intense and irreversible.

But would she be happy knowing, deep down, he was only marrying her out of a sense of duty?

Max was still privately congratulating himself on keeping his relationship with Sabrina a secret from his family. There was something deeply intimate about keeping their involvement quiet. The bubble of secrecy made every moment with her intensely special, as if they were the only two people left on the planet. He had never felt that close to anyone else before and it was both terrifying and tempting. Tempting to think it could grow and develop into something he had told himself never to aspire to because he didn't deserve it.

Worried he would somehow jinx it, destroy it.

It was still too early for Sabrina to be showing her pregnancy, but just knowing his baby was nestled inside her womb made him feel things he had never expected to feel. Not just fear, although that was there big-time, but flickers of excitement, anticipation, wonder. He caught himself wondering what their child would look like, who it would take after, what traits or quirks of personality it would inherit. He had even stopped avoiding people with prams and now took covert glances at the babies inside.

And he had gone to London's most famous toyshop and bought two handmade teddy bears—one with a blue ribbon and one wearing a pink tutu, because, for some reason, he couldn't get the idea of a tiny little girl just like Sabrina out of his mind. He was keeping the bears for when he and Sabrina came home from their first ultrasound appointment.

The day of the appointment, Max cleared his diary for the whole day because he was in no fit state to work even though it would only take up half an hour or so. He was barely able to speak on the way to the radiography centre as he was so lost in his tangled thoughts. His stomach pitched and pinched, his heart raced and his pulse rioted. What if there was something wrong with the baby?

He hadn't realised until now how much he cared about that little bunch of cells. The feelings ambushed him, making him wonder if other fathers felt like this. Men were mostly at arm's length from a pregnancy, distant from what was going on in their partner's body as it nurtured and sustained new life. But he felt an overwhelming sense of love for the child that was growing in Sabrina's womb. What was ahead for their child? What sort of person would they become? How could he as its father make sure it had everything it needed for a long and fulfilling and healthy life?

Max sat beside Sabrina in the waiting room, took her hand and rested it on his thigh. 'Nervous?'

She gave a wobbly smile. 'A little. Are you? You've been awfully quiet.'

He squeezed her hand. 'Sorry. I'm still getting my head around everything.'

A flicker of worry passed through her blue gaze and she looked down at their joined hands. 'I'm sorry about all of this… I can't help feeling it's my fault we're in this situation.'

'Sabrina.' He tipped up her chin and locked

his eyes with hers. 'It's not your fault. If it's anyone's fault it's mine.'

Max was relieved Sabrina had finally agreed to marry him. He wanted nothing more than to provide a stable and loving home for their child. And it would be a loving relationship, though perhaps not in the most romantic sense. He genuinely cared about Sabrina, she had been a part of his life for so long, and yet it had only been recently that he had found out the more complex layers to her personality.

He had been deeply touched when she'd revealed to him what had happened to her as a teenager. He wished she had told him that night in Venice but she hadn't and he had to accept it. Would he have still made love to her? He couldn't answer that question. The need between them was so strong and seemed to be getting stronger.

Sabrina's name was called and they were led into the examination room. Max continued to hold her hand as the sonographer moved the probe over Sabrina's still flat abdomen. How could a baby—his baby—be growing inside her? It didn't seem real until he saw the image of the foetus come up on the screen. He could barely register what the sonographer was saying. All he could think was that was his child floating around in the amniotic sac that would feed and nurture it until it was born in seven months' time.

His chest suddenly felt tight with emotion, his heart thumping with a combination of dread and wonder. What sort of father would he be? How could he trust that he would always do the right thing by his child? He had never thought this day would occur and yet here he was sitting with his wife-to-be and staring at a 3D image of their baby.

His wife-to-be. Sabrina, his fiancée. The mother of his child.

Sabrina's hand grasped his tighter. 'Isn't it incredible?' Her eyes shone with the same wonder he was feeling. 'That's our baby.'

Max squeezed her hand and smiled. 'It sure is.'

'You have a few more weeks to decide if you want to know the sex,' the sonographer said. 'It's usually pretty clear from about eighteen to twenty weeks.'

'Do you want to know the sex of the baby?' Sabrina asked Max after the scan was completed.

'Do you?'

'I asked you first.'

'I'm not a great one for surprises, as you probably know,' Max said. 'But I'll go with what you decide. It's your call.'

Her teeth did that lip-chewing thing that never failed to make him want to kiss away the teeth marks on her pillow-soft lips. 'I kind of want to know but I kind of don't. Does that make sense?'

He smiled and brought her hand up to his lips, kissing her bent knuckles. 'It makes perfect sense. At least you've got a bit of time to make up your mind.'

She nodded and gave a fleeting smile. 'It's a little scary now that I've seen the baby… I mean, it makes it so…so real, doesn't it?'

Max kept her hand in his. 'You don't have to be afraid, sweetie. I'll be with you every step of the way.'

She looked at the printed photo of their baby that the sonographer had given them. 'I wonder who it will take after? You or me? Or maybe a bit of both of us.'

'As long as it's healthy, that's all that matters,' Max said. And even then things could happen. Bad things. Tragic things. His gut churned at the thought and his heart started tripping and hammering again. Boom. Trip. Boom. Trip. Boom. Trip. Boom.

Sabrina must have sensed his disquiet and placed her other hand over their joined ones. 'You'll be a wonderful father, Max. I know you will.'

He tried to smile but it didn't quite work. 'Come on. Let's get you home so you can rest.'

Sabrina wasn't tired when they got home but she was concerned about Max. He had seemed preoccupied at the appointment and he'd kept looking at the photo of the baby since then with a frown pulling at his brow. Was he thinking of all the things that could go wrong even after a healthy baby was born? There were no words to settle his fears because no one could guarantee that nothing would happen to their baby. Even after gestation and infancy, there was still the treacherous landscape of childhood and adolescence. But worrying about it wouldn't change what fate had decided—or so she kept telling herself.

Max came into the bedroom where she was

resting a short time later, carrying two shopping bags. He sat on the edge of the bed and passed them to her. 'For the baby, whatever sex it is.'

Sabrina opened the first bag to find a handmade teddy bear wearing a blue ribbon. 'So you think it's a boy?'

He gave a one-shoulder shrug. 'I'm hedging my bets. Open the other bag.'

She opened the bag and pulled out another teddy bear but this one was wearing a pink tutu. It touched her that Max had already gone shopping for their baby. It made her wonder if his growing feelings for the baby would somehow, one day, include her. 'They're so cute, Max. That was so thoughtful of you.'

He picked up the blue-ribboned teddy bear and balanced it on his knee, his finger absently flicking the ribbon around its neck. 'Both Daniel and I had one of these. Our grandparents gave them to us.' Something drifted over his features like a shadow across the sky. 'Daniel's was buried with him; it sat on the top of his coffin during the service. I'm not sure if Mum kept mine or not. I think she found it hard to look at it once Daniel had died.'

Her heart ached at what Max must have felt at his baby brother's funeral. And she felt deeply moved that he had shared with her a little more about his childhood and the sadness he still carried. Sabrina took the bear out of Max's hands and set it beside the pink-tutu-dressed one by her side. She took his hand in hers and stroked the strong tendons running over the back of his hand. 'I have a feeling this baby is going to bring a lot of joy to both our families, but especially to yours. You'll be a fabulous dad. I just know it.'

He gave a ghost of a smile and lifted her hand up to his mouth, pressing a soft kiss to the backs of her knuckles. 'I wish I had your confidence.' He lowered her hand to his lap and circled one of her knuckles with his thumb, a frown settling between his eyebrows. 'I'll do my best to protect you and the baby. But what if I fail?'

Sabrina grasped his hand, squeezing it. 'You won't fail. Don't even think like that, Max. Everyone feels a bit daunted by the prospect of parenthood. It's normal.'

He gave another fleeting smile but a shadow remained in his gaze. 'That reminds me…' He let go of her hand and pulled a small velvet box out of his trouser pocket. 'I have something else for you.' He handed the box to her. 'Open it. If you don't like it we can change it for something else.'

Sabrina took the box and prised open the lid. Inside was an exquisite diamond ring that glinted as the light caught all its facets. Being in the business she was in, she saw lots of engagement rings but none had been as gorgeous as this one. 'Oh, Max, it's beautiful…' She glanced up at him. 'But it looks frightfully expensive.'

'And why wouldn't I buy you an expensive ring?'

Because you don't love me.

She didn't have to say it out loud. It was loud enough in her conscience to deafen her. She looked back at the ring and carefully took it out of its velvet home.

Max suddenly took the ring from her and lifted her hand and slipped it over her ring finger. 'There. What about that? A perfect fit.'

'How did you guess my size? Or is that another thing my parents have told you over the years?'

He gave a twisted smile. 'They might well have. But, no, this time I guessed.'

Sabrina looked down at the ring winking on her finger. She tried not to think about how different this moment might have been if they were like any other normal couple. A couple who had met and fallen in love the old-fashioned way. 'It's a gorgeous ring, Max. Truly gorgeous.'

A frown appeared on his forehead. 'Would you have preferred to choose one yourself?'

'No. This one's perfect.' She glanced at him again. 'But I'll have to only wear it in secret for another month because if either of our parents see this giant sparkler on my hand—'

'Maybe we should tell them.'

Sabrina frowned. 'But I thought we agreed to keep it quiet until the twelve-week mark?'

He took her hand and toyed with the ring on her finger, his inscrutable gaze meshing with hers. 'I know but we've had the first ultrasound and everything looks healthy so—'

She tugged her hand out of his and held it close to her body. 'No, Max. I think we should wait. It's only another month and then we can tell everyone about the baby and…and set a date for the wedding.' Every time she thought about the wedding she had a panic attack. How was she going to get a dress made

in time? What if she ballooned and looked nothing like the picture she had in her mind of the bride she had always wanted to be?

But it wasn't just about looking the part… what if Max *never* came to love her? People who genuinely loved you never deserted you. It was love that sheltered and sustained a relationship, not an overblown sense of duty.

Max captured her hand again and stroked it in warm, soothing motions. 'I don't want you to think I'm hiding you from my parents out of shame or embarrassment, like we're having some tawdry little affair. I'm proud to be your partner.'

Sabrina squeezed his hand. 'Oh, Max, that's so sweet of you. But I'm kind of enjoying our little secret. I'm surprised we've managed to keep it quiet this long. But I'm sure that's only because my mum and dad are away on holiday at the moment. I told Mum when she phoned me that I was moving out of my flat to stay with a friend. Unusually for her, she didn't ask which one, but it won't be long before she does.'

'But would it be such a problem to tell her you're staying with me? I don't want to come between you and your parents, espe-

cially your mother. And especially now you're pregnant.'

Sabrina rolled her eyes. 'You know what my parents are like, always telling me what I should do. I know they mean well, but as soon as they know I'm pregnant they'll whip out their medical bags and whisk me off to have every test under the sun. I just want to have time to get used to it myself. I'm enjoying the secrecy and the privacy for now.'

Max turned her hand over and traced a lazy circle in her palm. 'I'm enjoying it too.'

'You are?'

His eyes glinted. 'So much so, I think we should go away for the weekend.'

A bubble of excitement formed in her chest. 'Where to?'

'It's a secret.'

Sabrina gave him a coy look. 'You kind of like your secrets, don't you?'

He gave a quick grin that transformed his face. 'More than I realised. Can you take the time off work? I know you usually work on a Saturday but—'

'It's fine. My assistant Harriet is getting better all the time so she can take over while I'm away. I figured she's going to have to do more and more for me the further along I get with the pregnancy.'

Max stroked his hand over the back of her head. 'How long will you work? I can support you if you'd like to take more time off and—'

'I love my job, Max. Pregnancy isn't a disease. I'm perfectly healthy and—'

'I just worry about you doing too much. Running a business more or less single-handedly is not an easy task. You need to outsource so you're not overburdened with unnecessary work. We have a wedding to plan and a baby on the way and that needs to take priority, surely?'

How could he suggest she take time out from the business she loved as if it was nothing more than a fill-in job? Sabrina swung her legs over the edge of the bed and stood. 'Will you stop lecturing me about what I should do? You're starting to sound like my parents.'

'Yeah, well, maybe your parents are onto something.' Max's tone tightened.

She glared at him, stung by his betrayal in siding with her parents. 'What's that supposed to mean?'

He released a rough-sounding breath.

'Look, I don't want to argue with you. I'm just saying you need to do things a little differently. You're a talented designer, no question about that, but you can't possibly make every single dress yourself.'

'I don't make every one myself. I have a small team of seamstresses but I do all the hand-sewing myself because that's my signature touch.'

'Would it help if I set up a workroom for you here?' Max asked. 'You could work from home and get your assistant to run the shop so you can rest when you need to.'

It was a tempting offer. She had often thought of working from home without the distraction of phones and walk-ins who were 'just browsing'. Some of her hand sewing was complicated and painstaking work and she needed to concentrate. And truth be told, she had been feeling a little overwhelmed with it all even before she'd found out she was pregnant. 'You wouldn't mind?'

'Why would I mind?'

'I don't know… I just thought weddings weren't your thing.'

He came back to take her hands in his. 'There is only one wedding I'm interested in right now and that's ours. And the sooner it happens the better.'

Sabrina chewed the side of her mouth. 'But I need time to make myself a dress.'

'Don't you have one in stock you could use?'

She rolled her eyes and pulled her hands away. 'Duh. I've been planning my wedding since I was four years old. No. I cannot wear a dress from stock. I want to make it myself.'

He frowned. 'How long will it take to make one?'

'I usually have a six-month lead time for most of my clients. I'm only doing Holly's in a shorter time frame because she's my best friend.'

'Six months?' His tone was so shocked she might have well as said it would take a century.

'I might be able to rustle something up a little earlier but I want my dress to be something I can be proud of when I look back on our wedding day.' Not to mention her relationship with Max. But would she look back on that with pride or despair?

'You're stalling.' The note of schoolmaster censure was back in his tone. 'I don't want to wait for months on end to get married. We've made the decision so let's get on with it.'

'I am not stalling,' Sabrina said. 'Weddings are not dinner parties where you invite a few guests, cook some food and open some wine. It takes months of planning and—'

'So we'll hire a wedding planner.'

'Max, you're not listening to me,' Sabrina said. 'I want to plan my own wedding. I want to make my own dress. I don't want it to be a rushed shotgun affair.'

His jaw worked for a moment. 'I'd like to be married before the baby is born. I want it to have my name.'

'The baby will have your name regardless.' Sabrina sighed and came over to him, touching him on the forearm. 'Maybe we can compromise a bit. I can't say I want to walk up the aisle with a big baby bump on show. That's not quite what I envisaged for myself when I was growing up.'

His hands came to rest on the tops of her shoulders, his eyes searching hers. 'Would you be happy with a small and simple wedding, just family and a few close friends?'

She would have to be happy with it because she was starting to realise there wasn't time for her to plan anything else. How far from her childhood dreams had she come? 'Is that what you would like? Something small and intimate?'

One of his hands went to the nape of her neck, the other to cradle the side of her face. 'I'm sorry I can't give you exactly what you want but we can make do.'

Make do. There was that annoying phrase again. But Sabrina was increasingly aware of her habit of idealising stuff and ending up disappointed when nothing met her standards. Maybe it was better this way. To lower her expectations and be pleasantly surprised when it worked out better than she thought. She pasted on a smile. 'Then that's what we'll do. Make do.'

CHAPTER NINE

BY THE TIME the weekend came, Sabrina had almost convinced herself her relationship with Max was just like that of any other young couple in love and preparing for their marriage and a baby. Almost. He whisked her out of London on Friday afternoon, with their weekend bags loaded in the boot of his car, and drove a couple of hours into the countryside to a gorgeous Georgian mansion a few kilometres from a quiet village.

The mansion had been recently renovated for the garden was still showing signs of having had tradesmen's workboots and ladders and other construction paraphernalia all over it. But even in the muted late evening summer light she could see the neglected garden's potential. Roses bloomed in messy abundance, clematis and fragrant honeysuckle climbed rampantly over a stone wall, and along the pathway leading to the front door she could see sweet alyssum filling every crack and crevice in a carpet of white and purple.

'What a gorgeous place,' Sabrina said, glancing at him as helped her out of the car. 'Is it yours?'

'Yes. Do you like it?'

'I love it.' She breathed in the clove-like scent of night stocks and sighed with pleasure. 'Wow. It's just like out of a fairytale. I'm almost expecting fairies or goblins to come dancing out of that back section of the wild garden.'

Max took her hand. 'Come on. I'll show you around.' He led her to the front door, taking care she didn't trip over the cracked pathway. 'I bought it a while back. I've been coming down when I can to do some of the work myself.'

She gave him a sideways glance. 'Well, I know from personal experience how good you are with your hands.'

He grinned back and squeezed her hand. 'Cheeky minx. Careful, the sandstone step here is a bit uneven. I was going to replace it but I quite like the fact it's been worn down over the years.'

It was becoming more and more apparent

to Sabrina that Max was a traditionalist at heart. He was always careful in his designs to respect a building's history and incorporate it cleverly into any new development on the same site, just as he had done with his house in Notting Hill. And wasn't his determination to marry her because of the baby another indication of his commitment to his strong values?

Max unlocked the door and led her inside the house, switching on lights as he went. The interior had been tastefully decorated in mostly neutral colours, which brought in more light. The furniture was a mixture of old and new and she wondered if he'd chosen it himself or got an interior decorator to do it for him. He would certainly know plenty in the course of running his architectural firm. Most of whom would be female.

Sabrina swung her gaze back to his. 'You have excellent taste. Or did you get someone to do the decorating for you?'

He kicked at the crooked fringe on the rug on the floor with his foot to straighten it out. 'There's a woman I use now and again. She's good at listening to what I want and getting on with it.'

The big green-eyed monster was back and poking at Sabrina's self-esteem. 'Is that all you use her for?'

Max frowned. 'Pardon?'

Sabrina wished she hadn't spoken. She turned away and ran her hand over a beautiful walnut side table. 'Nothing…'

He came up behind her and placed his hands on her shoulders and turned her to face him. 'Sabrina. Listen to me.' His voice was gentle but firm. 'You and I are in a committed relationship. You don't have to worry that I'll be looking at any other woman. Ever. Understood?'

She chewed at her lower lip. 'I'm sorry but I can't help feeling a little insecure. It's not like we're in love or anything. How can you be so certain you won't fall in love with someone else?'

His hands tightened on her shoulders. 'Stop torturing yourself with unlikely scenarios. I realise this is a tricky time for you. You have crazy hormonal stuff happening and a lot has happened in a short period of time. But believe me when I say I'll remain faithful to our marriage vows. You have my word on that, sweetheart.'

Sabrina looked into his grey-blue eyes and wished there was a magic spell she could cast that would make him fall in love with her. It would be so much easier to relax and enjoy every facet of their relationship if she thought it was founded on the things that were most important to her.

He was offering commitment without love. Other men offered love and then reneged on the commitment. Could she continue to hope and pray Max would find the courage to relax the guard around his heart and love her as she longed to be loved? She stretched her mouth into a smile. 'Thank you.'

He inched up her chin and planted a kiss on her lips. 'Come on. I'll show you upstairs.'

Sabrina followed him up the staircase to the landing, where eight bedrooms each with their own bathroom were situated. The master bedroom was huge with a gorgeous window seat that overlooked the rambling garden and the landscape beyond. Sabrina knelt on the chintz-covered cushioned seat and looked at the wonderful view of rolling fields and the dark green fringe of forest and wondered if she had ever seen such a beautiful setting.

'Gosh, it's so private. Are there any neighbours?'

'Not close by,' Max said. 'That's why I bought it. It's nice to get away from the hustle and bustle every now and again.'

Sabrina rose from the window seat. 'Do you plan to live here one day? It's a big house for one person. I mean, you weren't planning on settling down and all.'

He reached past her to open the window to let in some fresh air. 'It's more of a weekender. I find it relaxing to be surrounded by nature instead of noise. It clears my head so I can work on my designs.'

Sabrina bit her lip and fiddled with the brass knob the curtains were held back by. 'As big as this place is, you might not get much head space when there's a wailing baby in the house…'

He took her hands in his, his thumbs stroking the backs of her hands. 'Are you nervous about being a mum?'

'A little…yeah, actually a lot.' She sighed. 'I know women have been having babies for ever but it's my first baby and I can't help feeling a little worried I won't be good enough.'

He cut back an incredulous laugh and

squeezed her hands. 'Not good enough? You'll be the best mum in the world. You're a natural nurturer.'

'But don't you worry about how this baby is going to change both our lives? I mean, a bit over a month ago we were both single and hating each other. Now we're having a baby and getting married.'

'I have never hated you.' His tone had a strong chord of gravitas.

But what did he feel for her? 'You certainly gave me that impression. Not that I can talk, of course.'

His expression was cast in rueful lines. 'Yes, well, with our parents watching us like hawks for any sign of a melting of the ice between us, I guess we both did or said things we regret now.'

Sabrina moved closer as his hands went to her hips. It never ceased to amaze her how neatly they fitted together like two pieces of a puzzle. 'You're being far too gracious, Max. I seem to remember being an absolute cow to you on a number of occasions.'

He dropped a kiss to the tip of her nose and smiled. 'You're forgiven.'

She smiled back, struck again by how much

a smile transformed his features. She lifted her hand to his face and traced the contours of his mouth. 'You have such a nice smile. I don't think I ever saw you smile at me before a few weeks ago.'

'Maybe you're teaching me to lighten up a bit.'

'By accidentally falling pregnant? Yeah, like that's the way to do it.'

He brushed her hair back from her forehead. 'What's done is done. We're moving forward now and it won't help either of us to focus on the negatives about how we got together.' He stepped back with a brief flash of a smile. 'I'm going to bring in our things while you settle in. I've brought some supper for us.'

Sabrina sat on the end of the bed once he'd gone, her thoughts in a messy tangle. Was she being too negative about their situation? She was a lot better off than many young women who suddenly found themselves pregnant after a one-night stand. Max was determined to stand by her and support her. He was bending over backwards and turning himself inside out to be the best partner he could be.

She was grateful he was standing by her,

but it didn't stop her hoping his concern for her and the baby would grow and develop into lasting love.

When Sabrina came downstairs, Max had unpacked the car and loaded the fridge with the food he had brought. She was touched by how much effort he had put into making their weekend away so stress-free for her. She hadn't had to do anything but pack her overnight bag.

He came back into the sitting room with a glass of fresh orange juice and some nibbles on a plate. 'Here you go. I've just got to warm up the dinner.'

Sabrina took the juice and smiled. 'Who knew you were so domesticated?'

'Who indeed?'

He sat down beside her and slung his arm along the back of the sofa near her shoulders. His fingers played with the loose strands of her hair, making her scalp tingle and her skin lift in a frisson of delight. 'Not too tired?' he asked.

She leaned forward to put her juice on the coffee table in front of the sofa, then sat back to look at him. 'Not too tired for what?'

His eyes did that sexy glinting thing. 'No way am I making love to you until you've had something to eat, young lady.'

Sabrina shifted so she was straddling his lap, her arms going around his neck. 'But what if all I want right now is you?'

He ran his hands down the length of her arms, his touch lighting fires along her flesh. 'Those pregnancy hormones really are going crazy, hey?'

She had a feeling it had nothing to do with her hormones. It had everything to do with him. How he made her feel. 'Could be.' She brought her mouth down to his, meeting his lips in a kiss that sent a river of flame straight to her core. She could feel the pulsing ache of her body pressed so close to the burgeoning heat of his. The surge of his male flesh reminding her of the erotic intimacy to come.

He drew in a harsh breath as if the leash on his self-control had snapped. One of his hands going to the back of her head to keep her mouth crushed to his. His tongue thrust between her lips, meeting hers in a hot sexy tangle that sent another shiver racing down her spine.

Sabrina set to work on undoing the buttons

on his shirt, peeling it away from his body so she could touch his warm hard flesh. He slid his hands under her top, the glide of his slightly calloused hands on her naked skin making her ache for his possession. He deftly unclipped her bra and brought his hands around the front of her body to cradle her breasts. His thumbs stroked back and forth over her nipples, turning them into achingly hard peaks that sent fiery shivers to her core.

'God, you're so damn sexy I can hardly control myself.' His voice was deep and sounded like it had been dragged over a rough surface.

'Don't control yourself, then.' Sabrina licked his lower lip, relishing in the way he shuddered at her touch. 'You can do what you want to me if you'll let me do what I want to you, okay?'

He didn't answer but drew in a ragged breath and brought his mouth back to hers in a long drugging kiss that involved tongues and teeth and lips and mutual desire so ferocious it threatened to engulf them both.

Sabrina wrenched at his belt fastening, finally getting it undone and tugging it through the lugs of his trousers. She tossed it to the floor over her shoulder and it landed in a snake-like slither on the carpeted floor. She wriggled down off his lap, quickly removing the rest of her clothes, a frisson passing over her flesh when she saw his eyes feasting on her. It amazed her how quickly his body responded to hers and how quickly hers responded to his. Even now she could feel the tight pulses and flickers of need deep in the core of her womanhood, the tender flesh swelling in high arousal, the blood pumping through her veins at breakneck speed.

'Take your trousers off.' Sabrina was a little shocked at how forthright she was being. Shocked but thrilled to be discovering her sensual power. For so many years she had doubted herself, felt ashamed and insecure. But with Max she felt powerfully sexy and feminine. There was no room for shame, only room for the celebration of her sensual awakening.

He stood and stepped out of his trousers, his expression a mixture of rampaging desire and caution at what she might do to him. She pushed him back down on the sofa, bending down on her knees in front of his seated form. 'Now I get to play naughty girl with you.'

Max sucked in another breath and put his hands on her shoulders. 'You don't have to do that—'

'I want to.'

'Oh, God…' He groaned as her hands encased him, moving up and down in massaging strokes the way he had taught her. But she wanted more. She wanted to taste him the way he had tasted her.

Sabrina gave him one long stroke with her tongue from base to tip, delighting in the whole-body shudder he gave. It gave her the impetus to keep going, to torture him with her tongue the way he had done to her. She stroked him again with her tongue, back and forth like she was enjoying her favourite ice cream, casting him wicked temptress glances from beneath half-mast lashes. His breathing rate increased, his body grew more and more tense, every muscle and sinew struggling to keep control. Sabrina opened her mouth over him, drawing him in, sucking and stroking until he was groaning in blissful agony.

Max pulled himself away before he came, breathing hard, his eyes glazed with lust. 'Not all the way, sweetheart.'

'Why won't you let me?'

He got to his feet and picked her up in his arms. 'Because I have other plans for you.'

She linked her arms around his neck and shivered in anticipation. 'Ooh, that sounds exciting.'

He gave her a glinting smile and walked up the stairs, carrying her as if she weighed no more than one of the cushions off the sofa. When they got to the master bedroom, he laid her on the bed and came down beside her, his thighs in an erotic tangle with hers. He cupped one of her breasts in his hands, bringing his mouth down to take her tight nipple into his mouth. He swirled his tongue around its pointed tip, then gently drew on her with a light sucking motion that sent arrows of heat to her core. He moved to her other breast, pleasuring her with the gentle scrape of his teeth and the flick and stroke of his tongue.

Sabrina moved restlessly beneath him. 'Please. I want you *so* much…' Her body was throbbing with the need to feel him inside her. The hollow ache between her legs was unbearable, every nerve primed and poised for the erotic friction it craved.

'I want you too, so damn much, I'm nearly crazy with it.' He moved down her body, holding her hips with his hands as he kissed her abdomen from her belly button down to the top of her mound. She drew in a sharp breath as his mouth came to the heart of her desire. He separated her with the stroke of his tongue, moving along her sensitive flesh in a series of cat-like licks that made every hair on her head shiver at the roots.

It was too much and it wasn't quite enough. Her nerves were tight as an over-tuned cello string, vibrating with the need for release. And then she was suddenly there, falling apart under the ministrations of his lips and tongue, shattering into a million pieces as the tumult of sensations swept through her. She cried, she laughed, she bucked and moaned and clutched at his hair, but still he kept at her until the very last aftershock left her body. She flung her head back against the bed, her breathing still hectic. 'Oh, my God…that was incredible.'

Max placed a hand on her belly, a triumphant smile curving his mouth. 'But wait. There's more.' He moved back over her, careful not to crush her with his weight, and entered her with a smooth, thick thrust, making her gasp all over again.

He set a slow rhythm at first, but then he increased the pace at her urging. She wanted him as undone as she had been. She moved her hands up and down the bunched muscles of his arms, then placed them on his taut buttocks, kneading and stroking the toned flesh as his body moved intimately within hers.

'You feel so damn good.' His voice was part moan, part groan as his mouth came back to hers.

Sabrina kissed him back, using her lips and tongue and even her teeth at one point. The intensity of his passion for her was thrilling. The movement of his body, the touch and taste of him delighting her senses into an intoxicating stupor. She arched her spine, desperate to get closer, to trigger the orgasm she could feel building in her body.

He slipped a hand underneath her left hip, lifting her pelvis and shifting slightly to change the contact of their hard-pressed bodies. And just like that she was off again in a heart-stopping release that sent shockwaves through every inch of her flesh. It was like fireworks exploding, fizzing and flickering with blinding light and bursts of colour like a shaken kaleidoscope.

Sabrina was conscious of the exact moment he let go. She felt every shudder, every quake, felt the spill of his essence and held him in the aftermath, listening to the sound of his breathing slowly return to normal. There was something almost sacred about the silence that fell between them. The quiet relaxation of their bodies, the synchronisation of their breathing, the mingling of their sensual fragrances and intimate body secretions was so far removed from her first experience of sex it made her love for Max deepen even further.

Max leaned on one elbow and placed his other hand on her thigh. 'Was that exciting enough for you?'

Sabrina smiled a twisted smile and touched his stubbly jaw in a light caress. 'You know it was.'

He captured her hand and kissed her fingertips, holding her gaze with his. 'I've never been with a more responsive partner. Every time we make love you surprise me.'

She aimed her gaze at his Adam's apple, feeling suddenly emotional. 'I know I've said it before, but I wish you'd been my first lover. I can't believe I let that jerk mess with my head so much and for so long.'

He cradled her close, his hand gently brushed back her hair from her forehead. 'Sweetie, if I were ever to find myself alone with that creep I would delight in giving him a lesson on how to respect women. What he did to you was disgusting and unforgiveable.'

Sabrina couldn't help feeling touched by the flare of righteous anger in his eyes. It was wonderful to have someone stand up for her, someone who respected and cared about her welfare. Even if he didn't love her the way she wanted to be loved, surely it was enough that he would move heaven and earth to take care of her and their baby? 'You're such a good man, Max.'

He pressed a soft kiss to her lips and then lifted himself off the bed. 'Stay here and rest. I'll bring supper up in few minutes.'

Sabrina propped herself up on the elbows. 'Are you sure you don't want some help?'

He pointed a finger at her but there was a smile in his eyes. 'Stay. That's an order.'

She gave him a mock-defiant look. 'You know how obstreperous I get when you issue you with me orders. Are you sure you want to take that risk?'

His eyes ran over her naked form in a

lustful rove that made her want him all over again. 'Are you spoiling for a fight, young lady?' His voice was a low deep growl that did strange things to the hairs on the back of her neck.

Sabrina got off the bed and sashayed across to him with a sultry smile. She sent her hand from the top of his sternum to the proud bulge of his erection. 'I was thinking more along the lines of making love, not war. Are you on?'

He shuddered at her touch and pulled her closer. 'I'm on.' And his mouth came down on hers.

CHAPTER TEN

AN HOUR OR SO later, Max sat across from Sabrina in the cosy kitchen of the cottage and watched as she devoured the supper of soup and fresh bread and fruit he'd brought with him. He wondered if he would ever get tired of looking at her. Her hair was all tousled where his hands had been in it, her lips were swollen from his kisses and her cheeks had a beautiful creamy glow.

She looked up to see him looking at her and her cheeks went a faint shade of pink. She licked her lips and then, finding a crumb or two, reached for her napkin and dabbed at her mouth. 'What?'

Max smiled and pushed his untouched bread roll towards her. 'I like watching you eat. You remind me of a bird.'

'Yeah? What type? A vulture?' She picked up the bread roll and tore it into pieces. 'Seriously, I can't believe my appetite just now. I'm starving.'

'Must be the hormones.'

She gave him a sheepish look. 'Or the exercise.'

His body was still tingling from said exercise. And that was another thing he wondered if he'd ever tire of—making love with her. 'I should have fed you earlier. It's almost midnight.'

'I love midnight feasts.' She popped another piece of bread in her mouth, chewed and swallowed, and then frowned when she saw his water glass. 'Hey, didn't you bring any wine with you? I'm the one who isn't drinking while I'm pregnant, not you.'

'That hardly seems fair,' Max said. 'I'm not a big drinker in any case.'

'Oh, Max, that's so thoughtful of you. But I don't mind if you have a glass of wine or two.'

'It's not a problem.' He passed her the selection of fruit. 'Here, have one of these peaches.'

After a while, she finished her peach and sat back with a contented sigh. 'That was delicious.'

He got up to clear the table. 'Time for bed?'

She smothered a yawn. 'Not before I help you clear this away.' She pushed back her chair and reached for the plates.

'I'll sort it out. You go up and get comfortable.'

She was halfway to the door when she turned around to look at him with a small frown wrinkling her forehead. 'Max?'

'What's up, sweetie?'

'Have you brought anyone else down here? Another woman, I mean?'

'No. I've only just finished the renovations.' He picked up the plates and cutlery and added, 'I wasn't going to share it with anyone, to be perfectly honest. Even my parents don't know about it.'

'Why haven't you told them?'

'There are some things I like to keep private.'

She chewed at her lip. 'I've been thinking... It must have been hard for Lydia, knowing your parents didn't think she was right for you.'

Funny, but Max could barely recall what his ex-fiancée looked like now. 'Yes, it probably was hard for her.' He frowned and continued. 'I sometimes wonder if I only got engaged to her to stop them banging on about you.'

Something flickered through her gaze. 'Not the best reason to get engaged.'

'No.'

'Have you seen her since?'

'No. What would be the point? We've both moved on.'

She gave him a thoughtful look. 'But have you?'

'Have I what?'

'Moved on.'

Max turned and loaded the dishwasher. 'You can rest easy, Sabrina. I have no lingering feelings for Lydia. You're my priority now.'

'But in a way, it's the same, isn't it?'

He closed the dishwasher with a snap. 'What's the same?'

'The way you felt about her is similar to how you feel about me. You weren't in love with her and you're not in love with me.'

Max didn't like where this conversation was heading. He wasn't incapable of love. He just chose not to love in *that* way. It wasn't called 'falling in love' for nothing. You lost all control when you loved someone to that degree. He was worried that if he fell in love he would eventually let the person down.

Hadn't he always done so? His parents? His baby brother? Even Lydia had been shortchanged and had gone off looking for someone who could love her the way she wanted.

'Sabrina.' He let out a long sigh. 'Let's not have this discussion this late at night. You're tired and—'

'What are you afraid of?'

He gave a short laugh to lighten the atmosphere. 'I'm not afraid of anything. Now, be a good girl and go upstairs and I'll be up in a second.'

She looked like she was going to argue, but then she let out a sigh and turned and headed upstairs.

Max leaned his hands on the kitchen counter and wondered if this was always going to be a stumbling block in their relationship. But he assured himself that Sabrina wasn't in love with him so what was the problem? If she had been, wouldn't she have said so? No, they were two people forced together because of circumstance and they were both committed to making the best of the situation. They had put their enmity aside, they liked each other, desired each other and respected each other. If that wasn't a positive thing, what was? Their relationship had a lot more going for it than others he'd seen. And it was certainly better than any relationship he'd had in the past.

Way better.

Sabrina spent the rest of the weekend with her mouth firmly closed on the subject of Max's feelings for her. She didn't want to spoil the relaxing time together because she could see how hard he was trying to do everything right by her. Her feelings weren't the top priority right now. They had a baby on the way and she had to somehow reassure Max he would be a wonderful father. She knew it still troubled him and she ached to ease that painful burden for him.

She consoled herself that in time he might relax the guard around his heart, open himself to loving her once he fell in love with their baby. Didn't most new parents say the experience of bringing a child into the world was a defining moment? A time when overwhelming love flooded their beings? It was her hope, her dream and unceasing prayer that Max would feel that groundbreaking love for their child and include her in it.

A few days later, Max left for a brief trip to Denmark, where he had a project on the go. Sabrina could sense his reluctance to leave her but she assured him she would be fine as she had work aplenty of her own to see to. Most days her nausea was only mild and if she was sensible about getting enough rest she was able to cope with the demands of her job.

Living at his house had far more benefits than she had first realised, not least the warm protective shelter of Max's arms when she went to sleep each night and when she woke each morning. Staying at his house was like living in a luxury hotel but much less impersonal. There were reminders of him everywhere—books, architectural journals he was reading, one with a feature article on him—and even the house itself with its stylish renovation that perfectly married the old with the new.

There was that word again—*marriage*.

But she couldn't bring herself to regret her acceptance of his proposal. She had to concentrate on what was best for the baby and put her own issues aside. Max cared about her otherwise he wouldn't have made such a fuss over her, looking after her, insisting on her living with him and doing a hundred other things for her that no one had ever done for her before.

The evening he was due to come back, Sabrina found a photo of him with his family in the study, taken before his baby brother had died. She had seen the photo at his parents' house in the past but somehow she hadn't really looked at it in any detail before. She traced her finger over Max's bright and happy smile as a seven-year-old boy and wondered if the birth of their baby would heal some of the pain of the past. There was no doubt in her mind that he would make an excellent father.

The sound of the doorbell ringing almost made her drop the photo frame. Max was due home any minute, but surely if it was him he would use his key rather than the doorbell? She placed the photo back on Max's desk and went out to check the security monitor in the foyer to see who was at the door. Her heart nearly jumped out of her chest when she saw it was her mother standing there with Max's mother Gillian. She had thought her mother would be away for another week in France… or had she got the dates wrong?

Sabrina stepped backwards away from

the monitor, hoping Gillian Firbank and her mother hadn't heard her footsteps on the black and white tiles of the foyer, but in her haste she stumbled and bumped against the hall table. She watched in horror as the priceless vase that was sitting there wobbled and then crashed to the floor, shattering into pieces.

'Max?' Gillian said, rapping firmly at the door. 'Is that you? Are you okay?'

Sabrina stood surrounded by the detritus of the vase, her heart hammering faster than that of a rabbit on the run. Should she open the door? But how could she explain why she was at Max's house? They were supposed to be keeping their relationship a secret. But if their mothers found her in situ at Max's home…

'Perhaps it's a burglar,' Sabrina's mother said. 'We'd better call the police.'

Sabrina had no choice but to open the door before her mother summoned half of London's constabulary to Max's house. 'Hi,' she said. 'I'm…erm…housesitting for Max.'

Gillian's and Sabrina's mother's eyes widened and then they exchanged a twinkly-eyed glance.

'Housesitting? For… Max?' Her mother's voice rose in a mixture of disbelief and hope.

'Yes. Just while he's in Denmark. He's coming back tonight. In fact, I thought he would be home before this. Perhaps his flight's been delayed.'

Gillian's mouth was tilted in a knowing smile. 'I knew something was going on with you two at my party.'

'Nothing's going on,' Sabrina lied, not very well by the look on the two women's faces.

'I wanted to show your mother Max's new renovations,' Gillian said. 'We were in the area and saw the lights on and thought we'd pop in. But if Max isn't home we'll come back another time.'

'You told me the other day you were staying at a friend's house.' Her mother's expression was one part accusatory, one part delighted.

'Yes, well, that's sort of true,' Sabrina said.

'So you two are friends now?' Her mother's eyes danced like they were auditioning for a part in *La Cage aux Folles*.

'Mum, it's not what you think—'

'Actually, it is what you think,' Max said as he came up the path to the front door carrying his travel bag with his laptop case slung over his shoulder. 'Sabrina and I are getting married.'

'Married?' The mothers spoke in unison, their faces so aglow with unmitigated joy they could have lit up the whole of London.

Max put his arm around Sabrina's waist and drew her close to his side. 'Yes. We haven't set a date yet but we'll get around to it soon.'

Sabrina glanced at him with a question in her eyes but he simply smiled and bent down to kiss her. 'Miss me, darling?' he said.

'You have no idea how much.' Sabrina bit her lip. 'I'm sorry about your vase…'

'What vase?'

She pointed to the shattered pieces of porcelain strewn over the foyer behind them. 'I bumped it when I was checking the security monitor. Please tell me it wasn't valuable.'

'Not as valuable as you,' he said, and kissed her again.

'Oh, look at you two gorgeous things.' Gillian grabbed Sabrina's mother's arm to lead her inside Max's house. 'We need to celebrate. Let's open some champagne.'

Sabrina gave him a *what do we do now?* look, but his expression remained calm. 'They had to find out sooner or later,' he said, sotto voce, and led her inside behind the older women.

Before she knew it, Max had efficiently cleaned up the pieces of the vase and Sabrina found herself sitting beside him on one of the sofas in the main sitting room. Her mother and Gillian were sitting opposite with glasses of champagne raised in a toast.

'Why aren't you drinking yours, Sabrina?' her mother asked after everyone else had sipped theirs. Max had only taken a token sip, however.

Sabrina cradled her glass in her hands, her cheeks feeling so hot she could have stripped the paint off the walls. 'Erm…'

'Oh, my God!' Gillian shot to her feet as if a spring in the sofa had jabbed her. 'You're pregnant?'

Max looked like he was the one suffering morning sickness. Sabrina's mother Ellen looked like she didn't know whether to laugh or cry.

Sabrina decided there was no point denying it. Besides, she wanted her mother to be one of the first to know and not find out some other way. 'Yes, I am pregnant but only eight weeks. We're not telling everyone until the twelve-week mark.'

There were hugs and kisses and hearty congratulations all round and finally, after promising they would only tell their husbands and Sabrina's brothers about the pregnancy, the mothers left.

Max closed the door on their exit with a sigh. 'I'm sorry. I forgot I told my mother to drop in sometime to see the completed renovations.'

Sabrina frowned. 'But why did you have to tell them we're getting married? Why not just say we're having a fling or something? You know how I feel about this. Now they'll be in full on wedding fever mode, telling everyone our business and—'

'I was thinking about it while I was away,' Max said. 'Trying to keep our involvement a secret is going to cause you more stress than you need right now. I figured it was safer to get this out in the open. I didn't realise my mother would twig about the pregnancy, though.'

Sabrina sank back into the sofa and hugged one of the scatter cushions, eyeing her untouched glass of champagne as if it had personally insulted her. 'If I hadn't broken that damn vase, trying to avoid them, we might still have kept our secret safe. Argh. I hate how out of control my life is right now.'

He hunkered down next to her and grazed his knuckles across her cheek, his eyes warm and tender. 'It was going to come out sooner or later. And there's no reason to think your pregnancy isn't going to continue.'

'Would you prefer it if I lost the baby?'

He flinched. 'No. How can you ask that?'

She shrugged one shoulder and tossed the cushion to one side. 'I've done a pretty good job of stuffing up your neatly controlled life.'

He straightened and then came to sit beside her on the sofa, his hand slipping under the curtain of her hair to the nape of her neck, his expression wry. 'Maybe it needed shaking up a bit.'

Sabrina could feel every inch of her body responding to his touch. She placed her arms around his waist, loving the strength and warmth of his body so close to hers. She rested her head against his chest and sighed. 'At least our families are happy for us.'

He lifted her face off his chest and meshed his gaze with hers. 'It's a good start.'

'But what if we make each other miserable? I mean, further down the track?'

He brushed an imaginary hair away from her face. 'We're both mature adults. We can handle the odd difference of opinion, surely? Besides, I quite like arguing with you.'

A smile tugged at her mouth, a hot tide of longing pooling in her core. 'Do you fancy a fight now?'

His eyes glinted. 'Bring it on.' And he scooped her up in his arms and carried her to the bedroom.

CHAPTER ELEVEN

A FEW DAYS LATER, Sabrina had left the shop early, leaving Harriet in charge so she could get home to make a special dinner. They had been eating out mostly but she wanted to have a night at home for once. She suspected he took her out for dinner so often so she wouldn't have to cook but she enjoyed cooking and wanted to do something for him for a change.

Max's once-a-week housekeeper had been through the house and left it spotless. Holly had given Sabrina some fresh flowers and she placed them in the new vase she'd bought to replace the one she'd broken.

He came in just as she was stirring the Provençale chicken casserole on the cooktop and she put the spoon down and smiled. How could a man look so traffic-stopping gorgeous after a long day at work? 'How was your day?'

'Long.' He came over and planted a kiss on the top of her head. 'Mmm…something smells nice.'

Sabrina held up the spoon for him to have a taste. 'It's one of your favourites. Your mum told me.'

He tasted the casserole and raised his brows in approval. 'Delicious. But why are you cooking? Shouldn't you be resting as much as possible?'

'I like cooking.'

'I know, but you don't have to wait on me. I could have picked up a takeaway to save you the bother.'

Sabrina popped the lid back on the pot. 'I'm not waiting on you. I just wanted to do something for you for a change. You've been so good about everything and I—'

'Hey.' He placed his hands on her shoulders and turned her so she was facing him. 'I like doing things for you. I want to make this relationship work.'

She bit down on her lip. 'I know. For the baby's sake, right?'

His hands gave her shoulders a gentle squeeze. 'Not just for the baby. For you. I care about you, Sabrina. Surely you know that?'

She gave an on-off smile. Would caring be enough for her? 'I know but—'

He placed a finger over her lips. 'No buts. I care about you and will do everything in my power to make you happy.' He lowered his hand and brought his mouth to hers instead, kissing her leisurely, beguilingly until she melted into his arms.

Sabrina wound her arms around his neck, pressing herself closer to the tempting hard heat of his body. Her inner core already tingling with sensation, his mouth triggering a tumultuous storm in her flesh. His tongue met hers and she made a sound of approval, her senses dazzled by the taste of him, the familiar and yet exotic taste that she craved like a potent drug. His hands cradled her face as he deepened the kiss, his lips and tongue wreaking sensual havoc, ramping up her desire like fuel tossed on a naked flame. It whooshed and whirled and rocketed through her body, making her aware of every point of contact of his body on hers.

With a groan Max lifted his mouth from hers. 'How long can dinner wait?'

Sabrina pulled his head back down. 'Long enough for you to make love to me.'

He kissed her again, deeply and passionately. Then he took her hand and led her upstairs, stopping to kiss her along the way. 'I've been thinking about doing this all day.'

'Me too,' Sabrina said, planting a series of kisses on his lips. 'I'm wild for you.'

He smiled against her mouth. 'Then what's my excuse? I've been wild for you for months.'

He led her to the master bedroom, peeling away her clothes and his with a deftness of movement that made her breathless with excitement. The touch of his warm strong hands on her naked skin made her gasp and whimper, his hands cupping her breasts, his lips and tongue caressing them, teasing her nipples into tight peaks of pleasure. The same tightly budded pleasure that was growing in her core, the most sensitive part of her hungry, aching for the sexy friction of his body.

Max worked his way down her body, gently pushing her back against the mattress so she was lying on her back and open to him. It was shockingly intimate and yet she didn't have time to feel shy. Her orgasm was upon her as soon as his tongue flicked against the heart of her and she came apart in a frenzied rush that travelled through her entire body like an earthquake.

He waited until she came down from the stratosphere to move over her, entering her with a deep but gentle thrust, a husky groan forced from his lips as her body wrapped around him. Sabrina held him to her, riding another storm of sensation, delighting in the rocking motion of his body as he increased his pace. Delighting in the strength and potency of him, delighting in the knowledge that she could do this to him—make him breathless and shuddering with ecstasy.

Max collapsed over her, his breathing hard and uneven against the side of her neck. 'You've rendered me speechless.'

Sabrina stroked her hands over his lower back. 'Same.'

He propped himself up on his elbows, his eyes still dark and glittering with spent passion. 'I mean it, sweetie. I don't think I've ever enjoyed sex as much as I have with you.'

She couldn't imagine making love with anyone but him. The thought appalled her. Sickened her. She snuggled closer, her arms around his middle, wondering if it were possible to feel closer to him than she did right now.

After a long pause he stroked a strand of hair away from her face, his eyes dark with renewed desire. 'How do you think dinner is holding up?'

She rubbed her lower body against his pelvis and smiled her best sexy siren smile. 'It'll keep.' And she lifted her mouth to the descent of his.

Max had a run of projects that urgently needed his attention. He'd been neglecting his work in order to take care of Sabrina, making sure she had everything she needed in the early weeks of her pregnancy. But his work could no longer be postponed. He had big clients who expected the service they paid good money for. He hated leaving Sabrina but he had a business to run and people relying on him.

Travelling out of town meant he would have to stay overnight and that's what he hated the most. Not waking up next to her. Not having her sexy body curled up in his arms, the sweet smell of her teasing his nostrils until he was almost drunk on it. He informed her of his business trip over breakfast and she looked up from buttering her toast with disappointed eyes. So disappointed it drove a stake through his chest.

Her smile looked forced. 'Oh… Thanks for telling me.'

He scraped a hand through his hair. Clearly he had some work to do on his communication skills. And his timing. 'I'm sorry. I should have told you days ago. I thought I could manage it at a distance but the client is getting restless.'

She got up from the table and took her uneaten toast to the rubbish bin and tossed it in. 'I know you have a business to run. So do I.'

'Why aren't you eating? Do you feel sick?'

She turned from the bin with a combative look her on face. 'I'm fine, Max. Stop fussing.'

He came over to her and took her stiff little hands in his. 'Do you think I really want to leave you? I hate staying in hotels. I would much rather wake up with you beside me.'

Her tight expression softened. 'How long will you be away?'

'Two nights,' Max said, stroking the backs of her hands. 'I'd ask you to come with me but

I know you're busy with Holly's dress. Which reminds me, we need to set a wedding date. My mother has been on my back just about every day to—'

'Yeah, mine too.' Her mouth twisted. 'But I don't want to get married close to Holly's wedding day. But neither do I want to be showing too much baby bump on ours. I don't know what to do. Ever since I was a little girl, I've dreamed of my wedding day. Not once in those dreams did I picture myself waddling up the aisle pregnant. I'm stressing about it all the time. Whenever I think about it I just about have a panic attack.'

He cupped her cheek in his hand. 'Oh, sweetie, try not to stress too much. We'll talk some more when I get back, okay?'

She sighed. 'Okay…'

Max kissed her on the forehead, breathing in her summer flowers scent. 'I'll call you tonight.' He touched her downturned mouth with his fingertip. 'Why don't you ask Holly to stay with you while I'm away? I'm sure she wouldn't mind.'

'She spends every spare minute with Zack.' A spark of annoyance lit her gaze. 'Besides, I don't need flipping babysitting.'

'I can't help worrying about you.'

She slipped out of his hold and picked up her tote bag where it was hanging off the back of a chair. 'You worry too much. I'll be fine. I have plenty to keep me occupied.'

Max placed his hands on her shoulders, turning her to face him. 'You'll have to be patient with me, Sabrina. I'm not the world's best communicator. I'm used to going away for work at a moment's notice. But obviously that's going to have to change once we become parents.'

She let out a soft sigh. 'I'm sorry for being so snippy. I'm just feeling a little overwhelmed.'

He brought up her chin with his finger, meshing his gaze with her cornflower-blue one. 'It's perfectly understandable. We'll get through this, sweetheart. I know we will.'

She gave another fleeting smile but there was a shadow of uncertainty behind her eyes. 'I have to run. I have a dress fitting first thing.'

He pressed a kiss to her lips. 'I'll miss you.'

'I'll miss you too.'

Sabrina was ten minutes late to her fitting with her client, which was embarrassing as it had never happened before. But she couldn't seem to get herself into gear. Ever since she'd found out Max was going away, she'd felt agitated and out of sorts. It wasn't that she wanted to live in his pocket. She had her own commitments and responsibilities, but she had come to look forward to their evenings together each day. She loved discussing the events of the day with him over dinner, or curling up on the sofa watching television. She had even got him hooked on one of her favourite TV series. She loved the companionship of their relationship. It reminded her of her parents' relationship, which, in spite of the passage of years, seemed to get stronger.

And then there was the amazing sex.

Not just amazing sex, but magical lovemaking. Every time they made love, she felt closer to him. Not just physically, but emotionally. It was like their bodies were doing the talking that neither of them had the courage to express out loud. She longed to tell him she loved him, but worried that if she did so he would push her away. She couldn't go through another humiliation of rejection. Not after what had happened when she was eighteen. But even so, she had to be careful not to read too much into Max's attentive behaviour towards her. He cared for her and he cared about their baby.

That was what she had to be grateful for.

Holly came in for her final fitting later that afternoon just on closing time. 'Hiya.' She swept in, carrying a bunch of flowers, but then noticing Sabrina's expression frowned. 'Hey, what's up?'

Sabrina tried to smile. 'Nothing.'

Holly put the flowers down. 'Yeah, right. Come on, fess up.'

Sabrina was glad Harriet had left for the day. She closed the shop front door and turned the 'Closed' sign to face the street. 'Come out the back and I'll do your fitting while we chat.'

'Forget about the fitting—we can do that another day,' Holly said, once they were out the back. 'The wedding isn't for another few weeks. What's wrong?'

Sabrina put her hand on her belly. Was it her imagination or had she just felt a cramp? 'I'm just feeling a bit all over the place.'

'Are you feeling unwell?'

'Sort of…' She winced as another cramp gripped her abdomen.

Holly's eyes widened. 'Maybe you should sit down. Here…' She pulled out a chair. 'Do you feel faint?'

Sabrina ignored the chair and headed straight to the bathroom. 'I need to pee.'

She closed the bathroom door, taking a breath to calm herself. Tummy troubles were part and parcel of the first weeks of pregnancy. Nausea, vomiting, constipation—they were a result of the shifting hormones. But when she checked her underwear, her heart juddered to a halt. The unmistakable spots of blood signalled something was wrong. She tried to stifle a gasp of despair as a giant wave of emotion swamped her.

Was she about to lose the baby?

Holly knocked on the bathroom door. 'Sabrina? Are you okay?'

Sabrina came out a short time later. 'I think I need to go to hospital.'

Max was in a meeting with his client when he felt his phone vibrating in his pocket. Normally he would have ignored it—clients didn't always appreciate their time with him being interrupted. Especially this client, by far the most difficult and pedantic he had ever had on his books. But when he excused himself and pulled out his phone, he didn't recognise the number. He slipped the phone back into his pocket, figuring whoever it was could call back or leave a message. But he only had just sat back down with his client when his phone pinged with a text message. He pulled the phone out again and read the text.

Max, it's Holly. Can you call me ASAP?

Max's chest gave a painful spasm, his heart leaping and lodging in his throat until he could scarcely draw breath. There could only be one reason Sabrina's friend was calling him. Something must be wrong. Terribly wrong. He pushed back his chair and mumbled another apology to his client and strode out of the room. He dialled the number on the screen and pinched the bridge of his nose to contain his emotions. 'Come on, come on, come on. Pick up.'

'Max?'

'What's happened?' Max was gripping the phone so tightly he was sure it would splinter into a hundred pieces. 'Is Sabrina okay?'

'She's fine. She's had a slight show of blood but nothing since so that's good—'

Guilt rained down on him like hailstones. He should never have left her. This was *his* fault. She'd been out of sorts this morning and he'd made it a whole lot worse by springing his trip on her without warning. What sort of job was he doing of looking after her when the first time he turned his back she ended up in hospital? Was there something wrong with him? Was there a curse on all his relationships, especially the most important one of all? His guts churned at the thought of her losing the baby. Of *him* losing her. Dread froze his scalp and churned his guts and turned his legs to water.

'Are you sure she's okay? Can I speak to her?'

'She's still with the doctor but I'll get her to call you when she's finished. She didn't want to worry you but I thought you should know.'

Damn right he should know. But he still shouldn't have left her. He had let her down and now he had to live with his old friend, guilt. 'Thanks for calling. I'll be back as soon as I can.'

'You're free to go home now, Sabrina,' the doctor said, stripping off her gloves. 'The cervix looks fine and the scan shows the placenta is intact. A break-through bleed at this stage, especially one as small as yours, is not unusual. Some women have spotting right through the pregnancy. Just make sure you rest for a day or two and if you have any concerns let us know.'

Sabrina tried to take comfort in what the doctor had said but her emotions were still all over the place. 'I'm not going to lose the baby?'

'I can't guarantee that. But, as I said, things look fine.' The doctor glanced at the engagement ring on Sabrina's hand and smiled. 'Get your fiancé to take extra-special care of you for the next few days.'

Her fiancé...

Sabrina wished Max were waiting outside instead of Holly. Her friend was fabulous and had swung into action as if she had been handling fretting pregnant women all her life. But the person Sabrina most wanted by her side was Max. She felt so alone facing the panic of a possible miscarriage. What if she had lost the baby? What if she *still* lost it? The doctor was right, there were no guarantees. Nature was unpredictable.

Holly swished the curtain aside on the cubicle. 'The doctor said you're fine to go home. Max is on his way.'

'You called him? How did you get his number?'

Holly patted Sabrina's tote bag, which was hanging from Holly's shoulder. 'I found his number on your phone. I didn't feel comfortable calling him on your phone so I called him on mine. I know you didn't want to worry him but if something had happened, imagine how he'd feel?'

Sabrina got off the bed, testing her legs to see if they were as shaky as they had been earlier when panic had flooded her system. 'He would probably feel relieved.'

'What? Do you really think so?'

'I know so.' Sabrina cast her friend a weary glance. 'The only reason we're together is because of the baby.'

Holly frowned. 'But he cares about you. I could hear it in his voice. He was so worried about you and—'

'Worrying about someone doesn't mean you love them,' Sabrina said. 'It means you feel responsible for them.'

'You're splitting hairs. That poor man almost had a heart attack when I told him you were in hospital.'

'I wish I had what you have with Zack,' Sabrina said. 'I wish Max loved me the way Zack loves you. But wishing doesn't make it happen.'

'Oh, honey, I'm sure you're mistaken about Max. You're feeling emotional just now and this has been a huge scare. You might feel better once he's back home with you.'

But what if she didn't?

Max risked speeding tickets and any number of traffic violations on the way back to London. He'd called Sabrina several times but she must have turned her phone off. He called Holly and she told him Sabrina was back at his house, resting.

'Can you stay with her until I get back?' Max glanced at the dashboard clock. 'I'm about an hour away.'

'Sure.'

'Thanks. You're a gem.' He clicked off the call and tried to get his breathing under control. But every time he thought of what could have happened to Sabrina he felt sick to his guts. Miscarriages were dangerous if help wasn't at hand. It might be the twenty-first century but women could still haemorrhage to death. He couldn't get the picture of a coffin out of his mind. Two coffins. One for Sabrina and another for the baby. How could he have let this happen? How could he have put his work before his responsibilities towards her and their child?

It felt like an entire millennium later by the time Max opened his front door. Holly had obviously been waiting for him as she had her bag over her shoulder and her jacket over her arm.

'She's upstairs,' Holly said.

'Thanks for staying with her.'

'No problem.' She slipped out and Max was halfway up the stairs before the door closed.

Sabrina was standing in front of the windows with her back to him, her arms across her middle. She turned when she heard his footfalls but he couldn't read her expression.

Max wanted to rush over to her and enfold her in his arms but instead it was like concrete had filled his blood and deadened his limbs. He opened and closed his mouth, trying to find his voice, but even that had deserted him. His throat was raw and tight, blocked with emotions he couldn't express.

'You're back.' Her voice was as cold as the cruel icy hand gripping his throat.

'I came as fast as I could. Are you all right?'

She was holding herself almost as stiffly as he was but he couldn't take a step towards her. His legs felt bolted to the floor, his guts still twisting and turning at what might have been.

'I'm fine.'

'And the baby?' He swallowed convulsively. 'It's still—?'

'I'm still pregnant.'

Relief swept through him but still he kept his distance. He didn't trust his legs to work. He didn't trust his spiralling emotions. They were messing with his head, blocking his ability to do and say the things he should be saying. Things he wasn't even able to express to himself, let alone to her. 'Why aren't you in bed? You need to rest.'

A shuttered look came over her eyes. 'Max, we need to talk.'

He went to swallow again but his throat was too dry. Something was squeezing his chest until he could barely breathe. 'You scared the hell out of me. When I got that call from Holly…' His chest tightened another notch. 'I thought… I thought…' In his mind he could see that tiny white coffin again and another bigger one next to it. Flowers everywhere. People crying. He could feel the hammering of his heartbeat in time with the pulse of his guilt.

Your fault. Your fault. Your fault.

'Max, I can't marry you.'

He went to reach for her but she stepped back, her expression rigid with determination. 'You're upset, sweetie. You've had a big shock and you'll feel better once you've—'

'You're not listening to me.' Her voice with its note of gravity made a chill run down his neck.

'Okay.' He took a breath and got himself into some sort of order. 'I'm listening.'

She rolled her lips together until they almost disappeared. 'I can't marry you, Max. What happened today confirmed it for me.'

'For God's sake, do you think I would have left town if I thought you were going to have a miscarriage? What sort of man do you think I am?'

Her expression remained calm. Frighteningly calm. 'It's not about the miscarriage scare. You could have been right beside me at the hospital and I would still have come to the same decision eventually. You were wrong to force your proposal on me when you can't give your whole self to the relationship.'

'Forced?' Max choked back a humourless laugh. 'You're having my baby so why wouldn't I want you to marry me?'

'But if I had lost the baby, what then?' Her gaze was as penetrating as an industrial drill. 'Would you still want to marry me?'

Max rubbed a hand down his face. He had a headache that was threatening to split his skull in half. Why did she have to do this now? He wasn't over the shock of the last few hours. Adrenaline was still coursing through him in juddering pulses. 'Let's not talk about this now, Sabrina.'

'When will we talk about it? The day of the damn wedding? Is that what you'd prefer me to do? To jilt you like Lydia did?' Her words came at him like bullets. *Bang. Bang. Bang.*

Max released a long, slow breath, fighting to keep his frustration in check. He couldn't talk about this now, not with his head so scrambled, thoughts and fears and memories causing a toxic poison that made it impossible for him to think straight. Impossible for him to access the emotions that went into automatic lockdown just as they had done all those years ago when he'd seen his mother carrying the tiny limp body of his baby brother. It felt like he was a dead man standing. A robot. A lifeless, emotionless robot.

'I put marriage on the table because of the baby. It would be pointless to go ahead with it if you were no longer pregnant.'

Nothing showed on her face but he saw her take a swallow. 'I guess I should be grateful you were honest with me.'

'Sabrina, I'm not the sort of man to say a whole bunch of words I can't back up with actions.'

Tears shone in her eyes. 'You act like you love me. But I can't trust that it's true. I need to hear you say it, but you won't, will you?'

'Are you saying you love me?'

Her bottom lip quivered. 'Of course I love you. But I can't allow myself to be in a one-sided relationship. Not again. Not after what happened when I was eighteen.'

Anger whipped through him like a tornado. 'Please do me the favour of not associating anything I do or say with how that creep treated you. You know I care about you. I only want the best for you and the baby.'

'But that's my point. If there wasn't a baby there wouldn't be an us.' She turned to the walk-in wardrobe.

'Hey, what are you doing?'

'I'm packing a bag.'

Max caught her by the arm. 'No, you're damn well not.'

She shook off his hold, her eyes going hard as if a steel curtain had come down behind her gaze. 'I can't stay with you, Max. Consider our engagement over. I'm not marrying you.'

'You're being ridiculous.' Panic was battering inside his chest like a loose shutter in a windstorm. 'I won't let you walk away.'

She peeled off his fingers one by one. 'You're a good man, Max. A really lovely man. But you have serious issues with love. You hold everyone at a distance. You're scared of losing control of your emotions so you lock them away.'

'Spare me the psychology session.' Max couldn't keep the sarcasm in check. 'I've tried to do everything I can to support you. I've bent over backwards to—'

'I know you have but it's not enough. You don't love me the way I want to be loved. And that's why I can't be with you.'

Max considered saying the words to keep her with him. How hard could it be? Three little words that other people said so casually. But he hadn't told anyone he loved them since he'd told his baby brother, and look how that turned out. He felt chilled to the marrow even thinking about saying those words again. He had let her down and there was nothing he could do to change it. He wasn't good enough for her. He had never been good enough and he'd been a fool to think he ever could be. 'Will you at least stay here for a bit longer till I find you somewhere to live?'

A sad smile pulled at her mouth. 'No, Max, I don't think that would be wise. I'll stay with my parents for bit until I find somewhere suitable.'

Later, Max could barely recall how he'd felt as Sabrina packed an overnight bag and handed him back the engagement ring. He hadn't even said, *No, you keep it.* He'd been incapable of speech. He drove her to her parents' house in a silence so thick he could almost taste it. His emotions were still in an emergency lockdown that made him act like an automaton, stripping every expression off his face, sending his voice into a monotone.

It was only days later, when he got back home to his empty house after work, where the lingering fragrance of her perfume haunted him, that he wondered if he should have done more to convince her to stay. But what? Say words she knew he didn't mean? He would be no better than that lowlife scum who'd hurt her so badly all those years ago.

But why did his house seem so empty without her there? He had got used to the sound of her pottering about. Damn it, he'd even got used to the mindless drivel she watched on television. He would have happily watched a test pattern if he could just sit with his arm around her. He could get through watching just about anything if he could hear the sound of her laughter and her sighs, and patiently hand her his handkerchief when she got teary over the sad bits of a movie.

But he would have to get used to not having her around.

* * *

Sabrina dragged herself through the next few days, worn down by sadness that her life wasn't turning out like that of the dewy-faced brides that filed through her shop. It was like having salt rubbed into an open and festering wound to see everyone else experiencing the joy and happiness of preparing for a wedding when her dreams were shattered. Why was her life destined to fall short of her expectations? Was there something wrong with her? Was she too idealistic? Too uncompromising?

But how could she compromise on the issue of love?

Moving back in with her parents might not have been the wisest move, Sabrina decided. She was engulfed by their disappointment as well as her own. It seemed everyone thought Max was the perfect partner for her except Max himself. But she couldn't regret her decision to end their engagement. She couldn't remain in a one-sided relationship. The one who loved the most was always the one who got hurt in the end. She wanted an equal partnership with love flowing like a current between them. Like it flowed between both sets of parents, long and lasting and able to withstand calamity.

No. This was the new normal for her. Alone.

And the sooner she got used to it the better.

A few miserable days later, Max went into his study and sat at his desk. He found himself sitting there every night, unable to face that empty bed upstairs. He sighed and dragged a hand over his face. His skull was permanently tight with a headache and his eyes felt gritty.

His eyes went to the photograph of his family before Daniel had died. There was nothing he could do to bring his brother back. Nothing he could do to repair the heartache he had caused his parents by not being more vigilant. His phone rang and he took it out of his pocket and swore when he saw it was his mother. The gossip network was back at work after a few days' reprieve. No doubt Sabrina's mother Ellen had called his mum to tell her the wedding was off. He was surprised Ellen hadn't done so the moment it had happened but maybe Sabrina had wanted things kept quiet for a bit. He answered the phone. 'Mum, now's not a good time.'

'Oh, Max. Ellen told me Sabrina called off the engagement.'

'Yep. She did.'

'And you let her?'

'She's an adult, Mum. I can't force her to be with me.' Even though he'd damn well given it a good shot.

'Oh, darling, I'm so upset for you and for her,' his mum said. 'I can't help thinking your father, Ellen, Jim and I have been putting too much pressure on you both. We just wanted you to be happy. You're perfect for each other.'

'I'm not perfect for anyone. That's the problem.' He let out a jagged sigh. 'I can't seem to help letting down the people I care about. You, Dad and Daniel, for instance. I do it without even trying. It's like I'm hard-wired to ruin everyone's lives.'

'Max, you haven't ruined anyone's lives,' his mother said after a small silence. 'I know you find it hard to allow people close to you. You weren't like that as a young child, but since we lost Daniel you've stopped being so open with your feelings. It was like a part of you died with him. I blame myself for not being there for you but I was so overwhelmed by my own grief I didn't see what was happening to you until it was too late. But you weren't to blame for what happened, you know that, don't you?'

Max leaned forward to rest one elbow on the desk and leaned his forehead against his hand. 'I should have known something was wrong. You asked me to check on him and he seemed fine.'

'That's because he *was* fine when you checked on him. Max, the coroner said it was SIDS. Daniel might have died in the next ten minutes and there was nothing you could have done to change that.' She sighed and he heard the catch in her voice. 'Darling, do you think I haven't blamed myself? Not a day goes past that I don't think of him. But it would be an even bigger tragedy if I thought you weren't living a fulfilling life because you didn't think you deserved to love and be loved in return.'

'Look, I know you mean well, Mum, but I can't give Sabrina what she wants. What she deserves. I'm not capable of it.'

'Are you sure about that, Max? Totally sure?'

Max ended the call and sat back in his chair with a thump. It was slowly dawning on him that he had made the biggest blunder of his life. His feelings for Sabrina had always been confusing to him. For years he'd held her at arm's length with wisecracking banter, but hadn't that been because he was too frightened to own up to what was going on in his heart? She had always got under his skin. She had always rattled the cage he had constructed around his heart.

And up until he'd kissed her he'd done a damn fine job of keeping her out. But that one kiss had changed everything. That kiss had led to that night in Venice and many nights since of the most earth-shattering sex of his life. But it wasn't just about amazing sex. There was way more to their relationship than that.

He *felt* different with her.

He felt alive. Awakened.

Hopeful.

His sexual response to her was a physical manifestation of what was going on in his heart. He was inexorably drawn to her warm and generous nature. Every time he touched her, he felt a connection that was unlike any he'd experienced before. Layer by layer, piece by piece, every barricade he'd erected had been sloughed away by her smile, her touch. Her love. How could he let her walk away without telling her the truth? The truth that had been locked away until now. The truth he had shied away from out of fear and cowardice.

He loved her.

He loved her with every fibre of his being. His love for her was the only thing that could protect her. Love was what had kept his family together against impossible odds. Love was what would protect their baby, just as he had been protected. His and her parents were right—he and Sabrina were perfect for each other. And if he didn't exactly feel perfect enough, he would work damn hard on it so he did.

Because he loved her enough to change. To own the feelings he had been too fearful to name. Feelings that he needed to express to her because they were bubbling up inside him like a dam about to break.

Sabrina's parents fussed over her so much each night when she came home from work that she found it claustrophobic. They were doing it with good intentions but she just wanted to be alone to contemplate her future without Max. Thankfully, that night her parents had an important medical function to attend, which left Sabrina to have a pity party all by herself.

The doorbell rang just as she was deciding whether she could be bothered eating the nutritious meal her mother had left for her. She glanced at the security monitor in the kitchen and her heart nearly stopped when she saw Max standing there. But before she allowed herself to get too excited, she took a deep calming breath. He was probably just checking up on her. Making sure she'd settled in okay.

She opened the door with her expression cool and composed. 'Max.' Even so, her voice caught on his name.

'I need to talk to you.' His voice was deep and hoarse, as if he had swallowed the bristly welcome mat.

'Come in.' Sabrina stepped away from the door to allow him to follow but she didn't get far into the foyer before he reached for her, taking her by the hands.

'Sabrina, my darling, I can't believe it has taken me this long to realise what I feel about you.' His hands tightened on hers as if he was worried she would pull away. 'You've been in my life for so long that I was blind or maybe too damn stubborn to see you're exactly what our parents have said all this time. You're perfect for me. Perfect because you've taught me how to feel again. How to love. I love you.'

Sabrina stepped a little closer or maybe he tugged her to him, she wasn't sure. All she knew was hearing him say those words made something in her chest explode with joy like fireworks. She could feel fizzes and tingles running right through her as she saw the look of devotion on his face. 'Oh, Max, do you mean it? You're not just saying it to get me back?'

He wrapped one arm around her like a tight band, the other hand cupped one side of her face, his eyes shining like wet paint. 'I mean it with every breath and bone and blood cell in my body. I love you so much. I've been fighting it because on some level I knew you were the only one who could make me feel love again and I was so worried about letting you down. And then I went and did it in the worst way possible. I can't believe I stood there like a damn robot instead of reaching for you and telling you I loved you that night you came home from hospital. Please marry me, my darling. Marry me and let's raise our baby together.'

She threw her arms around his neck and rose up on tiptoe so she could kiss him. 'Of course I'll marry you. I love you. I think I might have always loved you.'

Max squeezed her so tightly she thought her ribs would crack. He released her slightly to look at her. 'Oh, baby girl, I can't believe I nearly lost you. I've been such a fool, letting you leave like that. How devastated you must have felt when you told me you loved me and I just stood there frozen like a statue.'

Sabrina gazed into his tender eyes. 'You're forgiven, as long as you forgive me for being such a cow to you for all those years.'

He cradled her face with his hands and brushed his thumbs across her cheeks. 'There's nothing to forgive. I enjoyed every one of those insults because they've brought us here. You are the most adorable person in the world. I wish I could be a better man than I am for you, but I give you my word I'll do my best.'

Sabrina blinked back tears of happiness. 'You are the best, Max. The best man for me.

The only man I want. You're perfect just the way you are.'

He gave her a lingering kiss, rocking her from side to side in his arms. After a while, he lifted his head to look at her, his eyes moist with his own tears of joy. 'Hang on, I forgot something.' He reached into his trouser pocket and took out her engagement ring and slipped it on her finger. 'There. Back where it belongs.'

Sabrina smiled and looped her arms around his neck again. 'We are both back where we belong. Together. Ready to raise our little baby.'

He hugged her close again, smiling down at her. 'I'm more than ready. I can't wait to be a father. You've taught me that loving someone is the best way of protecting them and I can safely say you and our baby are not going to be short of my love.' He kissed her again and added, 'My forever love.'

EPILOGUE

A FEW WEEKS LATER, Max stood at the end of the aisle at the same church in which he and his baby brother had been christened, and looked out at the sea of smiling faces, his friends and family. He saw Zack sitting with Sabrina's family with a grin from ear to ear, having just got back from his honeymoon. Holly was the maid of honour so Zack would have to do without his new bride by his side while the ceremony was conducted.

Max drew in a breath to settle his nerves of excitement. The church was awash with flowers thanks to Holly. He couldn't believe how hard everyone had worked to get this wedding under way in the short time frame. But wasn't that what friends and family were for? They pulled together and the power of all that love overcame seemingly impossible odds.

The organ began playing 'The Bridal March'

and Holly, as Sabrina's only bridesmaid, and the cute little flower girl, the three-year-old daughter of one of Max's friends from University, began their procession.

And then it was time for his bride to appear. Max's heart leapt into his throat and he blinked back a sudden rush of tears. Sabrina was stunning in a beautiful organza gown that floated around her, not quite disguising the tiny bump of their baby. She looked like a fairytale princess and her smile lit up the church and sent a warm spreading glow to his chest.

She was wearing something borrowed and something blue, but when she came to stand in front of him he saw the pink diamond earrings he had bought her after they had found out at the eighteen-week ultrasound they were expecting a baby girl. They had decided to keep it a secret between themselves and it thrilled him to share this private message with her on this most important of days. One day they would tell their little daughter of the magic of how she brought her parents together in a bond of mutual and lasting love.

Sabrina came to stand beside him, her eyes twinkling as bright as the diamonds she was wearing, and the rush of love he felt for her almost knocked him off his feet. He took her hands and smiled. 'You look beautiful.' His voice broke but he didn't care. He wasn't ashamed of feeling emotional. He was proud to stand and own his love for her in front of all these people. In front of the world.

Her eyes shone. 'Oh, Max, I can't believe my dream came true. We're here about to be married.'

He smiled back. 'Our dream wedding.' He gave her hands a little squeeze. 'My dream girl.'

* * * * *

If you enjoyed The Venetian One-Night Baby
by Melanie Milburne
you're sure to enjoy these other
One Night With Consequences stories!

Consequence of the Tycoon's Revenge
by Trish Morey
The Innocent's Shock Pregnancy
by Carol Marinelli
An Innocent, A Seduction, A Secret
by Abby Green
Carrying the Sheikh's Baby
by Heidi Rice
Available now!